09/08 JBN

The Eye of Horus

The Eye of Horus

CAROL THURSTON

William Morrow
An Imprint of HarperCollins*Publishers*

HarperCollins books may be purchased for educational, business, or sales promotional use. For information please write: Special Markets Department, HarperCollins Publishers Inc., 10 East 53rd Street, New York, NY 10022.

FIRST EDITION

Designed by Nancy B. Field

Map drawn by Jeffrey L. Ward

Printed on acid-free paper

Library of Congress Cataloging-in-Publication Data has been applied for.

ISBN 0-380-97696-X

00 01 02 03 04 RRD 10 9 8 7 6 5 4 3 2 1

*Heaven and earth conspire that everything which has been,
be rooted and reduced to dust. Only the dreamers, who
dream while awake, call back the shadows of the past and
braid nets from the unspun thread.*

—Isaac Bashevis Singer

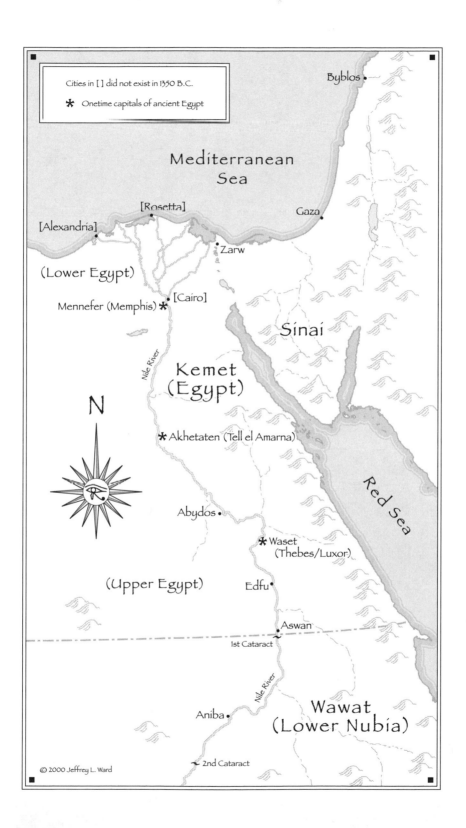

Cities in [ ] did not exist in 1350 B.C.

✴ Onetime capitals of ancient Egypt

Byblos •

Mediterranean
Sea

[Rosetta]

Gaza •

[Alexandria] •

• Zarw

(Lower Egypt)

Mennefer (Memphis) ✴ • [Cairo]

Sinai

Nile River

Kemet
(Egypt)

N

✴ Akhetaten (Tell el Amarna)

Red Sea

Abydos •

✴ Waset
(Thebes/Luxor)

(Upper Egypt)

Edfu •

Aswan
1st Cataract

Nile River

Aniba •

Wawat
(Lower Nubia)

← 2nd Cataract

© 2000 Jeffrey L. Ward

THE LAST PHARAOHS OF THE

EIGHTEENTH DYNASTY

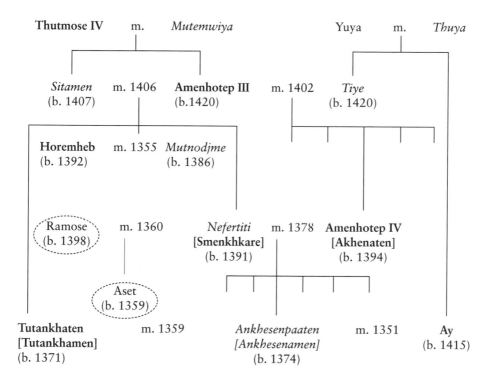

NOTE: Names of pharaohs in **bold**
Female names in *italics*
All dates B.C.

(Fictional characters)

The Eye of Horus

S he sensed that the line she'd just drawn was somehow wrong. What she didn't know was how to make it feel right. Too much was missing. Might always be missing. Rationally she knew that, too, yet she still couldn't accept that no one would ever know how Tashat came to die so young. Or what that man's head was doing between her legs.

Kate tossed her drawing crayon aside, got up, and walked over to the lighted viewbox, to trace the path of destruction again—from the linear fracture of the left humerus up to the comminuted clavicle, then down into the rib cage, where the fractures were not only multiple but displaced. In the end, though, it was Tashat's left hand that drew her eyes. Something else that was missing. Only it wasn't really, at least not in the same way. That hand appeared to be encased in something the X rays couldn't penetrate, like the gold fingernail stalls found on the mummy of Tutankhamen. But if that's what it was, why the entire hand? And why the left but not the right?

She stepped back from the head-to-toe X ray, hoping to find something "off" about the angle of the splintered ribs, or in the pattern of bone fragments scattered through the thoracic cavity—anything to suggest that the violence done to the young Egyptian had occurred after death rather than before. Otherwise, just trying to breathe would have been so excruciating it didn't bear thinking about. No one would have considered opening the chest back then, to remove the fragments of bone or repair a punctured lung. They still hadn't figured out that the blood flows through a closed system of veins and arteries, let alone how to control infection or shock. But they did know mandrake root and poppy juice—scopolamine and morphine—which raised the possibility that some ancient physician had given Tashat a drop too much, sending her central nervous system into the sleep of eternity.

Kate turned to glance at the tightly wrapped form lying on the workbench near the windows. For a minute the two images battled each other in her head—that painted face glowing with youthful vitality and the macabre death's-head she knew lay beneath it. Then, as if through an open window, she caught a glimpse of Tashat peering into a polished bronze hand mirror, to tuck a blue lotus blossom into her riotous black curls. A moment later, with a jaunty wave to someone Kate couldn't see, she disappeared from sight. Mesmerized by the image that had seemed so real, Kate continued to stare without seeing, willing the young woman to reappear—and was rewarded when Tashat came through the door of the whitewashed house into the bright sunlight of ancient Waset. As she started across the garden, Kate heard a muted click, like someone snapping their fingers. It wasn't until she emerged from the gate in the mud-brick wall that Kate noticed the little white dog trotting at her heels.

Then, sensing that Tashat would come toward her, Kate turned and waited. As they passed in the narrow street—really only a dusty alleyway—the irrepressible Tashat's luminous blue eyes lit up with a smile Kate thought she recognized. A smile so engaging it bordered on the mischievous.

A smile Kate couldn't help but return.

In the womb before the world began, I was a child among other gods and children who were, or may be, or might be.
—Normandi Ellis, *Awakening Osiris*

ONE

Year Two in the Reign of Tutankhamen
(1359 B.C.)

DAY 16, FOURTH MONTH OF INUNDATION

The sudden noise startled me. Not that there was anything unusual about someone pounding on my door in the night. It was just that my thoughts were so far from the concerns of the living as I sat recording everything I had learned only a few hours before, in the House of Beautification. What did come as a surprise was to find a great hulk of a man standing between two Nubian torchbearers, flames leaping in his eyes like an angry Anubis, come to wreak vengeance on one who dared desecrate his dead. An impatient man, with his fist raised to beat on the door again.

"Fetch the physician, Senakhtenre, and be quick about it," he ordered.

"I am Senakhtenre," I replied, and lifted my lamp to lighten the shadows cast by his beaked nose and heavy brow. I knew then that I had seen him before, for his is a face to remember with that white scar slashing across one bronze cheek to pluck at an unforgiving mouth.

"Then come with me at once. There is no time to waste."

"First I must fetch my bag of medicines."

"Just do not think to delay, *sunu*," he warned me, "lest the lady who kneels on the bricks this night be taken by Osiris. Should that come to pass, I can promise, you will end by wishing the light of Amen had never fallen across your door."

I held my tongue and left him standing outside, for it is always a lesser man who needs to sound important simply because he is not. I refilled the packets of herbs I would need to treat a woman who labors in vain, then extinguished all but the lamp in my shrine to Thoth before hurrying back to where he waited.

He set a fast pace, avoiding the streets and alleyways where people stood drinking and talking even after dark, celebrating the news that the young Horus on Earth has taken the Princess Ankhesenamen as his Great Royal Wife. It has been almost three years since the young boy who succeeded the Fallen One of Akhetaten changed his name and returned to the city of Amen, restoring Waset to its rightful place as capital of the empire. And where before there was only the fetid odor of starvation and decay, the city of my birth now bustles with commerce and hope. On the edge of town we took the path to the walled precinct of Amen, where my silent escort did not skirt the god's great temple as I expected, but went between the twin towers of Osiris Amenhotep's massive gateway, then across the courtyard to the path beside the Sacred Lake, without once pausing to pay homage to the god on whose holy ground we trod.

From there we traveled a way known only to the priests, making me wonder what a rich master such as his could want of an ordinary physician like me when he could have any of the exalted priests from the House of Life. But I did not question the self-important jackass who had come for me, knowing he would welcome any chance to put me in my place. When we passed through a gate in the far wall of the temple precinct, the darkness closed around us in earnest, until we came to still another wall and then a watchman's lodge set into it. At a shout from my taciturn companion, the gate swung open to reveal a grand white villa, unlike anything I had seen in my entire twenty-two years. In the torchlight it seemed a shimmering white butterfly with its wings outstretched to hover over a bed of blossoms. As we approached the tall center section I saw that the double wood doors bore the likenesses of the animals representing the seven gods of creation, carved and inlaid with carnelian, ivory, and ebony.

Once inside, the servant led me through a shadowy antechamber, lit only by the many shrines to the family's household gods, then down a long hallway that opened into a vast high-ceilinged chamber. Here the walls were pristine white. So were the six lotusbud columns supporting the dark wood rafters overhead, where colorful figures of the entire pantheon of gods danced and played in their heavenly garden. A room of unmistakable elegance, but what I found most intriguing was how it bristled with life yet at the same time felt profoundly serene, a contrast that produced harmony rather than conflict or chaos.

I was still trying to uncover the secret of such a paradox when a man rose from the padded sitting shelf on the far side of the room and started toward me. He looked to be in his middle thirties, though his sleeveless white tunic revealed the muscled arms of a man ten years younger. But it was the way he carried himself rather than his house or fine linen and gold armlets that made me know there was far more than some twelve or thirteen years between us.

It wasn't until he passed under the lamp hanging from one of the rafters that I realized his head was clean-shaven. Yet he wore red-leather sandals beneath his long white kilt—another paradox since it is a rare priest who covers his feet. "You are the physician Senakhtenre?"

I nodded and put my palms together without taking my eyes from his, which were the color of the afternoon sky.

"My lady's midwife and two servingwomen remain with her," he told me without ceremony. "All the others have been sent away." I could hardly credit that such a man would allow any of his women, even the lowliest concubine, to go without the incantations of the priests, and I suppose it showed in my face. "Yes, *sunu*, your reputation travels ahead of you, even here. But do not stumble over your pride. If you have need of anything or anyone, you must say so. Other than that I ask only that you treat whatever happens here tonight as a vision that comes while you sleep, without substance in the light of Re."

"As it is with all those I treat, my lord. Whatever you know of me came from their mouths, not mine."

"Then go to her. And may Amen guide you as well as my child." He nodded to his man, who waited in the doorway. "Pagosh will show you the way."

I followed the servant he named Pagosh up a stairway to the sleeping room of an apartment fit for a goddess, where the priest's lady lay curled in upon herself as once she must have been inside her own mother. Two servingwomen hovered over a birthing stool to one side of the room while a white-haired grandmother sat beside the canopied couch, crooning a mournful lullaby.

As I approached, she broke off and turned to greet me. "Thank Amen you have come, *sunu*. I am Harwa, midwife to the Divine Consort to the God's Father."

It hit me like an unexpected blow from a throwing stick—the man who had greeted me below was the priest named Ramose, overseer of Amen-Re's land and all it produces, not to mention the god's growing treasure of gold.

"But I fear it is too late even for one such as you," she added, "who knows the secrets of the great Imhotep himself, may his *ka* live in eternity." The midwife cast a furtive glance at the bulging figure of the pregnant hippopotamus in the wall niche beside her, but the lady lying on the couch never stirred, even in the restless tossing of one whose *akh* sleeps while the demons of the Netherworld torture her body. Only the babe within her moved, probably to protest his long confinement.

"I will undertake treatment," I muttered, making no pretense of consulting my scrolls, though I was committing myself to a favorable outcome—a reportable offense should I fail. I laid my fingers to the vessel in the lady's neck, then to the base of her throat. Even there I could feel no more than a faint flutter, like the whisper of moth wings on a warm summer night. I knew then that she would not deliver at all, let alone in a kneeling position, unless I could strengthen her heart.

I extracted a packet of dried hyena's tongue from my bag and instructed one of the servingwomen to bring me a pitcher of beer. "And you," I called to the other, pointing to the basin on a brazier in the corner of the room, "throw that out and fill it with clean water." After that I spread a hand over the lady's belly, to feel for the moment when it would begin to tighten. When a harsh growl rose from her throat, I looked her full in the face for the first time—and jerked my hand away as if from a flame.

For a moment I could only stare at the countenance I had believed gone from this life forever, except where she strides across the face of the pylon before the temple of Re-Horakhte. But the shadow of her royal father lay across her face, in her almond-shaped eyes and prominent jaw, and try as I might to doubt my eyes, I knew in my heart who she was. Nefertiti. Beautiful One. Daughter of the Magnificent Amenhotep. Great Royal Wife to the Heretic Akhenaten. Queen of the Two Lands. And then, near the end, Nefer-neferu-aten Smenkhkare, Horus on Earth.

Even now, without her majestic blue war crown, with her face pale as the linen she lay upon, she possessed the same ethereal beauty. But she was Queen no more, nor King, and I knew not how to address her even in the privacy of my own thoughts.

What I did know was that this babe was not her first, so that could not be the reason it refused to come. "Why is there no incense burning to sweeten the air?" I inquired of the midwife, for the stench of the rituals performed by the priests who had been there before me was like smoke to my eyes.

"Majesty does not—" Harwa began, then caught herself. "My lady complains that the smoke burns her eyes."

"Do it anyway," I ordered, to let her know I was in charge there now. Then I poured beer into my bronze cup, added a measure of crushed hyena's tongue, stirred it with a wooden stick, and set it aside to steep. After that I scrubbed my hands with the powder from Wadi Natron and positioned them again over the lady's bulging belly, this time to search downward for the curve of the babe's head.

It was not where I expected it to be. Nor were the babe's buttocks there instead, which told me all I needed to know. I took a piece of hollow animal horn from my bag, slipped the narrow end between her lips, and poured a bit of the drugged beer into it. As the liquid trickled into her throat, she choked, then her eyes flew wide open.

"Rest easy, my lady. I am Senakhtenre, the physician." She searched my face, then took the cup from my hand and drank it down. The next tightening brought her shoulders and knees curling up from the couch, yet still she made no sound. "It hurts nothing to cry out and might even help," I told her, since I could do nothing to ease her pain lest I weaken her will to expel the child. As the knot slowly untied itself I slipped my fingers inside the birth canal and found her cervix wide enough to let the babe pass through. With one hand outside and the other in, I next determined that her babe lay side to side within her.

"How long has she been like this?" I inquired of Harwa, leaving one hand spread over the lady's belly to learn how much the babe might move when another tightening began and ended.

The midwife glanced at the water clock. "Three, perhaps four hours. I would have sent for you sooner but for the priests having to consult their scrolls and mumble over their smoldering ram's hair, trying to call forth the Seven Hathors, until—" She broke off, worried that she already had said too much.

"Then surely Isis must be watching over him," I murmured.

"Listen well to me, *sunu*," the onetime Queen whispered, struggling to rise on her elbows. "I have heard much of your skills with women who labor, and not from the mouths of peasants. So do not believe you can fail me and live to tell the tale. This child must live, *will* live."

"Then you would do well to entreat Isis to watch over him a little longer, while I try to place his feet on the path into this world."

"I have no need to ask the help of any other god!" So did the Beautiful One claim to be immortal even in the throes of an act she shared with every mortal woman.

I waited for her uterus to soften, instructed her to take a deep breath and, with one hand cupping the babe's head and the other his buttocks, began to alternately stroke and push his head down. For a while then we worked as partners, me turning the babe little by little while each tightening grew stronger than the one before it. Still she never uttered the scream that must have clawed at her throat, until I stood in awe of her strength of will. At last a sudden sliding movement told me the babe had tumbled into a different position, and I placed one hand above the lady's belly, ready to press down.

A few minutes later I held a tiny girl in my hands. I wiped the mucus from her nose, ran a finger inside her mouth to open the pathway for her to breathe, and felt her little chest expand, just before she let out a loud, angry cry.

"You have a daughter," I told her mother, though that would come as no surprise after the six Nefertiti already had birthed, fathered by the Heretic.

I laid the infant across her mother's stomach, tied off the cord with two lengths of linen thread, and waited for the pulsing blood to slow. Then, using the knife Harwa had seared in the flames of the brazier, I severed the connection between them—the act I find most disconcerting of all those I perform as a physician, for in solitude do we all exist from that moment forward through all eternity. The little girl ceased crying and began kicking her legs, glorying in her newfound freedom. When I wiped her clean with a soft cloth she quieted and watched my face with the unblinking, unfocused eyes of a newborn. Then I handed her to Harwa and turned to attend to her mother.

"Leave me in peace, *sunu*," the priest's lady muttered, turning away from my hand. "My part of the bargain is finished." It seemed an odd thing to say, though I could not fault her for wanting to rest.

"Not until you birth the after-membrane."

She objected no more, leaving me to wonder why she turned her face from her new daughter as well. Perhaps she has become disillusioned, I thought, for the gods have not been kind to her as a mother. Her three youngest daughters by the Heretic were carried away by the same pestilence that had taken the last child of Queen Tiye, her mother by marriage. As if that were not enough, her eldest is said to have thrown herself into Mother River rather than bear her father another child, a story that gained credence after her eleven-year-old sister died giving birth. That left only one, Tutankhamen's new Queen. And now this tiny daughter by a priest of Amen.

I handed a packet of powdered kesso root to Harwa, to give her lady should she complain of pain, and instructed the midwife to have her eat leeks cooked in goat's milk to stop the bleeding. After that I asked after the babe's nurse-mother.

"Ani, go find Merit," Harwa ordered one of the serving-women. "Tell her the *sunu* would speak with her." When the young woman appeared, she called out, "Another daughter, Merit, just as I predicted."

Barely eighteen, if that, the wet nurse took the babe into her arms and offered the little girl her breast.

"Your own child fares well?" I inquired.

"He went to Osiris two nights ago," she whispered, eyes cast down.

"I am sorry for that." I had no choice but to press her further. "Can you describe how it was with him, whether he felt too hot or—"

"Harwa said he came too soon." She blinked back the tears flooding her eyes. "He could hardly catch his breath—" When the babe at her breast chose that moment to fall asleep Merit looked to me with her heart in her eyes. "This one also is too small?"

I shook my head. "She only needs to rest after her long, difficult journey." The young nurse-mother continued to hold the new babe close while I instructed her to pour all the water she used, for bathing or drinking, through a finely woven cloth. When I turned away to repack my bag, she waited, then asked, "Is that all?"

"Ohhhh," I breathed, pretending to think. "I suppose it would not hurt for you to hug and play with her from time to time." It took a moment before her eyes lit up with understanding and, finally, delight.

"I will do exactly as you say, my lord, in all things."

I put my palms together and touched my chin to my fingertips. "Then may the gods grant you a joyful body, a healthy mouth, limbs that are forever young, and a long, happy life."

When I left the house of Ramose a short time later, my heart was warmed by the knowledge that the babe I had just helped enter this world would be cared for by a woman with so much love to give. For I suspect the tiny girl will get little enough of that from the woman who gave her life, whose ambition is known to exceed that even of old Queen Tiye, Osiris Amenhotep's Great Royal Wife. Or from her father, the man who guides Amen's growing wealth.

How long will it be, I wonder, before he is in a position to make all his lady's dreams come true?

TWO

Kate glanced up and noticed that the workroom had gone gloomy, all but the drawing table where she sat and the oversize viewbox mounted on the wall behind her. The row of windows above the workbench faced east, so by early afternoon it always turned dim and dreary. Now, in the waning days of November, the monochrome pall invaded the room even earlier than it had back in September, when Dave Broverman first consigned her to this backwater of the museum. She narrowed her eyes and saw the scene around her as an old photograph, absent both contrast and definition— sepia-toned, since the entire two-story building exuded a musty brown smell, as if to live up to its name. The Denver Museum of Antiquities.

She'd tried to put her own stamp on the high-ceilinged space by consigning the dusty detritus left by those who had been there before her to the shelves lining the back wall, and then never turning on the overhead fluorescent lights. But like the evil spirits the ancient Egyptians once believed in, the aura of failure emanating from all the botched attempts at conservation was beginning to take its toll on her own work. She couldn't forget they were there. That's why, without mentioning it to anyone, she'd been working on the artifacts she knew how to fix. All the toy lion with the movable jaw had needed was a new-old piece of string, a small wooden dowel inserted into the two parts of his broken front leg, and someone with sense enough to knot the string so his lower jaw wouldn't fall open too far.

It was the ones beyond help that broke her heart. Like the painted wood head of the young Egyptian boy. The gesso had begun to flake loose from the wood, so someone had used a syringe to inject glue into the cracks, then pressed the brittle pieces back into place over his rounded cheeks, breaking the flakes into even smaller fragments. The ultimate insult, though, had been to abandon him before the glue dried, allowing it to seep through the cracks and run down his cheeks, where it hardened, making the once-joyful boy appear to be crying. Sometimes, when Kate sat looking at him, she did, too.

"I told him everyone else has already left for the day," Elaine complained, flipping on the overhead lights as she burst through the half-open workroom door. Kate blinked and looked down at the dun-colored floor to let her eyes adjust to the harsh glare.

"I'm only going to be in town a couple of days," the man following Elaine explained, "to settle my grandmother's estate. I'd really appreciate it if you could look at a couple of pieces of her jewelry, so I'll know whether to bother with them. I'd expect to pay your usual appraisal fee, of course." He stepped closer and extended his hand. "Name is Maxwell Cavanaugh."

It sounded to Kate as if she'd missed something, but she accepted that the way she shook his hand, without a second thought. "Kate McKinnon," she returned. Unlike his thick brown hair, Maxwell Cavanaugh's beard was shot through with white. It might be neatly trimmed, but it still obscured too much of his face.

She glanced at Elaine. "Why don't you go ahead and lock up the information desk? Just let me know when you're ready to leave." The museum volunteer nodded but gave him a hard look as she left.

"I'll be happy to look, as you ask," Kate told him, "but the person you really need to see is Cleo Harris, our curator of Near Eastern Art. Ancient jewelry is her special area of expertise."

"My grandmother was really passionate about archaeology, and this one looks Egyptian to me." He dug into the outside pocket of his tweed sport coat, which he'd paired with faded blue jeans and a white shirt that was open at the neck, and pulled out a long string of beads. "It—I thought it might even be ancient," he added, watching for her reaction.

The beads were glass, but one glance told Kate they were neither Egyptian nor very old, because she had a passion, too, for anything and everything to do with ancient Egypt. That was why she had taken this assignment. That and Cleo, her old college roommate. From the beginning they had shared a fascination with how the ancient Egyptians lived, for what they knew and when they knew it, not just their way of death. The glue that held the two friends together, despite all their other differences, was parents who were no longer married to each other. In the end, emboldened by each other, they had mustered the nerve to say no to fathers who didn't really care and spent their vacations cruising the museums, Kate making detailed drawings for her roommate's "artifact file" while Cleo supplied the where, when, why, and how. Now Cleo was a recognized authority on ancient jewelry from Egypt, Turkey, and Mesopotamia. She also was a vintage-clothes freak, which was why Kate felt pretty confident about the provenance of her visitor's necklace.

"The fat green beads are scored to resemble Egyptian hieroglyphs, so you're right, they do have an Egyptian look," she agreed, "but they're too symmetrical and shiny to be ancient." She pointed to the small white beads strung between the green ones. "These probably were intended to mimic a papyrus stem, but the stems of the bulrushes that once grew along the Nile were round. These are triangular in cross section, like the papyrus plants we grow here, usually in pots because they freeze."

He lifted a skeptical eyebrow. "My grandmother had an educated eye, not to mention a sixth sense for when something didn't ring true. I doubt she would have been taken in by tourist junk."

Kate had her own doubts—that an "educated" eye meant to him what it did to her. It was more than the fact that most people weren't trained to be consciously observant. Because what she saw was intermixed with how it made her feel. Like the summer she and Cleo had gone to Europe by boat, when she'd spent hours watching the churning blues and greens of the ship's wake widen and spread to the distant horizon. Somehow the smell of the ocean, breathing air that was like no other on this earth, had made her so intensely aware of being alive that she had dreamed every night about the coming dawn, seeing the sun rise on the eastern horizon. Re-Horakhte.

"I didn't mean that it has no value," Kate responded, trying not to offend him. She couldn't tell from his face if he intended to sound argumentative, was just being protective of his grandmother, or what. But she had learned to be wary around anyone—male or female—who felt the need to hide behind a hairstyle or beard. "This necklace is an example of what we call Egyptomania, which is very collectible. I'd say it probably dates from the late twenties or early thirties, after Howard Carter found Tutankhamen's tomb. That's when the Egyptian look influenced everything from jewelry to furniture. The tassel of beads at the bottom is a nice blend of the Egyptian look with twenties styling, when they wore necklaces down to here"—she held it up so he could see where it would fall to on her—"with those short, flapper dresses. Perhaps it was a gift from someone your grandmother was especially fond of."

"Maybe," he muttered as he pulled something else out of his pocket. This one was wrapped in tissue paper, which he unfolded with care to reveal the necklace a little at a time. Ivory, without question. But it was the two pieces forming the catch—a sleek ivory ram's head and slender oval ring that slipped over its neck—that caught Kate's attention. As she stared, all kinds of foreign yet strangely familiar images began stumbling over each other in her head, until she felt overwhelmed by a sense of—of what, confusion?

She glanced up to find Maxwell Cavanaugh watching her like a hawk. "Something wrong?" he inquired in a quiet voice.

She shook her head. "It's just, for a minute, I thought—the ram's head reminded me of—I don't know. It's really quite beautiful. And very old." She reached to take it from him and saw his eyes shift to something behind her left shoulder.

"What happened to *her*?" He circled Kate to get a better look at the X ray.

"What makes you so sure it's a her?" She needed to know if he was guessing.

"Shape of the pelvic cavity, also the flare of the ilium. It's a mummy, isn't it? Egyptian?" Kate nodded. "How old is she?"

"The inscription on her coffin says she was fifteen."

"I'd say she was closer to twenty-five, but I meant how long ago did she live?"

Anyone could have misunderstood him, Kate told herself, rejecting old habits. "About 1350 B.C., plus or minus twenty-five years. The end of the Eighteenth Dynasty. Why do you think she was twenty-five?" she asked, curiosity driving her tongue.

"Ends of the tibia, for one thing. I'm a radiologist."

"Oh!" Was he, really? She couldn't help doubting, if only because every M.D. she'd ever encountered—and that was a lot—would have identified himself as *Dr.* Cavanaugh the instant he walked through the door.

"Pretty hard to fathom, isn't it—that she lived more than thirty-three centuries ago, yet we're standing here looking at her!" He turned to look at Kate and she saw that his entire face had changed, had come alive. Especially his blue eyes. Not as blue as Tashat's, but close. His pupils seemed dilated, giving his gaze a penetrating quality that Kate found disconcerting. Even so, she couldn't bring herself to look away. "I suppose that explains the extensive damage," he added, pushing her to respond.

"Not necessarily. Her cartonnage doesn't have a mark on it. Even her wooden coffin has only a chip or two out of the paint, not what you'd expect if she was dropped or moved around a lot." He turned back to the X ray and pointed to the larger of the two bones in Tashat's upper arm. The left one.

"See this faint line running parallel to the length of the bone? About the only time you see a linear fracture of the humerus like that is from a hard fall"—he crooked his left arm and smacked the elbow with the palm of his right hand—"with the elbow bent. But her arm is lying straight at her side, so the elbow couldn't have been hit the way I just described, not after her body was wrapped. That means this one fracture, at least, happened while she was alive. Or else during mummification." He glanced at Kate again. "That is what you'd like to know, isn't it—whether any of this mayhem occurred before she died?"

As if her answer was a foregone conclusion, he turned again to the backlit transparency. "Fingertips of the right hand disappear into the shadows because that arm is folded across her chest with the fingers curving over one breast," he observed, continuing his inventory. "Her left hand is lying at her side but appears to be covered with something the X rays couldn't penetrate . . . unless it's a technical blip."

Kate hadn't even considered that possibility, but Dr. Cavanaugh seemed to take her silence for closure. "Sorry, but this is pretty fascinating stuff. Guess I got carried away," he apologized with a wry smile. "What was it you were saying about that necklace?"

He couldn't possibly have missed the extra head! Kate let the necklace slide through her fingers, barely aware of the buttery feel of the timeworn ivory until her fingers touched the carved ram's head. Glancing down at it, she was struck again by the timeless beauty born of utter simplicity.

"Do you have any idea where your grandmother might have gotten this?"

He shook his head. "I never saw it before, when she was alive I mean. I found a slip of paper in the box, but with just one word on it, in her handwriting. Aswan."

The ram's head didn't look Egyptian, but Aswan was where the First Cataract once had been, one of six rough passages that at times were unnavigable before any dams were built on the Nile. And the god of the First Cataract was Khnum, a ram-headed man.

"I think this could be a really important piece," Kate told him, "and that you definitely should show it to Cleo Harris, the curator I mentioned earlier. She knows old jewelry from that part of the world better than anyone else in this country."

"Yeah, I heard someone here was good on jewelry," he replied. "Are you sure it isn't fake, maybe a copy? I read an article on the plane coming up here from Houston about the traffic in fake netsukes—you know, those little ivory carvings Japanese men used to wear with their kimonos?" He waited for her to nod. "Apparently they can make ivory look really old by soaking it in tea—"

"This is older than any netsuke."

"More than four or five hundred years?" he asked, obviously testing her.

Kate nodded. "I also think the two pieces forming the catch could predate the rest," she added, to whet his appetite for bringing it back. Cleo would be absolutely ecstatic about a piece with such unusual iconography. "Anything made of ivory would be too valuable to throw away even if some of the original beads were lost. It probably was handed down from generation to generation, with people adding new beads as needed to replace those that went missing."

"I guess the question is who, then? Or is it when?"

"Both." She mentioned Khnum. "But he has slightly wavy horns that stick out sideways from his head. These are suppressed to the point of only being suggested."

"What about Amen, or Amen-Re? Wasn't he represented as a ram, too?"

She took her time, aware now that Maxwell Cavanaugh knew more about ancient Egypt than he was admitting. "Rams were symbols of male fertility, so they always exhibited prominent horns even when they're curled close to the head. This one is more stylized. More abstract."

"That's what I thought, but doesn't that mean the opposite—that it isn't ancient?"

What he implied touched on one of Kate's pet peeves, the knee-jerk denigration of ancient abstract forms as primitive. "No. By abstract I mean stripped of decoration, of everything but the essentials, like some of the early female fertility figures that are all breasts and belly, with tiny heads." She surprised a glint of humor in his eyes. "It's just that this doesn't strike me as typically Egyptian. That suggests it could have been influenced by some other culture, but then I'm no Egyptologist. I'm sure Cleo will know."

She handed the necklace back to him, and he let the beads drip into his palm, slowly, forming a puddle of old ivory. Then, as if he'd come to some decision, his fingers snapped closed over the necklace.

"What's the story on that head between her thighs? Any idea who *he* is?"

She felt, suddenly, like a balloon loosed to float up into the clouds, just because Maxwell Cavanaugh had confirmed her own inexpert opinion that the extra skull was male. "We don't have a clue," she admitted. "Sometimes they put a stillborn baby in the same coffin with a mother who died in childbirth, or the body of a relative or servant in the tomb of a pharaoh, but usually in a different chamber. Dave Broverman, the director of the museum, thinks it's probably an accident. In some other cases, he says, the extras turned out to be chicken bones. Leftovers from some embalmer's lunch."

Dr. Cavanaugh gave her a thoughtful look. "I take it you don't agree."

"That the same accident is likely to occur again and again? No."

"Can you tell if she was rewrapped, like all those pharaohs after their tombs and mummies were robbed?"

"Perhaps you'd like to judge for yourself." Kate pointed to the bench under the windows, where Tashat lay in all her eternal splendor.

Dr. Cavanaugh followed her across the room without a word, nor did he say anything as his eyes traveled the length of the carton-nage, then returned again and again to the head and shoulder mask—to the glowing countenance framed by straight bangs and a smooth fall of jet-black hair.

Tashat's painted face possessed a lifelike quality beyond any funerary portrait Kate had ever seen, even from the period called the Golden Age of Egyptian art, when a more natural style had come into fashion. The mummy mask was only intended to resem-ble the person beneath it, so Tashat's wandering soul could find the body it belonged to each night, yet it was that infinitely intriguing face that made Kate feel so sure the extra skull was no accident.

Tashat's body had been tightly swathed in linen, the outer lay-ers stiffened with gesso and varnished to seal out moisture, then covered with a series of colorful scenes framed by gold bands that imitated the linen ones beneath them—scenes that Kate thought might represent the landmarks in Tashat's short life, if only they could figure out how to read them. Cleo insisted they were just vari-ations on the standard themes of religious symbolism associated with the afterlife, but they reminded Kate of the dreamlike scenarios of Paul Delvaux, the Belgian surrealist whose visual signature was a common street scene containing one thing that didn't fit, forcing the viewer to reassess everything else in the scene. On Tashat's carton-nage it was the tiny figures squeezed into every odd-shaped space like fillers in an artistic design. But they also could be read as pic-tographs, and one in particular—the stair-stepped hieroglyph for the goddess Isis—appeared again and again, sometimes alone, other times perched on the back of a little white dog, like a saddle on a horse. Except the Egyptians didn't ride horses. At least not then.

"That necklace is called an Amarna collar," she said, breaching the silence to point to the radiating rows of blue cornflowers and green leaves. "It's one of the reasons we think she lived during or shortly after the reign of Akhenaten, the pharaoh who outlawed all their gods but Aten, the full face of the sun. He built a new capital city at Akhetaten—Tel el Amarna today. But all we really know is that she was the daughter of the doorkeeper at the great temple of Amen and the wife of a Theban noble."

"Don't those hieroglyphs tell you anything?" He pointed to the column of symbols running down the center of Tashat's cartonnage.

"They're sort of an epitaph, verses from the Book of the Dead, which the Egyptians called the Book of Coming Forth by Day." While she translated one from memory she watched his eyes. " '*At my death let the bubbles of blood on my lips taste as sweet as berries. Give me not words of consolation. Give me magic, the fire of one beyond the borders of enchantment. Give me the spell of living well.*' "

His lips moved as if he were about to speak, but his Adam's apple seemed to get in the way. When he swallowed, shook his head, then swallowed again, Kate guessed that he was discovering—as she had—that any words he could think of paled by comparison. For the first time, Maxwell Cavanaugh was at a loss for something to say.

In that moment she forgot he was a member of the cabal that had caused her so much grief and came to his rescue. "That style of sandal originated in Thebes around the middle of the fourteenth century B.C.," she told him, pointing to Tashat's papier-mâché-like foot mask. "More confirmation of her provenance." The palm-frond sandals had a low sidewall sloping in from the sole, like the beginnings of a shoe, and a braided strap curling up from the toe to form a T with the strap across the instep.

"Do you think she was his only wife?" he asked without looking up.

"A man could have however many wives he could afford. Since most people of her class would have a full pasteboard cartonnage over the linen wrapping, not just a head mask and a foot mask, that suggests a lesser wife, probably one of several."

"Maybe he didn't *want* three or four wives." A smile played at the corner of his mouth.

"What makes you say that?"

"Something about her eyes, or maybe it's her mouth—both, unless my imagination has gone through the roof. I suspect looking at her might do that to you."

"What . . . about her eyes?" Kate urged, trying not to prompt him.

"It's just, well, she has such a look of—" He paused, searching for the right word. "Call it intelligent curiosity combined with, oh, I'm not sure—as if there's a spark of mischief hiding behind that serious facade. Like she's smiling somewhere inside." He turned to Kate with a self-deprecating smile. "I hope you're not going to tell me it's just some stylized portrait they put on all the young women back then."

Kate watched his lips curve up, pulling a fan of lines at the outer corners of his eyes. Then the fold above them closed down while his cheeks lifted in a classic Duchenne, the only one of several well-documented smiles known to produce happy emotions, or at least a good mood—one more thing she knew about him, despite the beard. That and the fact that he was very good at reading X rays. Had to be to get gender from the skull alone with little more than a casual glance, which probably meant it wasn't as casual as he made it appear.

"No, she's definitely one of a kind," she answered, just as Elaine poked her head around the door.

"All locked up and ready to go."

"Okay, we're coming, too." Kate went to the closet for her coat and on the way out flipped the switch on the viewbox, letting the X ray go dark.

They walked down the hall together and through the reception area to the main entrance, where the security guard locked the door behind them. It was pitch-dark outside and felt near freezing. "I always forget how cold it can get here in November," Dr. Cavanaugh mumbled into his collar. "We were still running the air-conditioning when I left Houston."

"I heard it might snow tonight," Kate remarked, trying to think of some way to ask if he'd be interested in a trade—Cleo's appraisal of the ivory necklace for a professional reading of that X ray.

They were almost to the parking lot when he slowed and put out a hand to detain her. "Look, I know how you could learn a lot more about her, and without disturbing a hair on either head." His breath formed a cumulus cloud in the frigid night air. "Maybe if I could describe what I have in mind and you told me more about—" He glanced around as if searching for something. "It's too cold to stand out here. How about going someplace for a cup of coffee or a beer? Unless you have someone waiting for you at home?"

She did, and he wouldn't be a bit happy if she was late again. But a chance like this didn't come along every day. Sam would just have to wait.

Vince's Italian Ristorante specialized in Neapolitan pizza. Anything else, Vince had told her more than once, was a bastard—unworthy of the name. He greeted them from behind the cash register and suggested they pick their own table.

"Near the fireplace okay with you?" Dr. Cavanaugh inquired. Kate nodded and started across the room, relieved to see that only one table was occupied. She didn't want to miss anything he had to say.

Once seated he glanced around at the decor, taking in the red-brick walls and checkered tablecloths, then commented, "Smells great in here. Would you like something to eat?"

She assumed he was just being polite. "No thanks, but I'll have a glass of wine. The house red."

Vince had followed them and took their order. When he left, Dr. Cavanaugh sat back as if he expected her to make conversation while they waited. When she didn't, he volunteered, "This kind of weather is why I left Michigan after my residency."

The Michigan coincidence was almost too much, but Kate didn't want to divert him from what he was about to propose. Fortunately, a waitress brought their drinks right away, and he poured some beer into the frosted mug, then tasted it before glancing across at her. "If you're not an Egyptologist, what are you doing with that X ray?"

She was beginning to see a pattern in the way he *didn't* react immediately to something that puzzled him—first the head between Tashat's legs, then who or what Kate was at the museum. A cautious man, yet he obviously had acted on impulse as they were leaving the museum. Now it sounded as if he was having second thoughts.

"What I'm supposed to be doing are forensic illustrations to display with the mummy," she replied. "How Tashat's body probably looks right now, under the cartonnage, what she may have looked like in life, and an in-the-round head if I can get accurate enough measurements to duplicate her skull. Unfortunately, I need to get the story I'm going to tell clear in my head before I can draw it. With Tashat, that's not happening." She paused, anticipating his reaction, then took the plunge. "I'm a medical illustrator, on temporary assignment at the museum as a favor to Cleo Harris, a friend from college."

He came close to stuttering. "You're a phy—an M.D.?"

Kate didn't intend to confess to any stranger why she'd dropped out of medical school, let alone one of *them*. That the decision was hers to make didn't matter; that she had worked hard to succeed at something she really cared about and failed, did. Five years later it still felt as if she'd walked into an ambush, mostly because she had gone in believing she could work around her old nemesis just as she had in college—by observing how a classroom was arranged and manipulating most situations so she could concentrate on one voice at a time. And she had, until they started group hospital rounds. That's when it hit home that she'd never be able to trust herself—to know for sure she hadn't missed something crucial because too much was going on at once. Too much noise. Trying harder wasn't enough. She'd finally had to accept the reality of her own inadequacy.

"No, I'm not," she replied, opting for the truth but not the whole truth. "I know a lot of medical illustrators are, but I've got a solid grounding in physiology, plus I've been drawing for as long as I can remember." He watched her the way a cat eyes a bird, without blinking or moving a muscle. "I did give med school a shot," she continued. "Two years. By then my drawings were in such demand I decided illustration was what I really should be doing."

He continued to stare at her. Then, without a word, he lifted his beer and drained half the glass. Kate recognized the pattern. Worried that he might be backing off, she grabbed on to the first thing that came to mind.

"Were you at Ann Arbor?" He nodded, still watching. "It's an odd coincidence is all. That X ray of Tashat was taken by a team from the dental school in Ann Arbor back in the late sixties, when they took a portable unit over to study the effect of genetics on dentition in Nubian children. The people at the Egyptian Museum, in Cairo, asked them to return the next year, to x-ray the royal mummies and try to trace familial connections through dentition and craniofacial features. While they were at it they did several mummies that had been stored in an attic room for some thirty years, mostly priests and government officials from the New Kingdom. Tashat was among them."

"How did she get here?"

"She's nobody important and the Department of Antiquities needed money to modernize the Cairo museum, so they allowed an indefinite loan in exchange for the requisite baksheesh. Considering the pollution in Cairo, she's probably better off here." Actually, Kate wasn't too sure about that, given the budget constraints Dave Broverman was always throwing in her face to explain why they couldn't buy the equipment she needed, let alone do the one thing that would solve most of her problems—have Tashat scanned.

"Okay." He scooted forward as if he'd come to a decision. "That you're familiar with what I'm going to suggest only makes it easier. Can I call you Kate?" She nodded. "As I'm sure you know, a CT scan produces cross sections without the shadows cast by surrounding tissue or bone. We also can do three-dimensional images, of an entire organ or a single tooth. That's what I'd like to try on Tashat."

"Look, Dr. Cavanaugh—"

"Max."

"Max," she agreed. "It's been a while—five years—so I'm not really up on what the latest scanners can do." She pushed her hair away from her face and tried to slow down. "Would you mind if I ask a few questions?"

"Ask away," he invited.

"Is there any chance of determining which fractures may have occurred before she died?"

"Not unless we found some evidence of primary callus. Otherwise, we'd have no way of telling whether there's no new bone growth because she died right away or because the fractures occurred postmortem."

"I meant can the new scanners pick up bone growth the older X rays might have missed?"

He hesitated. "Maybe."

"How about whether that extra skull was wrapped before it was placed between her legs?"

"I'd certainly think so. How much contrast we can develop might be a question, if you're thinking of using the films as illustrations. I've never scanned a mummy, but if it's important, I can check the literature. Is it?"

She nodded. "That would be pretty compelling evidence against any accident." He waited for another question, but Kate was concentrating on how to approach the touchiest subject of all—money.

"At the very least," he continued, "we ought to learn whether that shadow on her right hip was caused by an injury or infection. It could even be an artifact of the conditions under which they shot the X ray, if they were using portable equipment." Kate hadn't even thought of that, which only brought home again how much they needed someone with Maxwell Cavanaugh's expertise.

"The problem is, Dr. Cavanaugh—"

"Max."

"I doubt my director would even consider shipping her—"

He was shaking his head. "I mean do it here, at an imaging facility I sometimes consult for. That way you and anyone else from the museum could help us interpret whatever we run into."

"I thought you weren't going to be in town very long."

"I can always arrange to stay a little longer, or else come back." His eyes stayed on her face. "The museum wouldn't be out anything except the cost of transporting her across town, if that's what's worrying you." He paused to see if that made any difference before adding, "I really would like to do this, Kate. It wouldn't be a one-way street, all give and no take."

She didn't feel comfortable asking, but obsessing over a woman who lived over three thousand years ago wasn't her usual thing, either. "Why?"

A piece of wood popped and he glanced at the fire, then back at her. "My grandmother was sort of the Auntie Mame type, I guess, and one year during the Christmas holidays she took me to Egypt. Just the two of us. I was twelve, but like so many kids, infected with the bug even before that. Wanted to be an Egyptologist, spent hours poring over pictures of mummies and tomb paintings. I must've read *God, Graves and Scholars* at least five times, cover to cover." He gave her a wistful smile, then shrugged the memory away. "Call it nostalgia, a chance to revisit a time in my life when everything wasn't set in concrete."

"When—what changed your mind about becoming an Egyptologist?"

"I suppose my fascination with mummies evolved. Still bodies, but living ones. I wanted to know what makes us tick—how the brain works, an organ the Egyptians hardly even talked about. As I recall, they believed the intellect resided in the heart." Kate finally let herself smile, but he wasn't through. "Look, you're not up on the latest scanners, and I'm not up on what three thousand years can do to human bones. I don't even remember what internal organs they left in and which ones they took out during mummification."

"No problem. I can give you a refresher course in fifty words or less. At the time we're talking about here, the priests in the House of Beautification went up the left nostril with a long spoonlike tool and punched through the spongy ethmoid bone into the cranial cavity. Without disfiguring the nose, I might add. Some people think they used the same narrow spoon to scoop out the brain, but I think it's more likely that they stirred the brain to liquefy it, then simply poured it out." She put her fingers to the left and a little below her navel. "They made an incision right about here to remove the lungs, liver, kidneys, stomach, and intestines. But not the heart. That had to stay in to be weighed against the feather of truth when it came time for Osiris to pass judgment on the deceased." She reached up to tuck a wayward strand of hair behind her ear. "After that the body was laid on a sloping table to let the liquids drain off and covered with natron, a crystalline form of sodium and calcium salts, mostly sodium carbonate. Same with the viscera. For forty days."

"I thought it was seventy."

"I'm not finished. After forty days in the natron, they washed the body with palm wine, closed the abdominal incision, and sealed it with resin. Wads of oil-soaked cloth were placed in the mouth and a piece of linen over each eye, before closing the lids. The nostrils were sealed with wax. Then came the adornments—rings, bracelets, wreaths of flowers—followed by the burning of incense to symbolically restore warmth and odor to the body. Finally, they began wrapping, first each finger and toe, followed by each arm and leg. With a male the penis was wrapped separately, too. In an erect position, of course."

He didn't even try not to smile. "Why do I get the impression you're looking for more than what you just asked me about?"

She didn't want him to think she was a New Age nut bent on making everything fit some half-baked theory like numerology, but she needed to test her hunch on someone whose roots weren't so firmly planted in the humanities. Cleo's virtue was flexibility, but her logic often was illogical since she could accept, or simply ignore, evidence Kate could not.

"I think the scenes on Tashat's cartonnage, perhaps the ones inside her coffin as well, may tell a story. A boat under sail is the hieroglyph for south, for instance, because the prevailing wind on the Nile is from the north. That's what made it possible for them to sail up the river against the current. Suppose Tashat traveled up the river for some reason? Certainly that would have been a major event in her life."

"Aren't boats pretty common in Egyptian mythology?"

He was right to point that out. "I know it's ambiguous if you view each scene alone, but there's more. The hieroglyph for the goddess Isis appears in every one of those panels"—she drew a stair-stepped shape in the air—"most of the time with a little white dog. But dogs don't figure in their religious iconography, unless you count Anubis, who watched over the embalming process. But he has a long tail and pointed ears and is always black, the color of death."

Max nodded, slowly, thinking while he continued to watch her. Then, as if he'd arrived at some conclusion, he picked up his glass and drained it, reached into his back pocket for his wallet, and put a bill on the check. When he glanced up his eyes were sparkling with eagerness. "Okay, so where do we go from here? Should I talk to your director? What's his name again?"

"Dave Broverman. But I'd like to bring Cleo in, ask her to arrange something for tomorrow if that works for you." Worried that Maxwell Cavanaugh might still slip through their fingers, Kate stopped short of spelling it out for him—that she was low man on the museum totem pole.

"Okay, but I need to contact my radiologist friend in Littleton before I talk with whoever has to give us the go-ahead, and see how the scheduling looks there so I can be more specific about when. How about if I call you in the morning?"

"Sure." She pulled a paper napkin from the holder, took the pen he handed her, and wrote down her number at the museum. "I should know something by ten." Maybe even sooner, she thought, since it was Thursday, the night Dave's wife played bridge.

THREE

Dave had agreed to a magnanimous fifteen minutes for Max at three o'clock. Kate considered the way he'd worded his response as borderline insulting, but it didn't seem to bother Max. He had called from the clinic in Littleton, and said he would come early "so you can clue me in on what he'll probably want to know."

By noon she was feeling too jumpy to eat, but forced herself to go to the museum café, where she nibbled on the crackers that came with her salad. Then, worried that she might miss him, she gulped down some hot tea and hurried back to the workroom. She needed to get a grip and the only way to do that was to draw. First she tried sketching the street scene with Tashat and her little white dog, but it had already begun to fade, like a dream that disappears from memory upon waking. She ended up doodling, letting her hand wander without purpose until an image slowly began to form in her mind's eye.

Flipping to a clean page, she drew with quick strokes, hoping to catch the essence of Maxwell Cavanaugh before he, too, could slip away. A few minutes later she knew she had him. Not his face but the attitude of his body, which spoke louder than words. He moved with a kind of controlled deliberateness, yet his stance was relaxed, which suggested he was at peace with himself—without the simmering insecurity that made Dave Broverman such a control freak. She pictured Max's broad square hands, the flash of excitement in his eyes, and realized they were of a piece—that the one out-of-tune note was the mustache and beard. What was that? Some kind of midlife rebellion against a wife or job that had gone stale?

"Am I interrupting?" She turned to find him peering around the half-open door. She shook her head, aware that he looked different. It wasn't until he came on in that she caught the full impact of his mouse-colored suit, and wondered if he planned to overwhelm the lion with meekness.

"The clinic in Littleton has one of the new high-resolution machines," he told her right off, "so we can slice her down to one millimeter if we need to. It'll have to be at night or a Sunday, though, and the sooner the better. Come December, Phil Lowenstein spends every weekend on the slopes."

"Your friend wants to be there, too?"

"Either him or a technician, and I'd rather have him." He looked all around while he spoke, as if seeing the workroom for the first time. "I'm not licensed in Colorado."

"You can't even x-ray a mummy without a license?"

He shrugged, then moved to the workbench where she'd spread some watercolors to dry. "Can I look or would that be a breach of protocol?"

"They're just studies for a larger illustration, but help yourself."

He examined them one at a time, taking so long that Kate decided he wasn't going to say anything. Not that she was looking for compliments. But they were perfectly ordinary anatomical renderings, without any abnormalities that might send him into his silent mode.

"Jesus, Kate," he said finally. "These are really exceptional." He laid one down and picked up another. "You caught every muscle and tendon exactly right. Arrested, yes, but not for long. I get the feeling it could even be a trick of my imagination, that you stop-framed this one so I could see how the muscles elongate but it's just on the verge of reversing itself, of contracting. They're just so—so exquisitely right!" He glanced at her. "Do you know those anatomical studies by da Vinci, the ones he did with this same red pencil?"

"Conté crayon."

"Whatever. That's what I mean about the way you've captured the fluidity of the human body in motion." Like Re-Horakhte rising on the eastern horizon, a smile started somewhere behind her eyes, bathing the whole room in its brilliant white light. Max didn't seem to notice. He was holding up the portrait she'd done with transparent washes.

"Do you think her eyes actually were blue? Weren't the Egyptians a dark-eyed people, like Middle Easterners today?"

Kate had wrestled a long time with the color of Tashat's eyes and still worried that she had let herself be influenced by personal experience, because her own eyes were yellow with brown flecks—unlike anyone else in her family, which her father never let her forget.

"It may be politically correct to describe them as a mosaic instead of a melting pot, but there had to be a lot of intermixing in an empire that extended north to the Euphrates and south up the Nile to Khartoum. They traded all over the Mediterranean and brought prisoners of war home as slaves, so blue eyes may not have been common but there must've been some."

"In that case why give her curly hair when it's straight on that mask?"

"That's probably a wig. I'm guessing she would choose something different from her natural hair." Kate shrugged, felt a strand of curly hair fall across her cheek, and reached up to push it behind her ear. "I know I would."

She caught the smile in his eyes before he glanced at his watch. "So fill me in on your director. Anything I should try to make a point of, or avoid?"

This was not the time to tell him that Dave Broverman feared new information the way the Egyptians feared the plague, in case it should topple the house of cards on which he'd built his reputation. Now, with feelers out to several universities, Dave would be especially wary of anything that sounded risky. But she was counting on Cleo to remind him that the "gift" Maxwell Cavanaugh was offering actually could tip the scales the other way. The Antiquities Museum operated in the shadow of Denver's pride and joy, the Museum of Natural History, where a newly installed Egyptian exhibit included not only a mummy but films from a CT scan carried out at a local hospital. That scan had revealed very little they didn't already know, which Dave knew, but just by doing it the

Antiquities Museum would rise to its level. Finding something new, not to mention sensational, could put Dave's operation on the map.

"You might want to reassure him about this procedure, that it carries no risk of damage to the mummy," Kate suggested. "Also, if he asks how the scanner works, try not to make it too complicated. Cleo's the same way. Anything very technical turns them off."

"Okay. Anything else?"

She pulled the *X-Ray Atlas of the Royal Mummies* from the shelf where she kept the books she'd borrowed from the Denver Museum of Natural History library, something else Dave's budget couldn't support. "You might want to glance at some of the shots taken by the University of Michigan team." She handed it to him and reached for another book, this one entitled *Evidence Embalmed*. "This, too, in case Cleo brings up the Manchester study."

"Your friend's going to be there?" Kate nodded. "Anybody else?"

"Me."

"Good. Why Manchester?"

"The museum there got together a group of people from different fields to conduct autopsies on a couple of their undesirables— mummies in plain brown wrappers so they're not prized for display. Anyway, they did a pretty thorough job. Blood grouping, histology, carbon dating, and even developed a way to rehydrate tissue so they could lift fingerprints from the dermis rather than the epidermis."

"Okay." He sat down at her drawing table and started on the atlas.

Twenty minutes later Dave was doing his predictable best to downplay the whole idea. "I'm not sure she's worth all the trouble, Dr. Cavanaugh, but I'd be interested in hearing what you think we could learn that we don't already know."

"We'd eliminate the guesswork about what she looks like right now, under the bandaging."

"An image composed of multiple cross sections?" Dave glanced at Kate. "Do you think that's aesthetically wise?"

Max answered for her. "We can produce some pretty impressive composites, too, of any part or the entire body, from any angle."

"But still a computerized image," Dave insisted, fingering the knot of his tie. Satisfied that it was straight, he checked his cuff links next, making sure they were aligned with the buttons of his coat sleeves. "What about cause of death?"

"That depends on what it was. But we'd establish an age range for that second skull, and learn whether it was wrapped before it was placed between her legs."

Dave flicked a glance at Kate, as if to let her know that he knew where that came from. "I assure you that is the result of rewrapping, or else an embalmer's mistake."

"Then we could confirm that she *was* rewrapped," Max persisted.

Cleo arrived at that moment, mumbling apologies for being late, and Max rose from his chair to greet her. "This is Cleo Harris," Kate began, hoping to get the introductions over with quickly. "Cleo, meet Dr. Maxwell Cavanaugh."

Max beamed as Cleo offered her hand. "That wouldn't be short for Cleopatra, would it?" To Kate it sounded like something he would say to put a new patient at ease.

"A self-fulfilling prophecy," Cleo replied with an assessing glance, then took the chair beside him, "but don't let me interrupt." She had on a velvet tunic and long bias-cut skirt, mixing vintages in different shades of green that made her copper-colored hair look even more so, with platform shoes she didn't need.

"I was just telling Dr. Broverman that scanning Tashat would resolve a number of questions about that male skull," Max explained for her benefit. "What he has in his mouth, for instance. Or do you already know?"

A stunned silence greeted his little bombshell.

Kate kept her eyes straight ahead, wondering why he hadn't mentioned that the day before. Was it just his brand of insurance, as Cleo was hers?

"Oil-soaked pads, most likely," Dave supplied, eyes darting sideways between Maxwell Cavanaugh and Kate.

"I thought MRI was the preferred imaging technology these days," Cleo put in.

"For resolving soft tissues, yes," Max agreed, "especially the brain. But magnetic resonance depends on aligning the hydrogen molecules in water. If there's no water left in the body, the results could be unreliable. X-ray tomography, on the other hand, is better for resolving the cranial sutures, the seams where the plates of the skull come together. Those and the growth plates in the long bones are what we need to see to clear up the confusion about her age."

"But we already know how old she was," Cleo pointed out, leaning around him to peer at Kate. "Didn't you tell him?"

"She told me," Max replied. "I can't be absolutely sure from that old X-ray, but the third molars appear to be partially in. If so, that would make her at least twenty. If they're all the way in, she's even older, not fifteen. Maybe her coffin was intended for someone else. That happened sometimes, didn't it? Seems like I read about one where the original face had been scraped off and repainted. Akhenaten, wasn't it, the pharaoh they call the Heretic?"

The back of Dave's executive chair snapped to attention. "If you mean KV Fifty-five—that's Valley of the Kings tomb number fifty-five, Dr. Cavanaugh, in case you're not familiar with our notation system—yes, that coffin does appear to have been intended for someone else. But the body was Smenkhkare, not Akhenaten. A lot of amateurs, even graduate students, confuse the controversy over who the coffin belonged to with the identity of the body it contained."

"The inscription had been changed, too, from female to male," Cleo added. "So that coffin probably belonged to Meritaten, Smenkhkare's wife and Akhenaten's daughter, which would explain why his name was on some of the grave goods."

"I stand corrected then," Max murmured. Without missing a beat, he asked, "How did they establish the identity of the mummy?"

"An autopsy and radiological examination carried out by three very reputable scholars working as a team," Dave replied, "who verified it was a male no younger than eighteen and no older than twenty-three."

"I understand those remains were in pretty bad shape even a hundred years ago, when the tomb was found. Do you happen to know which—"

"Both age and gender were determined not only by the pelvis," Dave said, anticipating him, "but the state of development of the sacrum. Akhenaten had to be at least thirty by the end of his reign. Even more compelling is that this body was of the same blood group as Tutankhamen, which means the elusive Smenkhkare was Tut's brother. Some of us believe Smenkhare was not only Akhenaten's coregent but his lover." That little kicker didn't even faze Max.

"Blood grouping indicates kinship," Max agreed, "but not whether two men are brothers, father and son, or even cousins twice removed. Didn't Akhenaten have an older brother who died?"

"You're an Egyptologist as well, Dr. Cavanaugh?" Dave inquired, making a point of his own.

"No, of course not. I only—"

"You're probably too much the rational scientist to appreciate the ancient Egyptian mind," Dave continued, an insult masquerading as a compliment. "But to preserve a man's *ren*—his name—was to allow his spirit to live on after death. To blot it from memory was to destroy him forever, a powerful form of an ancient curse."

For Kate the words were flying back and forth so fast they began to pile up in her head, like cars on a superhighway that suddenly narrows, forcing them into one bumper-to-bumper lane. A sensation she recognized. Next would come the static. She closed her eyes to shut everything out so she could concentrate on stopping the rush of words before they collided and burst into unintelligible noise, and tried to bring up an image of Tashat. Instead, another face appeared in her mind's eye, one more familiar than her own. Sam.

"That is why," Dave said, "when Horemheb and the priests of Amen set out to rid the Two Lands of the Aten heresy, they tried to eliminate all evidence that the Amarna kings ever existed—not only Akhenaten but Smenkhkare, Tutankhamen, and Ay."

Kate suspected he was warming up to say no. She opened her eyes and turned to Max. "Computerized tomography could give us a true-to-life dimensional map of Tashat's skull, isn't that right?" He nodded, then waited to see where she was going. Kate looked at Dave. "That means I wouldn't have to extrapolate or just plain guess in some places to re-create Tashat's skull."

"That's right," Max agreed, following her lead. "The data from the scanner can even be fed to a computer-controlled milling machine, to carve an exact replica of the skull out of styrene or some other rigid plastic. Then there's laser sintering, where a computer-guided laser beam duplicates whatever shape it's told to by polymerizing a powdered plastic. A surgeon I know in Houston uses that technique for the parts he needs in reconstructive surgery." He glanced at Kate. "No offense intended, but you'd get a more accurate armature for building that head, and much faster."

Kate looked around him to Cleo. "Not only the skull. Think of it, Clee—Tashat dressed and adorned as she might have been thirty-three centuries ago, walking the streets of ancient Waset—Thebes to the Greeks—with her little white dog. A blue lotus blossom tucked behind one ear, to match her eyes. All with *exquisite* accuracy." The little smile plucking at one corner of Max's mouth told her he remembered using that very word.

For a moment Cleo just sat there, letting her imagination take up where Kate left off. Then, unable to sit still, she jumped up and began pacing back and forth across the end of Dave's big desk, skirt swirling around her ankles.

"Picture it, Dave. An entire room"—she used both arms to draw a huge square—"or rooms, devoted to life as a young Theban woman lived it during the Golden Age of Egypt! We could open with a series of X rays and cross sections from the scan, intermixing them with poster-size images of what Tashat looks like now—the composites Max mentioned. Follow that with drawings or photographs of each step in the reconstruction process. Next would be Kate's sketches and colored portraits of Tashat, adorned with different wigs and jewelry, all building to the grand climax—a fully realized figure from life in her natural setting. All done with unassailable accuracy!"

She stopped pacing, braced her hands on the desk, and spoke directly to Dave. "What the Egyptians really looked like remains controversial because the ethnic mix is speculative at best. We still don't know how literally to take their reliefs and paintings, or Akhenaten's physical abnormalities—the pear-shaped torso and elongated face. How much of that was real versus symbolic? Or was it just artistic convention?" She pushed free of the desk and went back to pacing. "With Tashat as the cornerstone, plus a few important loans, I'll bet we could get a corporate grant to underwrite the whole thing."

Dave began to nod, slowly, eyes focused inward on his own fantasies—a cushy professorship at Chicago, if not Harvard or Yale.

"Yes," he murmured finally, smoothing a hand over his dark, razor-cut hair, "it does present some very interesting possibilities."

"Of course you'd have to write the monograph to go with it," Cleo reminded him, adding fuel to the fire she'd lit under Dave's ego. "From what Dr. Cavanaugh says, we might even discover something about the extra head that points to a death ritual nobody's ever seen before."

Kate watched Max watch Cleo stack the deck in their favor. "The scanner is available this Sunday, day after tomorrow," he put in, "if that works for whoever you'd get to transport her from the museum."

Dave stood up suddenly, signaling that he'd come to a decision. "Cleo is right. This could be an invaluable tool for educating the public. And that, after all, is our primary reason for being." All smiles now, he came around his desk to seal the deal by shaking Max's hand.

As they all began moving toward the door, Cleo flashed Kate a self-satisfied grin, as if to say "See, I told you not to worry." Dave almost caught her when he turned and dropped a proprietary hand on her shoulder. "I know you'll want to be there, Cleo, so I'll leave all the arrangements to you."

Kate had heard enough. Craving quiet, she started back to the workroom, and was halfway down the hall when Cleo caught up with her.

"I know you want this, Katie, but be careful. From what I heard in there, I'd say this one is cut off the same bolt of cloth as those clinchpoops you ran into back in med school." Cleo favored vintage terms of endearment, too. "Besides, he's too old for you."

"I don't care if he's forty or four hundred, Clee. I'm not interested. Not the way you mean, anyway."

"Well, he's interested in you."

Kate just shook her head and veered off into the workroom, leaving Cleo heading for the stairs to the second floor.

By the time Max showed up it was finally beginning to sink in—
Dave had actually said yes. She was going to see Tashat as she really
was. What excited her most, though, was the realization that she
would be able to re-create Tashat as she once actually looked, without all the guesswork that had clouded her vision for the past two
months. Not one of those vacant-eyed mannequins either, she told
herself, thinking of the forensic heads she'd seen, some so impersonal their own mothers wouldn't recognize them.

"Boy, am I glad your friend is on our side!" was Max's first
comment.

"Me too." Kate had to smile despite a new worry that had
occurred to her—that they might learn something she didn't want
to know. Something that would put the lie to Tashat's cartonnage
portrait and destroy the young woman who had begun to come
alive in Kate's head. A kind of second death.

"Was it my imagination, or is something going on between
those two?"

"You might call it that."

He shrugged. "Thought that was a wedding ring he had on."

"So what else is new?" Kate responded, hoping he would drop
the subject.

He did. For a minute Max pretended a consuming interest in
the little wooden lion she kept on the corner of her drawing table
because she liked being able to reach out and physically touch a
time long past. Now he pulled the knotted string, making the lion's
jaws open and close, until the silence began to feel uncomfortable.

When she caught Max glancing at his watch, she blurted out,
"When are—" just as he said, "Would you—"

"Sorry," he apologized. "I was going to ask if you'd like to have
dinner with me." She wondered if Cleo might be right, until he
explained why. "I've got a few questions, thought I might try to get
a better handle on what we're likely to run into Sunday. I brought
my laptop with me and plan to plug into Medline before then, see
what I can find in the literature. If you're busy that's okay. It's not
important."

It was to Kate. "No, I'd like to. But I need to go home first—"
She stopped, remembering how much he seemed to enjoy tossing

that little bombshell back in Dave's office. "To fix Sam's supper. He gets upset when I'm late too many nights in a row."

Max looked confused, then apologetic. "That's okay, we can let it go."

"Why don't you come with me? It's only a few blocks from here. So close I even walk to work most of the time, or else jog. But not today. That way we wouldn't have to take both cars." She could tell by the way he hunched his shoulders that he was backing away. Closing a door. "Besides, meeting you would be a real treat for Sam. You two have a lot in common."

"Sure," he agreed. "Be glad for him to come along if he'd like."

Kate shook her head. "He'd only be bored. Besides, he needs to learn that throwing a temper tantrum won't get me to stay home."

Kate drove into the driveway of her rented brick bungalow, then waited on the front porch while Max parked at the curb. It was ominously quiet inside, too quiet, making her wonder what Sam was doing. As Max came up the steps, she pushed the door open and called, "Sam? Where are you?"

The dog came shooting out of the bedroom hallway, made a beeline straight for Kate, and slid to a stop against her ankles. Then, wagging his tail with pure delight, he put his forepaws on her knees and leaned his head into her hands.

"I brought a friend home to meet you." She patted his chest, a signal for him to get down. "Max, meet Samson. Sam for short."

"You're a breed unto yourself, aren't you, boy?" Max muttered to the dog as he squatted down to pet him. "Just like her."

Sam had the thick, sturdy body and short legs of a Welsh corgi, the pointed ears and nose of a fox, and velvety brown eyes that had been Kate's undoing. Black-and-brown fur waved down his back, ending in a long, silky tail that was sweeping the floor.

"No telling what he was up to in my bedroom," she said. "Last night he tore his bag of dry snacks and scattered crunch all over the kitchen floor." Max started to stand, but Sam put out a paw, pleading for more. "He likes you," Kate observed.

The living room was empty because it faced north and was

always dark, besides which she didn't have much furniture. Now she saw it through Max's eyes and realized how it must look to him—not only bare but temporary. "Want something to drink while I fix his supper?" she asked, an excuse to move to another part of the house. "I've got wine in a box and beer."

"A beer would taste good."

Sam led the way to the kitchen and sat beside his bowl while Kate took a plastic container and can of Olympia from the refrigerator, then handed the beer to Max.

"Did you name him Samson because he's strong or just strong-willed?" he asked, watching Kate scoop some beef stew into Sam's bowl.

"I didn't know that at the time. I found him at the city shelter right after I got here."

"How long ago was that?"

"Two months." Kate had never had a dog, yet the idea came to her shortly after she started work at the museum. At first she assumed it was empathy, a subconscious attempt to understand the significance of what puzzled her most—the little white dog on Tashat's cartonnage. Now Sam was just one more reason, besides Tashat, to believe that coming to Denver was simply meant to be— that Cleo had served as handmaiden to something more powerful than friendship.

"One look at those big brown eyes," she added, smiling at Sam, "and I could no more walk away than—"

"—than you can walk away from Tashat without trying to find out what happened to her?" Max finished.

"Tashat grows on you with time. With Sam it was love at first sight. His name comes from the Hebrew *Shimson*, which means 'like the sun.' I thought it fit."

"Is that one of the things we have in common?" Max inquired, dipping his head to where Sam was sitting up on his haunches, front paws folded in supplication. She realized then, if she hadn't before, that Max felt the supplicant in his bid to scan Tashat.

"It just seemed—" she began, embarrassed, then decided to spit it out. "The Egyptians thought too much hair, on man or dog, was the mark of a barbarian."

Max burst out laughing but gave her shoulders a friendly

squeeze to let her know he wasn't offended. "Feel free to look around if you want," she suggested, "while I put Sam's supper in the microwave to take off the chill. The glassed-in porch through that doorway is where I work and watch TV and read and just about everything else."

He wandered out onto the enclosed porch that ran all across the back of the house, but soon returned holding a sheet of watercolor paper. "Tell me about this."

"It's the Egyptian Judgment Day. That one is from Tashat's coffin, but it's fairly typical. The heart of the deceased—the double-handled jug on one side of the scale is the hieroglyph for heart—is being weighed against the feather of truth, the symbol of Maat, goddess of order and justice. We'd say what's moral or right." She pointed to the dog-headed man. "That's Anubis, watching to see that the heart doesn't use any trickery, and the man with the head of an ibis is Thoth, the god of wisdom, who invented writing. He records the judges' decision, while Horus, the son of Isis and Osiris, waits to escort her to Osiris, who will read her the verdict—whether she'll be allowed into eternity. Heaven. The part-lion, -hippo, -crocodile crouching near the center post of the scale is Ammit. If your heart is too heavy with all the sinful things you've done, Ammit will devour it, and that's the end of you."

"Guess Tashat passed then, since her heart is lighter than the feather."

"Usually the scale is evenly balanced, probably because the gods are supposed to pass judgment, not mere mortals. Dave thinks it's just sloppy workmanship."

"Dave Broverman is full of it!"

A laugh caught in her throat at the unexpected outburst. "I hope you realize you were treading on hallowed ground this afternoon."

He grinned, an admission in itself. "Not at first, but yeah."

She set Sam's stew on the floor. "Well, next time you ride into battle over that particular mummy, if there is a next time and you really want to live dangerously, try dropping Nefertiti's name—Akhenaten's Queen, the famous one in that beautiful painted head?"

Max nodded. "Why?"

"Some very respected Egyptologists think *she* was Smenkh-kare."

"Jesus, I wish I'd known that this afternoon!" Motioning for her to follow him, Max went back out onto the porch, to the walnut table she used as a desk.

"What did you mean by plus or minus twenty-five years? Doesn't the inscription on her coffin say when she died, or at least when she was born?"

"Yes and no. The Egyptians wrote dates as Year One or Year Five, or whatever, of a particular pharaoh's reign, but there are three different dates on her coffin. Two of them are suspect, but still—"

"Suspect how?"

"Most Egyptologists think Akhenaten ruled seventeen years, yet—here, I'll show you." She pulled a piece of paper toward her and wrote three names, adding the length of each pharaoh's reign in parentheses. Then, following each one, she wrote the date from Tashat's coffin.

Akhenaten (17)	Year	18
Smenkhkare (3?)	Year	4
Ramses (2)	Year	1

Max caught on right away. "So there shouldn't be a Year Eighteen for Akhenaten, or a Year Four for Smenkhkare?"

Kate nodded. "It's not just a list of kings, either, because three pharaohs are missing—Tutankhamen, Ay, and Horemheb, in that order—between Smenkhkare and Ramses. Horemheb is considered the last pharaoh of the Eighteenth Dynasty because he married into the royal family. There are twenty-four years, at least, between Smenkhkare—whoever he or she was—and Ramses."

"So the first Ramses begins a new royal line, the Nineteenth Dynasty?"

Kate nodded again. "Another military man, like Horemheb."

"If Ramses wasn't in line to inherit, then whoever wrote those dates had to be alive to know that he ever sat on the throne. That means the Ramses Year One is the most telling date."

She was beginning to appreciate that Max Cavanaugh was no mean practitioner of the diagnostician's art. "I agree, but that still doesn't explain why there are three dates instead of one."

"And the question mark after Smenkhkare?"

"No one knows for sure whether he followed Akhenaten or was only his coregent. If it was the latter, Smenkhkare's reign was simultaneous with the final years of Akhenaten. Nefertiti *did* disappear from public view during the last three years of her husband's reign, but nobody knows where they started counting with a coregent, either. That's one reason there are different chronologies of the pharaohs."

"Too damn many pieces of the puzzle are missing," he muttered, threading his fingers through his hair. "Too much we may never know." Worried that he was beginning to feel overwhelmed, Kate tried to think of something she could give him to hold on to, that wasn't in doubt.

"I'll admit to some wishful thinking, but I can't accept the reasoning of someone like Dave Broverman any more than you can. Not yet. Because there's another verse on her cartonnage." Kate paused, then began to recite it for him.

"*At first a voice cried out against the darkness, and the voice grew loud enough to stir black waters.*

"*It was Temu rising up, his head the thousand-petaled lotus. He uttered the word and one petal drifted from him, taking form on the water.*

"*He was the will to live. Out of nothing he created himself, the light. The hand that parted the waters, uplifted the sun and stirred the air.*

"*He was the first, the beginning. Then all else followed, like petals drifting into the pool.*

"*And I can tell you that story.*"

FOUR

Year Five in the Reign of Tutankhamen

(1356 B.C.)

DAY 12, SECOND MONTH OF HARVEST

The priest's servant came for me again, but while Aten sailed high in the sky. This time we went around the priest's main residence, to a smaller house connected to it by a covered walkway, where he led me to a large room guarded by life-size statues of the ram-headed god—Amen in his ancient form. The sleeping couch in the center of the room was shaped like a kitten with its tail arrested in mid-swing while its head turned to watch over the little girl on its back.

"How long since you first noticed something was amiss?" I asked the girl's nurse-mother, who I recognized at once for she had changed little in the nearly four years since I saw her last, except for the deep shadows beneath her eyes.

"Three days. First she fussed about a piece lost from one of her games, or when Tuli did not come the instant she called, which is not her way."

"She also would not eat," Pagosh put in, "and stopped talking.

That is not her way, either." I could feel the heat from the girl's body even before I put my fingers to her neck, so it did not surprise me that her heart spoke too fast.

"She felt too warm to my hand," Merit continued, "but who does not when Re takes so long to cross the sky?"

"Are any of the other children sick?"

"There are no other children in the house of Ramose. Only this one"—Merit's voice faltered as tears flooded her eyes—"small girl."

"Bring a lamp so I can see into her mouth. And you—Pagosh— see that a brazier is lit, but outside. Then uncover the windows and have someone bring a fan, since there is no breeze for the wind-catcher on the roof to capture."

Holding the lamp in one hand, I squeezed the girl's cheeks, and saw that her throat was swollen and inflamed. But it was the white spots on the back wall of flesh that concerned me most. "Let her lie on the ropes and continue bathing her with water," I instructed Merit, "while I prepare a draught for her throat. Wet her face, neck, and chest, even her legs, then turn her over and do the same again."

Pagosh brought a servant girl with an ostrich-feather fan, then led me to the terrace where he had lit the brazier. I handed him a bronze ewer containing dried sage and bark of willow, instructed him to fill it with clean water, and set it over the flame. "Your lord cannot spare another servingwoman to help her nurse-mother care for his daughter, even when she is sick?" I inquired.

"Merit does not trust anyone else with Aset. Only me, so say what you need."

I scooped two spoons of pulverized soil from an old cattle pen into my mortar, along with a few pieces of rotten bread. "A pitcher of beer will do for now."

"Later, *sunu,* after you tend to the girl."

The stiff-necked lout thought I meant to drink the beer myself! "You really expect me to believe that Merit trusts the girl with you?"

He gave me a hard look, yet he spoke in a softened voice. "Merit is not only my wife and the mother of my son, may his *ka* live in eternity, but the beloved of my heart. She knows I would pro-tect Aset as if she were the child of my own loins, for she was a gift from the goddess after Osiris took our son."

Understanding hit me like the gust of a hamseen blowing in from the Western Desert—Merit's dead babe had been this man's son. "Merit also trusts me, does she not?" I asked. He nodded. "Then we have little choice but to trust each other." The least I could do was put him at ease about what I intended, I thought, and why. "We must replace the fluid burned away by the fever. That is why she will need more than the few sips of beer she gets with this decoction for her throat. Perhaps you could ask one of the kitchen servants to press the juice from a pomegranate."

He nodded and hurried away to get the beer. When he returned I poured some into my bronze cup and added three measures of the powder from my mortar. "I must give her this first, while you take the willow tea from the brazier. When it has cooled bring it to me."

He lifted the hot pot with his bare hand, set it on the tiled table, and covered it with a cloth. "I will return for it when you say."

We found Aset thrashing about, trying to escape the flames that threatened to consume her. I dipped a goose feather into the pitcher of cloudy beer and let it drip between her parched lips, praying all the while that Re would sail faster to give ease to this child of his brother Amen. That thought soon gave birth to another.

"Her mother knows she is sick?" I asked Merit, who shrugged and refused to meet my eyes. "What of her father?"

"He comes both day and night, and makes offerings to Amen for her life."

The afternoon passed into twilight and then darkness while I dripped beer, then willow tea and fruit juice down the girl's throat. Merit finally agreed to rest on the pallet Pagosh placed on the floor while I continued to drag the wet cloth over Aset's body, again and again, praying all the while that Thoth had guided my hand. For all rotted animal dung is not the same.

I lost all sense of time then, until I sensed another presence in the room and turned to find the priest standing behind me. "She will live?" he asked in a low voice.

"Only Thoth can know that," I replied, wondering if he felt true fondness for his daughter or only concern for the means by which he might gain greater power. "If Osiris does not take her in the night, she will be better by morning. Now I battle the fever with the only weapon left to me, the water of life."

How long Ramose remained I never knew, for he disappeared as silently as he had come. I glanced around to relieve the stiffness in my neck and back, and noticed the baskets filled with the little girl's toys. One contained rag dolls and a wooden puppet with movable limbs, her only playmates if what Merit said was true.

"Please do not leave me!" she cried out suddenly, bringing Pagosh to his feet. "Oh, Tuli . . . please come back!"

"Who is this Tuli she calls for?" I asked him.

"A street dog who has become her shadow. He even sleeps on the foot of her couch. Yesterday he seemed to know she was sick and whined until I put him out."

"Only come back and I promise never to leave you again, Tuli," she cried again, "not even to go across the river with my lady mother."

"Go find the dog and bring him here," I instructed Pagosh.

A few minutes later he returned with a small dog straining at the leash, though in truth he looked more like a rat, from his half-chewed ears and dirty gray coat to his nearly hairless tail. Only his eyes distinguished him, one blue and the other amber. I motioned him up onto the couch, and put one of her hands to his back.

"He just appeared one day, a pup not fully grown," Pagosh explained, "with his ribs sticking out and a great tear in his belly. Aset had me carry him to the physician-in-ordinary to my lord's cattle and slaves, but he refused to treat the animal, so Aset cared for him herself, by pouring sour wine on the wound and feeding him scraps of meat. That night nothing would do but I must fix a pallet for him in here, so she could keep a lamp burning against the darkness—'when all snakes bite and every lion leaves its lair.' By morning she had named him what he is, she said—brave." I thought the story a bit overblown, and I suppose he must have read it in my face. "If you doubt that one so young can know what it is to be brave *sunu*, it is because you do not know her."

He returned to his place by the door and the drip of the water clock seemed to grow louder after that. I began to ponder how we measure time. Since day and night each are divided into twelve parts, the length of an hour varies with the season. But we are in the season of long days, when the hours of the night are shorter than at any other time of year, so why did they *feel* so long? I was still mulling that question when Osiris rose up on the other side of her couch, to stand with his arms crossed over his chest, crook in one hand, flail in the other.

"You cannot take her!" I protested.

"Why not?" The Lord of the Netherworld appeared unperturbed by my outburst.

"Because it would break poor Tuli's brave heart." My eyes fell on the lock of hair Merit had pulled back and tied with a strip of leather and a carnelian amulet—the knot in the girdle of Isis, talisman of her namesake and guardian. "Surely you would not deny the mother of your son, the mighty Horus who avenged your death!"

Like smoke, he curled in upon himself, mingling with the shadows in the corner of the room. That surprised me, too, for I was taught that Osiris takes when and where he pleases, without appeal. I continued to wet the cloth and drag it across her chest, until at last it seemed to me she felt a little cooler. After another hour or so her cheeks finally gave up their angry color. I knew then that I had chosen well, and let the cloth fall back into the bowl, drew a thin blanket up to her chest, and sat back to rest a bit.

When next I opened my eyes, the light of Re-Horakhte was streaming through the clerestory windows. I looked first to see if the girl still breathed, and found her watching me with eyes the color of the afternoon sky. Surely they are a gift from her father, I thought, though hers are a clearer blue, unsullied perhaps by all his eyes have seen. She lay still except for the hand stroking Tuli's ear, and showed no fear at waking to find a stranger beside her couch. Even so, I stayed quiet so as not to alarm her, until I saw the hesitant beginnings of a smile. She seemed to be testing me, so I returned her gift in kind—and was rewarded with a smile of such joy that I was helpless to do anything but try to match it.

That was how Pagosh found us when he came to see how she fared. "Paga!" she whispered in a scratchy voice, raising her arms to him. He bent to hug her, but mumbled, "You are not to get up, little one, until the physician says you are healed."

"He is a *sunu*?" she whispered, blue eyes suddenly too big for her face.

Pagosh nodded. "The one named Senakhtenre. Remember what Merit told you about the night you came into this world?"

Still she stared at me, causing me to wonder if she saw in me the physician who had refused to treat her dog. "My friends call me Tenre," I offered, to calm her fears.

"Is that what *you* call him, Paga?" she whispered into his neck.

"It is an honor to be offered the friendship of such a man," Pagosh replied, avoiding a direct answer.

"Then you can call me Aset, for that is what *my* friends call me. Isn't it Tuli?" The dog wagged his tail, then licked her foot.

"Aset?" Merit rose from her pallet, then began laughing and crying at the same time when Pagosh handed the girl into her keeping. "I will fetch a cup of broth and some fruit," he muttered, though I suspect he went to inform Ramose.

"You are squeezing me too tight, Mother," Aset complained, "and those ropes have scratched my back." Merit reached for a blanket and wrapped it around her.

"Put fresh padding on her couch," I told Merit, then spoke to Aset. "Will you promise to drink all the juice and water Merit brings you?" She nodded. "And rest when you feel tired?" This time she was not so quick to agree. "Tuli is impatient for you to be well, so you can play with him. So am I." At that, laughter sparkled in her eyes, all the reward I needed for sitting through the night with a sick child.

I handed a packet of dried sage to Merit to steep in hot water, to help soothe her throat. "You also can have all the fruit you want," I told Aset. "Do you like watermelon?" She nodded, making her curls dance. "Then rest for now." I pointed to the dog. "Him too." I picked up my goatskin bag. "I will return tomorrow to see if you have followed my instructions." By the time I reached the door her eyes were closed in pretend sleep.

DAY 13, SECOND MONTH OF HARVEST

I was down by the river, tending a man who had dislocated his shoulder while loading one of Pharaoh's trading vessels, when I heard someone call my name.

"Tenre! Hallo."

I was sure my ears deceived me. Then the crowd of soldiers and vendors parted, and I caught a glimpse of a familiar face. "Mena!" I shouted, and ran to him.

"You said this was where I would find you when I returned." He clapped me on the back, pulling me into the embrace of brothers, then made a show of drawing away to cast his eyes over me. "Let me see how you fared without me."

Mena and I first found kinship in playing ghoulish pranks on the priests in the temple school. Later, it had been his unfailing optimism that sustained me through the lower grade of the priesthood, a requirement for entry to the Per Ankh and medical training. But once there, neither of us could stomach the decision not to treat, so we set out to test every prescription handed down from the time of the great Imhotep, and ended by bribing a slave in the Per Nefer to look the other way while we discovered for ourselves how the great vessels lay between the heart and lungs.

"Did you just arrive?" I asked, fearing that he had long since returned to Waset and now was about to embark again, without even seeking me out. I could see that he was much changed, more by his eyes than the white at his temples.

He pointed to where three bearded slaves coaxed a pair of skittish horses from the deck of a twin-masted ship. "With General Horemheb. Have you not heard that he comes to take the Princess Mutnodjme for his wife?"

"I beg most humbly that you will forgive my intolerable ignorance, Lord Merenptah." I bowed my head to hide the grin I could not keep from my face. "Surely the messenger you sent ahead to announce your glorious coming must have been waylaid by pirates on the Great Green Sea. Otherwise, with or without the General who names himself Greatest of the Great and Most Powerful of the Powerful, every whore in this backwater of Pharaoh's great empire would have been waiting to greet you."

He burst out laughing, a sound I have sorely missed these past five years. "Thank the gods you are not changed, Tenre. Do you still spend your nights with your scrolls instead of a woman, or is it a wife that has turned your brown eyes so solemn?"

"Hardly," I scoffed. "Most women I see are already big with child, but perhaps with you here my luck will change—unless you are the one who has settled into middle age." I caught a glimpse of the boy he used to be before his face turned serious again.

"Not yet and not likely, though I confess I grow weary of seeing men spill their guts and brains for no good reason. I can still hear their moans in my sleep, and wake with the noxious odor of their rotting flesh in my nose. But if you are through twisting that poor fellow's arm, let us go find a cool mug of beer."

I nodded, anxious to hear where he had been and what he had learned, for we had made a pact the night before he sailed. He would learn all he could from the wounds men suffer in battle while I did the same from the ills of the men, women, and children who tend Amen's fields. On his return, we would combine our newfound wisdom to rewrite the scrolls of the ancients.

"I swear I do not remember it being so infernally hot here," he commented, as we settled in the garden of the Clay Jar, a tavern popular with soldiers and seamen. "But tell me how you earn enough to eat by treating women and children?"

"Everyone prospers since the young Pharaoh returned to the city of Amen." I paused to wet my throat. "You remember Nofret, my widowed aunt? Well, it is our habit to take the evening meal in my garden, where she regales Khary, the man I have hired to cultivate my herb garden, and me with gossip. So I'll wager I knew before you that your General would take the Princess for his wife. What I want to know is how you came to be with him."

"I was sent to our garrison at Zarw, where my General prepared a campaign into Canaan. One day when he was practicing with his bow, the shaft of an arrow splintered as he released it, driving a thin sliver of wood into the soft underside of his arm. Horemheb is not one to take notice of such a small thing, so by the time I saw it the wound had gone putrid and looked as bad as it smelled. I poulticed it with moldy bread, mumbled a magic spell, and had him eat radishes sufficient to send ten men to the latrine. He believes I saved his life as well as his arm, and so must have me always at his side."

I smiled, remembering how it has always been with us, but in the next instant his face changed from day to night. "The ambassadors of our onetime allies may have returned to court, Tenre, but they come without treaties or tribute because Tutankhamen has nothing to bargain with." Word of the General's failure to regain the territory lost by the Heretic Akhenaten had already filtered back to Waset, but Horemheb returned triumphant anyway because he brought long-owed tribute from the Canaanites and their Shasu brethren. "My General comes to acquire more than a royal princess," Mena continued. "He needs more troops, and Ay will see that he gets them." He sat back. "Once Horemheb chases the Hittites back to Hattusas, the throne will be his."

I knew Mena too well to believe he spoke in jest. "Akhenaten taught the priests of Amen a lesson they mean never to forget," I reminded him. "It will take a clever hand to tame a lion and crocodile at the same time."

"Horemheb will pull their teeth. Power lies with the strong now, Tenre, not in the blood. Do not forget that the General rose through the ranks under the wily old Master of the Horse, who now sits on Tutankhamen's right hand."

"Ay sat beside Akhenaten as well," I reminded him, "and look where *he* is!" That we spoke of the Beautiful One's first husband was proof to me that the gods play games with our thoughts. "But since you mingle among the high-and-mighty, tell me what has happened to the Heretic's Queen."

"Mutnodjme's royal sister? I have heard only that she lives somewhere in the land of the lotus, likely not far from here."

"Then perhaps I can tell *you* something, though it must be as physician to physician." With those words I bound his tongue and could trust him not to share the confidence. "She is Consort to a God's Father named Ramose, keeper of Amen's accounts, and has borne him a daughter."

Shock and then chagrin crossed Mena's bronze face, so he understood full well what an alliance between a powerful priest of Amen and a daughter of the Magnificent Amenhotep could portend. "Like a cat, that one always lands on her feet."

"Her claim to the throne is without equal," I reminded him, "not only as the daughter of Osiris Amenhotep but because she once sat at Akhenaten's side. Now she plays a new game of Jackals and Hounds, this time with the High Priest of Amen."

"Did you hear that bit of gossip from your widowed aunt as well?"

"I attended the babe's birth."

"You?" Mena almost fell off his stool. "What do you take me for, a witless ox? No offense, Tenre, but the priest you describe would never allow one such as you anywhere near his woman, not when he could have a physician from the House of Life."

"So I thought, too. But you know how it is. Birthing is for mid-wives. The exalted ones from the Per Ankh are not called until it is too late and so have little experience of a woman who labors. And no wish to acquire it."

"How long ago was this?"

"On the very day her other daughter became Tutankhamen's Queen." I decided not to mention that I had gone to Ramose's house again only the night before.

"Nearly four years." He gave me a look to see if I pulled his leg. "For an ordinary physician, my friend, you seem to have acquired anything but an ordinary reputation." Then, without warning, he sailed in a different direction. "I have learned that dried crystals of honey will save many a hacked limb, by taking up the fluid from a deep cut."

That he remembered our youthful pact made my heart sing with joy. "I, too, have much to report. An ointment made from the blood of an ox mixed with fat from a black snake will stop a man's hair from turning white. You should try it."

Before I knew what he was about he had slapped my cheek in play. "How I have missed you," he said.

"As I have missed you," I admitted, warmed by his words.

He glanced up at the sky. "I must go learn where I am to lodge this night, and find a bath before I show myself at Pharaoh's palace."

It was my turn to gape. "You go to Tutankhamen's House of Jubilation?"

"He is to accept the tribute Horemheb brings and reward him for his service. Also for taking his sister off his hands." Mena sent me the ingenuous grin that once fooled even my father into believing him an innocent.

"If royal blood counts for so little," I asked, "why does

Horemheb wed a princess? Surely it is common knowledge that she has lain with every man in the Two Lands, except for you and me. Or perhaps I should speak only for myself."

"I see your skill at finding the holes in an argument is still sharp as a razor," he muttered as we got up to leave. "Once my General impregnates her it will no longer matter. Soon he must sail to Upper Nubia to inspect the garrisons that secure the territory above the Second Cataract, but until then they cruise on the royal barge."

"You will go with him to Kush?"

"Not this time, and perhaps never again." His face was hidden from me as we passed from the garden. "I find myself lying awake at night, wondering—should Anubis come for me tomorrow—what I leave behind to mark my existence, with no wife to mourn my absence nor any children to say my name." He handed the tavern keeper a chit to cover our beer, and we went out into the hot, dusty street.

"It is the wisdom Imhotep left to those who have come after him that endures," I reminded him. "But while you ponder which good woman to choose for your wife, it might clear your vision to spend an hour or two in the marshes . . . unless your throwing arm grows weak with age."

"At our usual place," he returned, taking the bait, "just as Re-Horakhte shows his face above the horizon?"

I nodded, but could not resist pricking him again. "Do not forget to eat some cabbage with your meat tonight, lest a throbbing head spoil your aim."

"Not even a dancing girl will lie with me if I stink of cabbage. Better to chew almonds and kill two birds with one throw, remember?"

With that he started toward the river while I stood feasting my eyes on his familiar stride, letting the memory of other times and other taverns engulf my heart. Especially the night we set out to discover whether eating almonds would prevent the sore head that comes from too much wine and at the same time produce an erection to rival that of the god Min himself. Then I turned and made my way to the path to Amen's temple.

• • •

Pagosh stepped forward to greet me as I passed through Ramose's gate. "So, *sunu*, what kept you?"

My heart jumped into my throat. "Her fever returned?"

"No, but if you believed it might, why leave her to last?"

I willed my heart back down into my chest. "And because of that you withdraw the hand you extended to me in the night?"

"You speak in riddles," he muttered, turning to lead me toward the priest's house.

"I think you understand me only too well, *friend*."

"Then come . . . Tenre." It did not come easy for him. "My lord wishes to speak with you first, and the little one grows impatient. She has been waiting all day with her Jackals and Hounds, ready to play."

"Your little goddess thinks I come to play games?"

"Aset is not one to lie."

"No, she does not lie," I agreed, vowing to guard my tongue more carefully. "But Jackals and Hounds is no game for a child."

He gave me an indulgent look. "She has a kind heart and probably will let you win the first game."

I followed him to the big room where the priest had awaited me before. "I am forever in your debt, Senakhtenre," he said in greeting. Nor did he keep me standing this time, but invited me to join him on the padded sitting shelf. "Pagosh believes you are wise beyond your years, and I see the proof of that in my daughter's eyes." His generous mouth hinted at the rare smile to come, and I caught a glimpse of Aset in her father's face. "Since the will of Amen has brought us together not once, but twice, it appears that our destinies have been joined. I would be a fool to turn away from you again, so I ask you now to become physician to my household." I stared at him, wondering if he jested at my expense. "Your first duty would be to care for my daughter, though I would expect you to attend the other women, as well. Merit, for one."

It is common enough for a wealthy man to employ an ordinary physician to tend the sickness and injuries suffered by his servants, fellahin, and animals, but that was not what he was asking. "I am not—" I stopped and began again. "If you believe I can perform miracles, my lord, you have been misled."

He waved that away with an impatient hand. "I admit that I made it my business to learn why you are not like the others, and questioned every man I sent to you for treatment. So I leave the miracles to Amen. It is the wisdom you have gained from your endless questions and experiments that I desire from you. In exchange, I offer you a house of your own and food from my kitchen. Beer from my brewery and wine from my vineyard." Ramose paused, but my thoughts ran in every direction at once. "All the eggs you need from the fowl yard," he added, watching me with those all-seeing blue eyes. "Ten rations of beef and double that of grain each month."

He offered me riches beyond any I ever expected in this life, but the man sat on Amen's Sacred Council, and I have no love for priests. *He also sent the priest-physicians packing when they allowed his royal wife to walk near the western horizon*, a voice reminded me. My *ka*, I suppose.

"I see you hold back for another reason. Tell me, then, for I must be well fortified indeed if I am to disappoint both Pagosh and my daughter."

"It is not that I do not wish to care for your daughter, my lord, but that so many others depend on me."

"What if I find another *sunu* to serve them, could you not teach him your ways?"

"Perhaps, but no one else can honor the promise I made my assistant, whose wife soon will bring forth their first child." Should he chide me for playing the role of midwife after calling me to attend his own lady, I would have the measure of the man and find it easy to refuse his offer.

"You speak of your man Khary?" I nodded, wondering what else he knew of my affairs. "Then have him send for you when her time is at hand."

It was not until Khary came to work for me that I discovered he could read and write, and that behind his tawny cat's eyes and gentle hands lies a wit sharp enough to hone my own. In the end I hired a second man to till my soil and have been teaching Khary to prepare my pills and potions. I did not wish to give up the idea I have been considering for some time, of dispensing our medicines and herbs to all those in need.

"I would need to maintain my house in town," I told him, testing how deep his desire for my services might run, "and go there to replenish the medicines my assistant prepares."

His eyes narrowed at that, but in the end he nodded. "Anything else?"

"I must be allowed to treat *all* your workers and their families, since whatever pestilence attacks them could be visited on those you wish most to protect." I dared much should Ramose take as heresy what I said about the spread of pestilence among rich and poor alike. Perhaps some sixth sense told him I would not come otherwise.

"Then I rely on you to do as you see fit. Only be sure you do not neglect my daughter." He gave me a thoughtful glance. "My animals, too?"

"If I am to gain the confidence of your daughter."

He almost smiled. "We are agreed, then?"

"I would like to consider my decision over the night, if you will permit it."

"Then think about this, as well. I do not fault Merit for loving her overmuch, but she cannot protect Aset from the cruelties she will encounter in the temple school, from both the priests and her schoolmates. At times, perhaps, even from me. I do not wish to see her spirit crushed, nor do I want her spoiled by indulgence, and the path between is a narrow one. The same path you often walk in hurting a child in order to heal."

"But I have no experience in the raising of children, my lord."

"You do not give over easily, do you, *sunu*? Another reason I need you. Call it an experiment, then, if that is what it takes. Give me a year. At the end of that time we will talk again." He glanced up at the clerestory windows. "It is time for me to bid Amen-Re farewell, while you see to my daughter. We will talk again tomorrow, but whatever you decide, Senakhtenre, be assured that you have a friend in the house of Ramose."

An hour later I found myself bargaining with his daughter as well. "Bastet refuses to nurse her kittens," she insisted. "If I do not feed them, they will cry all night."

"Tomorrow," I repeated, watching her replace the carved wooden sticks. Was there some advantage in playing the floppy-eared hounds I didn't know about? "The chill of evening soon will lie upon the land."

"But evil demons hide in that dark corner and only wait for you to leave to make me sick again." Tuli let out a pitiful howl, adding his voice to hers.

"Then put on something to keep warm, and I will take you up on the roof," I told her, while Pagosh listened in silence.

"I am warm enough." She jumped off the kitten couch, ready to go. She looked at me, and ran to a clothes chest. Grabbing the first tunic she found, she slipped it over her head and wriggled it down to her knees.

"Where are your sandals?" I asked.

"I don't need any." Apparently one look was all it took for her to tell I would not give over on this, either. "Why?"

"So you will form the habit of wearing them. There are worms in the dirt, and one kind can enter your body through breaks in the skin between your toes."

"Oh!" Her eyes widened. "But my sandals hurt my toes. Sometimes they make me fall. What if I should break my arm or my head? Surely that is worse than having a worm crawl between my toes."

"Then we must find you a pair that do not hurt." While she slipped on her sandals I reached into my goatskin bag for one of the carved animals I carry to distract a sick child. "A blind man carved this from a piece of papyrus root." I held out the little lion.

"Truly? How, if he cannot see?"

"By feeling with his fingers until the shape fits the picture he carries in his memory. Just because a man loses his sight does not mean he cannot remember what he has seen." She closed her eyes and ran her fingers over the animal's body and legs, stopping to test his ruff of dried papyrus heads, and finally the tail. Then she opened those blue eyes and gave me a smile I shall never forget. "You may keep it if you like."

"I will treasure it always. Will you tell the blind man that for me?"

I nodded, pulled a blanket off her couch, and lifted her in my arms. Pagosh led us to the steps leading up to the roof, with Tuli running ahead, then circling back. He was too excited to go slowly but unwilling to let Aset out of his sight.

The fiery orb of the sun was just beginning to slide behind the western cliffs, and a cloud of dust hovered over the red sand, like smoke rising from the burning desert. I lowered her to a bench beneath the palm-frond canopy and for a while we sat taking in the scene around us. As boys Mena and I used to climb the red cliffs that guard the Place of Truth, to stand high above the mud-brick houses below and look across the river to the Eastern Desert and distant mountains, wondering what lay beyond them. Now we looked toward the fine houses around Pharaoh's palace and the village of the necropolis workers nestled in the low, rocky hills.

"Look, Tenre." She pulled one arm free of the blanket. "See the canal to Pharaoh's House of Jubilation? That is where my sister Ankhesenpa lives, and Merankh."

I stared at the rambling complex of royal apartments, understanding for the first time what she meant when she had promised Tuli not to leave him, even to go across the river with her lady mother. "Ankhesenpa?" I repeated, since she used the Queen's old birth name, which had been changed when she married her mother's brother, Tutankhamen.

"Pharaoh's Great Royal Wife. Now that I am well I will visit her, to cheer her up. Her little babe came into the world asleep, and none of Pharaoh's physicians could wake him. Ankhes is the one who taught me how to make rag dolls, for Tuli, so he will not be so lonely when I am at the temple."

"And Merankh?"

"He is Tutankhamen's great huge hunting hound. Except he barks when he is not supposed to and scares the birds away before my uncle can loose an arrow or throw a stick. At times he even knocks me down with his tail, though he does not mean to."

For a while we sat watching Re sail his boat toward the western horizon, listening to the stillness. It seemed to me as if every living creature held his breath, waiting for the goddess to cry—except Tuli, whose tongue lolled from the side of his mouth while Aset stroked his back with a bare foot.

I was trying to think of a story to amuse her when my eyes fell on a lotus-covered pond. Banked to contain the water flowing into it from a nearby collecting tank by way of a canal, it contained a thin sheet of water even with the harvest season near an end.

"Do you know what those are?" I asked Aset, pointing.

"I think—" She stretched taller and whispered what sounded like, "Yes, but where could they have come from?" Then in a voice full of excitement she exclaimed, "It is a great herd of elephants! See how they flap their big ears to fan themselves in the heat?" She glanced at me. "Don't you see them, Tenre?"

I glanced down to find her watching me with the unwavering gaze of a child who never gets enough to eat. "Of course, I only wanted to be sure. They appear to be the rarest kind, too—the ones with blue eyes."

"As blue as mine?" Still she watched me.

"Uh—no, not quite," I replied, after looking again. The big green leaves did look like elephant's ears. "But then I have never seen any as blue as yours, even on a monkey." She laughed with delight, a soft sound that bubbled in her throat.

To keep her smiling I told her about the vervet monkey Khary was training to pick figs from the sycamores, who eats two for every one he puts in his basket. By the time I finished, the sky was awash with color and the shadows below the red cliffs were reaching across the valley, like fingers trying to hold on to the thin strip of river.

"Did you know that before the world began there was nothing but water, anywhere? Until one day a blue lotus rose from the water." Apparently she thought it was her turn to tell me a story. "When the lotus opened its petals, a beautiful goddess was sitting in its golden heart—the one we call Re. Light streamed from her body to banish the darkness. But she was lonely, so she imagined all the other gods and goddesses, and gave them life simply by naming them. Nut, our Mother Sky. Geb, the earth, and Shu, the air that separates them." She paused. "Did you know the lotus blossom closes its petals every evening and vanishes back into the water? One day perhaps she will not return at all and there will be nothing but darkness ever again."

All the wriggling had caused her blanket to fall to the bench, so I wrapped it around her shoulders and tucked in the corner. "The lotus blossom opens in the morning and closes in the evening. Some never reopen, others do for perhaps three or four days. Then it sinks under the water, where it gives birth to a number of seeds, so there is no reason to worry or feel sad."

"How can you know that?"

"When I was a boy I spent many an hour watching the blossoms open and close."

"Why?"

I lifted her onto my lap to shield her from the breeze as Re reached between the cliffs to kiss Mother River farewell, setting the sky afire with streaks of crimson and gold. "My father had me learn my numbers by counting the lotus blossoms in our pond. When a seed is ready, tiny sacs of air lift it to the surface of the pond, where it drifts until they dry and pop open. In that way the seed falls to the bottom In a new place, where it puts down roots and sends up another plant."

"How I wish I could have been there with you, to watch the seeds bob to the surface of the pond." She sighed, then was quiet for so long I thought she had fallen asleep. Reluctant to disturb her, I sat watching Re spread a blazing sheet of orange across the quiet surface of the Nile, until—without warning—she twisted around to peer at my face.

"Must I always be sick before you will come to see me?" I knew then that my decision had been made for me, with just one word. Why?

"Soon I will be here every day, for I am to become physician to your father's household. Perhaps then you will come to visit *me*." A brilliant smile lit her enormous blue eyes, making me want to give her something more. "But next time I will take the Hounds, while *you* play the Jackals."

FIVE

They were crowded into one of two side rooms that looked out through a glass window to the scanner, where Tashat lay with her head just inside the gantry of the huge white cylinder—like an ancient sacrifice about to be sucked into the gaping maw of some hungry monster.

"Let's begin at five millimeters," Max suggested to Phil Lowenstein, who sat at the control console, "from the vertex of the skull to the cervicothoracic junction. I want enough measurements to produce an exact replica."

"You name the tune and I'll play it." Phil's long fingers moved over the keyboard, sending commands to the scanner. He was taller than Cleo, with a lanky build and feet to match his hands.

"That's the equivalent of snapping a picture every five millimeters," Kate whispered to Cleo, "from the top of the skull to the base of her neck." She calculated how many "slices" that would produce and came up with 125—of the head alone!

With his part done, Phil swiveled around on his stool, hardly able to keep his eyes off Kate's old roommate. Cleo had dressed conservatively for the occasion in a beige ribbon-knit sheath and fringed silk piano scarf that dipped almost to her knees in back, a twenties collectible that pointed up her Irish-setter red hair. "Do you think that's how she really looked in life?" Phil inquired.

"The Egyptians believed the spirit left the body each morning and returned in the evening, so the funerary mask had to at least resemble the person it belonged to. But how closely?" Cleo shrugged and spread her hands, setting off the castanetlike clicking of a half-dozen Bakelite bracelets.

"Here comes the first one," Max announced, moving back so Kate and Cleo could see each image or "slice" as it came up on the monitor. "Keep in mind that what we're seeing on the left is Tashat's right side. This rounded shape is the outline of the carton-nage"—he leaned forward to point to the wavering gray lines—"and these are layers of bandaging. This thicker outline is the skull, which shows white because the radiodensity of bone is high compared to the soft tissues."

New images came and went at a fairly fast clip, requiring their eyes to constantly process and release each complex image, usually before Kate was ready. Max let several go by before he spoke again

"Remember what I said about the seams or sutures in the skull closing at different ages?" He glanced at Cleo. "The first starts closing at twenty-two, the second at twenty-four, and the last one at twenty-six. See this line?" He pointed again. "This is the second suture. It looks fuzzy because the edges are starting to feather. That means it's beginning to close."

"You're saying Tashat was Kate's age?" Cleo inquired.

Max sent Kate a quizzical glance. "If you mean between twenty-four and twenty-six, yes," he confirmed. "I don't see any sign that the last suture is beginning to close, but I'll wait until we see the epiphyses before making a final judgment."

"Epif—what's that?" Cleo mouthed to Kate.

"The growing ends of the long bones in the arms and legs, hands and feet," Phil replied, "where the soft cartilage eventually turns into bone."

Cleo glanced at Max. "Okay, but if the last one starts to close at twenty-six, how would you know if someone is—oh, say your age?"

Kate wanted to kick her, but Max took no notice of Cleo's heavy-handed remark. "The sutures reach closure in the same order—at thirty-five, forty-two, and forty-seven—so we'd extrapolate more or less the same way. Generally we have the most success between twenty and fifty-five, since other changes occur with puberty and senility. In females the epiphyses close three to four years after menarche, for instance."

"Yeah, the clavicle is among the last to unify," Phil added, "at its medial end, where it meets the sternum. Usually between twenty-three and twenty-five."

"What about race?" Cleo persisted. "Doesn't that have to be taken into account?"

Max shook his head. "I'd expect more difference between males and females. But we don't have any reliable statistical difference in either case, race or gender. I suppose there might be some effect from the difference in nutrition then and now, but not nine or ten years."

"I don't understand why you need so many measurements. Most physical anthropologists do discriminant function analysis with only eight." Aware that Cleo didn't know zip about statistical analysis, Kate almost laughed.

"Sure, if all you're looking for is gender and race," Phil answered. "You could even get by with five if they're the really crucial measurements—total facial height, sinus breadth, bigonial and bizygomatic breadth from a posterior-anterior shot, plus one from a lateral." Kate didn't dare look at Max, afraid she would break up. "Listen, guys who work for the police, like that famous Dr. Snow," Phil continued, as if he hadn't just snowed Cleo with jargon, "actually get to handle the bones people dig up. Nothing like what we're doing here."

Max came to her rescue. "Discriminant analysis gets sex right about ninety-five percent of the time but on race the success rate drops to eighty percent. And that's broadly speaking—Caucasoid, Negroid, or Mongoloid—without ethnic breakdowns."

If Cleo was searching for some way to discredit what they found, she was fishing in the wrong pond, Kate was thinking when Max put a hand on Phil's shoulder. "Wait up, Phil. Can you stop that before it gets away?" He motioned for Kate to come closer. "Look between the eye sockets."

Unaccustomed to viewing the skull in cross section, Kate tried to identify the thin, spidery lines. "It looks almost spongy." Then it dawned on her. "Ethmoid air cells?"

Max nodded. "The ethmoid is intact. They didn't enter the brain vault."

"Sometimes they removed the brain through a hole at the base of the skull," Cleo put in, "though not until several hundred years later . . . we think."

"We'll watch when we hit the foramen magnum, then, where the spinal cord joins the brain."

The conversation continued to flow around her, but Kate concentrated on what she could see.

"Pretty good teeth, considering," Max commented at one point. "Very little decay found in any of the mummies, but sand in their food wore their teeth down, caused a lot of abscesses, which they treated with turpentine and ground mandrake root." He paused. "What d'you think about those third molars, Phil?"

"I'd say they're in."

Max watched several more images come and go. "Nothing unexpected in the soft tissues around the cervical spine." He waited a second. "Okay, let's go to a composite of the entire head."

Kate turned away while the computer carried out Phil's commands, dreading what she knew was coming—Tashat as she looked right now, under the bandages and that mask.

"Left anterior oblique view coming up," Phil announced.

Knowing what to expect didn't compare with the actuality, a ghostly white apparition, disembodied, hovering in a black void. Cadaverous, with retracted lips, sunken cheeks, prominent cheekbones, and mandible all clearly visible through the shroud of leathery skin.

Kate stared, fascinated and repelled at the same time. It hardly looked human with all the cross sections stacked like geologic strata, giving the silhouette a stair-stepped edge. She shut her eyes, trying to hold on to the image of the vital young woman who lived in her imagination, fearing that she might never get it back—that Tashat's death might intrude on her life. In the blackness behind her lids, she worked at erasing the macabre image that pulled her like a magnet, against her will.

She didn't open her eyes until she heard Max instructing Phil to take a reading every millimeter through the thoracic cavity, "to see if we can pick up any primary callus."

He turned to Cleo and Kate. "I'll put together what I can as we go along, but I'm not going to catch everything on this pass-through, especially with those displaced ribs coming in at odd angles."

For several minutes no one said a word. "Clean break in the clavicle," Max commented. Putting his finger on the bright spot above Tashat's heart, he added, "This is about where that amulet showed up on the old X ray."

"A scarab to protect the heart, either serpentine or jasper since they were green," Cleo supplied, then thought to add, "usually."

"Her arms are wrapped inside the outer bandaging," Max continued. "Right one is folded across her chest, which we already knew from the X ray." He glanced at Cleo. "Isn't that a sign of royalty?"

"Wrong arm," Cleo answered. "Even if it wasn't, that's not conclusive after the middle of the Eighteenth Dynasty. Too many female mummies have turned up with their left arms folded for all of them to be royal. Some randy old pharaoh probably granted the privilege to his favorites and the practice caught on."

"You mean the king had an annual honors list, like Queen Elizabeth, where he named his favorite bedmates?" Phil asked, momentarily breaking the growing tension.

Cleo didn't think it was funny. "I was only suggesting how the practice might have gotten started."

Max cast a sideways glance at Kate. To accept something by inference without eliminating other possibilities didn't sit any better with him than it did with her, especially if Max was right about Tashat's age. That one discrepancy alone put everything else they thought they knew about her in question.

"Tips of the fingers on the right hand are wrapped in something with a high radiodensity," Max observed, as a different image appeared.

"Oils and gums pretty much destroyed everything except Tutankhamen's face, fingers, and toes," Cleo said by way of explanation, "which were protected by gold-foil stalls and that solid gold mask."

"Hey, Max, what do you make of this?" Phil pointed to a faint gray line. "Watch the next one. See, there it is again. And again."

"Looks like something flat between the layers of bandaging. I'll try collating the images later, but let's get the distance in from the surface so I can focus down on it when I do the standard radiography." He looked at Kate. "Can't promise we'll get anything, but we might as well try. See if there's any writing on it."

"The ink would need to have an appreciably higher radiodensity than what it's written on to show up," Phil warned.

"Iron oxide for red, carbon for black since they used soot," Kate told him.

By then they were well into the rib cage, and no one said another word until Phil breathed a soft, "Uh-oh!"

"Yeah, a couple of the ribs are impacted," Max confirmed. Keeping his eyes on the monitor, he translated for Cleo. "That's where one fragment of bone has been driven into anoth—wait up, Phil. Freeze it." He paused. "Now improve the contrast if you can, then move in on this area, right here." He put his finger to the monitor and with his other hand pulled a pair of half glasses from his shirt pocket. "Age is a factor in how fast a bone mends, but even in children it's rare to see any callus in less than two weeks."

He motioned for Kate without shifting his eyes. "See here? And here? That's primary callus. How long would you say, Phil?"

"Three weeks max. One of those ribs could have punctured a lung or torn the liver, maybe even the spleen, but that's not a conclusive cause of death."

"Just the opposite if she stayed alive long enough to form callus." Max turned to Kate. "Don't you agree?"

She nodded, overwhelmed by an unutterable sadness. That meant Tashat had died a slow, painful death, probably by suffocation, or massive infection.

"It's still more than likely that most of the other damage occurred postmortem," Max reminded her before turning back to the monitor. "Okay, Phil, let's move on."

The images changed again and again, keeping time to some relentless beat set by the computer, a machine with a slice of silicon for a heart. And no soul.

"From here on we're into Phil's area of expertise," Max said, inviting his colleague to take over the commentary.

"Well, to begin, we've got a fracture of the posterior lip of the right hip socket, which could result in dislocation and scatter minute granules of bone into the joint, probably what caused the shadow on that old X ray." He pointed to a yellow spot on the monitor. "This is the pubic symphysis, where the bones meet to form the pelvis. And this indentation here tells us she had at least one child. She's also past eighteen."

Kate felt like a voyeur watching Tashat's most intimate secrets revealed one millimeter at a time.

"What the hell is that?" Phil exclaimed, thrown off stride by the sudden burst of light from the monitor.

"Looks like the entire hand is encased in something." Max glanced at Kate. "Could she be wearing some kind of glove?" Distracted by the images blossoming on the screen in quick succession, she didn't answer. Neither did Cleo. A few seconds later Max let out a long sigh. "Jesus!"

Kate didn't have to ask why. She had seen all the fractures come and go, too fast to count, some with lateral slivers of bone that meant Tashat's hand had been crushed. Yet the bright rings around each finger hardly changed from one axial image to the next.

"She was alive then, too," Kate murmured, barely aware that she spoke aloud, "because there's not the slightest dent in that gold glove. That's why she's wearing it—to protect her broken left hand."

Phil nodded and spoke to Cleo, but Kate couldn't make out what he said, partly because of the muted hiss of forced air, which reminded her of the subtle deafening effect of boarding a plane. When Max joined their conversation she tried to separate out what he was saying from the clacking of Cleo's Bakelite bracelets and relentless on-off hum of the machine as it moved over Tashat's desiccated remains. Instead, all she could hear was unintelligible gibberish. Then even that was blotted out, only to be replaced by a roaring storm of sound, fast-moving, like snow on a TV screen. The muscles in her neck tightened until her entire body felt like a vibrating string, sending a shiver of pain into her temples. The next thing she knew, Max had slipped off his sport coat and was draping it around her shoulders.

"These machines put out a lot of heat is why the air-conditioning is going full blast. You okay?" Another practiced response from the ever-solicitous caretaker?

Kate nodded. "I've been standing still too long. Think I'll go find the rest room."

"It's time for lunch, anyway," Phil put in. "Why don't you girls go powder your noses while we shut down here? It's just a few doors that way, on your right."

Cleo shot Kate a manic-eyed grimace and mouthed an exaggerated "GIRLS?" then let her eyeballs roll up into her head. Kate got the message.

As they started down the hall, Cleo mumbled, "Too bad. He's got fantastic buns."

Kate pushed through the door of the "Ladies" and into a stall. "He's also tall and has a full head of hair," she pointed out through the partition. "Of course that would mean you'd have to stop complaining about having to look down on some guy's bald spot." She hit the lever and let a rush of water end the discussion.

"So what do you think, Katie?" Cleo asked as she joined Kate at the next sink.

It was too good an opening to let pass. "What I think is that you let Dave talk you into something, and now you can't figure a way out that won't cost your job."

Their eyes met in the mirror. "Okay, I'll give him through lunch," Cleo agreed.

Freed from the demands of his control console, Phil allowed his attraction to Cleo to blossom. Once it came out that he was divorced, the two of them engaged in a pas de deux that might have been choreographed by Balanchine, with Cleo testing his intellect as well as his tolerance for the outrageous while Phil countered every thrust with a sense of humor that seemed to surprise even Max. Through it all he sent sometimes amused, other times amazed looks at Kate, sharing his thoughts as openly as if she had been an old friend. By the time Phil laid his credit card on the check, Kate figured her old roommate had met her match.

"It's going to take most of the afternoon to finish up," he commented as they got up to leave, "so if you two girls are bored—"

Cleo didn't bat an eyelash. "Bored? You must be joking! I haven't come across anything this exciting since my last dig, in western Anatolia. The land of the Hittites. Turkey. Asia Minor."

"Yeah? So what'd you find that was so interesting?" Phil inquired, swallowing her bait. Kate glanced at Max and knew what he was thinking—the dance isn't over.

"A man and woman, caught in flagrante delicto, with his penis still engaged, preserved in a peat bog . . . for almost a thousand years. Can you imagine?" Cleo gave Phil a wide-eyed, innocent look. "She was wearing a heavy gold anklet, primitive but absolutely gorgeous." He started grinning. "As for later, I hate to impose when you've already done so much, but I'm sure questions are going to come up. Maybe we could talk occasionally, about the scans, I mean."

"Sure, anytime," Phil agreed. "I'm off Wednesday afternoons. How about if I come by the museum this week, let you show me around? That way I could answer any questions you think of between now and then." He dug for his wallet again, extracted a card, turned it over, and scribbled a number on the back. "That's my unlisted number at home, in case you need to reach me after hours."

As they walked toward the parking lot, Phil commented, "A thousand years, huh?" He gave Cleo an appraising look. "That gold anklet must've really been a dilly."

Back at the clinic, Max and Phil picked up where they left off—near the top of the male skull. For a minute utter silence pervaded the small room, as if all of them were holding their breath, waiting.

"There's the second skull," Max murmured, then let several images come and go before adding, "wrapped every bit as neatly as Tashat." He turned to Kate. "I didn't see any evidence of rewrapping on her, did you?" She shook her head, aware that he was deferring to her.

"He's also old enough to be her father," Phil put in. "That second suture looks fully closed, but the last one is—what do you think, Max?—halfway?"

"I'm not very keen on estimating age from skull sutures alone, but the first one is almost obliterated. That makes him past forty but shy of forty-seven." He sent Cleo a knowing grin. "Pretty ancient."

"He also has more than teeth in his mouth," Phil observed. "Whatever it is, it reads like bone. Any idea what it could be?" He looked to Cleo, who shook her head.

"I'll play with the contrast later, see what I can get," Max said. "Browridges and mastoid processes confirm sexual determination. So do the shape of the arch and size of the teeth. His cusps also show more wear than hers, which fits his age."

Phil crooked a finger at Cleo, motioning her to come closer. "Want to show you something. Cartilage is opaque to X rays, so it looks like this. The growth plates are really just connective tissue, to allow the long bones to grow. When a kid stops growing it means the cartilage has formed bone, which is more porous, like this. That happens first in the hands and feet, last in the collarbone, also earlier in girls than boys. Anyway, the point is, Max is right. Everything from the metacarpal and phalangeal epiphyses in her hands to the distal ends of the humerus and tibia, the long bone here"—he touched his upper arm—"and the shinbone says she had her full growth. She had to be at least twenty."

"Great," Cleo mumbled, "I can hardly wait to tell Dave."

Max glanced at his watch. "I'd like to do one more composite, so Kate can see what's under that foot mask."

A few seconds later another ghostly apparition materialized in the black void of the monitor.

"Her feet must be tightly bound," Phil commented, manipulating the image to view Tashat's feet and ankles from the front, then the back, left and right profiles, and finally from below—the soles. "Could those lines be folds in the skin, Max?"

Max mimed wrapping them with his hands, first one way, then the reverse, and shook his head. "They run almost at right angles to the creasing you'd expect with folds. Anyway, those edges appear to be cut." A silence so profound it sounded loud descended on the small room, almost like waves crashing onto a rocky shore. A second later Kate realized it was the blood pounding in her ears.

"I'd say we just learned *why* she died," Cleo concluded, "even if you can't determine the medical cause of death."

"How do you figure that?" Phil inquired.

"The head between her legs plus the slashed feet add up to an unfaithful wife. Cutting the soles of women who strayed has been a common practice in the Middle East and the Maghreb for centuries. Even in China."

Like a streak of lightning that comes and goes so fast it leaves only the memory of light on the retina, Kate caught a glimpse of a colorfully painted tower jutting high into the brilliant blue sky.

"No!" Anguish overwhelmed everything in its path. "It wasn't like that at all!" Kate hardly recognized her own voice and couldn't think how to explain what she'd just seen, not without sounding like a silly, impressionable—

She glanced at Max and caught the wide-eyed look he sent Phil Lowenstein. "I thought adulterous women were stoned to death," Phil remarked, giving her time to recover her equilibrium. "Seems like I read about that happening to some princess in Saudi Arabia a few years back. Or was it her lover?"

"In Turkey it's still not unheard of to slash a woman's feet, then tie her in a gunnysack and throw her into the Bosporus," Cleo replied, blithely unaware of Kate's acute discomfort.

"Why bother, if they're going to drown her anyway?" Max asked, joining in.

"So she can't run away again, even in the Afterworld. Look, let's assume for a minute that Tashat was a nubile young woman married to a rich man, probably a good deal older and wealthy enough to have more than one wife. Say he's spreading himself so thin sexually that she doesn't get enough attention to satisfy her, even if she was partially circumcised. The question is, who would her wandering eye be likely to fall on? Servants, relatives, and friends of her husband, maybe an occasional business associate, that's who. Wives, concubines, and children all lived together in the harem, the women's quarters, but they weren't locked up as they were later, in Turkey. Egyptian women could own property and walk freely about town. On social occasions the men ate with men while women ate with the other women, but in the same room." She paused for effect. "Say her husband is cuckolded by someone he knows, an even greater betrayal. He makes sure the transgressor gets his just deserts, has his head put between her legs, and tosses the rest to the crocodiles."

Phil shook his head. "Why not just throw him to the crocodiles, period?"

"Not the Egyptian way," Cleo insisted. "Putting her lover where her husband found him but without the equipment to do anything about it—" she stopped and snapped her fingers. "That has to be what's in his mouth—his genitals!—so he couldn't lie his way into the Afterworld."

"Talk about eternal damnation!" Phil muttered, shaking his head.

"How do you explain that judgment scene on her cartonnage, then?" Kate protested, still not ready to accept Cleo's little scenario. Or the evidence before their eyes—Tashat's slashed soles. "Surely a husband bent on such terrible vengeance would have insisted on the scale being tipped the other way, to let the gods and everyone else know she brought shame on his name." A bemused smile played around Max's lips, all the encouragement she needed. "Instead, he paid an exceptionally talented artist to paint a portrait so natural and vital that he gave her a different kind of eternity. To me that mask is the legacy of love, not betrayal and revenge."

Max nodded, letting her know he agreed. "Didn't the Egyptians believe that the head was the seat of reanimation, when they would come forth into the light of a new day? And in the Egyptian lexicon, wasn't the open eye synonymous with knowing?" He looked at Cleo, waiting for her nod. "Well, maybe it's my advanced age, but I just remembered something I forgot to mention earlier. Our anonymous friend's eyelids were never closed. He's traveling through eternity with his eyes wide open."

SIX

Year Eight in the Reign of Tutankhamen (1353 B.C.)

DAY 11, THIRD MONTH OF PLANTING

The basket maker's son wore a rough tunic over his loincloth, which meant he was no longer hot with fever. Even so, the skin around his swollen ankle still oozed fluid, attracting a swarm of flies. "It hurts," he whined.

"Then you know how the *eeyore* felt when you hit him with the stick," I told him. By the time I finished placing the leeches where the flesh was engorged with blood, he had quieted, I thought because curiosity got the better of self-pity. I was wrong. It was the sight of the girl he knew to be the lord's daughter.

"My name is Aset," she told him with a shy smile, "and this is Tuli." The dog beside her wagged his tail when he heard his name. "Would you like to see him do a trick?" Ipwet's son could barely nod, let alone speak. They both were six years old, yet Ruka was twice her size, with broad, coarsened hands and feet. Aset touched Tuli's muzzle, then drew three quick circles in the air. The dog flopped down on the hard dirt floor, rolled over three times, scrambled to his feet, and trotted back to nose her hand.

"How did you make him do that?" Ruka wanted to know.

"In the beginning I showed him how, and I always reward him."

"I didn't see you give him anything."

She dropped a hand to Tuli's back, pointed first to Ruka, then Ipwet, then to me, and finally to herself. "Count the people, Tuli. How many?"

Unlike most street dogs, Tuli can speak. And that is what he did, four times. Then he looked to Aset. When she nodded, he wagged his tail and sought her hand again. She hugged him and whispered in his ear.

"He understands that you promise him a bone," Ruka decided.

"It is how I touch and speak to him that makes Tuli happy. That is the way it is between friends, and he is my dearest friend in this world . . . besides Tenre. Would you like to be my friend?" I understood then that she intended more than to teach him a lesson about animals, for her father denies her the company of other children, even of her own kind.

I removed the leeches, sponged Ruka's ankle with sour wine, and covered it with goose grease laced with ground mandrake root to numb the pain. Too entranced by the girl and her dog, Ipwet hardly noticed what I did until I said I would return the next day.

"Must you go, too?" Ruka asked Aset.

"Yes, but we will come tomorrow, too, if your mother will allow it." She glanced at Ipwet. "Couldn't he teach me how to prepare the palm fronds for your baskets?"

"You are welcome anytime, but not to do my work."

"Tomorrow, then, Aset, don't forget," Ruka called after us.

As we set out for town, Tuli ran circles around us, lagging behind to sniff at the base of a doum palm, then running like the wind to catch up, only to be distracted again by a crumb of bread some bird had dropped. We encountered only two worshipers carrying offerings to the temple of Re-Horakhte, and I saw that the enclosure wall had cracked, exposing its mud-brick core. Even the paint flakes from the stone pylon where Nefertiti tromps over the nine enemies of the Two Lands, wielding a scimitar while her onetime husband favors the crook and flail, symbols of peace. But if Aset recognized the figure as her lady mother, she gave no sign, perhaps because she was too excited at the prospect of visiting Khary and his monkey.

Pagosh waited at the edge of town to put a rein on Tuli's adventures. "Does he *have* to wear a leash?" Aset protested. "He always comes when I call."

"How do you think his belly got torn?" he asked, and attached a length of twisted hide to Tuli's collar. "Too many of his brothers roam the streets ahead. Because they belong to no one, they must find enough to eat wherever they can."

As we passed along one side of the market, Pagosh had to restrain Tuli from attacking the red-eared baboons used by the police to patrol for thieves. When one bared his teeth at us, Aset slipped her hand into mine. "Did we do something to make him angry?"

"He warns us away because that is what he is trained to do. We need only keep our distance."

"My uncle's baboon steals food from the kitchen."

"Then perhaps it takes a thief to catch one," I replied.

Nofret awaited us with a basket of honey cakes made fresh that morning and took Aset to the garden while I went to my workroom. It was my day for checking the accounts and signing orders for what we do not grow ourselves—myrrh gum from Nubia, red sandalwood from Kush, olive oil from Mycenae, saffron and sage from Crete, and cinnamon and ginger from beyond the Red Sea. When I finished, I wandered out to the garden, relishing the sense of contentment I always find there, perhaps because I fashioned the place to suit myself. Khary and Aset sat cross-legged in the shade of an old acacia tree, forming bread dough into little balls, so they paid no attention when I stretched out on the grass nearby and crooked my arm over my eyes, to contemplate whether I should hire another man, perhaps to chop the raisins and dates Khary forms into medicine-laced sweets.

"How do you know which medicine the pills contain once they are baked?" Aset asked him.

"The ones for children with worms I roll in sesame seeds. These I mark with a cross, like this." He scored the top of a tiny ball with an ivory needle. "If in doubt, I can always taste one, but—" Before he knew what she was about, Aset had popped one into her mouth. An instant later she spit it back out. "Icckkkh!" She rubbed her mouth with the back of her hand. "Is it the bitter taste that drives the sickness away?"

"You are never to put any medicine in your mouth unless Tenre says so," Khary warned. "And those are to be swallowed rather than chewed, because of the taste. I wish it were otherwise because most little ones gum them until they soften, then do just what you did—spit it out."

Aset stopped what she was doing and sat blinking her eyes, a sure sign that she was thinking. "I have an idea." That was nothing new, either, and I had been up half the night with an old man, holding his hand until he passed through the reeds, so I closed my eyes, intending only to doze a few minutes.

"—and I would like to become an outline scribe," she was saying when I came awake, "but not if I have to make the eye of an *eeyore* like that." She pointed at the ground with the stick she had used to draw something.

"Then do as I did," Khary suggested. "I was taught to write by an old scribe, along with several other boys who took classes in his home. The charcoal seller fed his brazier in the winter, the weaver kept him in clothes, and mine supplied him with faience amulets and *ushabti,* to serve him in the Afterlife. But I did not wish to sit cross-legged in the dust all day, counting *khars* of wheat for Pharaoh's tax collectors, so I decided to learn everything I could, to be ready when the day came to follow where my heart led me. I did not know it then, but that turned out to be here, with our friend." I could feel his eyes on me and hoped he could not tell I was listening.

"But why did you have learn to write if you wanted to be a gardener?" she asked.

"I wanted to be a healer, but my father followed Aten and believed, as did the Son of Horus who fled the Two Lands, that his god would heal all ills. I mean no disrespect, but I believe the gods—whether one or many—are too busy to care for each and every one of us. That is why I decided to learn all the old scribe could teach me, to keep faith with my *ka.* Perhaps you could do the same."

I let a couple of minutes pass, then stretched to make a show of waking and shaded my eyes against the blinding blue sky as I slowly sat up—and saw that the rush sieve on the ground was filled with pills shaped like tiny birds and fish.

DAY 23, SECOND MONTH OF HARVEST

Mena's throwing sticks are a wonder to behold, with brightly painted likenesses of crocodiles and hippos and other fierce beasts, as befits the chief physician to Pharaoh's palace guards, while mine are the unadorned tools of a common laborer, fashioned by his own hands. But they came to me for services rendered, so I prize them as highly as Mena does his, and our friendship remains without envy because we live different lives by choice.

We drifted quietly instead of clapping our sticks together to flush the birds, preferring to pit our wits against theirs by watching and waiting. The world around us was blue, both above and below the black land from which we draw sustenance, as if Mother Sky had mated with the Netherworld, transforming that dark place into the twin of her heavenly abode. The river only mirrored the cloud-less sky overhead, of course, and underneath was turgid with silt, but the daily reawakening of life always has a magical effect on me, renewing my spirit in a way I can neither explain nor understand. As the face of Re-Horakhte kissed the tip of Hatshepsut's silvery needle, shooting a brilliant arrow of light across the placid water, Mena imitated the call of a cormorant to his mate on the nest. I crooked my arm to be ready for the first bird to take wing, and lis-tened for the slap of feathers. In the instant I caught sight of a duck rising from the reeds, I felt our skiff tilt beneath my feet and knew Mena had bested me. Still, I let fly a moment later, heard my stick hit, and saw the bird falter before nosing into a dive.

Mena poled us through the reeds, each of us keeping an eye on where his bird had fallen while searching for his stick at the same time. With the need for quiet past, I decided to test whether he might still be persuaded to go with his General, who prepares another campaign. "Are you not worried that this young assistant you speak of so highly may displace you in Horemheb's affections?"

"Senmut may lack experience on the battlefield, but he has an eye that cuts to the bone. Like you. As for how he gets on with the

General—" Mena shrugged and let the skiff glide. "If you think I grow bored with besting you at fowling and wish to be away from here, it is because you cannot know the joy I find in Tetisheri and Nebet."

In the nearly three years since he returned to Waset, Mena has had the good fortune to find a wife with the wit and charm to match her beauty. He also has fathered a daughter named Nebet, who shines like gold to his eye despite her deformed hip. "Our time in this world is short," he warned me, "and twenty-eight years of it are gone already. Do not leave it too late to get any children of your own, Tenre."

In appearance we are as two strangers, yet in other ways we are like twins, so I am never surprised to hear him voice my own thoughts. But he does not know that I have been visiting a young widow named Amenet, who I find pleasing in both face and disposition. Nor is she coy about offering me her body as well as a meal.

"How does Nebet fare with the new splint?" I inquired, since we have put our skills together to find some way to hold the ball of her thighbone in its socket yet still allow her to move. Now, since her second feast day, with Nebet able to take a few steps and needing more freedom, our latest device is lighter and more flexible than the one before it, to let her muscles grow strong enough to replace the brace.

"She tests herself on the steps leading to our sleeping room, so our privacy soon will come to an end." He sent me a wry grin, since I know of his unorthodox habit of sharing his couch with his wife through the night. He reached into the water, grabbed his duck by the legs, and bound them with a cord, then tossed the bird into the bow of the boat with the others. "Anyway, the General is content for me to stay behind to look after his wife, should he leave her with child. Since the Queen lost another babe, he wants someone nearby he can trust. He believes the fault lies with her physicians, though I am not so sure." I knew he alluded to Ankhesenamen having conceived her first child by her father, to the same end.

We paddled to where my bird should have been and in time found him thrashing about in the water, only stunned. I gave him his life and motioned for Mena to pole us into the backwash of the main channel, where we began another wait. "You know the Queen is with child again?" he asked after a minute, keeping his voice low so as not to warn off our prey. I nodded and watched the thicket of reeds ripple like ripening wheat in the cool morning breeze. "Perhaps it will go better with her this time. I hear Ramose has offered Pharaoh the services of his own physician, a man he swears can bring forth a live child if any can."

"It is not for me to judge who Ramose chooses to—"

"He names the physician Senakhtenre. Did he not tell you?"

"Me, attend the Queen?" I stammered, not sure I understood him.

"Sheri says Ankhesenamen intended to ask for you even before the priest came forward, at the urging of her little sister."

"Aset?" I must have sounded the village idiot, for he hooted with laughter, setting our reed skiff to rocking. It is ideal for skimming ponds and marshes, but lacks the stability provided by a keel. "The laugh will be on you if you dump our catch in the water," I reminded him, knowing he would not want to lose his favorite meal.

"Sheri insists that you attend the banquet we plan for the General, to wish him well on his forthcoming campaign."

Mena's residence is near the palace, a place as foreign to me as the lands beyond the Red Sea. "I thank you, truly, but I am not at ease among people in high places, nor are they with me."

"Then hide yourself in the crowd if you must, until the Queen and Tutankhamen grace us with their presence . . . unless you prefer greeting her for the first time from between her legs. Besides, you could do me a favor by speaking to my wife, who refuses to heed her father or me. She still believes Nebet's hip, or worse, will be visited upon another child."

"In his own house, even a wise man is green as a young shoot," I said, then sat thinking for a minute. "All right, I will come to your fancy affair." To make sure he did not feel too satisfied with himself, I added, "But there is little chance that Horemheb will leave Mutnodjme with child so long as she uses a pessary of ground acacia spikes."

His face was reward enough for the teasing I suffer at his hands. "How in the name of Thoth could you know that?"

"She sends a servant to the Eye of Horus, the name Khary has given our dispensary. Every packet of powders and herbs now carries that mark." I strung my tale out on purpose. "His sympathetic ear and helpful suggestions loosen many a servant's tongue, so if I can be of assistance to you at any time"—I kept a straight face as a grin broke across his—"to uh, determine the proper treatment for one of your rich patients, I shall be more than happy to do so. For a price, of course." It is only with Mena that the boy I once was, who still lives somewhere inside me, dares make himself known.

"Then pray Thoth you succeed with the Queen where others have failed, if you want to keep your little goddess from the claws of the vultures. It matters not if it is another girl, Tenre, only that the babe should live."

DAY 14, FOURTH MONTH OF HARVEST

"The priest kept her," Pagosh explained before I could ask why Aset was late coming home from her classes at the temple.

"What was it this time?"

He shrugged. "You will have to ask Tuli. But while I stood waiting for her in the temple courtyard, I saw some boys from her class playing a game. One had his left arm bound to his side while the others laughed and jeered at whatever it was he drew in the dirt with a stick."

"I will have the truth from her this time," I vowed. Pagosh did not move. "What else?" I asked.

"Why do you refuse to let her go with you to visit those who are sick in the village of her father's fellahin, when you did not deny her before?"

"All pestilences are not the same. Some content themselves with attacking one man or one child. Others afflict many people, like fleas. How I do not know, but I have seen the sickness that runs among the field hands and their families before, and know it to be as painful as it is deadly."

"Then why does the flea not jump on *you*?"

"At one time or other I suffered similar ailments, but the truth is, I do not know, despite your high opinion of my skills."

"Perhaps," he agreed grudgingly "but you are alone in admitting it. I will make sure she does not go there, then—with or without you."

Later, when Aset accompanied me to the workshop of Ramose's potter, she told me that "Mahu, a boy in my class, says my lady mother once was a man, so she cannot possibly be my real mother." She skipped to catch up with me, while Tuli lagged behind to sniff the trunk of a tree. "He says my father only puts that about in order to proclaim me a royal princess. Could that be true, Tenre? Surely *you* must know."

"You are the child of her body," I assured her.

"But how *could* she be my mother if she once was a man?"

I believe she looked for a way to explain why Nefertiti feels no affection for her, but I had none to give. "Your lady mother once was Queen of the Two Lands. Then, for a while after her first husband, the Pharaoh Akhenaten, named her his coregent, she pretended to be a man, just as you dress up to act the great lady."

"Oh!" She seemed to accept that, for she went on to something else. "Mahu knows many secrets, but he tells them only to the other boys. Today none of them could solve the numbers problem the priest gave us, so Mahu agreed to tell me his best secret if I would give him the answer." She looked up at me. "He says I am to be wife to a priest of Amen, so the High Priest and his Sacred Council can put one of their own on the throne of Horus."

A cold fist tightened around my heart, but I held my stride. "Whose son is this Mahu that he gossips like an old woman?"

"Neterhotep, the mayor of Waset. Why?"

"Because the mayor should teach his son to control his flapping tongue and attend to his numbers, that's why. Why were you late again today?"

"Because I entered the sanctuary, where only Pharaoh and the High Priest are allowed to go."

"If you knew it was forbidden to enter the sanctuary, why did you go there?"

"To see the zoo Mahu is always talking about, in a chamber behind the sanctuary, but I lost my way in the dark. My teacher says I ask too many questions, Tenre. Do I?"

I always answer when she asks why I give this herb or that pill, but the priests believe that to question signifies dissatisfaction with the accepted ways, and I did not want her punished for some heresy she learned from me. "That depends on what you ask, and why. Some things are done for no reason except habit or a tradition so old that no one remembers why. There also are private matters that do not concern you."

"Like what Pagosh tells Merit about what he feels in his heart?" I nodded. "Does that mean I should never tell anyone what my *ka* and I say to each other?"

"That is a question better asked of your father."

"He says we all have a voice somewhere inside us that only we can hear and we must never ignore it or we might do something that is not *maat*. But when the *sunu* refused even to try to heal Tuli's wound, my *ka* asked me why. So it is my *ka* who asks all these questions, not me."

"Do not try to put the blame for what comes out of your mouth somewhere else. No matter what the voice inside you says, you and your *ka* are one. What did the *sunu* say when you asked why he refused to treat Tuli?"

"That Osiris would take him anyway and—" She stubbed her toe and fell to one knee. Tuli heard her cry out and came racing back. "It is these accursed sandals that cause me to fall, *senu*," she muttered. The first time she called me that I thought she only twisted her tongue while saying *sunu*. But I have heard her use many other words from the Akkadian language since then, so she called me "shoe" and believed me ignorant of her intent.

"We will go back and wash the dirt off your bloody knee." I bent to pick her up.

"I am not a baby, and there is no need to go back," she said, jerking away from me. "Ipwet lives just over there."

Ruka came bursting through the door calling, "Are you hurt, Aset?" Clumsy oaf that he is, the boy's heart overflows with love simply because she calls him friend.

After Ipwet cleaned the dirt from her knee, Aset pointed to an oblong shape made of folded strips of palm fronds, obviously the start of a basket. Ramose's basket maker handed it to her, then watched Aset turn it over and over, examining it from the top, then the bottom and finally from the side.

"Could you weave a sandal shaped like this," she asked, "but with the wall leaning in rather than out, so it would keep my foot from sliding off the sole? Surely that would be better than those old things." She made a face at her discarded sandals.

"It takes no time to weave such a little thing," Ipwet agreed, eager to repay Aset's kindness to her son, "but it would not stay on without a strap."

"Perhaps," Aset replied, "but not one that rubs my toes. I will think on it and let you know what I decide . . . tomorrow."

DAY 16, FOURTH MONTH OF HARVEST

"Does she admit to what she did?" Ramose asked.

I nodded, then told him about the boy who talked of a chamber behind the festival hall of the great Thutmose, where his outline scribes had created all manner of exotic birds and strange animals. "I suspect she wanted to see how they were drawn."

"The priest who is her teacher says she is skilled at outlining," Ramose agreed. "He also complains that she sows the seeds of rebellion in others by refusing to copy the figures in the proper way."

"Pagosh says the boys in her class imitate how the priest binds her left arm to her side to keep her from using it. Apparently they find amusement in seeing her humbled."

His face flushed with anger. "I will—" He stopped as a child's voice came from the hallway, followed by a sharp slap. A moment later, Nefertiti burst into Ramose's library, dragging her daughter behind her. She jerked Aset's arm, causing her to stumble and cry out in pain.

"See what a thieving little beggar your precious princess has become!" she spat at her husband. "She not only pilfers my jewelry but paints herself as a woman of the streets."

Aset stood rubbing her shoulder with one hand, looking so pitiful it was all I could do to keep from going to her and taking her into my arms. The wig she wore had slipped askew and both cheeks were streaked with green from her eyes. When she dropped her hand I saw that a smear of henna stained the sleeve of her white gown.

"Yesterday was not enough?" Ramose inquired, revealing that

he knew about her transgression at the temple. Aset lifted her chin to brave his piercing gaze. "You went to your lady mother's apartment, as well, though you have been instructed not to?"

"Yes, because everyone is going to Mena's banquet but me. Tuli and I decided to have our own party." Her voice began to quiver. "I meant only to borrow her necklace, just for tonight."

"You disappoint me, daughter." Ramose's words cut deeper than any knife, causing Aset's tears to overflow and run down her cheeks.

"I will not tolerate such chaos in my house!" her father burst out. "You are never to come before me in tears again."

Wide-eyed at his display of anger, Aset darted a glance at me as Nefertiti went to Ramose and began stroking his arm—to soothe his temper, I thought. When she slid her hand beneath his arm and then over one bare breast, I realized she intended something else entirely.

"You will go to your room and reflect on why you insist on intruding where you are not wanted," he told Aset, getting himself under control—at least where she was concerned, and motioned me to take her away. I bowed first to him and then his lady, who had already turned away, and took Aset's hand.

As we passed from the room I glanced back and saw Ramose approach the Beautiful One from behind, grasp her breasts in his hands, and pull her against his aroused body. In the hallway I slowed my stride and would have lifted Aset in my arms except for the look on her face.

Once we reached her room I removed the necklace and wig, then cleaned her face and scrubbed the henna from her palms. Still she refused to meet my eyes, to hide how much she was hurting.

"Do you remember the little girl I told you about who cannot run or play because she must wear a splint on one leg?" Aset's eyes flew to mine. "Nebet will have no one to play with tonight while her parents entertain their guests."

"You will take me with you?" she whispered. I nodded. "Tuli, too?"

I nodded again and tried not to let her see that I was worried about him. "Do you know where he is?"

"My lady mother ordered Paga to cut his throat and throw him on the trash heap, because he tried to bite her. But Paga will not let anything bad happen to Tuli." She searched my face "I can go . . . truly?"

The word has become our way of sealing a bargain, and once given cannot be taken back. I hesitated only because to defy her father's orders is an act I cannot undo, either. But Ramose charged me with looking after not only her body but her *akh,* the spark of life that is hers alone, and in my heart I knew what I did was *maat.*

"Unless you find Nebet is too young. She is not yet three, while you soon will celebrate your seventh feast day." Aset was already shaking her head. Suddenly transformed into an imp with sparkling blue eyes, she bounced on her toes.

"Nebet has no brothers or sisters, either?"

"Not yet. I will call Merit to help you dress and brush your hair. I would not have you shame me before my friends." I only said it to give her an excuse to wear something special, but when she ran to her clothes chest I saw that she held her left arm to her body. "But first I must have your word on one more thing."

She turned back to me. "I promise to stay with Nebet so my father will not see me," she vowed, revealing that she understood more than I intended.

"Come here." When she stood before me again I took her left hand in mine. "If ever the priest ties this to your side again, you must come and tell me."

"But it is wrong for me to form the sacred signs of the language of the gods with my left hand. Isn't it?"

"Is it wrong that one of Tuli's eyes is blue and the other yellow?" I shrugged. "Who are we mortals to deny how the gods formed us?"

She started to giggle, but Tuli chose that moment to come running across the room and they both went down in a heap of intertwined limbs. I turned to find Pagosh in the doorway.

"I will pole you across the river, but not until it is dark," he said, as I passed him on my way out. "Ramose will not expect you to go against his orders, but his lady has eyes in the back of her head."

. . .

Merit had brushed Aset's short curls and tied her youth lock with a yellow ribbon and carnelian *tyet* to match her saffron linen dress. She wore sandals made from gazelle hide painted the same colors as her wide collar, and looked a highborn lady in all but the coarse linen bag swinging from one shoulder. Tonight it held not only the little papyrus-root lion and ivory scribe's palette, a gift from her father on her fifth feast day, but a woven straw box filled with fruit candies.

As we approached the entrance to Mena's compound, I took the path to the lesser gate and Nebet's rooms. When Aneksi, her nurse-mother, came to the door, I told her I brought a surprise— "the company of another child, which may prove to be the best medicine yet for our little friend."

We found Nebet pulling a wooden crocodile across the tile floor, holding to the edge of the sitting shelf with one hand while jerking the string with the other to make his long snout open and close. "Watch out he does not eat one of your toes," I called out.

"Tenre!" she shrieked. I went down on one knee and opened my arms while Aset stood back with Tuli, watching Nebet lift her splinted leg free of the floor and swing it around in front of her. Then she let go of the sitting shelf and came straight toward me, balancing herself with each step while she lifted her splinted leg and placed it in front of the other one. Our game had started as a way for me to watch her walk alone, to see how the splint allowed her to move, but now it is that and much more. She was still some distance away when she reached out, trusting me to catch her, which I did, then swung her up and around in a circle.

"I have missed you, little lotus bud," I whispered in her ear. "You are growing so fast you soon will be as tall as your mother, and just as beautiful." Embarrassed, she tucked her face into my neck and in that moment caught sight of Aset.

They stared at each other until I set Nebet back on her feet, holding her hand while she found her balance. A *wah* collar of saf-flowers and persea blooms circled her neck, like those her parents offered their female guests on such occasions, but she was wearing a short tunic so Aset could see the jointed brace. It extended from her ankle to her hip and was made of a thin bundle of reeds bound with gum-soaked linen, for lightness and flexibility.

"My name is Aset, and this is Tuli." She clicked her fingers, and he sat up on his haunches. Nebet covered her mouth with her hand to hide a smile. Next Aset dug in her bag for the papyrus-root lion. "Would your crocodile like to play with my lion?" she asked, holding it out to the other girl. Nebet has always been fearful of strangers, and I could not be certain she would accept the offer of friendship. But Aset seemed to sense that she was shy and let her take her time.

When Nebet reached for the lion, Aset held out her arm and said, "Here, you can hold on to me." Nebet is tall for her age while Aset is small for hers, so they were not so far apart in height. "I promise not to let you fall. And you are not to worry about your hip. Tenre will fix it. Truly. He gave me life when no one else could. Even Paga says there is no one his equal in all the Two Lands. Except your father, of course. Tenre says *he* is the best physician in this world. Then when you can walk better, we will go all sorts of places together. Would you like to pretend that Tuli is our baby brother? We could tie this piece of cloth around his hips for a kilt. If he is good, you might even give him a piece of the candy I brought you."

I left them then and went around to Mena's garden, where his other guests stood about, women with other women and men with men, sipping wine and talking. Tall for a woman, Mena's wife stands eye to eye with most men, and disarms them with her penetrating insight as well as her beauty. Tonight Tetisheri wore a white gown fringed with blue, a gold necklace inset with lapis lazuli, and a wreath of flowers like Nebet's.

"It has been too long, Tenre." She touched her cheek to mine and whispered, "Now that you are here to keep the hyenas from attacking his back, I can relax and enjoy myself."

"Fear not, Sheri. It was your husband who kept the crocodiles from eating me when we were boys," I murmured, holding her close long enough to explain about Aset.

"Do you seduce my wife before my very eyes?" Mena called, clapping me on the shoulder as he slipped his other arm around Sheri. That she chose him amazes Mena still, I think, for it has changed him in ways that neither of us could have anticipated. I made a show of inspecting him, from his gold armlets to the hem of his pleated hip wrap and purple belt, the ends weighted with nuggets of turquoise.

"Take care, my friend, lest one of your soldiers mistakes you for a woman." He laughed and slapped my cheek, a familiarity he does not visit on anyone else.

"Come, let me get you some wine and introduce you to our guests." He led me to three tall clay jars standing like soldiers at attention, their bottoms planted in a bed of wet sand. "We have Antyllan, but the Ymet is better."

"I have the tongue of a peasant, so I will leave the choice to you." I spoke in jest, then realized it was true. "I do not belong here, Mena."

"It was your pure heart and good sense that took Ramose's eye, not your taste in wine." He grinned, knowing he had me in the palm of his hand. "Ymet it is then—the white gold from Lake Mareotis."

Several men attended the guest of honor, but Mena did not hesitate to interrupt. "It is my pleasure, General, to present my friend Senakhtenre, physician of Waset like his father before him." He began to recite Horemheb's titles. "Commander of Pharaoh's Armies of the North and the South, First—"

I noticed that Horemheb has eyes like a bird, with lids that stand wide open and irises as black as the pupil, leaving them without depth. He also is so big that only one man stood taller. The Nubian.

"You are too short," Horemheb said to me. "Our host speaks so highly of your skills I expected a man at least twice your size."

I risked a glance at Mena and found him grinning like a fool. "In that case, General, he has misled us both. The last thing I expected of you was a sense of humor." The Commander of Pharaoh's Armies honked like a goose while Mena's ruddy face turned even darker.

He hurried to perform the other introductions, leaving the Nubian to last. "And my aide, Prince Senmut, son of the King of Aniba." In all the talk of his young assistant, Mena never had mentioned that he was royal or from the province above the First Cataract. But Senmut did not wear his hair bobbed above the ears like his countrymen, and his skin is black as night, not brown. Indeed he is fortunate in his wide mouth and straight nose, both suggesting that his forebears came from Punt, the land near the mouth of the Red Sea.

Mena guided me across the garden to the cluster of men standing with the High Priest, Ramose among them. "You have heard me speak of my physician, Senakhtenre," he said to Paranefer.

"*Sunu*," the High Priest intoned, putting me in my place. Tiny red worms crawled beneath the skin of his fleshy nose and his yellow fingernails curled over the ends of his fingers, both signs that his time in this world grows short.

As we moved on, Mena mentioned the tomb Paranefer builds in the Place of Truth. "A pyramid, no less, though a puny one compared to those of the ancients. He claims only to want a view of Amen's northern temple, but I say he wants to remind those who would usurp the power of Amen that *he* is the one who turns men into gods."

"He could pass as brother to the Pharaoh who strides across the walls of more than one temple, so perhaps he has reason to ape the old ones."

"You have as much taste for intrigue as the rest of us, Tenre, despite your protest to the contrary." We both saw Sheri motioning him to come to her. "Which means you are capable of fending for yourself while I see what my wife wants. I see Senmut has become bored with politics and watches the dancers. Go talk with him."

A grassy area beyond the tile-lined pond had been roped off for the dancers and musicians. The torch flames danced to the music, as well, while the palms fronds waved like lazy fans in the evening breeze. Even the serving girls weaving in and out among Mena's guests moved to the music, offering dates dipped in cinnamon, grapes and sliced melon, or fried balls made of bean paste.

Senmut seemed engrossed in one dancer in particular, who followed the rising beat with ever more erotic moves. "See that leg?" he asked when he saw me.

The girl he pointed to wore a likeness of the god Bes tattooed on her thigh, but otherwise looked like all the others, with the same string of hollow beads around her hips. "A good-luck charm," I said, stating the obvious.

"She will need it. Look at her spine, just to the left of the dimple. The leg with the tattoo is shorter than the other, though she makes up for it with the pliant muscles of youth. But give her a few more years and she will be crooked as an old crone." I saw that he was right. "What would you do to stop that from happening?" he asked.

When he turned to me, I was struck again by the handsomeness of his face. "To attach something to one foot would only bring attention to her affliction and put an end to her dancing," I replied. "No house of pleasure would take her in, nor would any man want her for his wife, knowing she might visit her affliction upon his children. How would she eat?"

"Soon she will barely be able to hobble," he snapped. "How will she eat then?"

"Given the choice, I would prefer to find pleasure while I can, rather than have my legs match and starve now. What about you?" I held his eyes, challenging him to admit what he did not want to, that neither solution satisfied.

"Perhaps," he muttered. "But I do not like your choice. It is not *maat*."

"Exactly," I agreed, throwing caution to the winds because I understood for the first time that it was Senmut's restless curiosity and impatience with ignorance that endeared him to Mena. "And the only way we are likely to find a better answer is to somehow learn to ask the right questions."

He gave me a sheepish grin. "I only wanted to hear you reason with my own ears. Your name is too much like honey on Mena's tongue, especially when he talks of your experiments." That Mena entrusted such secrets to him surprised me. "I came here tonight to tell you I would consider it an honor if you would let me help. Only say what you want me to do."

"I hear the Hittites cleanse their hands with plant ash dissolved in water, while the Babylonians boil olive oil, ashes, and natron together to make a washing paste. Perhaps you will encounter someone who knows which is better, and why."

He nodded and waited. "You can trust me, Senakhtenre. Truly."

I almost capitulated then, but he was a stranger, and the habit of caution is an old friend. "Which teacher in the House of Life did you find most enlightening?" I asked, to see if he played politics with me.

"Khay-Min, Chief Physician of the South, who is as gifted in examining with the hand as he is fortunate in his daughter." He pointed to Sheri. "But I have learned even more from Mena."

"Who taught you what you consider to be most useless?" It was a trick question, intended to reveal his true color no matter how he answered. Again he turned, seeking someone. "That one standing with Neterhotep and Aperia, watching the baboons. The one who dresses like a peacock is Neterhotep, mayor of Waset. It is the other one I mean, Bekenkhons, who oversees the cutting of boys who are to become priests."

"Then he is a *ka* priest, not a physician in the House of Life," I pointed out, "and would have no part in your training."

"He demonstrated how he cuts the labia and clitoris on the women of his harem, saying it makes them more tractable. But he takes pleasure in the maiming as well since he spilled his seed even as he wielded the knife. On some women he cuts everything away and seals the vagina, leaving only an opening the size of a slender reed for urine and blood to pass. The woman has to be forced open by her husband, not a pleasurable task for any man except one bent like him."

"Surely you jest. Mena would never invite such a man into his house."

"He came in the retinue of the High Priest, not by personal invitation."

A burst of feminine laughter drew our attention to a group of women. Only Nefertiti among them veiled her body with a robe that outlined her breasts, abdomen, and thighs when she moved. The woman beside her with one breast uncovered had to be the General's wife, since Mutnodjme is known to keep two female dwarfs constantly by her side. It is because of them that she is rumored to be the prostitute depicted on the wall of a recently deceased noble's tomb. But she was not alone in cheering the two red-eared baboons who fought each other off while one and then the other tried to copulate with the third, a female whose hindquarters glowed bright red.

"Neterhotep and Bekenkhons are not the only ones who enjoy Horemheb's baboons," Senmut observed. "The General sent them over for tonight's entertainment because the female is in heat." While we watched, Nefertiti turned, seeking Ramose with her eyes. "That one breathes fire when she so much as looks at the priest, so you can be sure *she* is intact. She only appears calm and serene on the surface," Senmut added, "while underneath she seethes like a banked fire, needing only a little stirring to burst into flames. I hear she is so demanding the priest has no seed left for his other women."

"Never doubt that Ramose is a willing accomplice in whatever scheme the priests are plotting," Mena put in from behind my shoulder. His words sent a chill down my spine, reminding me of what the mayor's son told Aset—that the Sacred Council planned to put "one of their own" on the throne. "But if either of you had a woman of your own, you would not have to speculate about what other men do with theirs. Come, the roast goose awaits us inside." He squeezed my shoulder. "Sheri asks you to look in on one of the servants first, Tenre, who has gone into labor."

I invited Senmut to come with Mena to my house in town, and went in search of Tetisheri. A delicious odor pervaded the house, especially when a serving girl hurried past me with a roasted goose. Another followed her carrying honey cakes speckled with nuts and seeds, and small loaves filled with coddled eggs. But Sheri was nowhere about, so I went to Nebet's rooms instead. Before I reached the door I could hear the two girls talking and giggling. I found them on the floor with chips of limestone scattered all about, so I knew that Aset had been entertaining Mena's daughter with her picture stories, as she does more and more lately when accompanying me to visit a sick child.

Aset saw me first and jumped to her feet. "Is it time to go already?"

Before I could answer, Sheri arrived with Pagosh close behind her. "It is the Queen, Tenre. No one else is to be called until after you examine her, to learn whether her babe still lives. Then the priests and others must be summoned. So Mena must remain here lest someone suspect. Pagosh will show you the way."

My thoughts raced in anticipation of what the next few hours might bring, not only for me but all the people of the Two Lands. But first I went down on my knee to Aset. "You must stay with Nebet until Pagosh returns to take you home."

"Is it time for my sister's babe to come?" she asked, her big eyes solemn. I nodded. "Then you must ask Mena to lend you his bag of medicines, just for tonight." Until that moment it had not occurred to me that I had come away empty-handed. "Don't forget the itasin ointment," she added.

I nodded, drawing courage from her confidence in my skills. "What would I do without you?" I whispered, and waited for a smile to light her eyes. Instead she threw her arms around my neck and gave me a fierce hug. Then, just as quickly, she stepped back to let me rise to my feet.

And so, because one small girl had such unwavering faith in me, I made my way to the palace with my back straight and chin held high—as befits the physician to Ankhesenamen, Queen of the Two Lands and Great Royal Wife to Neb-khepru-re Tutankhamen, Lord of Upper and Lower Kemet, Son of Horus on Earth.

SEVEN

"Even if the Jews did pick up the practice of circumcision in Egypt," Kate told Cleo, who stood watching her fit narrow strips of clay between the tissue-depth blocks already in place on the replica of Tashat's skull, in a pattern similar to the supporting structure of a geodesic dome, "there's no evidence that the Egyptians ever performed clitoridectomies on their women, partial or otherwise. Despite the pharaonic label attached to one style of genital mutilation today."

"Herodotus says they did," Cleo countered. "And modern Sudanese and Somali women, even those who have had their clitoris cut away completely, claim they feel *something*." Kate didn't even look up. "Anyway, I only threw it in to rev up Phil's motor." Cleo watched her press a strip of clay into place and blend the joint. "What comes next, after you get all those strips in place?"

"I'll fill in the empty spaces, except around her mouth and eyes, where I plan to sculpt in the musculature, since certain muscles determine the angle at which the eyes appear to slant. Also the inner and outer corners of the eyes. That's where the really iffy part is, around the eyes and mouth."

"Okay, say she *is* twenty-three or twenty-four. That's still young enough to want more sex than she's getting. It *is* unnatural not to need it, you know."

"Leave it alone, Clee," Kate warned, not wanting to hear any more lectures about how a monastic lifestyle goes against the nature of innately social animals.

Cleo waited for her to scrape and measure and scrape again to get the thickness exactly right over one browridge. "It's just that I hate to see you get involved with an older man. He may be in halfway decent shape now, but give him ten years and his batting average will be in the basement, just when you're hitting your prime."

Kate shook her head. "The only reason I brought up that it's been three weeks since we've heard anything is because I'm anxious to see the workup he promised."

"I can call him if you want, ask if he's found anything to do with that necklace among his grandmother's papers, then kind of offhandedly mention the workup."

"I'm sure he'll get to it soon as he has time," Kate assured her, "and I have plenty to do." She could tell Cleo was keyed up by the scatterbrained way she jumped from one subject to another, probably excited about spending the weekend with Phil.

"Listen, Clee, I've gone over both the coffin and cartonnage with a magnifying glass," Kate told her, "comparing them every way I can think of. I'm sure they were painted by the same hand. A switched coffin just won't wash. There has to be another explanation for the discrepancy between that inscription and her true physical age."

"The same artist probably painted hundreds of masks and coffins, Katie!"

"I also think they were painted by a woman."

Cleo pursed her lips and blew out a puff of air. "Okay, let's hear why."

Kate couldn't explain why any more than she could explain the fragmented images that came to her in the night—black flies crawling over the torn belly of a little dog, white-robed men bent under the burden of pulling a loaded sledge across the barren desert.

"I just think we should look at all the possibilities before we jump to some knee-jerk conclusion, like those boobs did with the mummy in Tomb Fifty-five. First it's Queen Tiye because the left arm is folded and they found grave goods bearing her name—until a professor of anatomy happens along and points out that it's a male. Right away everybody jumps to the conclusion that it's Akhenaten. Except it turns out he would've been too old, which leaves the elusive Smenkhkare. With half the ancient sites in Egypt untouched, why does it always have to be one of the above instead of we just don't know?"

"Point taken," Cleo agreed, knocking the wind out of Kate's self-righteous sails. "Anything else?"

"I didn't mean to preach, but, well, I don't want to see you slip in Dave's dirty water. Scientific technology has brought archaeology out of the dark ages, yet dinosaurs like Dave are the first to attack any scientist who dares suggest that his precious theory leaks like a sieve." She straightened and dropped her voice. "I'm afraid you're too much the rational scientist, Dr. Cavanaugh, to understand the ancient Egyptian mind. That's the defense of a desperate Egyptologist—accuse the messenger of garbling the message."

"I already asked Larry to search the literature for any mention of females with an arm folded across the chest, beginning with Amenhotep Three," Cleo responded, pulling the plug on Kate's ballooning indignation.

Kate laughed and give her friend a hug. "Have fun."

"Let's have lunch Monday. I'll tell you all about it." Cleo glanced at her watch. "Got to run. Phil is picking me up at four." Kate waved her away but called, "Don't break a leg!" as she left.

With no more distractions, Kate's thoughts wandered to the painted floor of Tashat's coffin. Ptah was the patron of craftsmen and artists, said to have created the world by thinking, which made him the god of imagination. The other figure was Khnum, the ram-headed form of Re, who had fashioned the body and soul of man out of clay. But if Tashat was an educated woman, why Ptah instead of Thoth, the god of learning and wisdom? Could there be some connection between Tashat's broken fingers and how she used her hands? Surely the wife of an aristocrat would never be a potter, but what about an outline scribe, the closest thing to an artist the Egyptians had?

"Mind if I watch?" Startled, Kate's hand jerked, gouging a hole in the clay strip she was smoothing. "Sorry," Dave mumbled. "I figured you heard me come in."

"That's okay." She pinched off a small piece of clay to patch the hole.

He watched her for a while, then, "How can you tell how big to make her nose with nothing to go by except a hole in the skull?"

"In a Caucasoid, the width of the bony aperture is about three-fifths of the total nasal width across the wings. And the projection of the nose is about three times the length of the nasal spine, measuring from the lower edge of the nasal opening to the tip of the spine. The exact shape of the nose is always something of a guess, though, even if the length and width are not."

"What about the lips?"

Kate guessed where he was heading, but she wanted him to spit it out. "The width of the mouth depends on where her canine teeth were, also on the distance between borders of the iris. The mouth slit is about a third of the way up the upper incisors, but the lips themselves—the red part— is guesswork. Not that I won't be keeping several other things in mind."

"How would you know if she was fat or skinny?"

"Unless a person was so obese it affected the curvature of the spine or knee joints, we have to go with an average based on size of the skeleton plus age."

"She could have been black, you know," he murmured, finally getting to it.

"Then the nasal opening would be heart-shaped, and it isn't."

He watched a curl of clay roll up in front of her looped-wire tool. "The extra skull is Caucasoid, too?" Kate nodded. "No room for doubt on the gender?"

"Men generally have thicker skulls," she said with a straight face. "There's an overlapping area where it could be either male or female, but this one is beyond that, where the chance of finding a female is extremely remote."

"Even so, don't you think it would be wise to get a second opinion before we stick our necks out?" He sounded edgy. Kate wondered if the rumor she'd heard was true—that the Oriental Institute at Chicago was about to make him an offer.

"Sure, if you want to that's fine with me. But even Cleo couldn't push Max to commit himself without at least one piece of corroborating evidence."

"I don't suppose you know where she is. Secretary said she left early."

Kate made a pretense of sighting along one of the strips. She didn't like lying, even for Cleo, but when Dave interpreted the dip of her head as a negative answer she decided to let it be.

"Listen, there's something I'd like to ask, if you have a minute." She pointed to the lid standing next to the open coffin with the inside facing out, where the painted scene showed a flower-lined road, the traditional symbol of a spiritual journey. "What do you make of these cartouches? They look like two footprints, side by side, walking up the road. Didn't cartouches always contain the names of pharaohs?"

"Plus three queens. Hatshepsut, Nefertiti, and Cleopatra," Dave agreed as he moved closer. "But this mummy is *not* Nefertiti, if that's where you're headed. I hear you've been teaching yourself to read hieroglyphics, so how would *you* read them?"

"The little pot is n-w," Kate ventured, naming the letters rather than trying to pronounce the word. The written language of the ancient Egyptians contained no vowels, so how the words sounded was a guess. "The arrow over the pot makes it s-n. Or s-w-n. With the seated man, that makes it s-w-n w. Physician." It was the determinative that made the difference in whether the other signs stood for medicine or the person who administered it. And since physicians had to know how to write, the seated man—a scribe—pointed to the person rather than a disease or treatment.

"*Sunu*," Dave confirmed, adding the vowel sounds Kate was shy of voicing, "an ordinary lay physician with no priestly titles or royal appointments."

"What about the cartouche with a loaf of bread in place of the arrow?"

"Just another way of writing the same thing."

"Can't it mean shoe . . . or sandal?" She was fishing, but the cartouches looked like footprints, Tashat's cartonnage was fitted with palm-frond sandals, and the soles of her feet had been slashed.

"I said *sunu*. *Senu* means shoe in Akkadian, an early form of cuneiform that originated somewhere between the Tigris and Euphrates. Are you trying to learn that, too?" He seemed to find the idea amusing.

She wasn't about to tell him that languages had always come easy for her, or that she was taking a class at Denver University. "Then how do you explain the word "physician" in a cartouche? Even if it's used symbolically to mean that some physician reigned in her heart, it still doesn't make sense. There's no way her husband could be called ordinary. Or her father."

"Papyrus was a lucrative export. That's why Akhenaten ordered everyone to write hieratic, to save space. From then on hieroglyphs were used only for sacred writing. So put this in the religious context. Pharaohs were named sons of Amen-Re when they took the throne and became gods themselves. Akhenaten considered himself the son of Aten, and wore a gold bracelet inscribed with his immortal father's name inside the double cartouches of a pharaoh. He preached that Aten was the ultimate healer. That's why the practice of medicine went downhill during his reign. Sunu is a kind of generic word for physician, so enclosing it in cartouches probably means something like 'God is the physician who heals all ills.' "

"I guess that does make sense," Kate agreed, giving Dave his due.

He surprised her by responding in kind. "Don't get discouraged, McKinnon. You're not doing half-bad for a beginner."

Kate had gone only two blocks when it started snowing, small icy flakes that stung her face like windblown sand. By the time she reached her street she couldn't see two feet in front of her, her toes had gone numb, and she could hear a squishy noise with every step she took.

Sam heard her stomping around on the front porch and began jumping against the door. Once inside she hugged him close and let her cold fingers sink into his thick fur. Then she started through the house, turning on lights as she went. In the bathroom she peeled off her wet panty hose and pitched them into the sink before heading for the kitchen. "Come on, Sam, let's put some crunch in your bowl so I can go get warm in the shower."

She was letting the needles of hot water pummel her back when she heard him barking, reminding her that she had forgotten to let him out. She was drying herself when she heard the door chime, gave a quick swipe down each leg, slipped into her robe, and padded barefoot across the living room to the front door.

"Quiet, Sam," she whispered, and put her eye to the peephole viewer. It had stopped snowing, and a pristine white blanket covered everything in sight, except for the dark shadow in her driveway. A car with its parking lights on. A movement caught her eye and she saw a figure moving away from her front steps. In that instant she recognized the way he moved and started fumbling with the dead bolt, trying to get the door open before he reached the car.

"Max?" she called, stepping out onto the icy porch. Sam shot past her ankles, lost his footing at the bottom of the snow-covered steps, then scrambled to right himself.

The shadowy figure bent to catch the dog. "Sorry I got you all upset, boy." The voice was right, and Sam was wagging his tail off, sending snow flying in all directions, but when Max straightened and started toward her, she didn't recognize his face.

"Uh, listen, I didn't mean to interrupt anything. Thought I'd just swing by for a minute on the way to my hotel"—he kept glancing over her shoulder into the lighted house—"and let you know I was here."

Shivering, bare feet freezing, she wished he would hug her the way he had Sam. "I didn't recognize you without the beard."

"Oh! Yeah, I shaved it off." He hesitated, obviously at a loss for words. "I should've called before coming. It was a stupid idea."

"You caught me in the sh-shower"—her teeth started to chatter—"trying to get warm. I just walked a mile in the snow."

He nodded. "I noticed your shoes."

"They were brand-new." A rush of tears hit her at the thought that Max was standing on her front porch acting like a stranger. "If you don't turn off those lights and come inside right now, I'm going to catch pneumonia and die. *That* would be stupid."

"You're sure?" A familiar smile started in his eyes and Kate decided he looked younger. Not so sure of himself. She nodded and went back inside, leaving Sam with Max. A few minutes later man and dog burst through the door, grinning like a couple of kids.

Max dropped his briefcase on the floor, peeled off his all-weather coat, and tossed it over the back of the only chair in the room. As if that was a signal, Sam took off like the devil was after him, tearing across the living room to the kitchen, where they heard him crash into a chair. Then he was back, heading straight for Max, who opened his arms only to have Sam swerve aside at the last second and circle toward the kitchen again. Bemused, Kate watched Max play Sam's game a few more times, until he glanced over at her bare feet.

"Why don't you go put something on while Sam gets this out of his system?"

Kate was bursting with questions, so she made quick work of a pair of faded blue sweatpants and top to match, gave her hair a lick with the brush to tame the Shirley Temple look, and glanced in the mirror one more time. It was after ten, and she didn't want to give Max a bum steer about why she'd invited him in.

She found him in the kitchen talking to Sam. "Where do you suppose your Kate would keep the makings for hot chocolate, assuming she has any?"

"Right in front of you, on the shelf with the coffee," Kate supplied. "If you had let me know you were coming—" She stopped, shocked at hearing herself repeat her mother's favorite refrain.

"Need to get something hot into you." Max glanced down at Sam. "Wouldn't want her to get pneumonia and die, would we, boy?" He took a wooden spoon from the basket on the side of the cabinet and added cocoa mix to the milk he already had heating. "I was on call this weekend, but one of my partners needed to trade so it was a last-minute deal. How about getting us some cups?"

Kate took two stoneware mugs from the cabinet, opened a bag of marshmallows, dropped two into each one, and set them on the stove. After that she let Sam out the back door, stalling for time so she wouldn't sound too anxious.

"I haven't had hot chocolate with marshmallows since I was a kid," Max remarked as he handed her a steaming mug. "Anyway, we sat on the ground in Lubbock for a good three hours waiting for Denver to clear the runways. Didn't know if I was even going to get here." He took a careful sip, then drilled her with an accusatory look. "What the hell were you doing out walking in the dark alone?"

"I worked late." The picture in her head was doing battle with his naked face.

"Couldn't you have called Cleo or someone?"

"She's in Aspen. Phil's teaching her to ski."

He grinned. "I wonder why that doesn't surprise me."

"Did you finish the workup?"

"Yeah, it's in my briefcase. Still no cause of death, though." He paused. "How's it going with the head?"

"Good. The closer I get the harder it is *not* to work on it." She watched him slosh the marshmallows around in his mug, not looking at her, as if he felt ill at ease—and decided she didn't want to hear any excuses.

"Would you like to see some pictures?" she offered, starting for the sunporch.

As she passed him he caught hold of her arm. "In a minute. I need to say something first."

"That's okay, Max, we didn't expect—"

He gave her arm a little shake. "Just listen, will you? It's just, well, the last time I called I—you sounded sort of distant, remote, like you didn't much want to talk to me. I thought maybe I was pushing too hard, asking too many questions, or—" He paused. "D'you want the real reason I didn't let you know I was coming? So you couldn't say 'just put it in the mail.' "

"Dave was in the workroom when you called."

"I never even thought of that." He began shaking his head at how far off the mark he'd been. "But it doesn't change anything. What I'm trying to say is—I'd like to stay involved, Kate. Do whatever I can to help, but only if you want me to. You, not Dave."

"Why did you shave your beard?"

"You called me a barbarian."

"I was teasing, and you know it. And it's not going to help for you to retreat from the field of battle without ever engaging the enemy"— she waved in the direction of the front porch—"the way you did out there!"

Taken off guard, he couldn't help himself. He laughed. "I should've kept the beard. Those cat's eyes see too damn much." He lifted a hand as if to touch her, then let it drop. "Gimme a break, will you? I've never been around anyone like you."

"Then we're even." They just looked at each other, until Sam scratched on the back door.

When Kate went to let him in, Max followed her to the sunporch. "Where are those drawings you wanted to show me?"

"Not drawings. Photographs. Pinned up on the wall around my worktable."

He twisted the switch on the flex-arm lamp, stretched it almost straight, and directed the light at the giant mosaic covering the wall on either side of the table, blowups in full color of Tashat in all her forms. The cartonnage viewed from the top and underside, then the outside and inside of her wood coffin, including the lid and floor.

"Wow!" He stepped back. "This is what her coffin looks like?"

Kate nodded. It was the usual mummiform shape except where Tashat's face and wig were articulated in plaster, but the predominant color was light blue, the color of royalty. "On the left is the underside of the lid. The two figures on the right, Ptah and Khnum, are on the floor of the coffin."

He leaned forward to examine something she had tacked up over the table. "Don't tell me—" He held up a hand and glanced from the pink blossoms she'd cut from a seed catalog to the garden painted on the inside of the lid. "This is one of the plants in that garden, right?"

"Foxglove. Except they called it hyena's tongue."

"Must be those yellow-ringed brown spots spilling from the throat of the flowers. Not that I've seen a hyena's tongue. Are all the plants medicinal?" It was common knowledge that foxglove contained digitalis, a heart stimulant, so she wasn't surprised that he'd made the connection.

"You tell me." She pointed to a gray-green patch. "These are poppies."

"Opium. Morphine and codeine, to sedate or deaden pain."

She pointed to another spot. "These with the yellow flowers and forked root are mandrake."

"Hyoscyamine. Numbs the central nervous system." He sounded like he was really enjoying this.

"And the castor plant?"

"The oil is a purgative but the beans contain ricin, one of the deadliest poisons around."

"They burned the oil in their lamps, but they must've known about the beans," Kate agreed, before moving her finger again. "Garlic."

"Heart problems again?" Max guessed.

Kate shook her head. "Insect bites and tapeworms. And this one, with the lacy leaves and clusters of tiny white flowers, is an acacia tree."

"Contraceptive."

"Uh-uh, intestinal worms."

"If you say so. But the spikes contain gum arabic. And fermented gum arabic gives you lactic acid, which immobilizes sperm. Acetic or tannic acids are more effective, but—"

"Where in the name of Thoth did you learn that?"

He shrugged. "Read it in some journal I suppose. Are there any more?"

"Onions for dysentery, but most workers were paid in bread, beer, and onions." She pointed to a dark green area. "Parsley for urinary incontinence. Leeks to stop the bleeding after miscarriage or childbirth. Sage to treat a sore throat. Saffron and ginger for stomach disorders. Cabbage to prevent a hangover, and lettuce to stimulate the sexual appetite. I know," she added before he could, "it's not like any lettuce we know. Too tall."

"Stranger still if it affected the libido." He swung around to face her. "It's not just your ordinary ancient Egyptian garden?"

"Hardly. Sage and saffron came from Crete, ginger from beyond the Red Sea."

"Interesting, but where does it get us? Unless we can find some way to tie that coffin to Tashat—" He let the words trail off when he caught her grinning. "Show me."

Kate adjusted the lamp downward, to where the flower-bordered road began. "This path symbolizes the road to eternity, and this is the beginning, where the road emerges from a pond of blue lotus blossoms—the symbol of rebirth. See where the little girl is drawing in the sand with a reed or stick? She's using her left hand." Next Kate pointed to the man and woman farther along the road, seated side by side with a scroll unrolled across their laps. "Their legs are crossed, the traditional way of depicting a scribe, and she's using her left hand again. It has to be the same person."

"Unless it's her mother and father," Max pointed out.

Kate drew in a quick breath. "I forgot handedness can be familial."

"More often than not it's the result of a stressed birth."

"It's a stretch, but I think the lotus blossom in her hair signifies a new beginning for her, a kind of rebirth as an adult. From here on they're always shown side by side and the same size. Yet artistic convention demanded that a wife, even a queen, be shown behind her husband and smaller, with their children behind and smaller than her. The only exception is a relief where Nefertiti is standing beside Akhenaten with her arm around his shoulder."

"You don't think Tashat might be Nefertiti, do you?"

Kate shook her head. "Cleo says they're probably Isis and Osiris. The stair-stepped throne in the woman's headdress is the hieroglyph for Isis, who the Egyptians called Aset. But there's nothing to identify him as Osiris—no green face, no tightly wrapped body or sheaf-of-wheat headdress."

She pointed to the cartouches and told him about her conversation with Dave. "But *sunu* is a title, not a name. Pharaohs had two names, the one given to them at birth and another when they took the throne. That's the reason for the double cartouches. But why the same word over and over, even if it takes two different forms?"

"Maybe the words aren't really identical. What about two physicians but with different specialties?" With Max, trying to solve a puzzle was like a game of leapfrog, each player able to jump ahead because of the other.

"To differentiate status, maybe," Kate agreed, "but they didn't have specialties in the Eighteenth Dynasty like they did earlier, in the Old Kingdom, when they had titles like Shepherd of the Anus." She ducked her head to hide a smile. "I guess that makes proctology the second oldest profession."

"Okay, suppose she *was* left-handed. So what?"

"I don't want to sound like some New Age nut, but I think we could be looking at a kind of puzzle, where each piece contributes to the meaning of the whole—and we should be looking for how she might have used that hand." She searched through the mess on her worktable for a piece of paper, and scribbled *swnw* on it.

"That's the word for physician." Next she wrote *swnw.t.* "T is the feminine particle, so now it's a female physician. For a long time Egyptologists insisted there weren't any, that the extra character was just scribal error, until a French doctor in Cairo connected it to a physician he knew was female from other evidence." She paused. "What if the arrow is masculine and the bread is feminine?"

"Two physicians, a him and a her?"

"Whoever painted that mask had to be someone close enough to Tashat to know that her idea of heaven was a garden filled with medicinal plants. The coffin inscription says she was a well-educated woman, or words to that effect. Why couldn't she have been a physician, a healer? It's a place to begin, isn't it? A working hypothesis?"

"Why not? I say run with it, see where it takes you."

Kate let out her breath and gave a little laugh. "Oh, Max, I'm so glad you came. Otherwise, I might never have—" She almost threw caution to the winds and hugged him, but Sam started barking and jumping up, wanting in on the fun, so she grabbed his front paws and danced him around on his hind legs. "Cookie time for you, Samson, while Max and I celebrate with a glass of wine."

She stopped suddenly and dropped Sam's paws, leaving him watching her with a puzzled tilt of his head. "If Tashat is the cartouche with the loaf of bread, then the cartouche with the arrow is the head between her legs. They're traveling the road to eternity together. But surely no one would dare put an adulterous lover on her coffin."

"Who else could he be? Her father? I know they had priest-physicians back then, but why the hell would anyone put *his* head between her legs?" He started shaking his head again. "Jesus, and I thought I was hooked before."

Kate realized he meant it—that Maxwell Cavanaugh couldn't walk away from Tashat any easier than she could, not without examining every possibility, including some that sounded pretty far out, not to say unlikely. More than that, questioning the conventional wisdom, no matter how sacrosanct, was as much a way of life to him as it was for her. The only way.

"Join the crowd," she murmured, covering her eagerness to

accept his offer with a cliché. She might be overjoyed at the prospect of having Max as a cohort, but that didn't mean she trusted him completely. Not yet.

"Enough for now," he decided. "Let's go have that wine." Crooking a comradely arm around Kate's neck, he guided her toward the kitchen.

Sam tagged along, not ready to let either of them out of his sight.

EIGHT

"Aside from the evisceration, her body struck me as relatively undis-turbed," Max told Dave, who had agreed to meet them at the museum even though he didn't usually come in on Saturdays. "We can see soft-tissue collections in the orbits, extending posteriorly. Probably the remains of the globes and optic nerves. In the end we had thirty-four measurements to plug into the formula to establish age, so we're confident that she was somewhere between twenty-two and twenty-five. With only the teeth and cranial sutures to go by on him, we have to stay with a wider range—forty and forty-eight."

"What about that canopic bundle in his mouth?" Dave asked. "Did you find out what that is?"

Max shuffled the stack of plastic sleeves that held the X-ray film—color transparencies presented twenty to a sheet, four across and five down—searching for the axial images he wanted. When he found it he slid the sheet onto the lighted viewbox, the reason they had moved from Dave's office to Kate's workroom.

"I passed these around to my partners in Houston, but we all came up empty-handed. Maybe you'll recognize something. This is the base of the maxilla, and here's the missing molar I mentioned. And here, dead center of the arch, is some rectangular object—see how the shape stays the same from one image to another? The wrapping conforms to the contours of the mouth, but the rectangle inside it has the radiodensity of bone. There's also a hollow, tube-like object inside it." He traced the gray circle inside the white rectangle. "Only thing I can think of is a box of some kind."

Kate had an idea what both objects might be, if the diameter of the tube stayed constant along its entire length, but she didn't want to interrupt Max's presentation.

"Could it be a penis?" Dave asked. "Yes or no."

"I doubt it."

"Thought so, or Cleo would have been here strutting like a peacock."

"Do you attach any significance to the fact that Tashat's child wasn't mentioned in that coffin inscription?" Max inquired.

"Because it was fathered by her lover? Hardly. The child probably died in infancy, or was a girl. In case you didn't notice, there's no mention of her mother, either. Females were of little importance unless they were royal."

Max flipped the switch on the viewbox. "Well, that's about it, then. We estimate she stood four feet, ten inches tall, with no obvious skeletal abnormalities . . . unless you consider being left-handed abnormal. The ulna and radius generally are a little longer in the dominant arm, in this case the left one. Same with the humerus."

The significance of what he was saying hit Kate like a clap of thunder, leaving behind a profound silence. Why, if the skeletal evidence showed Tashat was left-handed, had he let her go on about it last night, building a case on those painted figures alone?

"Also the humeral head tends to be a little more rounded," Max continued for Dave's benefit, before he finally looked at Kate—and couldn't keep a straight face any longer. It dawned on her suddenly that he was paying her back for Sam!

"What's the joke?" Dave groused.

"Kate got there a different way, that's all," Max replied, "a way that ties up another loose end. The coffin wasn't intended for someone else, then for some reason got switched and ended up with Tashat."

"How so?" Dave inquired.

"The girl, then woman, on the inside of the coffin lid—they're both left-handed."

Dave stalked over to where the lid leaned against the wall and squatted down to see for himself. When he stood up his face was an unhealthy pink except for the ring of white around his lips. "Have to give you credit, McKinnon. That's pretty good detective work for an amateur. But you're still just a hired hand, so don't go expecting to get your name on any publications coming out of this project."

"Oh, by the way," Max put in, saving her from saying something she might regret later, "I found those articles you gave me pretty fascinating reading."

"Well, that's nice to know," Dave replied, losing interest in Kate.

"Was Akhenaten stark raving mad or what? Have to be, wouldn't he, to go for another man when he had a looker like Nefertiti for a wife?"

Kate froze, not daring to look anywhere but out the window. Max was engaging the enemy on his own territory!

Dave shrugged. "Maybe there's something to the genetic thing, after all."

"Intrigued me how you fit all the pieces of the puzzle together—" Max went on, disarming Dave with an admiring smile. "Nefertiti's disappearance, making Smenkhkare his coregent, that relief showing two pharaohs fondling each other, giving him her throne name. After what you said about names being so important, that must've been the ultimate dirty trick." Like a warning shot across the bow, something in Max's voice sent a shiver down Kate's spine. "I was just wondering what she did to provoke that kind of retribution?"

Dave exhaled a nervous chuckle. "One thing you have to live with in my field, Dr. Cavanaugh, is rarely having all the evidence you'd like. Don't you ever have to deduce something from whatever you've got, incomplete as it may be?"

"Sure, I guess we all do. But it makes even more sense for two pharaohs to be shown in an embrace if they were husband and wife, and for her to keep the name he gave her when she became queen, along with the name he gave his coregent."

Rendered momentarily speechless, Dave sputtered like a dying sparkler. In the end he sought refuge in maligning the messenger. "That theory is not the first absurd notion to come from one of the Egyptologists who put it forward in the first place."

"But doesn't it make more sense to send a royal heiress to Thebes rather than a homosexual lover, to pacify the Amen priests who are stirring things up?"

"Queen Tiye was on occasion referred to as an heiress, too, and she was a commoner. So a little knowledge sometimes can lead you astray." Dave glanced at his watch, then rose and extended his hand to Max, bringing their encounter to a close. Still, he couldn't resist a parting shot. "I'm afraid I don't have time for any more history lessons today, Dr. Cavanaugh, but we do appreciate all you've done."

Once outside Max took off so fast Kate was hard-pressed to keep up with him. He also kept muttering under his breath, but the only thing she heard clearly was, "Blood grouping my ass, with pharaohs sleeping with their sisters, even their own daughters!"

"I wonder if that's really true," Kate volunteered, just to distract him. She was seeing a side of Maxwell Cavanaugh that surprised her, a man who let it all hang out. "They're supposed to have used the same word for sister and wife, but I think it's more likely that our ability to translate their language is flawed. Academics argue over how to interpret some minor variation in a symbol—is it just a mistake, something unintended, or does it have a different meaning?"

He jammed the key in the car door, then pulled it open for her. "Do you have to put up with that kind of crap all the time or does something about me bring out the worst in that bastard?" He went around to the driver's side, started the motor, and drove out of the parking lot as if the hounds of hell were on his trail. A man with a temper.

"I think he suspects something—you know, with Cleo. He's been coming by the workroom every day, watches what I'm doing for a few minutes, then leaves without a word. I'm worried that he might get riled up about something I do or say and use it as an excuse to send Cleo packing. Museum jobs are scarce as hen's teeth these days, even with a Ph.D., which she doesn't have."

He took his foot off the accelerator so fast it felt like he'd hit the brake. "I'm sorry, Kate. I didn't much cotton to the way he treated you the last time, but I figured he was busy, had other things on his mind. When he called you a hired hand I just saw red, wanted to hit him where it would hurt most."

"It's Tashat I care about. I can live without Dave's good opinion."

"Is that why you were quiet in there?"

She shook her head. "Mostly I was afraid I might put my foot in my mouth. Didn't sleep too well last night."

"Too much medicinal garden?"

She shook her head. "Crazy dreams. Part sleeping-dream, part waking-dream, if you know what I mean. You're the doctor. You tell me what's going on when that happens."

"Mostly too much." He didn't say anything for a block or two, then, "Are you spending the holidays with your family?"

"Maybe. I haven't decided yet. I know Christmas is less than a week away, but I've been too busy to make any plans. Cleo and Phil are cooking a turkey and want me to have dinner with them."

"Where do your folks live?" he persisted, fishing.

"They're divorced, so I don't see either one very often. Mom moved to California and my father lives in Ohio. He has two boys from his second marriage." She had intended to give ancient Egypt a rest, but any port in a storm. "I wonder what it was like to be left-handed back when everyone believed in magic spells and evil spirits. Could that be why it was damaged?"

"Like driving a stake through the heart of a vampire or burning a witch at the stake?" Max shrugged. "Possible, I suppose. A lot of lefties are marked in ways that don't appear to be related to handedness. One syndrome includes alcoholism, epilepsy, and autoimmune disorders, for instance, probably the result of a stressed birth that affects the left hemisphere of the brain. Remember George Bush? A high incidence of dyslexia among lefties might explain his syntax problems. He also has Graves' disease, an autoimmune disorder. We know right-brain hemispheres in lefties don't perform exactly the way left hemispheres do for right-handers, but we're still trying to track all the ramifications of that."

"Track how?"

"Looking at the neurological activities of the brain under conditions where we control the stimuli and can map the response."

"You mean you're involved in research in addition to your practice?"

"Yeah, with a group at the UT Medical School." He barely paused. "So how much time do you have off?"

"Five days, but I'll probably stay here and work," she answered, wondering why he kept asking. "I'm really anxious, now that we're about to see what Tashat actually looked like."

That was true, but Christmas was for kids and families. Just not the kind she had. Now that she was twenty-eight her father treated her with studied politeness but with none of the warmth he exhibited toward her two half brothers. But then they hadn't failed him . . . yet. Worse was the guilt she felt, even now, about letting her mother down.

"How about coming to Houston for a couple of days? I could show you some stuff you won't see outside a big teaching hospital. A colleague of mine uses a computer to plan how he's going to rebuild the skulls of patients with malformed faces. All we'd have to do is plug our measurements into his software and you could play with the tolerances on tissue depths, try out different lashes and brows, hairlines, lip shapes—on both heads, if you want."

It was a reminder that she was fast becoming obsolete, that technology soon would supersede everything she could do. When that happened she'd be lucky to get a job at McDonald's, given her Achilles' heel—her inability to deal with noise. Not that anything was wrong with her ears, as her father liked to remind her every chance he got. Max's voice brought her back from a place she didn't want to be.

"You don't need to decide right now, but think about it, okay?"

She nodded, relieved that he wasn't going to push. Relieved, too, that the session with Dave was over. She needed a breather from Egypt and Tashat, though nothing she had tried so far was working. Last week she'd been driving the back road to Boulder— the open fields on either side covered by a thin blanket of snow, Flatirons looming straight ahead, sharp as a scissors-cut silhouette against the Milky Way—when a hushed stillness came over the car. Suddenly, everywhere she looked, the snow had turned to sand. The broad valley became a vast, lifeless desert, except dead ahead, where the massive red cliffs stood guard over the Place of Truth.

Now, as if triggered by that memory, the same stillness muted the noise around her. She waited, but nothing came, neither familiar nor imagined images, only a vague sense of something about to happen. That's when she decided she was going to Houston.

"Kate? What do you think?" Max asked.

"Sorry. I was somewhere else."

"How about swinging by to get Sam, then drive up into the mountains a little way, clear Dave out of our heads."

"Two of Sam's all-time favorite things are riding in the car and getting to sniff out all the prairie-dog holes in some high meadow." She smiled, pleased that he would think to include her dog. Sam was going to be more than a little unhappy when Max left. Truth to tell she was going to feel a little let down herself, back to going it alone.

Three godlike sparrows swoop and spin above the banks. Even the frogs are dancing.

Normandi Ellis, *Awakening Osiris*

NINE

Year Nine in the Reign of Tutankhamen

(1352 B.C.)

DAY 16, SECOND MONTH OF INUNDATION

The face of Re-Horakhte burst above the horizon with an exuberance that matched my own, as if he, too, felt the excitement that caused my heart to thump against my ribs. Today marks the second month of life for Pharaoh's son, when he honors those who have served him above all others. And the name at the top of his list is a certain Senakhtenre, physician of Waset.

Mena served as my escort, on Pharaoh's orders, he claimed, and as we neared the royal precinct he tried to put me at ease. "The honor does you no harm with Ramose, since any glory that falls on his physician shines on Ramose as well. But you could not have dissuaded Pharaoh even had you tried. Aside from showing off his son, he signals that he is taking the reins of power into his own hands, simply by flaunting the skills of an ordinary *sunu*. It is his way of letting everyone know that he no longer depends on the old men around him to direct his every move."

More important to me at the moment was how to behave when Pharaoh called me before him. "Are you certain my appearance will not embarrass him, or the Queen?" I asked, though I wore a tunic of fine linen over a short pleated kilt and painted leather sandals. They were the best I owned, yet I worried they were not good enough.

"You will not shame either your King or your employer, if that is what you ask," Mena assured me, "though I suspect you are more concerned with two small girls. If left to them, you could cover yourself in rags and it would be the rest of us who are out of fashion." He paused. "I am not inclined to jealousy where my daughter is concerned, Tenre, but can you say the same for the priest?"

If he meant to give me more to worry about, he succeeded, but we were entering the palace grounds and my thoughts flew ahead of us, beyond the fragrant shrubs and brilliant flowers. I could not imagine that Pharaoh's house could be grander than the Queen's apartments, where marble steps sparkled with streaks of pink and black, and the walls portrayed the movement of life rather than the stillness of eternity—tiny birds darting among fruit-bearing trees, a herd of galloping gazelle—yet an awesome majesty pervaded my senses as we came into the huge throne room.

At the far end were only columns, making the vast hall one with the courtyard outside, where a light breeze ruffled the leaves of sycamores and acacia trees. A milling throng already had gathered, but ornately inlaid chairs lined the edges of the room, exposing rich carpets that hushed our footsteps and voices, while on the walls hunters stalked their prey in the desert or poled skiffs through the marshes, their throwing sticks at the ready.

At that moment the assembled guests bent like a field of wheat in the wind, so we did likewise as Nefertiti and Mutnodjme moved toward the dais and took their places, followed by the women of Pharaoh's harem. "Pharaoh's sisters are much together since the General sailed down the river," Mena observed from behind his hand.

Next came the Royal Ornaments and favorites wearing crowns of blue lotus blossoms. All but Aset and Nebet, who had draped themselves with garlands of blue cornflowers and white daisies. At seven Aset remains small for her age, so the two girls stood shoulder to shoulder and looked almost like twins in identical white gowns.

Both wore the palm-frond sandals Ipwet had fashioned to Aset's liking, as well, which turned out to be exactly what Nebet needs since, with her uneven gait, the built-up edge around the sole keeps her foot from sliding off to the side. They searched the crowd for us and were about to wave when Tetisheri laid a restraining hand on each shoulder and then smiled at Mena, sharing her delight in their daughter.

"See how well she goes with the new brace?" he whispered, fighting to keep his head bowed when his eyes hungered for his wife and daughter. "Even better when she walks beside her friend. Together they make more than two, as if each adds something to the other. Whatever magic lies behind those blue eyes, I begin to understand why she fills your heart—though she is the child of another man." He leaned closer. "Not only that, but from the night you brought Aset to our house, Sheri comes to me with eagerness again. For that alone I will thank you to the end of my days."

A parade of youths threaded their way through the crowd to take their places before the dais. "Children of the *Kap*," Mena explained, "led by Hiknefer, Crown Prince of Aniba and friend of Tutankhamen since they were boys." I knew of the custom of having the sons of Kemet's vassals attend the palace school with Pharaoh's own children and those of favored nobles. But what interested me most was that Senmut's brother wore wild cattails on each arm, ostrich feathers in his white headband, and gold tassels hanging from his ears. He also kept his frizzy hair trimmed above his ears.

"That one is cut from a different piece of cloth than his brother," I remarked.

"Same father, different mothers," Mena replied as the heralds raised their horns to announce Pharaoh's coming.

"Neb-khepru-re, Living Son of Amen-Re," the Herald called out, "Tutankhamen, Son of Horus on Earth, Beloved of Maat, Lord of Upper and Lower Kemet, Lord of Ipet-isut and Ruler of Waset." We dropped to our knees and touched our heads to the floor as Pharaoh and his Queen moved toward the dais. Tutankhamen held himself erect, arms crossed over his chest, the crook of the South in one hand and flail of the North in the other. He wore the blue leather crown bearing the serpent goddess of Upper Kemet and a

Nekhbet pectoral on his chest, its feathers inlaid with lapis lazuli, and gold lotus buds weighted the belt of his hip wrap. But it was the magnificent bracelet circling his left wrist that caught and held my eyes—a great green stone surrounded by tiny granules of silver that flickered like fireflies in the night.

Then the Chief Herald started his litany of titles for the Queen—Great Royal Wife, Beloved of Neb-khepru-re Tutankh-amen, Lady of the Two Lands, and so on. The Queen cradled her son in her arms, but I hardly recognized her delicate features beneath the elaborate wig with its hundreds of narrow plaits ending in tubes of gold that tinkled like bells.

"Until now the Queen rarely appeared at official ceremonies," Mena informed me, "to show that Pharaoh returned to the old ways. So he sends another message simply by having her present."

My eyes wandered from Tutankhamen to Mutnodjme and Nefertiti, then back to the young king, noting the similar shape of their eyes, for other than that there is little to show that they issue from the same mother and father. When I looked at him again the King was beckoning for me to come forward. "He does not wait for his steward to announce the order of presentations," Mena mut-tered. "Your time is at hand."

"You would throw me to the wolves alone?" I tossed back as I started toward the throne, leaving him to catch up. When I dropped to my knees before Pharaoh I saw Mena doing the same just behind me.

"I give you leave to stand in my presence, Senakhtenre, as a sign of the high esteem in which we hold you." I hurried to comply though I felt like a pair of leather sandals stiffened by too much paint. Tutankhamen handed his crook and flail to Ay, onetime Master of the Horse to the Magnificent Amenhotep who now serves his son, and exchanged them for a carved wooden staff. After that he looked out over the crowd and raised his voice. "As the fellahin sow their seeds in the black soil of the Two Lands, so Pharaoh planted his seed in his Great Royal Wife, who in her time brought forth a bountiful harvest, a son she has named Thutmose—may he be wise as Thoth and bring honor to his namesake, the builder of a great empire. Now I honor the physician who accompanied my son on his hazardous voyage through the dark waters of chaos and brought him safely into the light of Amen-Re, king of the gods from whom all life flows."

Contrary to what the young king said, I believe there is an ebb and flow in the organ of life as regular and predictable as the rising and waning of the moon, but it was not my place to correct a god, even a mortal one. Surely the man before me in no way resembled the youth I had encountered outside his wife's door, trembling under the weight of his decision. For to deny me admittance could mean the death of another child of his body, yet to allow me to enter alone went against the ways of his father and his father before him, which demanded the presence of a priest and priestess in addition to the one named Physician to the Queen.

Ay stepped to Pharaoh's side bearing a small bronze tray on which lay a necklace of gold and blue beads. "From this day forward," Pharaoh intoned as he placed the collar around my throat, "let it be known to all the People of the Sun that Senakhtenre, physician of Waset, is named Special Companion Who Goes In and Out of the Palace." The title conveyed on me the privilege of entering the palace at will, whether called there by the babe's nurse-mother or anyone else. In this way Pharaoh declared that I am to oversee the welfare of his son though I continue as physician to Ramose's household, an arrangement that suits us both without raising the enmity of the palace physicians.

I bowed and mumbled every word of gratitude I knew, but instead of dismissing me Tutankhamen withdrew the dagger he wore under the belt of his kilt. "The Goddess Maat also commands me to give him this mighty blade, for no other is a fitting match for the wisdom of his heart and gentleness of his hands." He pulled the blade halfway out of its sheath and laid it across my open palms. The ivory hilt was topped by a crystal pommel, while the gold sheath bore an embossed scene of hounds and lions attacking an ibex. But it was the blade itself that made it a priceless treasure, for iron holds a sharp edge, while bronze must constantly be honed.

Stunned by the magnitude of such a gift, my thoughts scattered like overripe lotus petals before the wind. Then Aset was standing before me with laughter dancing in her eyes, a perfect match for the cornflowers around her neck. "The Queen wishes to acknowledge her debt to you as well," Tutankhamen announced, "with a gift selected by her little sister."

Aset pushed the gold casket into my hands. "Open it." I lifted the lid and thought I looked at a puff of smoke held captive in a box, until I recognized the dried blossom of a plant I have only read about.

"Our little sister informs us that in the land beyond the Red Sea," Pharaoh explained, "the plant called *Khatun* is believed to contain much magic."

"I am humbled by Your Majesty's generosity," I murmured, struggling to conceal my ignorance of court protocol so as not to embarrass myself in front of Aset, who watched me with that glorious smile lighting her eyes. I could only guess at where she had learned about the plant, probably in one of her father's scrolls, but what truly warmed my heart was knowing that she understood why I prize such things more than any riches or titles Pharaoh could bestow upon me. I tried to tell her that with my own smile.

When I looked back at Tutankhamen he had turned to Mena. "I look forward to besting the both of you, then, in three days' time," he murmured, lowering his voice, "when Hiknefer and I fly our falcons against yours." He stepped back, signaling Aset to return to her place. Mena and I bowed, then backed away from the dais until we were swallowed up by those surging forward to see who would be next.

"Who shall I return this blade to?" I asked when we got clear.

"Re-return it?" Mena stammered.

"Surely Pharaoh meant that part only for show. What would someone like me do with such a precious thing?"

"Obtain enough credit to add to your house and find yourself a wife. With the title Pharaoh just handed you, many a father will jump at the chance to sign a contract for his daughter if you but sail while the breeze is fresh."

"You believe it was a mistake, then, to marry out of love for the woman you took for your wife?" I asked, hoping to trap him in his own net.

He ignored my question. "By the way you clasp that casket I doubt you have any intention of giving *that* back. Knowing what Aset had to choose from, that puff of nothing speaks louder than any words. Your little goddess knows you very well, indeed." He gave me an appraising look. "Is it enough, then, to be father to another man's child?"

"If not me, who will guide her through the cataracts that could dim the light that shines from her eyes? If in return I warm myself by her fire—" I shrugged. "As it is with Aset and Nebet, we each supply something the other lacks and needs."

He nodded, but he was not finished with me. "Now that you are rich you at least can afford some new garments, something a bit more adventuresome, perhaps. A red belt for your kilt, or a fringed cloak to enhance your girth and thereby your importance?"

That he still jested at my expense despite my new status made me want to laugh with joy. That I had doubted him made me feel ashamed. "The day you see me in such a cloak," I replied through clenched teeth, "you will know that evil spirits have invaded my body and taken control of my wits."

DAY 19, SECOND MONTH OF INUNDATION

Pharaoh led the way south from the palace barracks, along the line of palm trees marking the boundary between the open pasture where his cattle grazed on what little grass remained and the barren desert beyond. Hiknefer stayed almost axle to axle by him, while Mena and I rode some distance to the left to escape the cloud of dust raised by their clattering wheels. Behind us came Ay and a half dozen other officials, followed by several palace guards, and the handlers with our birds.

The Festival of Opet was but a week away, yet already the fertile water started to recede, leaving the backbones of old mud dikes sticking out like the ribs of a starving dog. As we passed the great stone lion guarding the western horizon of the city, the clang of hammers echoed across the valley from where the necropolis workers were cutting Pharaoh's tomb from the rock. Despite this reminder of his own mortality, he seemed in rare high spirits, and when the straight sweep of sand opened before us he gave his horses their heads. A moment later Hiknefer touched his whip to his blacks and took out after him, both yelling like boys as they raced across the sand.

Mena shouted, "Grab hold," and touched his whip to his team's backs, with me cheering him on. Like the others, his pair are palace-bred, for both strength and speed, so we had no trouble catching up. Pharaoh turned to see us gaining on them and motioned his boyhood friend to spread out, a ploy to force us into a wider path should we attempt to pass them, at a cost of both distance and time. Instead, Mena looped the reins tighter around his fists and waited his chance, then charged straight through the narrow space between the two royal chariots. By the time they realized what was happening, we had pulled ahead, giving them a taste of *our* dust. But almost at once Mena slowed his team to let Tutankhamen regain the lead, making it appear that his animals were blown.

Later, when we slowed to a walk to pass through a narrow defile between some sandy hills, Ay raised a fist to salute Mena's skill. We could hear each other then without yelling, and I remarked on the two Nubians—Senmut and Pharaoh's boyhood friend. "Hiknefer plays the palace pet while his brother stands outside, an observer with a passion for healing. So they differ in more than their mothers."

"Tutankhamen's friend came to manhood in the palace, hostage to his father's allegiance to the old Pharaoh," Mena reminded me, "while Senmut was a youth of some fifteen years when he arrived in Waset. And he came for one purpose only."

"The House of Life?" I guessed.

He nodded. "It is the custom among his mother's people to cut the clitoris and inner labia of their girls. Afterward they rub the outer lips raw with a stone and skewer them with thorns until they grow together. It not only makes a woman difficult to penetrate, but causes many of their babes to lose their breath before they can come forth, oftentimes taking their mothers as well."

"His mother died in childbirth?"

"No, his little sister, after they cut her. The one he loved above all others. He could do nothing to stop it. Or the bleeding."

"No wonder." I sighed, recalling his bitter words about Bekenkhons.

Our destination lay at the edge of the vast open expanse of bleached sand, where migrating birds come in low to seek respite in the trees and gardens just beyond. Small rodents and snakes also hide from the sun among the hillocks of rock and clumps of brush. And while falcons prefer ducks and ptarmigan—and to catch their prey in flight—they will go after small animals on the ground in order to feed on their hearts, which they tear into while still pulsing. Endowed with sharp hearing and eyes that see better and farther than any other living thing, the falcon is capable of stunning an animal as big as a jackal. Especially the female, who is half again larger than the male and the stronger of the pair.

Tutankhamen pulled his team to a stop, jumped from his chariot, and stood tapping the handle of his whip against his thigh, impatient for the rest of us to arrive. He wore a short kilt and striped nemset bearing a hawk fashioned of thin gold leaf across the top, its beak pointing toward his face and wings spread from ear to ear. Otherwise, Pharaoh bore no ceremonial trappings except a bracelet with the iron eye of Horus and a sheathed dagger strapped around his hips. He handed the reins to a guard and strode to where the birds and trainers were just coming to a stop.

Mena's horses are trained to stand when he ties their reins to the rail of his chariot, so we left them and went to uncage our own hawks. Mine was bred in captivity and taken from the nest as a fledgling, but the best hunters are captured in the wild after they have learned to fly and hunt—betrayed into captivity by a pigeon worth no more than a pair of papyrus-reed sandals. As a result they display more spirit, even though it takes longer to overcome the birds' natural fear of man. In the end, though, the falcon learns to trust the man who trains her, so it is rare for one to return to the wild. Mena slipped his hand into the thick horsehide sleeve and took the hooded bird from his falconer and calmed her with the sound of his voice.

"See how she ripples her feathers in anticipation of the kill? She smells it coming—that one exhilarating moment when she flies in search of prey. It is what she lives for, even if she must spend the rest of her life in the darkness of the hood, waiting, kept hungry and fed only when she returns to me with the weighted lure."

"It is true, then," I asked, since he gave me the opportunity, "that men take pleasure in subjugating the female falcon to their will because they see in her a wild, abandoned woman?"

"Perhaps," he agreed, as we carried our birds to where the others gathered, "but the most fascinating woman of all is both wild and shy. And the truth, my abstinent friend, is that your balls will shrivel from disuse unless you start discovering such things for yourself."

By then we were too close to the others to chance a response in kind, so I held my tongue for the time when I could return the jibe. Merankh, the king's big hunting hound, stood at his side, his long tail moving in a lazy swing whenever Tutankhamen fondled his drooping ears. He wore no leash, having been trained to his master's voice. "I like to come here," Pharaoh said to a man I did not recognize, "because to hunt where the game is neither plentiful nor what she prizes most is a challenge for my Horus of the Sky. At this time of year, of course, the migrating birds descend on our fields." He glanced at me with a quickening smile, reminding me that Aset was of his blood. "Even so, I will give you both a count of ten before I release my Horus of the Sky."

"As will I," Hiknefer agreed.

Mena started to protest, but Tutankhamen raised his hand. "No, it is only *maat*. Our birds know the terrain while yours do not." With his free hand he fingered the leather thongs attached to his bird's legs, causing the golden hawk to dance in anticipation. "Shall we wager that the one whose bird captures live prey first forfeits a jar of the finest wine to the others?"

So did he mask his acquired arrogance with innate generosity, and for the first time I saw the god in the man. I smiled, daring to believe that I could give him something as rare to him as his gifts were to me—the camaraderie of friendship.

"And the first to return her prey to her handler?" I inquired, suggesting a possible imperfection in his hawk's performance. "Shall he forfeit the same?"

He laughed. "Agreed." He waited for Mena and Hiknefer to do likewise, then Mena and I lined up to match the time of our release, while Tutankhamen and Hiknefer moved some distance off to do the same. The instant the hoods came off our birds, Tutankhamen started his count, to a chorus of ecstatic screeching and flapping wings.

A moment later he pulled the hood free and we all stood in awe, watching his hawk climb into the blue sky. For what appears to be reckless abandon to man is perfect control on the part of a hawk, who by nature is equipped to rise higher and higher on the eddying breezes and shifting winds.

It was almost eerily silent, except for the distant creaking of leather harness from our horses, as one by one our birds scribed loops in the air, turning upside down at the top of each one in a display of style and grace unmatched by any other beast. Or by man, with his feet bound to the earth even when he walks the path to eternity. Was that only because the priests lack the imagination to let him soar, I wondered, even in the company of Shu, god of the air, and Nut, goddess of the sky—and so made Amen a jealous God, resentful of his own brothers?

Mena's Beautiful Lady was first to swoop out of a wide loop, giving chase to a small heron, a bird that is lighter-boned and therefore capable of rising in smaller rings. A worthy opponent because the falcon has to climb in wider circles and at a higher speed, to get above the other bird in order to strike her target.

Pharaoh stood separate from the rest of us, an anxious look on his face, nor did he breathe easy until Mena's Lady overflew her quarry and circled up with her talons empty. By then Tutankhamen's Horus of the Sky had soared so high she was only a dark spot against the brilliant sky. For a time she glided, changing direction as she caught one air current and then another. Then, suddenly, she folded her wings and stooped, as if bowing to the Lord of the Two Lands, and came plummeting toward earth in a spectacular show of speed and power.

I could hear the wind ruffle her feathers, until she changed the angle of her dive and appeared to be heading straight toward us, gaining momentum as she came. When I saw her prepare to strike her quarry, I thought it a trick of the sun on her golden feathers. But in the next instant I heard a loud crack, from somewhere close by, and spun around to see the young Pharaoh stagger where he stood. His eyelids fluttered, then his eyes turned up into his head and he crumpled like a rag doll.

Mena and I started for him at the same time, leaving the others paralyzed with shock. Or disbelief. Except Hiknefer, who let out a howl of anguish and dropped to his knees beside his friend.

"Do not touch him!" Mena yelled. I ripped off my kilt and wadded it into a ball, then dropped to my knees and pressed the cloth to Pharaoh's bleeding cheek while Mena put his fingers to the hollow at the base of his throat.

"Shallow. And too fast." He looked around, searching for Ay, who stood rooted to the spot where we left him. "Bring his chariot," Mena yelled. "We must get him back to the palace." The old man turned and ran across the sand while Merankh licked his master's face in an attempt to wake him. Mena had to push him aside in order to remove the cloth headdress, revealing a swelling the size of a goose egg.

"Perhaps the blow only knocked him unconscious for a few minutes," he mumbled. But neither of us could forget the sound of the falcon's hind talon—like a rock flung at a hollow gourd—as it struck the young king's skull. "Lift his shoulders while I support his head. Hiknefer can take his legs." With tears running down his brown cheeks, the Nubian prince could only nod. "Under the knees and thighs," Mena added, "to support the lower part of his body."

Ay pulled up in a cloud of dust, turned Tutankhamen's team, then backed them toward us. "One of us must hold him," I told Mena. "Thank the gods his chariot is larger than most or it would not hold two men standing, let alone a third on his back. Someone must hold him, and no one at the palace will take orders from me. You go ahead of us, to have a litter ready."

I squeezed past him, braced one foot against the side of the chariot, and took Tutankhamen's head and shoulders against my chest. Merankh tried to climb in as well, but Mena pushed him away, then looped a piece of rope across the open bed, rail to rail, for me to hold to.

"Take the racecourse back. It will not jostle him so much," he told Ay. "And don't waste any time." Then he was gone, running toward his horses.

To me it seemed a journey without end. I tried to keep Pharaoh still by taking the bumps and jolts with my own body. And all the while I looked for any movement he might make himself, whether an arm or leg or even the flutter of an eyelid. But my thoughts returned to the place where Tutankhamen loosed the hood of his golden Horus of the Sky. My eyes followed her again as she rose higher and higher, then came plummeting toward earth. I knew then that the truth lay in the instant I looked away. I tried closing my eyes, to see if my ears remembered what my eyes could not—and heard the silence of the desert broken by the creak of harness, the whisper of feathers ruffled by the wind, and a soft, barely audible whistle. Not high and sharp but low, like the purr of a cat. The sort of signal a falconer might use so as not to startle his bird while in the act of swallowing, yet sufficient to train her to associate it with feeding. Or was it only a trick of the wind, blowing through the crevasse of an outcropping of rock?

When I looked at the young king's face again I found his eyes wide-open. "Stay as you are," I warned, putting my lips to his ear to make sure he heard me. "You were knocked from your moorings for a few minutes is all. We take you back to the palace."

"In . . . good hands. Gift from . . . gods." The words came one or two at a time, then his lips went slack, and his eyelids fell. His face took on a serenity I had not seen before, and for the first time in my twenty-nine years I found a man beautiful. A few minutes later he spoke again, without opening his eyes. "Legs . . . cold."

A shiver ran down my spine though the sun burned hot on my back. "Do not try to move," I warned. "Mena waits at the palace, and he knows more about the injuries men suffer in battle than any other physician in the Two Lands."

"I . . . battle? Anubis?"

"With your Horus of the Sky," I replied, though his eyes had closed again.

At the barracks Mena waited with six palace guards and an oxhide litter. Ay tossed the reins to one of the guards and hurried off, probably to summon the palace physicians. When the guards started away with him, Mena followed, with me close behind.

"He wakes from time to time," I told him, keeping my voice low, "but moves only his eyes and mouth, and can say only a word or two at a time—to complain of cold in his legs." Mena gave me a sharp look, then started into the antechamber of the royal apartment. "I will wait out here, in case you need me."

"No, I need you now. No one will deny you so long as Tutankhamen lives."

Word of the accident spread like fire before the wind, and we barely had time to lay him on his couch before we were shoved aside by Djehouty, Chief of Physicians in the palace, and Kemsit, Physician to Pharaoh. Behind them came Ay and Nakhtmin, Tutankhamen's Fan Bearer and Chief Royal Scribe, trailed by a gaggle of lesser priest-physicians.

The room was quickly shuttered and incense lit in the wall shrines, while they huddled to argue among themselves. Before they could decide how to treat him, Tutankhamen's entire body began to shake, sending the chanting priests scurrying lest the evil spirits take possession of them as well. No one considered that he might be cold, or what that could mean if he was. In the end it was the Queen who ordered a servant to bring blankets to cover her husband, then sat at his side holding one of his cold hands in hers. Merankh padded from one side of the couch to the other, pleading in vain for his master's touch, until Ankhesenamen finally ordered him to sit by her feet, where he whined and nosed their clasped hands.

A few minutes later, one of the physicians went to the foot of the couch, lifted the blanket from the young King's feet, and plunged a long needle into the end of his big toe. Tutankhamen did not move.

Mena motioned for me to follow him and like a shadow he moved around the edge of the room to a balcony overlooking the king's private garden, located to take advantage of the breeze from the north.

"She is too accepting," I murmured, relieved to be away from the priestly incantations and sweating bodies.

"Perhaps," Mena agreed, then cut to the bone. "You think his neck is broken?"

"Who can say without examining him? It could be an injury to the brain. You saw the contusion." He looked at me straight, then dropped his eyes and nodded, once.

"What would you have the Queen do?" he asked in despair. "Shriek and tear her clothes? Will that will bring him awake, able to laugh and walk again?"

I stared out over the roofs of the grand villas surrounding the palace, to the western cliffs standing black against the glowing pink sky. Re was dying. Taking his son with him. "Do not blame the bird for doing what she was trained to do," I said.

"Not here, you fool!" Mena whispered, giving me a knock on the shoulder. A mournful howl rent the silence, followed by a high, piercing scream. We rushed back inside only to be met by a chorus of voices—priests chanting prayers, his women shrieking and Ankhesenamen lying across her husband's still form, blood already oozing from the scratches on her arms.

It had been Merankh who first sensed when his beloved master's *ka* departed his earthly body, and let out that long, mournful howl of protest to his brother Anubis.

As we put our foreheads to the floor I remembered Mena's prophecy that power soon would belong to the strong. But what of the goddess Maat—did she simply turn a blind eye when the bird folded his wings to stoop?

My thoughts went backward in time to when I set eyes on him as a nine-year-old boy, standing before the great pylon of Ipet-isut on the day of his coronation. Naked except for the meanest loincloth, he came burdened with the sins of his half brother, the hated Heretic. Yet he had passed without fear through the copper-plated timber gates into the courtyard of the temple, where priests masked as gods waited to lead him into the sanctuary, where they would instruct him in the mysteries that would make him Amen-Re's son on earth, half-god and half-man. When finally he emerged, the young Tutankhamen's human aspect had been transformed forever by the symbols and raiment of royalty, a heavy weight to place on any man's shoulders, let alone one so young.

Now the priests in the House of the Dead will transform him once again, gutting him like a senseless beast to make him one with Osiris.

As for me, I will remember the Lord of the Two Lands the way he was when this day began, laughing while he raced his team across the desert, not as a statue made of stone. For the gods granted me the privilege of seeing the joy in his eyes as well as the fear he felt in going against his elders. I knew him to be capable not only of the arrogance of youth but generosity and love. That is why, in my heart, I weep for the boy who was allowed so little time to learn how to live before his time came to die.

*I am keeper of the book of my becomings: what was, what is,
what will be. I am a child, the rememberer of my father,
forever changing, eternal as day, everlasting as night. Can it be
said more plainly? Life and death are one.*

—Normandi Ellis, *Awakening Osiris*

TEN

Osiris Tutankhamen

DAY 13, THIRD MONTH OF INUNDATION

Pharaoh's ministers and advisors go unshaven in the bluish white
garments of death, and the taverns and pleasure houses all have
closed their front doors. Paranefer and his council pray for the
Pharaoh's safe journey to eternity, while Maya's outline scribes
labor day and night to finish the abandoned tomb of Nefer-neferu-
aten Smenkhkare, a gift to her brother in his time of need. Nor will
the priests hold any classes in the temple until the seventy days of
mourning are used up.

An unnatural quiet has come over Aset since Merankh, the
clumsy hound with the *akh* of a lovable puppy, grieved himself to
death in order to join his master, but most days she spends across
the river with her beloved sister, leaving mine without direction or
purpose. This morning I visited the potter's shed for the bowls I
ordered last week, only to have Resh hand me a small flask "for the
lord's little daughter." Shaped like a pomegranate, it had been left
the color of the baked clay except where the creamy glaze coating

the inside spilled over its narrow neck. I naturally assumed she had ordered it made, for the fruit is a favorite of hers.

"No, but she believes I have magic in my hands, like Khnum, who created the People of the Sun." His shy smile revealed a side to the man I had never seen before. "And I thought, since she is partial to pieces that have been kissed by the fire—" He was pointing to a black smudge on one side when Pagosh called out to us from some distance away.

"Have you seen Aset?"

"She is across the river," I answered when he drew closer.

"I brought her back not an hour ago," he puffed, out of breath from running. Or was it fear? "The Queen's babe has gone to Osiris."

The words came like a blow from an assailant who sneaks up from behind. "Prince Thutmose? What happened?"

"His nurse-mother found him as Re-Horakhte crested the eastern horizon, when she went to give him her breast. Some say his tongue grew too big for his mouth, others whisper that he fought with evil spirits who came for him in the dark, leaving his face one great bruise." He watched to see how I would take that.

"The babe's tongue protruded from his mouth?" I asked.

He nodded. "Aset refused to let anyone take him, said she acted for the Queen." That meant she had seen the babe with his face all bloated and black, for to be robbed of breath in that way is not a pretty sight. "I brought her away, but she did not want to leave her sister and accused me of disloyalty. We must find her, *sunu*." He tried to hide the hurt behind his gruff manner, but I knew him too well.

"Try the fowl yard and aviary. It is the beekeeper's day to collect honey, so Resh can go there while I search the barn. We will meet back here."

As I approached the stables I noticed Ruka loitering nearby, but paid him little attention until I saw him roll his eyes toward the closed end of the barn, where Sepi stabled Ramose's horses. Once inside I stopped to let my eyes grow accustomed to the dimmer light, and heard a murmur coming from the last stall, where I found her sitting on the floor with her legs crossed and Tuli wedged tightly against her. As I watched, he reached up to lick her face, trying to dry her cheeks.

"I am seven years old and no longer need a nurse-mother to watch over me," she told him. "Anyway, Merit and Paga only do what they are told, like any other servants." She must have sensed something, for she glanced up and saw me, then hid her face and began sobbing in earnest. A low growl came from Tuli's throat until he recognized my scent. Then he started to whine, pleading with me to fix whatever was wrong.

I rounded the partition, dropped to the hay-covered floor beside her, and lifted her onto my lap. "The demons c-came in the d-dark," she stammered, "and s-stole his breath away. They entered his nose backwards, turning their faces so they would not be recognized, and pretended they wanted to kiss him. Or quiet his cries."

I suppose she could find no other explanation for what happened to the babe she had come to love as a little brother. "Where did you hear such nonsense?" I murmured. "Thutmose was a strong babe. Perhaps he got tangled in his blanket."

She shook her head against my chest. "I saw no blanket."

"His nurse-mother would have tried to free him," I argued, even if I did not believe it myself, any more than I believe Tutankhamen's demise was the kind of misfortune that sometimes simply happens, without intent or reason. What I did not understand was why it never occurred to me that his son would be next.

"I can still see his face, even with my eyes closed . . . like the blind man could see my lion. Surely my sister's heart will break, like Merankh's. And mine."

"Mine, too," I murmured against the top of her head. Tears burned my eyelids, whether for the Queen's babe or her little sister I cannot say, and before I could blink them away she turned to look at me.

"Oh, Tenre, I am so sorry. I thought only of myself. I forgot you were the first to greet Thutmose when he came into this world." She put her arms around my neck and hugged me until I could not swallow. "Tuli thinks we should run away," she whispered, "but I would never leave you."

"Where would you go?"

"To a place where no one knows who we are. He thinks I should take a new name. Tashat, perhaps. What do you think?" It came to me then that she feared for her own life. "Poor Ankhes has no one to cry with, to make *her* feel better."

"Surely your lady mother stays with her."

She shook her head but refused to meet my eyes. "She has gone to General Horemheb's villa, to be with her own sister. I heard her tell my father that Ankhes must accept that she will never bear a child that lives, because my sister's royal blood is tainted with the blood of her grandmother, Osiris Amenhotep's Great Royal Wife, the Israelite. That means Ankhes is not fully royal, doesn't it?" She dared to look at me finally. "Does that mean I am tainted, too, and can never have a child who lives because my father is not royal?"

It taxed me not to say what I truly think of a mother who shows such a hard heart to her freshly bereaved daughter. Nor did I want to admit that I shared her fear. "You know better than that. I will go across the river to see what I can learn." I set her bare feet on the hard-packed dirt floor. "But I will take you to Nebet's if you promise to wait there and do nothing foolish."

"You forget that I am almost eight years old."

"No, you are the one who forgets. Merit knows what it is to lose a babe, yet you did not seek her wisdom. Or her love. Pagosh brought you away because he could not watch over you in the Queen's apartments, for he is more father to you than servant. And you know it." Fresh tears began to run down her cheeks, and I had to force myself to continue. "He and Resh have been searching all over for you. Even now they wait for me by the potter's shed, not because your father ordered them to but because they care for you. So make your peace with them first, before you go to Merit."

"I will, I promise. I am sorry, Tenre, truly."

"Then tell them that. And don't forget your sandals and a shawl to keep warm, for it will be dark by the time we return." I motioned her ahead of me in the passageway between the stalls.

"Would you take something to Ankhes for me?" she asked as we went. "After she saw the sandals Ipwet made for me she could talk of little else, so I tried on one of hers when she wasn't looking, to see how far it stuck out beyond my toes and know how long to tell Ipwet to make them."

DAY 17, FOURTH MONTH OF INUNDATION

When I consider what she has endured, I wonder that Ankhesenamen never tried to take her destiny into her own hands before. Who can blame her if she believes her babes all died because they were fathered first by her own father and then by her mother's brother? Certainly an alliance with another powerful ruling family would bring vigorous blood to the royal line. Whatever the reason, the Queen sent a message in secret to Suppiluliuma, King of the Hittites, asking for one of his sons to sit beside her on the throne of Horus. That she thought it possible to keep the message a secret is naive enough, let alone that Ay and Horemheb would allow such a marriage ever to take place. Or that the High Priest would accept a Hittite as the son of Amen-Re.

Mena believes that the scribe who wrote her message betrayed the Queen to Nefertiti, who carried the tale to Ramose and, probably, to Mutnodjme as well. However it was done, Ramses, who is Horemheb's deputy in the North and commander of the military fortress at Zarw, was waiting when Prince Zannanza stepped onto our soil, putting an end to the young Hittite's dreams of glory and empire.

Now two legions of Suppiluliuma's army march toward the border of Canaan, and poor little Ankhesenamen is caught in a trap of her own making.

DAY 2, FIRST MONTH OF PLANTING

A chorus of priests chanted prayers to Amen while the Chief Lector Priest placed the gold mask over Tutankhamen's face, marking him the son of Re. It was a softly burnished likeness of the young man I had come to love, with eyes of quartz and obsidian. His eyelids and brows had been inlaid with lapis lazuli, as were the stripes of his gold nemset. On his brow was the entwined serpent and vulture of Upper and Lower Kemet, to protect him from his enemies. Under the false beard of the god Osiris lay a broad collar of lapis and green feldspar beads. Aset came forward with a rope of blue cornflowers, draped it around her uncle's shoulders, and honored him with one last bow. Then the Lector Priest ordered that Pharaoh's two golden hands, holding the crook and flail, be sewn to the linen over his chest, ending the rites at the palace.

The funeral cortege was led by the Nine Friends of the King, followed by his council of ministers, his Fan Bearer on the Right, and viziers of the North and the South, then the priests who presided over the beautification of his body. Behind them, Paranefer and Ramose poured milk on the ground as they went, preparing the way for the six red oxen pulling the sled that bore the King's linen-swathed form. After the first canopied sled came another, this one bearing a gilded wood chest with the four alabaster coffins that held the King's liver, lungs, stomach, and intestines, pulled by eight white-robed priests. At the corners of the gilded chest stood four gold statuettes of the goddess Selket, her face so filled with tenderness that to look on it brought tears to my eyes. Perhaps it was her gently turned head and the position of her arms, stretched out to protect her precious cargo, but such exquisite work could only have come from the workshops of Akhetaten, the city the Heretic dedicated to his god. There refuse from every home and place of business was collected and burned, and public baths and shady gardens were open to everyone. Yet this heaven on earth was conceived by a man said to be afflicted with a fevered brain.

After the second sled came the Queen and her mother, then Horemheb's wife and Aset, followed by his secondary wives and concubines, including the foreign princesses sent by their fathers to Pharaoh's harem to curry favor with the Lord of the Two Lands. They wore the same white mourning sheath, now torn and sprinkled with dust from the road. Strung out behind them were the dead King's advisers and other high officials and, finally, his courtiers and nobles, where I took my place because of the title he had bestowed upon me barely two months before.

A crowd gathered on the banks of the river to watch us embark on the symbolic pilgrimage to the four holy cities, a long and tiring journey up and down both banks of the river. By the time we reached Tutankhamen's half-finished funerary temple, where Aset,

Nebet, and Tetisheri waited, the sun was high, erasing the shadows that give the earth depth and form. There, after a quick repast of fruits and breads, Mena and I again joined the line of mourners, leaving his wife and daughter behind lest the rough journey endanger Sheri's unborn babe or Nebet's fragile hip.

Once beyond the village of the tomb workers, we began the long trek across the incorruptible plateau of rock and sand to the Place of Truth, over terrain littered with chips of white limestone from the stones cut for Tutankhamen's funerary chapel—his life finished before the building. By the time we arrived at the place where he will live through eternity, several tents had been erected for the royal family, Paranefer, and his sem priests. Servants spread rush mats in what little shade they could find, so the women could pass the time gossiping and dozing while the men carried Pharaoh's grave goods into the cool, torchlit chambers.

I carried a painted wood head of him as a child, a coffer bearing his birth name, and a toy box with a secret lock, all souvenirs from his childhood as the rites demanded, along with a jar of sweet wine from Aten's vineyards in Zarw. One chamber already contained his two stillborn babes, and I took consolation from knowing he soon would be joined by the son who had given him such joy, and so would not be alone in that silent place.

Before leaving it, I paused for one last look at the walls in his chamber, skipping over the representations of Osiris and the other gods and goddesses, to where the living man skimmed through the marshes in a reed boat, his wife sitting at his feet. In another scene he hunted lions in the desert with his faithful Merankh, and afterward took his rest in a gilded chair, enjoying the attention of his Queen. Such representations often go against the truth, but I believe they did truly honor each other. If what they shared fell short of what I see between Mena and Sheri, that is because they had no say in the choosing. Still, given more time, who can say what might have been?

The guests gathered as Osiris Tutankhamen, adorned now with garlands of cornflowers, olive leaves, and blue beads, was raised to stand before the entrance of his eternal home. A chorus of young priests began a chant of supplication to Osiris, but when an Anubis-masked priest stepped forward to put a great white bull to the knife, a hushed silence fell over the crowd of mourners.

I glanced to where Aset stood and saw her eyes grow wide with fear and shock as the man she must have recognized as her father jerked the beast's head up and back, then with one quick slash opened his throat. Hot blood spurted from the wound, dropping the bull to his knees. Again the Anubis-priest wielded his knife, and a moment later presented the beast's forefoot and still-beating heart to the dead Pharaoh, causing several women to spill the contents of their stomach on the ground. The sour odor of vomit along with the stench of hot blood was enough to make the strongest stomach uneasy, but Aset only stared, wide-eyed with disbelief—as if she beheld a scene of such horror that it robbed her of the will to look away.

Next came Nachtmin, to speak the words that would make his master's name live forever, an honor that usually falls to the dead Pharaoh's eldest son or daughter. After him, Ay came forward draped in the leopardskin of a sem priest to perform the sacred gesture of opening the mouth—always the first act of the new Pharaoh—and a low murmur rippled through the crowd.

Astute as Ramose has been in recovering their former wealth, the priests of Amen do not yet command enough support among the provincial nomarchs, mayors, and judges. Instead, the grizzled old Master of the Horse held the governors in the palm of his hand because he controlled the royal treasury and storehouses during the seventy days of mourning. When the military commanders threw their support to him as well in order to secure the throne for General Horemheb, who still fights the upstart Syrian princes, the High Priest and his Sacred Council had little choice. Ay may once have served the Heretic and his god, but he has no children to follow him and, at sixty-two, little chance of getting any on Ankhesenamen. And since Nefertiti is said to seethe with frustration at being unable to alter this turn of events, it is certain that she had no part in Tutankhamen's demise, which leaves only the man who takes his place.

Ay spoke the dead king's throne name, followed by his birth name. Then he touched the bronze blade of the sacred adze to the dead King's mouth, to return speech and sight to Osiris Tutankhamen's now imperishable body, reuniting the six parts of a whole man. As he did so he recited the words given to him by the High Priest.

"You live again, young once more and forever."

The boy had lived on in the man, to laugh at the playful antics of his clumsy hound and boast of the deadly skills of his Horus of the Sky. Where is he now, I wonder. Does he stand before Osiris and his forty-two judges, declaring his innocence?

I told no falsehood, nor robbed any man. Neither have I killed or given the order to be killed.

By the time the God-masked priests carried him into his eternal home, Re had slipped behind the cliffs, creating narrow canyons that stretched to where we stood. Aset's hand crept into mine when Ankhesenamen tried to stop the priests with the words they had taught her.

"I am your wife, O Great One, do not leave me! Is it your pleasure, my husband, that I should go far away? How can it be that I am to go away alone? I would accompany you, but you remain silent and speak not!" Only the Queen was allowed to trail after the priests to where her husband would be enclosed within a sealed gold case, to me an even greater hypocrisy on the part of the man responsible for his end.

Aset never uttered a word as we joined the trail of mourners making their way back to his funerary temple, nor did she loosen her hold on my hand. Perhaps she feared the encroaching darkness of night on the Western Desert, I thought, remembering the time she had recited a line from the Heretic's Hymn to Aten.

In the dark every lion leaves its lair and all snakes bite.

Now, trudging across that landscape without pity, surrounded by an enormous nothingness, unchanging and eternal, those words did not sound nearly so fanciful as they had then. Nor did the line that follows them.

And the earth is silent, like the dead.

ELEVEN

Kate was washing the clay off her modeling tools when the phone rang, but she grabbed a towel and picked it up on the first ring. "Do you happen to know how that jug with two handles got to be the hieroglyph for heart?" Max asked without identifying himself.

She didn't miss a beat. "It evolved over time from a drawing of the heart with the large blood vessels attached, the same way the glyph for childbirth did. That one started as a woman kneeling on two stacks of bricks with the head and arms of an infant emerging beneath her. Eventually it was simplified to three down-curving lines representing the baby's arms and head, over two open squares—the bricks."

"S'that right?" he drawled. "Interesting. Thanks. Talk to you later." She was left with a dial tone and the impression that he was working on something. But what?

That night Kate called him, late, when she was sure he'd be home. He had given her the 800 number at the clinic, but she was reluctant to call there in case he was with a patient. "The hieroglyph for many is a lizard," she said soon as he picked up the phone.

"Hi, glad you called. I've been trying to read, but I keep going over the same line again and again. When the phone rang I was dreaming up a new game for Sam and wishing I could see what you got done today."

"I'm taking pictures every step of the way. Have been from the very beginning. You could always look at them."

"Not the same thing, but yeah, I'd like to see them. What was that about a lizard?"

"It's the glyph for many." She glanced at the page from his pocket notepad, which he'd left on her worktable. His writing met the requisite scrawl for physicians, so it had taken her a while to decipher, except for the word DOG at the top. Below that he'd made a kind of list.

1) Appears 13 times. Number significant? *What's the sign for many?*
2) Anubis (dog) is son of Osiris by Nepthys (O's sister)=adultery AND incest
3) Possible parallel with Tashat?

"Oh, you found my note. I guess that means there were a lot of them around. Listen, something else I meant to ask you—was it kosher to name an ordinary person after a god?"

"I guess, but combinations were more common. Amenhotep, for instance, which means Amen is content or satisfied. Thutmose translates as son of Thoth."

"Mose is Egyptian for son?"

"Or heir, since it can go either way, male or female."

"Does that mean the biblical Moses was branded fatherless just by his name, because he was found floating in the bulrushes?"

"Maybe. Not necessarily. I don't know." Without thinking, she asked, "Are you wearing your reading glasses?"

"Yep." He sounded amused. "Why?"

"I was just trying to picture you while we're talking. What were you reading?"

"An article by an archaeologist who's been digging in the Egyptian Delta, where the cities built by the Jews held in bondage by Pharaoh were supposed to be. He claims no such cities or towns existed in those places at the time of the Exodus."

"Aahhh, but when was the Exodus?" Kate breathed. "Who was the pharaoh of the Oppression? One theory has it that the volcanic eruption on the island of Santorini in 1483 B.C. explains the parting of the waters and tower of fire seen by the Israelites as they wandered in the wilderness. Another puts the Exodus just before the Eighteenth Dynasty, when the Hyksos, the foreign rulers—maybe—who brought the composite bow to Egypt, and horses—another maybe—were driven out. Others say it occurred three hundred years later, during the reign of Ramses the Second, or his grandson. Some people think Akhenaten was Moses, or else one of his followers. Freud, for one."

"Uncle! I get it. I get it!" Max yelled, making her laugh. "Egyptology and medicine have too damn much in common—too much we don't know. Oh, something else. Does the bandaging pattern the priests used to wrap her body tell you anything?"

"I don't know, but I can ask Cleo. Or Dave."

"Better not wave any more red flags in front of the bull," Max advised. "I'll put the question to the Egyptologists' Electronic Forum, on the Internet. They're a pretty solid bunch even if some of the academics on the list get pretty pedantic at times."

"All I know is that they knew every pattern we do, ways of wrapping that your medical colleagues think *they* originated for a particular wound or part of the body. But then bandaging the dead was tied to the central myth of their lives. Osiris and Isis."

"I have to confess I find all that pretty confusing, with Horus the Elder, and—"

"Basically, Osiris was murdered and his body hacked to pieces by his jealous brother, Set, who scattered them up and down the Nile. Except his phallus, which Set fed to the fish. Isis, who was both sister and wife to Osiris, searched until she found all the pieces, bound them together, and turned herself into a bird to fan the breath back into his body with her wings. Osiris took the form of a bird, too, and impregnated her before he returned to the Netherworld. That's why their son Horus has the head of a falcon. Think of them as the Egyptian trinity. The resurrection of Osiris is symbolized by new crops that follow the annual flood, said to be the tears of Isis mourning her husband. Isis is the goddess of love, a nurturing deity with the magic power to heal."

"Women with magical powers sure go back a long way," Max teased, a smile in his voice.

"So do witch doctors," Kate returned without missing a beat. "The priests had a lock on medical training and practice back then, too."

He laughed. "Sounds like your engine is running too fast."

"I know. I may never get to sleep tonight. Listen, did you notice anything special about that little dog on Tashat's cartonnage?"

"Just that he's all over the place, like you said."

"I think he was her pet and went everywhere she did."

"Suggestive," he agreed, "but not conclusive. They're all male. They're also all wearing fancy collars, but each one is different. That points to more than one dog."

Max was definitely a detail person, she decided. "It also could mean one dog with several collars, because there's writing on them. Always the same word—Tuli, which means brave. I think that's his name, like Prince Valiant in the comic strip."

"I didn't notice any hieroglyphs on the collars."

"Because there aren't any. It's written in hieratic, a more abstract, cursive form of writing. I missed it, too, until I got to thinking about what Dave said—that Akhenaten ordered everyone to use hieratic script as an economy, except on monuments or the sacred texts copied out by the funerary priests for people to put in their tombs. Dave advised me to put those cartouches in a religious context, yet the dog's name is written in hieratic. That casts a distinctly secular light on him. Maybe that's how we should be looking at those painted scenes."

"Okay, but does that really change anything?"

"Most gods had more than one face. Hathor was a cow, Thoth a bird, Amen a ram. Remove the religious slant and we're looking at a menagerie of animals at play in a medicinal garden—a zoo." She paused and heard her heart beating in her ears. "I made a reservation on a flight to Houston a week from today, the Monday after Christmas, but they're just holding it for me. I can change it if you're busy then."

"No, that's good," he said without hesitation. "I'll have Marilou reschedule the few appointments I have. How long can you stay?"

"A couple of days. I'm hoping to finish the head this week. The closer I get the harder it is to do anything else, even go home at lunch to let Sam out."

"Bring your photographs, also some drawings to show that surgeon I mentioned." Kate was trying to decide if she should ask him to get her a motel room or do it herself, when he added, "I'll reserve a room for you at the Warwick. It's half a block from the art museum and close to the Medical Center. Not far from my place either. Which airport are you coming into, and what time?"

"Hobby. Two-twenty-five, but—"

"I'll be there," he said, cutting her off. "Have you tried going to sleep with some problem on your mind, then wake up with the answer?"

"Doesn't everybody? Some nights that's the *only* reason to go to bed."

He laughed as if he were shaking his head, indulging her. "Time for you to hit the sack, Mac. I'll talk to you tomorrow."

Cleo suggested they try Vince's for lunch Tuesday, but Kate wanted to go home to check on Sam. "He didn't eat his breakfast, and I'm worried that he might be sick. Why not come with me and we'll fix a sandwich?"

Fifteen minutes later they found Sam squirming with excitement at hearing more than one set of footsteps. Cleo grabbed his paws, but Kate could tell his heart wasn't in it. He had been hoping it was Max.

"Phil says I have the build and coordination to be really good," Cleo prattled as she followed Kate to the kitchen and let Sam out the back door.

"So how did Dave take it when you told him?" Kate asked as she washed her hands and got out the sandwich makings.

"I didn't. He's tied up with family stuff during the holidays, so it didn't come up." Kate didn't say anything, so Cleo changed the subject. "I talked to Max this morning. No luck on finding anything more on that necklace among his grandmother's papers. I told him the truth—that it's museum quality, primarily because of the unique melding of iconographies in that ram's-head catch."

"Could it have been carried to Egypt as trade goods?" Kate asked after they sat down. "Aswan was a source of marble and a major way station for trade up the Nile."

"I doubt it. Three things are happening in that piece. One is the willingness to modify form for the demands of function—the need to suppress the horns to allow that oval ring to pass over the ram's head, and the unnaturally elongated nose to hold the ring in place. That's very un-Egyptian. Or so we thought," Cleo admitted with a wry smile. "But it still feels Egyptian, influenced by some other sensibility. Assyrian, maybe." She pinched off a bite of her tuna salad sandwich for Sam and set it on the edge of her plate. "I told Max what I thought it might bring at auction, and said we'd like to have first shot on an offer. Guess what he said."

"That it wasn't for sale—at any price."

Cleo shook her head and nodded, then carried her dishes to the sink. Kate did the same, and broached the subject she'd been dreading. "Listen, Clee, if you haven't changed your mind about going home between Christmas and New Year's, would you mind keeping Sam for a couple of days?"

"Sure. Where are you off to?"

"Houston. Max wants to show me some special equipment they have at the Medical Center there."

Cleo gave her a knowing grin. "Okay. Bring Sam along when you come for dinner on Christmas, so he and Bastet can warm up to each other before you have to leave him."

Kate nodded. Sam didn't much care for Cleo's cat, with good reason, which made Kate feel guilty. While Cleo went to the bathroom, she let Sam in and put cottage cheese in his bowl, then added some tuna salad as a special treat.

On the way back to the museum Kate mentioned that she was picking up the wigs later that afternoon. "Come by the workroom before you go home and I'll show them to you." The museum would be closed Friday, for Christmas, but she hoped to finish the head before then.

"Okay, I'll bring Max's necklace, too," Cleo replied, "so you can take it with you to Houston. Better carry it in your purse, though, or else wear it. It's too valuable to put in your luggage."

Kate worked without interruption until closing time, and was getting her coat from the closet when the phone rang.

"Did you know there's a description of angina in the Ebers Papyrus, including the pain in the left arm?" Max asked, without bothering to say hello—tacit understanding that they each recognized the other's voice by now. "Like you said, it's pretty tough trying to strip away all the stuff we take for granted and imagine what it was like without even the crudest microscope, when all you had was the naked eye plus your fingers and nose. Makes you wonder, though, if they traced the source of that pain to the heart, how the hell they could think those same vessels carried everything from blood, air, and saliva to urine and feces."

"Hippocrates didn't live for another thousand years, and *he* thought the vessels carried both air and blood," Kate reminded him.

"Yeah, but the Egyptians eviscerated their dead."

"That's not dissection. The priests who performed that part of the ritual were outcasts and had to live away from the rest of society, but they only made an incision and groped around inside with their left hands." It wasn't until she heard herself say it that she realized what that could mean. "Oh, God, Max, do you think—"

"Look, right and left has always had another meaning—right and wrong. But even if natural lefties *were* ostracized, her father was in a position to protect her, had to be if he managed to marry her off to a Theban nobleman." Max paused. "See what Cleo thinks. I've got to run. Talk to you later."

Later turned out to be nearly midnight. The first ring sent Sam racing for the front door.

"What's with Sam?" Max asked.

"He was asleep, really out of it. I think he mistook the phone for the door."

"What are you doing up so late?"

She could hear the smile in his voice. "Duplicating Nefertiti's blue war crown. It feels like ten people have moved into my head, and they're all talking at once. Arguing. I thought doing something mindless with my hands might make me sleepy."

"Arguing about what?"

"How much my feelings have influenced what I've done. Something keeps niggling at me, about Tashat's face, but I can't figure out what, or why, so I'm trying reverse psychology, hoping it will come to me if I don't think about it."

"Okay, so tell me about this crown you're making."

"Remember the straight-sided crown Nefertiti is wearing in that painted head? It looks black there, but supposedly it was covered with blue-enameled disks. She designed her own crown, probably because the traditional one wasn't very flattering. Too bulbous. Anyway, I made one out of Bristol board, a card stock that holds whatever shape you give it. Now I'm sticking blue-paper dots all over it to get the same effect."

"If you say so, but you'd probably get sleepy faster by reading today's paper."

"If you're looking for evidence that they had the concept of a pump," Kate told him, "you won't find it in the Ebers Papyrus."

Silence, then, "How the hell did you know that's what I'm looking for?"

Because we operate on the same wavelength, she thought, and realized that had been true all along, even if she hadn't been consciously aware of it.

"What you said about the vessels," she answered. "It doesn't make sense that people who lived next to a river and watched it rise and fall, who used the shaduf to lift water from a lower level to a higher one—which means they knew the principle of the fulcrum—who built ponds to capture the water and canals to direct it, wouldn't catch on to the idea of recirculation. Maybe it's like evisceration and dissection. How far is one from the other—recirculation and the concept of a pump—and what does it take to get there?"

"I knew I shouldn't call so late."

Kate could tell he was teasing. "Put your brain to work on that while you sleep," she suggested. "I'll talk to you tomorrow."

It was still dark when she woke the next morning. She took Sam for a run, ate a cold breakfast, fixed herself a sandwich, and headed for the museum, which wouldn't open to the public for another three hours. Once there she let herself in through the shipping-room door and ran through the long dark halls, to get the circulation going to her brain. In the workroom she got out all the materials and brushes she would need, filled a couple of jars with water, and waited for the sun to rise a little higher—when the light was perfect for what she needed to do.

Like river rocks exposed to the air, acrylic paints turn dull when the sheen of wetness disappears, so one of the guesses she had to make in mixing was how much the color would change as it dried. Flesh tones were the hardest to predict. Too much white turned the paint opaque, without the translucent quality natural to living flesh. Sometimes she added gel extender to enhance transparency, but too much produced a sheen that looked equally unnatural.

As the light changed through the day she had to count that in as well, so the sun was her clock, telling her the time by what it did to the colors she was mixing. She worked near the bank of windows to take advantage of the natural light as long as she could, even after the sun passed to the other side of the building. She took a short breather around three—two o'clock Houston time—and called the clinic, only to be told that Max was at the UT Health Sciences Center. The receptionist offered to give her his number there, but Kate demurred and went back to work. Around four, she finally had to give in and turn on the overhead fluorescent tubes, which she thought of as leeches because they paled all colors, bleeding them of vitality.

When the museum closed she went home to feed Sam and grab a snack. After that they went for a longer run, back to the museum, where she smuggled him in through the same door. He'd been there before and settled down on the small rug she'd brought from home in an effort to soften and warm the drab, lifeless room. Lying with his paws stretched out before him, head erect, Sam appeared to be keeping guard over the dead. Like his brother Anubis, she thought, then chided herself for getting carried away. A dose of reality would fix that.

She switched on the viewbox and stared at the X ray. Could Tashat have committed not only adultery but incest?

Why did she find that so hard to believe? The shattered hand, that's why, Kate realized, answering her own question. But her brain felt tired from weeks of trying to make connections where none existed. What she needed was to walk away for a while, which she was going to do.

Three hours later she had Tashat's face ready for the final embellishments. As she washed out her brushes, preparing to leave, she felt a growing sense of relief, at knowing she was finally bringing something to completion and could put the constant wondering to rest. Even if it didn't answer all their questions.

After another restless night she woke up early again but tried not to just eat and run. She scrambled a couple of eggs, one for her and one for Sam, and read the morning paper while she ate. The only thing that really registered was the date. December 24. The day Tashat would come forth to live again.

She ran to get dressed, dropped a container of yogurt into her purse, and gave Sam a fierce hug. "Be patient one more day, sweetie. I'll be back soon as I can, so no crazy stuff, okay?"

It was barely light when she left the house and felt cold as the North Pole so she drove to the museum instead of walking or running. Once there she peeled off her coat and gloves, turned the revolving platform until Tashat faced the windows on the east—to greet Re-Horakhte as he emerged from the darkness of the Netherworld—and sat down on a stool to wait and watch. As the white light of dawn flooded the workroom, she kept her eyes on Tashat's face, to catch the subtle variation in flesh tones across her cheeks and nose. Then, finally satisfied, she reached inside the head to remove the temporary plastic balls she had used to form the eyelids.

It was time to make the final transformation, from a forensic reconstruction to an archaeological portrait. She picked up one of the eyeballs with the blue irises, slipped her hand up through the neck again, and fitted it into place. Next, keeping her gaze on the other eye socket, she inserted the second one and stepped back enough to adjust them—to get the direction of sight exactly right so the eyes would look focused.

Kate was vaguely aware of familiar noises in the hall and knew the museum was coming awake, but homestretch jitters were causing her hands to shake. She turned and walked away from the head, to make a pot of herb tea.

"Did you ever go home last night?" Elaine inquired from around the half-open door.

Kate nodded. "Not that I could sleep."

Elaine came in for a closer a look. "She's way beyond those

heads the police come up with, but she still doesn't look real, does she?"

"I don't know why you'd say that," Kate joked, "aside from no eyebrows or eyelashes, and no hair." She glanced to where the wigs stood waiting on their stands.

"It's the lack of wrinkles. I know she was young, but—"

"I'm doing the eyes first so she won't look quite so—so vacant."

"Beats me how you'd know where to put them, anyway, but I guess that's where being an artist comes in, huh?" The thoughtless comment rubbed Kate the wrong way. Forensic reconstructions had fallen into disrepute back when the tissue depths were based on measurements taken from cadavers, but that had changed in the late eighties after a German professor named Richard Helmer used ultrasound on living subjects to establish more accurate average figures.

"I'm planning to add laugh lines at the corners of her eyes, because of the dry air and brilliant sun," Kate explained, partly to convince Elaine that there was a reason for everything she was doing.

"If you say so." The museum volunteer hefted the foil-covered pan she was carrying. "Don't forget the staff party this afternoon, after the cafeteria closes. Bring her along, and we'll drink a toast to both of you."

After Elaine left, Kate went back to outlining the eyelids, the cosmetic convention worn by everyone—men, women, and children alike—to protect their eyes from the bright sun. Women who could afford it sometimes painted their lids with a paste containing manganese oxide, giving it a slightly purple cast, or powdered malachite, which was green. But black was more common.

While she worked, Kate kept a book open to the color photograph of Nefertiti, but when she got to the eyebrows she parted company with the Beautiful One's sculptor, feathering the arching lines to make them look more natural, especially from a few feet away. After that she added artificial eyelashes, then stepped back to decide whether the brows needed to be heavier.

Time passed without notice except when her stomach grumbled in protest, forcing her to stop long enough to spoon down the yogurt. It was a little past two by the time she was ready for one of the wigs. She took care positioning it, not wanting to spoil her first view of Tashat by having the bangs crooked or too high above the brows. Finally, when she had the long straight wig exactly the way it looked on Tashat's cartonnage, she turned and walked a good fifteen feet away, took a deep breath, and closed her eyes, to wipe the slate clean before swinging around for her first real look.

Stunned by what she saw, Kate felt a rush of tears and a gale of conflicting emotions sweep over her, even as a smile broke across the surface of her mind long before it reached her lips—emotions born of the satisfaction of knowing that Tashat no longer lay in darkness.

Tashat's mouth was smaller than Nefertiti's, yet her lips struck Kate as every bit as sensuous, partly because of the way they lifted at the corners in a not-quite smile. Something about the set of her jaw suggested intransigence or strength, but what Kate found most beguiling were the contradictions that gave Tashat a persona so unlike Nefertiti's, despite the similarity in their cranial configurations—a young woman of intelligence and irresistible charm, with her clear blue eyes reflecting light from the windows exactly as the outer curve of the living eye did.

Kate stared, mesmerized by the echoes of something familiar, that she'd seen before, like hearing the harmonics of a pure tone. Then, driven by the vague sense of having known Tashat, or else someone who looked very much like her, she went to the mirror over the workroom sink to examine her own face. And came away shaking for another reason entirely.

Without thinking, she moved toward the workbench and the book she'd left open to the Berlin head, where Nefertiti wore the tall, straight-sided crown of her own devising and an Amarna necklace of petal-and-leaf-shaped glass beads. Found in the sands of central Egypt, in the remains of an ancient sculptor's workshop, it had survived with only slight damage to the ears and a missing brown iris in one eye, yet it showed enough similarity, especially through the jaw and chin, to suggest that Nefertiti and Tashat were of the same racial mix. That unexpected happenstance had led Kate to assume that Tashat's skin was no darker and could even have been lighter, given the color of her eyes. But Nefertiti's almond-shaped eyes were slightly hooded at the inner corners, giving her an almost melancholy expression, while Tashat's were not only blue but rounder. The result was that Tashat had a more open, more in-your-face sort of look—the look of a woman willing to dare a great deal.

Until that moment Kate had believed that two artifacts alone argued against the conventional wisdom that Egyptian art was conventional and individually uninspired. Now she added another—the cartonnage portrait of Tashat—which captured the sense of humor or intellect or whatever it was that was the source of Tashat's incredible vitality. Surely whoever painted her cartonnage and coffin had been an artist of rare insight, able to portray the essence of Tashat's spirit as well as her physical presence.

For a moment Kate immersed herself in the glow of discovery, indulging in the satisfaction of knowing that she had done an inspired job—not that she would ever say that to anyone else. Then she got out her camera to capture Tashat in the ornately braided wig, from several different views. After that she switched to the short curly wig. When she finished, she glanced at the exposure counter and saw that she still had two left, so she removed the wig and set Nefertiti's blue war crown on Tashat's head, and took one straight on and one in profile—for Max.

A movement at the edge of her eye caught Kate's attention, and she glanced up to find Dave Broverman standing a few feet away. Like a car accident you can see coming but do nothing to prevent, she knew he had noticed the open book and was going to jump to the wrong conclusion.

"Christ, McKinnon!" he exploded. "If you think I'm going to buy into your fantasies, that you can convince me this insignificant piece of dung"—he turned and pointed an accusing finger at the mummy—"is Nefertiti, you're out of your cotton-picking mind!"

"It's not what you—" she began, trying to mollify him. "I do *not* think she is—"

"Damn right she isn't. I'd have to be a fool—or is that what you had in mind? You and Cleo." He took two quick steps, swung his arm, and knocked the blue war crown off Tashat's head. It flew across the room, hit the floor, and bounced once, then rolled back and forth in a wobbling arc.

Stunned by the viciousness of his attack, Kate didn't move, though she had a crazy urge to laugh at the incongruous "cotton-picking" if not his infantile tantrum. "You never listened to a god-damned thing I said, did you? Just went your own pigheaded way. Some expert that doctor friend of yours turned out to be." Expecting him to calm down once he'd blown off some steam, Kate thought she might only make things worse by arguing with him. "Come to think of it, you're too much the lead foot to dream this up by yourself. Don't think I haven't noticed you and Cleo slipping out to lunch together—"

That did it. "I do *not* think Tashat is Nefertiti. If you'd let me explain—"

"I've had it with you, McKinnon. Up to here." He wedged an open hand against the bridge of his nose, eyes darting back and forth, looking anywhere but at Kate. "Come closing time today I want you out of here for good. Don't even think about hauling off anything that doesn't belong to you, either. I know you've been squirreling away supplies to use in the work you bootleg on the side." He strode toward the door, then turned around for one last jab. "Don't expect any more paychecks, either. You damn well better count yourself lucky I'm not inclined to be vindictive, or I'd bring suit to recover every penny we've paid you." He slammed the door behind him, sending shock waves reverberating around the room.

Shaking her head in disbelief, Kate edged down onto a stool, legs too weak to hold her up any longer. Her cheeks burned with shame, yet she felt like laughing at the stark lunacy of Dave's paranoid attack. The next instant she was raging at herself for not making him listen. At the very least she should have told him she could account for every piece of paper and tube of paint—and had the sketches and photographs to show how she'd used them—so there was no way in hell he could get a judgment against her.

That's when it began to sink in that she'd done it again, only this time it was not only Cleo but Max she'd let down. Rationally she could accept that there was a limit to how much anyone should have to put up with . . . even mothers and fathers. She knew she'd been an unpredictabe combination of the tortoise and the hare, one moment racing ahead and the next slowing to a crawl, so she didn't really blame her parents for deciding that their only child was among the lame and halt, if not a total failure. An emotional investment that never paid off. What she couldn't accept was the way they disappeared from her life. Now the King of Boobs was casting her adrift, too. What hurt most, though, was the thought of deserting Tashat—of letting it all come to nothing.

Kate glanced at the replica of the living Tashat and was hit by a sudden storm of thoughts and ideas, like gusts of wind blowing from every direction at once. *More drawings at home. Some different, some duplicates. Photographs of everything. Can repeat everything I've done here, so she won't be consigned to the dark forever. Except I'll never be able to do anything with them. Not without Dave's permission. And I just ripped any chance of that.*

Mind racing, she got up from the stool and with all the care she could muster placed the straight wig on Tashat's head, then set the wooden tripod in a corner of the room. After that she took a few deep breaths and sat down to sort through her sketches and watercolors, dividing them into two piles. One she slid into a large envelope. The other she left on the bench after leafing through each one to make sure they all carried her trademark signature—*KmcK*—where it couldn't be trimmed off. Next she marched down to the shipping room for a cardboard box, came back and filled it with her personal belongings—a few clay tools and brushes, the brown envelope, several books, her camera and portable radio, the small throw rug and the porcelain teapot.

Finally, she retrieved the blue crown from the floor, set it on top of the box, put on her coat, and laid her keys in the center of the empty table. After a last glance around to see if she'd overlooked anything, she picked up the box and started for the door. As she reached for the light switch she turned back for one long, last look at Tashat—then flipped off the lights and closed the door behind her. As she crossed the reception hall she glanced toward the cafeteria and saw several volunteers getting ready for the Christmas party but didn't even pause.

As soon as she got home she canceled her flight to Houston. Then she left two phone messages, one for Max on his answering machine at home, and the other for Cleo. The first she purposefully kept vague. "It turns out I can't make it to Houston after all. Something has come up. I'll give you a call sometime next week." The second was more succinct. "Dave just blew his stack and gave me my walking papers. If I were you, I'd lie low for a few days, come down with the flu or something until he cools off. Anyway, I'm out of here, taking Sam with me. Not sure for how long, but I'll call you next week. Promise. Or the week after." Then she unplugged the phone, poured herself a glass of wine, cleaned out the refrigerator, ate a sandwich, and started packing.

By sunup the next morning, she and Sam were on the interstate heading south, toward the blue skies of Georgia O'Keeffe country. The Red Land of New Mexico.

TWELVE

Year Three in the Reign of Ay

(1349 B.C.)

DAY 21, SECOND MONTH OF PLANTING

At six Nebet seems all arms and legs, like a boy who grows too fast to remember where his toes end. Or perhaps she only seems so to me next to Aset, who at ten years moves with such purpose and grace. That the two girls remain close despite the difference in their ages surely is due to the affinity of one lively intellect for another— that and the natural compassion that caused Aset to reach out to Nebet in the first place, to free her spirit from the fetters imposed by her body.

It was Aset, too, who encouraged Nebet's talent for drawing, a skill so unique that Tetisheri worries should it cause rivalry between them and bring their friendship to an end. But Aset makes pictures to a purpose—to tell a story—while Nebet turns a barren desert into a mysterious place of shifting shapes and colors that only she can see. So I have no such worry, for I believe the rock on which their friendship stands is their innate understanding of each other's need to stray beyond the boundaries of the way things are and always have been. Just as it has always been for Mena and me.

Nofret brought out a platter of cakes containing bits of nuts and dates, a treat she had prepared in anticipation of our coming, while Mata, Khary's assistant, trailed her with a pitcher of beer and a basket of fruit. When Pagosh joined us under the garden canopy, Khary left off harvesting the leaves of a young willow and the girls flopped down on the grass beside the small table, to help themselves to a cake.

"Sit and ease your back, woman," Khary ordered my widowed aunt, whose joints now ache with age. "Otherwise, you will be waking me in the night again, begging for one of my magic potions."

"The stew should cook a bit longer," Nofret agreed, easing her ample buttocks down on the bench beside him, "time enough for one of Aset's stories." She motioned to Mata. "Bring some chips and a piece of charcoal from the fire." She looked to Aset. "Surely you have a new one to tell us, sweetie."

"Let me think," Aset mused, slipping the last of her sweet bread to Tuli while she waited for Mata to bring the limestone flakes Khary keeps to figure our accounts before he enters the sums on papyrus. Then she selected a piece of charcoal and began outlining a hound, a mastiff in all but his short legs.

"Reliable's mother and father were nomads who wandered across the plains and mountains, following their sheep. *Some* people would call them street dogs, I suppose, since they had no country to call their own." Pagosh gave me a wry smile, knowing she chided him for his poor opinion of her ill-begotten companion. "But they learned many things in their travels and grew very wise, so when they saw how fertile our Black Land is, they decided to settle down and raise a family."

"Reliable was the runt of their first litter. His legs were too short and his ears too big, but he never let any of his father's sheep get lost. That is how he got his name." She set the stone flake on the ground where we all could see what she had drawn. "Anyway, like his father before him, Reliable was the best herder in all the Two Lands. His highborn masters rewarded him well for his faithful service, and in time he even could wear a collar of gold." Working upside down, she drew a collar around the hound's neck. "But his lady wife was never able to give him children, and that made him very sad." Next she added tears below his eyes. Earlier, when Reliable's parents became wise, her voice had deepened. Now her mouth drooped at the corners. "His fur grew shaggy and his muzzle turned gray. Finally, hair began to sprout like wild wheat from his eyebrows and ears, causing him to look like a heron about to take flight, and everyone began to call him Old Reliable."

She picked up another chip and started a new drawing. "Then one day his eye fell on one of Tuli's cousins, a girl-dog named Northwind, a beautiful young thing with a coat the color of Aswan marble." This time the dog she drew was delicate of limb and demeanor, and walked upright on her shapely hind legs. "Reliable's other wife had gone to Osiris by then, so he made Northwind his wife—because she made him feel young and strong again. He gave her many wonderful gifts, and so the gods decided to let him have the child he had wanted for so long."

She drew an elaborate bead collar around Northwind's neck and a round disk dangling from her ear, with lines radiating out from it. Even without the hands ending each ray, no one could mistake the symbol of Aten. Nor, from the moment she mentioned the hair sprouting from his eyebrows and ears, did any of us doubt that Old Reliable was Ay—the onetime Master of the Horse to several "rich masters" who in the end succeeded them on the throne. Or that Ankhesenamen was Northwind, the constant breeze that enables our boats to navigate upstream against the current of the Nile, which I took for the royal hand that guides the course of the Two Lands.

"No hound could possibly reach such a great age without making many friends, and one was a cat named Bastet, a majestic beast with the bearing of a great lady. She was so beautiful, in fact, that the gods who created her were always arguing about whether they had given life to another god by mistake, rather than a *meow*. Though she was no longer young, her tawny fur hid her sharp bones, and her great yellow eyes and dainty pink tongue drew males the way honey draws bees." Aset set the third chip next to the other two. "One day when Bastet came to visit, Old Reliable decided to consult her about his wife, because Bastet had been a mother many times over and he believed her wise in the ways of females. His beloved was spitting up every bite of food she swallowed, until he feared she might vomit up his child." Aset met my eyes for the first time. "Tenre and Mena know better, of course, but Old Reliable thought Bastet might favor him with some secret spell known only to mothers, out of gratitude for all his years of loyal service."

She paused, making us wait while she added a few more lines. "So you can imagine what a terrible shock it was when Bastet told him the reason his lady wife sickened was that Northwind had allowed other hounds to mount her." Nofret caught her breath and inched forward on the bench, eager to learn the identity of the young Queen's lover, but Aset had sketched three playful puppies. One was a miniature Northwind, another resembled Reliable, and one looked like Tuli with a spotted coat.

"When his wife brought forth a spotted cur, every person in the Two Lands would know that Old Reliable was not the father of Northwind's puppies, Bastet told him, and advised him to send Northwind far away lest he risk being shamed."

"Old Reliable agreed?" Nofret guessed, anticipating Aset.

"At first he refused to believe her and even scolded Bastet for repeating such street gossip. But she told him she had seen North-wind and her lover in the very act of making puppies." She glanced at Nebet, then me. "Bastet is a natural hunter, you see, because her yellow eyes allow her to see in the dark." The next drawing showed Reliable and Bastet standing on their hind legs, swiping at each other with their front paws. "Old Reliable demanded that Bastet tell him the name of the traitor who dared mount his wife, but she refused. Instead she offered to come live with him in Northwind's place, out of fondness and respect for his age, and to save him from public embarrassment. All men everywhere would envy him then, she said, since the gods soon would make her one of them." She picked through the limestone chips, looking for a smooth one. "You will never guess what Old Reliable did then. He—" She paused, shook her head, and smiled to herself.

"What? Get on with it, girl!" Mena burst out, though he knows she does it on purpose to hold us in her hand.

"At first Bastet believed the thought of lying with her was simply too much for his old heart, for already he had suffered one blow—that Northwind's puppies were not his. But Old Reliable was laughing, so hard that tears began to run down his cheeks, and he could hardly get his breath." She paused to draw a few lines. "When finally he could speak again, Old Reliable gazed at her with his watery grandfather's eyes and said, 'You have waited too late, Bastet. It is my time now, after all the years of sitting on the banks of Mother River watching the others come and go in their magnificent pleasure boats. My place is assured, for whatever the color of Northwind's issue, the royal scribes will name them mine.' " The last piece of stone showed Old Reliable with a wide, satisfied smile. "And then he said something I thought very strange indeed. 'You forget that Northwind's children will carry the blood of *my* father no matter who fathers them, something I could never be sure of with you.' "

Amid the boisterous laughter and questions that followed, Mena leaned closer to tell me Pharaoh had received a message from Zarw that Horemheb would soon return to Waset. "He sent the Hittites running for Hattusas already?" I asked.

"Only to the Euphrates, though he loosed two entire regiments against a much smaller Hittite-Syrian force. Worse yet, while he marched over land with his troops, the thieving Myceneans stole into Ugarit and sailed off with his great new ship."

"What of Senmut?"

"He travels to Waset with the General." He paused to watch Nebet and Aset, who now sat kicking their feet in my garden pool. "It is not like Horemheb to be so careless about guarding his back. The need to get here before Osiris comes for his old mentor must be nagging him like a rotten tooth."

"What will he do when he hears about the Queen's condition?"

He shrugged, then a wry grin twisted Mena's generous mouth. "Have you seen her? I would not have believed Ay could keep word from leaking out for so long."

"Perhaps he worried that Horemheb would return with troops at his back," I suggested, never sure of my footing when it comes to palace intrigue.

"Why worry about a man in Canaan or Syria when Paranefer and his Sacred Council sit waiting just across the river, like a flock of hungry vultures? A month or more ago Sheri began regaling me with tales of how Pharaoh sips the nectar from a different flower in his harem every night. I thought she only painted suggestive pictures to heat my blood, for they did that. When finally I told her to cease lest I be tempted to acquire a few exotic blossoms of my own, I discovered it is not a subject my wife takes kindly to, even in jest. She suggested it would be a frivolous expense at best, since I cannot begin to match the old man's stamina, let alone his inventiveness— that he knows many ways to please a woman, not just two or three." He looked chagrined even in the telling. "I turned tail and sued for peace at once. Later I learned the stories came from two of the Queen's favorite Royal Ornaments, who serve as her companions. But after the story Aset just told us, I suspect he planted the stories just to make sure no one doubts the babe is his. Pharaoh is sixty-five, don't forget—an age when most men have lost the vigor to service a woman."

DAY 7, FOURTH MONTH OF PLANTING

Mena is a frequent visitor to my house in Waset on the days I go there to replenish my supply of medicaments, but Senmut's unannounced appearance sent Nofret scurrying to prepare a proper offering for our royal guest.

"I made the mistake of telling him about our map," Mena explained, barely able to contain his ingenuous smile. "He insisted on tagging along to see it for himself."

"Mena talks of little else, until he repeats himself like a feeble grandfather," Senmut shot back. Mena and I exchanged a grin, for it was apparent that more than Senmut's eyes and smile remain the same.

"We learned many things while you were away," I said, to whet his appetite. "This, for one." I grasped Mena's forearm, turned his hand back side up, and supported it level with mine. Then I applied my forefinger to a vessel that lies just under the skin, between the second and third fingers. As blood filled it the vessel began to bulge, but only in the direction of his fingertips. Toward the wrist it flattened and became less visible with each passing moment.

"He has no cut on his hand or arm through which the blood can run out?" Senmut asked. I shook my head. Mena held his tongue as well, for we tested ourselves now. "Unlike urine or feces, the blood does not demand out. Yet it appears to flow like a river," Senmut mumbled to himself, "so where does it go?" He glanced up. "That is the question, isn't it?"

I laughed only because his answer pleased me beyond measure. "Yes, but—"

"Show him the map," Mena said, so we went at once to my examining room, where I unrolled a long scroll. The idea to make a map of all the vessels that contain blood—only blood, not air or urine or anything else—was Aset's. But to locate them properly within the outline of the human form took all the notes and sketches Mena and I have made over the years, knowledge drawn from the bodies in the Per Nefer as well as the wounds we treated.

"It is only in the red vessels that we hear the voice of the heart," Mena pointed out, to explain why Aset had painted some vessels red and others blue. Senmut forestalled him with a raised hand, preferring to find his own way. First he traced a path with his forefinger, from the heart up into the neck and the brain, then from the heart to the groin and down a leg. "The *metu* that you painted red contain the bright red blood that spurts from a wound," he decided, still leaning over my table.

"They also have thicker and tougher walls," Mena added.

"While the blue ones are soft and carry the darker—"

"Tenre?" Aset called from the garden, just before she appeared in the doorway. "Paga has come to take me across the river." Her eyes came to rest on Senmut's back. "Oh, I am sorry."

I motioned her in. "This is Prince Senmut."

She put her palms together and bowed. "Are you the physician who returned with General Horemheb?" Senmut nodded, caught the full force of her bright blue eyes, and broke into a smile that has its own power to startle, simply because his black skin makes his teeth look so white. "My name is Aset," she murmured, returning his smile.

Something about the look they exchanged reminded me that it will not be long until her monthly bleeding begins. She has read about the changes taking place within her body, but Pagosh says she has been asking Merit the kind of questions only another woman can answer, such as what it feels like to have a man's penis enter her body. I do not worry that Merit will frighten her with the horrors some women experience at the hands of a brutal man, for Pagosh loves his wife with a tenderness I find rare among men, but I plan to instruct Aset in how to keep from getting with child, to assure that she will have some say in her own destiny. But whichever high-and-mighty lord her father chooses for her husband, I doubt it will be a Nubian prince—beautiful as he may be in her eyes.

Hoping to distract him, I pointed to the map. "This was Aset's idea."

"But sh—she is just a girl!" Senmut stammered.

Aset's eyes met mine. "My sister sends for me. I am to spend the night with her."

"Again?" I did not like it but could not tell her why. "Pagosh—"

She anticipated me. "You know he is not allowed into her private apartment, Tenre. No man is. Except Pharaoh." Her eyes flashed with mischief. "And you."

"Go on, then, but I must speak with your father if you continue to miss your classes. Perhaps he will want to hire a tutor to come here instead."

"Why not let her attend the palace school with Nebet?" Mena suggested.

"My lady mother already spoke to my father about it," she told him, news to me. "He said no daughter of his was going to be a Royal Ornament, to serve others." That, on the other hand, did not surprise me. "He fears they will teach me some ungodly heresy, though he knows I do not believe everything my teachers tell me. And I do not need any tutor but you, Tenre." She glanced at Senmut, all girlish innocence. "Not everyone is so fortunate, of course, so they still have much to learn, especially about girls!" She put her palms together and bowed to Senmut, then Mena and me.

Senmut waited until she was well away. "That is the daughter of the Heretic's Queen, the one whose name is forever on Nebet's tongue? Is she always so—"

"So what?" Mena inquired.

"Simple, I suppose. Transparent."

"As transparent as the Nile at full flood," Mena agreed, trying to keep a smile from giving him away. "Supposing our worldly friend ever manages to find his tongue in her presence, Tenre, how long would you give him before she ties it in knots?"

I pretended to give the question serious thought. "Two minutes at most. Less, if he encounters her and Nebet at the same time."

Senmut took our teasing with good humor, so I gave him a friendly push toward the door. "You must sample Khary's latest brew. It will make a man of you."

DAY 8, FOURTH MONTH OF PLANTING

I came up from my couch like a striking cobra to see a shadow jump back in alarm. In the same instant I recognized his form and muttered, "Have a care, my friend. The night may come when my heart stops just at the sight of you. What is it this time?"

"The Queen," Pagosh whispered. "Aset sends for you."

It was only then that I remembered she had gone to the palace. I leaped to my feet, grabbed my hip wrap from a nearby stool, and fastened it around me. "Does the Queen bleed?" I asked, and started to my examining room for my bag of medicines.

"Aset said only that she cannot rouse her."

I looked up at the clerestory windows. "Why try at this time of night?"

"I did not stop to ask, *sunu*." Every time he calls me that I feel a chill in my bones. "I warned Ramose," he continued, "but he cannot refuse her. The she-cat who gave her life puts more distance between them only to let him know who holds the reins."

By the time we reached the palace the half-formed suspicions that feed my dreams had blossomed into a fearful premonition. Every window and balcony glowed with light, while black tongues licked at the path across the courtyard—shadows cast by enough torches to light a royal procession. "If it is as I think," Pagosh murmured as we approached the Queen's apartment, "send her out and I will take her to the house of your friend, for she will need the arms of a real mother to hold her on course this night."

It did not surprise me to find Ankhesenamen's physicians clustered in her sleeping room, consulting their scrolls, while a trio of priests chanted prayers at the foot of her couch. She lay on her back with a white linen sheet covering her legs and the swell of her belly, leaving her small breasts exposed. As I pulled the insect netting aside I noticed a folded blanket across the foot of the her couch. Everything, it seemed, had been straightened and neatened, including the Queen.

I put two fingers to the base of her throat and found her already cool to the touch. Even so, I peeled back one eyelid to confirm what my fingers told me, then stared at her countenance in silence. As I did so, I heard the creaking harness of restless horses, then the muffled whistle from somewhere behind me, before Tutankhamen's Horus of the Sky came plummeting toward earth. My eyes burned with the salt of my tears as my heart cried out to the gods. How could Isis and Hathor allow one of their own to suffer such grievous hurts? Wasn't it punishment enough, whatever Ankhesenamen's sins, to lose one babe after another, then her young husband and, finally, her only son?

When my eyes cleared again I noticed the tiny red vessels crawling beneath the skin at the edge of her nostrils, and before anyone could stop me, I bent to examine the soft inner lining of her lower lip. There I found more tiny vessels engorged with blood—and felt the hair rise on the back of my neck.

Still the Queen's physicians continued to consult their scrolls, though they must have known that her *akh* had departed her body. Perhaps they sought to save her babe, I thought, and put my ear to her belly, followed by the open palm of my hand. I felt nothing but an overwhelming sadness.

"My sister has gone to Osiris?" Aset asked from across the Queen's couch, though she had been nowhere in sight when I arrived. I nodded. "Her babe, too?" I nodded again. "That is what I thought, but I told Pharaoh to wait for you if he wished to be certain." She spoke with the calmness of a wounded animal who faces his executioner with resigned acceptance.

I circled the royal couch and held out my hand, all I dared offer her in the presence of the priests, for I could tell the child in her was weeping even if the woman she was becoming held her tears in check. "Pagosh waits to take you to Nebet and Sheri." She let out a shuddering sigh as we left with Tuli at our heels, and only turned back for one last glimpse of her beloved sister as we passed from the room.

We were in the hallway leading to her sister's antechamber when a rustle of voices announced Pharaoh's coming, and every forehead touched the floor. A moment later he was upon us with his entourage of advisers trailing behind him.

He saw Aset and stopped. "So, little sister, your physician finally has arrived." Deep creases ran from his nose to the corners of his mouth, and white hair sprouted from his ears. Old Reliable. I met his eyes for the first time since the falcon hunt that ended with me holding a dying Tutankhamen in my arms. "Well, speak up, *sunu*. What about my son? Can you not at least save him?"

"I am sorry to be the bearer of more bad news, Majesty, but he passed through the reeds with the Queen. The babe would have been too small to live outside her body in any case."

"That is what the others said." He sighed, as if releasing his last hope of eternity. "But after all the tales our little sister spins about the magic you can perform, I expected more from you."

"It is not my doing, Majesty Grandfather, if you mistake wisdom for magic." I wished Aset would hold her tongue, for I wanted to be away from that place.

"Spoken like a true princess." A smile touched the old man's lips, and I saw that he indulged her out of affection. "But tonight changes everything, for you as it does for me. You would do well to stay far away from this place, for there is nothing to be found here but sorrow." He bent to scratch Tuli's ear, and when he straightened all softness was gone from his face. "But you will come with me, *sunu*. I have need this night of one who can distinguish between the smoke of illusion and a failing of the flesh."

DAY 9, FOURTH MONTH OF PLANTING

I went to Nebet's rooms first, where Tetisheri rose like a ghostly nimbus from a chair near the doorway. "Oh, Tenre," she whispered as she put her cheek to mine, "how my heart weeps for her. She holds Tuli so tight he can hardly breathe."

"Did she tell you anything?" I kept my voice low since the doorway to Nebet's sleeping room stood undraped.

"Only that you instructed her to wait for you here."

I nodded and stepped through the doorway. A shielded lamp

had been lit in a wall niche, and I saw that she lay with Tuli tucked into the curve of her body.

"Is that you, Tenre?" she whispered.

"I thought you were asleep," I said, smoothing the curls from her face as I squatted beside her. "Are you ready to go home?"

"Do I have to?" She sat up, dumping Tuli off on the floor. The dog trotted through the doorway, probably to go relieve himself, so I motioned for her to scoot over and sat on the couch.

"No. Where were you when I arrived at your sister's apartment?"

"Behind the curtain of that little alcove where we often played games, on a pallet her servingwoman fixed for me. Ankhes liked for me to stay nearby."

I enclosed one of her hands between both of mine. "Why were you trying to wake her in the night?"

"Tuli kept nudging me with his cold nose, and he doesn't do that unless—Ankhes always had to use the latrine in the night, and I thought she might have called me, or needed something. I found her lying all crooked, with Thutmose's blanket halfway over her face, so I pulled the blanket away. But I could not hear her breathe, even when I put my ear to her chest. I did shake her, but very gently."

"Where were her servingwomen?"

"Ankhes does not—did not—like to have anyone else in her room. She said their snoring kept her awake."

"You folded the blanket and laid it across her feet?"

She nodded. "I put my finger into her mouth, too, the way you taught me, so as not to push anything down her throat." She raised up to see my face in the dim light. "She was not breathing yet her heart spoke to me from the great vessel in the side of her neck, Tenre, truly, though I do not see how that could be." The anguish in her voice tore at my heart. "I was trying to decide what to do when it—it just stopped."

"Did you touch her anywhere else?"

"I turned her on her side and patted her back while one of her women went for the palace physician, so she would know someone was with her. Did I do something terrible?" So did she reveal the paralyzing fear that had taken hold of her, that she had in some unknown way sealed her sister's doom.

"I would have done the same. It may be that her heart grew weak from carrying the burden of a babe. I will ask Mena what he thinks, but you must go to sleep now. Sheri stays nearby, in the other room." I tried to comfort her with the touch of my hands as I urged her back down, then bent to brush her cheek with my lips. "I have seen many a physician lose his wits when confronted with such a situation. You did well."

"Truly?" she whispered, clasping my arm to hold me there.

"Truly," I replied without hesitation, for I did indeed speak the truth. Without warning she raised up to wrap her arms around my neck and gave in to the tears in her heart. I held her small body and stroked her back while she sobbed a stream of barely intelligible babble about the gods "taking everyone." As for the rest, I understood only a name here and there, including mine.

By the time Tuli returned, she had succumbed to exhaustion, so I signaled him to jump up beside her and covered them both. Afterward I stood watching her, wondering what she might have seen that she could not speak of it, even to me—and saw her pull him against her, needing even in sleep to be sure the gods did not take him, too.

When I joined them a few minutes later, Mena was reclining on the sitting shelf in his library while Pagosh paced about like a caged lion.

"Sit and refresh yourself," Mena invited, pointing to the persea fruits, dates, and breads on the table next to him, along with a carafe of wine and two empty goblets. I filled both of them and handed one to Pagosh.

"Well, did you learn how the dirty deed was done?" he muttered.

I told them all I had seen and let them chew on that while I did the same with a piece of bread.

"Aset denies that she saw anyone," Pagosh stated, "but I know better."

Mena leaped up like a man stung by a scorpion. "You saw someone go into the Queen's sleeping room? Why in the name of Set didn't you say so?"

Pagosh ignored him. "Aset has never been one to dissemble and so gives herself away when she does. She refuses to see what she cannot bear to know." He was right, and there was only one person she ever lied about, to herself as well as others. But I wanted to hear him say it.

"For Thoth's sake, spit it out!" Mena yelled, impatient with Pagosh's cryptic ways.

"She must have seen her mother," Pagosh said. Mena looked to me.

I nodded. "Aset found a blanket over the Queen's face, and I found a thread from that same blanket caught in the torn nail of her forefinger. There were other signs as well—engorged blood vessels in her nose and mouth—that something was used to cut off her breath, probably the blanket. In her condition it did not take long."

Pagosh turned his tired eyes away. "Poor little Ankhesenamen was safe so long as her mother believed she could bear only still-born babes. Then Tenre brought her son into this world alive . . ." He stopped, letting us draw our own conclusion.

I could not help wondering if Ramose had been in league with his lady. "Did her father know Aset had gone to stay the night with her sister?"

"I took her across the river on his orders, and the message asking for Aset came from the Queen, not her mother."

"So Nefertiti could not have known Aset would be there?"

Before Pagosh could answer, Mena turned to me and blurted out, "How far do you trust this man? Aset's eyes are blinded by love, but yours are not. Do not forget that he serves Ramose as well as his daughter."

Pagosh refused to meet my eyes, as if he feared that all the years we have conspired to the same purpose counted for nothing with me now, in the presence of my boyhood friend. I took my time, searching for the right words, and remembered the first time Pagosh had come to my door, his heart eaten by grief over the loss of his son. The child of his loins. And then that day almost four years later, when we fought Osiris for Aset's life—the child of his heart.

"I doubt there is anything Pagosh does not know about what I do or think," I told Mena, "yet I sleep like a babe, as he himself can attest."

"I only needed to be certain before I spoke." Mena motioned Pagosh to the stool beside me and reached for the carafe of wine.

"Nefertiti takes the advantage wherever she can find it, and used Ankhesenamen's message to the Hittites to gain favor with Ay—to put him in her debt."

"Aset tried to tell us what was going on," I recalled, too late. "Remember what Old Reliable said? 'It is my time now, after years of watching the others come and go in their magnificent feluccas.' "

"Now Pharaoh eats the fruit of his own arrogance," Pagosh put in, "for he has lost both Northwind and his chance to found a new royal family." He let out a sigh. "The Sacred Council will wait no longer."

"For what?" Mena inquired.

"To position themselves to claim the throne of Horus, what else?"

That brought Mena to his feet. "You can't be serious!"

"Thanks to Ramose, Amen holds more land now than before the Heretic stripped them of their fields and gold. But that does not mean they can never again be thrown into the streets like so much dung. For that there is only one way—to hold the throne themselves. Why else would Ramose ally himself with the Heretic's Queen?"

"But if Nefertiti already had what she was after with the priest," Mena argued, "why try to strike a bargain with Old Reliable?"

Pagosh shrugged in that detached way, which I know to be a false front. "She may have scented something rotten in the air, for the priests do not trust her and never will. Not so long as Akhenaten lives." That he evaded my eyes made me fearful that more disasters were yet to come. "That is why Ramose will put her away and take his own daughter for his wife."

The words fell like pebbles on the surface of a quiet pond, plummeting to the bottom of my soul. I heard Aset's voice as if from afar. "*Mahu says I am to be wife to a priest of Amen, even though I am not fully royal.*"

"May Osiris turn a deaf ear to Thoth first!" Mena cursed. "If her mother gets wind of this—and you are right about what happened to Ankhesenamen—Aset will be next!"

"Not if, when," Pagosh added. "The she-cat has more spies than Tuli has fleas."

I felt like a man swept away by the Inundation. That Ramose

might actually desire his daughter warred with the realization that I would rather it be him than any other priest. He, at least, took pride in her love of learning. An idea came to me then, a possible way out of an impossible dilemma.

"I have a plan," I said, "but we must act quickly." I looked to Mena. "Are you sure that Ay has no child to succeed him, even by one of his other women?"

"I asked Sheri the same question. She says not."

"Then we must give Nefertiti the weapon she needs to force Ramose to meet her demands, lest she reveal everything to Horemheb or the old Pharaoh."

"But that would give her even more reason to be rid of Aset," Mena objected.

"Not if we shape the weapon to our purpose," I told him. "We know the priests had no part in the death of Tutankhamen's son, or the Queen. Since Ankhesenamen was Nefertiti's daughter, the Sacred Council probably sees Horemheb's hand behind both deeds. So we must make sure Ramose learns the truth—that it was his wife who stole the breath from her own child and grandchild—and in that way come to realize that *his* daughter could be next."

"The question is, will Ramose believe it?" Mena asked, still in doubt.

"If he is told by someone he trusts," Pagosh assured him.

"Me," I said. "Ramose is sure to hear that I was called to the palace tonight. He will expect to hear what I learned there from my own lips. I will suggest that he send Aset away for a time, perhaps down the river to the priestesses of Hathor. When he asks why— and he will—I will tell him."

"And Nefertiti?" Mena asked. "Who will she believe?"

"Her servingwomen," Pagosh volunteered. "They consider my wife to be simple and so do not guard their tongues in her presence. Nor would it occur to them that she uses them to her own purpose."

DAY 3, FIRST MONTH OF HARVEST

Mena brought Senmut during the hours I receive the sick among Ramose's workers, to tell me something that could not wait, he said.

"On the plain near Kadesh," Senmut began, "I came upon a

fight that ended with one man stopping the breath of another." He glanced at Mena. "Has the General always distributed *kat* leaves to his men before a siege?"

Mena nodded. "A practice he learned from your people, who believe it gives them the strength of a god."

"What it does is make them forget they cannot fly with the falcons, so they go into battle without the fear that makes men cautious. I suppose it could have been the *kat,* but his heart still spoke in the big vessel below his ear. I thought he might start breathing again, but after a few moments his heart slowed and then stopped." Mena and I exchanged a look. "Are you going to tell me—" Senmut started, when a scream rent the quiet morning, followed by the furious yelping of a small dog.

Senmut rushed for the door with me right behind him. We followed our ears to the brewery, then through the narrow passageway between it and the breadmaker's rising shed, where we came upon an old lean-to. A Nubian shaman stood before the rags draped across one end, jabbing at Tuli with a long stick. Barking and snarling all the while, the dog darted in and out, trying to sink his teeth into the black man's leg.

Senmut sent the old man sprawling, scattering cowrie shells and animal teeth in every direction, and pushed his way through the rags. I signaled Tuli to stand guard over the shaman and followed Senmut inside, where a sputtering oil lamp cast flickering shadows across the face of an old Nubian hag. In her gnarled fist she held a sharpened piece of flint, which she waved at us in an eerie kind of greeting.

"Old Nanefer knows how to put her right, you'll see," she rasped, heedless of the blood dripping from her knife. "It is the worm disease that keeps her from becoming a woman." Two younger Nubians kneeled on Aset's shoulders to capture her hands, while two other women held her legs spread wide.

"Please make her stop," Aset pleaded in a pitiful voice. I knocked aside the two women who pinned her arms while Senmut pushed the Nubian hag out of the way and took her place between Aset legs. Rising as best she could, Aset clung to my neck as sobs shook her body. Torn between wanting to see what the old crone had done and the need to comfort her, I put my lips to her hair.

"Hush, *meri*, hush. She will not touch you ever again, I promise. And Senmut will make it right, whatever she has done." I had no way to know if I spoke the truth except when I called her beloved.

Senmut lashed the old crone in her native tongue, his voice harsh with anger, while Mena drove the other women from the hut, cursing them and the man outside. When I slipped my arm under her knees Aset stiffened with pain, causing my entire body to shake with such rage that I almost dropped her.

Ruka came running as we crossed the courtyard, his face contorted with worry and fear. "Is she hurt bad? Please Amen, don't let it be bad. Is it, Tenre?"

I ignored his question. "Have you seen Pagosh?"

"He takes the Consort to the God's Father across the river."

I saw it all then. When Nefertiti learned of the High Priest's plan to set her aside, she knew the priests had beaten her at her own game—to use Ramose to regain the throne. They had used *her* instead, to beget a granddaughter of the Magnificent Amenhotep, intending all along to discard Nefertiti when the time was right. And knowing from experience what her husband desired most from a woman—that the fire in her body burn as hot as the one she lit in his—she had arranged his punishment to fit his crime.

"Stay by the watchman's gate," I told Ruka, as we passed through the gate to my garden, "and send Pagosh to me the moment he returns."

I laid Aset on my examining table and turned to Senmut. "Say what you need."

"Water and the oldest wine you've got. Also some olive oil. Soft cloths that have been dried in the hot sun."

"Anything else?" He would know what I meant.

"She is bleeding too much to tell for certain, but it appears the old crone sliced away only a piece of the inner labia." I nodded and hurried to gather what he needed while Mena stood with one hand on her shoulder, stroking her tousled curls. Afterward I stood holding her hand, but try as I might, I could not blind myself to the visions that formed behind my eyes. With them came a desire for revenge so overwhelming that I could actually taste it—the sweet ambrosia that drives a man to maim or kill.

"All will be well," Senmut murmured, so low I was not sure she heard him. "The wound will quickly heal. A few days of tenderness and some burning when she urinates, both easily treated. As for the other—" He glanced at me and shrugged.

"What does he mean?" Aset whispered, begging me with her eyes.

"If you want more than her body to heal," I told him, "you must tell her everything, what you do and why." He cocked an eyebrow, questioning the wisdom of that, but he does not know her as I do. To let what the old woman did to her stay hidden in darkness would allow it to fester like a putrid sore.

"I pour sour wine on the wound to clean it," Senmut told her.

"I want to know what she did to me."

"A woman is made like a flower, and little harm is done by taking only a petal away. It is the bud in the center that is the seat of pleasure for a woman."

Aset turned her head toward me. "I read nothing of that in your scrolls."

"Perhaps the physicians in the House of Life did not find it a seemly topic."

Next Senmut described how she must treat her raw flesh. "The oil will keep it supple and also prevent the cut edges from growing together. A scar does not stretch, so you must clean yourself with warm water several times a day and apply more oil." He paused. "Do you know why we want it to be able to stretch?"

"To allow a babe to pass through?" she guessed.

"Also, when the time comes, for your husband's penis to penetrate your body without hurting you. There is little pleasure to be found in pain, for you or him, unless—"

"I know about men who take pleasure in causing pain, or in suffering it." She showed no embarrassment in talking of what most women do not discuss even with their husbands. "But Tenre never told me—"

"Told you what?" I asked. She shrugged, avoiding my eyes.

I watched him sprinkle finely sieved wheat flour over her wound to stop the bleeding. Then he came to face Aset and squatted in order to bring his eyes level with hers. "In the land of Punt and also some places in my own country, it is the practice to cut the young girls before their monthly flow begins. Why?" He shrugged. "The reasons differ, but are passed from mother to daughter, generation after generation. In Kush, where that old woman is from, they say a girl who is small for her age cannot grow because of a worm, so they cut away her female parts to release the worm and make her able to conceive a child. But you are no ignorant tribeswoman to believe such rubbish."

Aset searched his face. "Don't the women in your country learn to read or write?" He shook his head. "Would *you* want a woman like that for your wife?"

He smiled for the first time. "Before a week was out I would be forced to banish such a woman from my house, bringing the wrath of her father down on my head."

She returned his smile. "I begin to understand why Nebet holds you in such high regard. She even insists you will be the equal of Tenre, one day, as a physician, I mean." She brought my hand over her lips, perhaps to hide from him that she was teasing. "But you can never ever hope to rival the wisdom of her father." I knew then that she was whole again, and glanced at Mena to find him grinning like a fool.

By then Senmut was, too. So his education continues, as does hers.

DAY 14, SECOND MONTH OF HARVEST

Re was sailing toward the western cliffs when I started back from the village of Ramose's fellahin. It wasn't until I encountered a line of pickers coming in from the orchard where the vines grow between the trees that I realized the wine making had begun. Soon I could hear the racket of clapping sticks mingled with singing and laughter, sounds of merriment that reminded me of the times I went to my grandfather's vineyard as a child. There my cousins and I would jump into the big stone vats to tromp on the grapes while our mothers and fathers, aunts and uncles, clapped out the rhythm with wooden hands. I hurried my step, eager to relive those happy days even as a spectator, and was barely through the gate in the wall when I spotted Aset in one of the vats—holding to Ruka's arm to keep from slipping down while she stomped to the beat.

The sight brought a smile to my heart, for she wore only a loin-cloth, like the boys, with the point pulled between her legs and tucked under at the waist. How much she has changed since her tenth feast day! Her hips and thighs grow rounder and softer while her face thins, bringing out her cheekbones and strong jaw. In that way she resembles her mother more every day. Only her eyes remain the same—so transparent a blue that the light of her *akh* shines forth from within.

I moved closer and joined in the clapping, to blend in with the others who crowded around, and saw her look up at Ruka and laugh. I felt my heart swell with regret that this might be her last chance for such childish abandon. Then I happened to glance around at the crowd, and saw a figure on the roof of Ramose's villa. My breath quickened with dread, for he has always denied her the company of his workers' children. Yet now, when he saw her consorting with them in the lowest way, baring her budding breasts for all eyes to see, I stood like a dumb ox—until Pagosh nudged me.

"Ramose awaits you in his pleasure garden," he mumbled for my ears only. "Bastet has him by the balls and begins to squeeze." We dropped back from the others, pretending a nonchalance neither of us felt. "He sends Aset away but not to the priestesses of Hathor. She goes to the harem of a rich noble instead." My heart leaped into my throat, making me gasp for breath, but when I turned to question him he shook his head, warning me off. Then he disappeared into the crowd, probably to keep watch on Aset.

I found Ramose staring into his lotus pond. He has changed little over the years, though it would not show had his hair gone pure white. The same can be said of his true motives, which is why I trust him no more now than I did before.

"Do you have a friend you would trust with all you possess, Senakhtenre, even your life?" he asked when I drew near.

I learned long ago to be wary of priests who sidle up to a subject, wrapping their true meaning in a veil of innuendo or mystery, so I told him what he already knew. "I have been fortunate, indeed, my lord, for my father was such a friend to me. And Mena."

"To think I once believed I knew all there was to know about you!" He shook his head, but his eyes crinkled at the corners, as if he made light of his own naïveté. "I do not try to trick you into tripping over your own tongue, Tenre. It is only that I must find the answer to a question. The right answer. For what I decide here and now will weigh heavily in the decision of Osiris and his judges, when my time comes to face them." He turned to me. "The question is, can I trust you with a treasure that is dearer to me than all the gold in Nubia, no matter what direction the wind may blow in the months ahead?"

"Probably not," I replied, for I would use whatever riches he entrusted to me to protect his daughter, even from him. "I am like any other man, my lord, in some ways stronger than others but in other ways weaker than most."

"Sometimes, *sunu*, I see too much of you in my daughter," he mumbled under his breath. "She, too, knows how to disarm with honesty."

"I beg your forgiveness if I gave offense." My deviousness lacks the refinement that comes with practice, while repentance is a well-worn habit.

He shook his head. "It is just that, in a world filled with self-seeking men, you become a master of obfuscation simply by speaking the truth. Perhaps one day before the water of our time in this world runs out, you and I will have the luxury of engaging in a real battle of wits. For now I must be content with the evidence before my eyes—my daughter, who I trust above all others . . . even my god." I could not have uttered a word had my life depended on it. "I, too, have a friend like your father," he continued. "He is old now, yet he loves me still, and I him. So Aset will become his Second Wife—"

"But she has not yet begun her monthly flow," I protested, raising my voice over the sudden pounding in my ears, for I cared little if my skull should split open if only the gods would allow me to live long enough to find another way.

"That is of no importance to him, and I do what I must to keep her safe. After the episode with the old Nubian—" He raised his hand to forestall any more objections. "It is done. The contract has been signed." I wanted to rip the tongue from his mouth. "You have served her well, my friend." He looked me in the eyes. "You are that, Tenre, are you not?"

I knew then that we had arrived at the crux of the matter. "I have tried to be, though I admit there were times when I went against your instructions. But not what I believed to be your true intent—that I keep her *ka* whole as well as her body."

His mouth relaxed in a wry smile. "Thank Amen I was right about one thing at least." Again he held my eyes. "What I ask of you now could cost you dearly, Tenre. More perhaps than you are willing to give. If so, I will not question your decision, but will do all I can to help you rise to the top rung of the ladder, if that is your wish."

"Then cease torturing me and get to it."

"The friend I send her to is both generous and wise, but he is old. Aset must disappear for a while, yet I cannot bear to coop her up with his unmarried daughter and two sisters, who are simple at best. Could she go to your house in town once her presence in Uza-hor's harem has been established?" The words began to flow from him like water from an upended shaduf. "Surely Merit could change her appearance so no one would be the wiser, perhaps by cutting her hair like that of an apprentice?"

"Or the man who manages my dispensary," I suggested, falling in with his plan. "What about Pagosh? And Merit."

"They will take up residence in her husband's villa. Aset must appear there from time to time, so her husband can show her to his friends, but her dowry will be available to you through his factor. Use it to add a room to your house, hire servants, or whatever you require. Ipwet and her son would take up service in your household, I am sure." So he already knew that Aset befriended his workers.

"Pagosh has agreed?"

"It was his idea. See that Tuli stays inside your walls and then she will, too." He seemed intent on plugging whatever holes I might find in his plan.

"Won't her new husband object to such an arrangement?"

Ramose shook his head. "He does this for me, no other reason." I was skeptical, but I had no other choice, so I followed him to his big house, where he motioned me though the door ahead of him. "Pagosh was to bring her to my library."

Aset jumped up as we entered the room, as if she had been caught doing something she was not supposed to. Which she had. "Tenre! I thought you went—?"

"We have been discussing your schooling," Ramose told her. "But let Pagosh bring us a cool drink first. Then we will talk."

"I will help him," she volunteered, and ran after him. She had slipped on a short tunic, which did not hide her juice-stained ankles.

When they returned Ramose told her what she needed to know and no more. "But why do I have to be Uzahor's wife?" she protested.

"Because your lady mother says it is time. And to put you under his protection by law, in case something should happen to me."

"But if Tuli can come with me to Tenre's, why not Paga and Merit?"

"So everyone thinks you remain with Uzahor." Pagosh never said a word, though I suspect his heart was in tatters. "You leave tomorrow, and will stay there until the tongues of the gossips find a new tale to wag about."

When she glanced at me, it was all I could do to nod. "Then I better help Merit pack our things, if we are to be ready when Re-Horakhte appears."

"As you wish," Ramose agreed, "but first I must have your word that you will do as Tenre says in all things, not just your studies."

"Only if he will answer my questions as before." I recognized that for what it was, a brave face to hide her fear.

Ramose nodded. "Also you will speak to no one of this."

"I have to tell Tuli so he will understand why he must stay within Tenre's walls."

A smile lit Ramose's blue eyes. "Tuli, but no one else." He went down on one knee. "Come here." Aset went to him and clasped her arms around his neck. "I will miss you, my little Nile goose," he murmured into her hair. "Now leave us in peace."

"That is all?" she asked, as he set her away. "Did you not see my feet?"

"I noticed, just as you intended." I saw the smile he tried to hide. So did Aset.

Later Pagosh told me Ramose took pleasure in informing Nefertiti that it was her history of consorting with the priests of Aten that tainted their daughter, making it impossible to find any man willing to accept Aset as more than a minor wife.

"But the bitch is not done. She must be sure the High Priest will deny Horemheb the throne, and cannot wait until the old Pharaoh's clock runs dry. That means Paranefer will be next."

I begin to understand Pagosh's constant state of restrained fury, since I, too, taste the bitterness of a truth I have long denied—my own helplessness. Not to prevent the disasters decreed by the gods, but by mortal men . . . and one woman.

THIRTEEN

Kate hit the city limits of Houston around four-thirty and let several exits go by before she took one, then followed the access road until she came to a service station. The pay phone was set out away from the pumps, so she steered straight for it, turned off the motor, and dug in her purse for a coin. Then she rolled down the window so that Sam could stick his nose out and told him to "stay." By the time she punched in the number at the clinic, her heart had jumped into her throat.

"Imaging Center."

"This is Kate McKinnon. Is Dr.—"

"Can you hold please, Miss McKinnon?" Kate assumed the receptionist had someone on another line. If Max was tied up, she'd just leave a message, then get a map and cruise around on her own, maybe find a motel where they would allow dogs.

"Kate?" He sounded out of breath. "Are you all right? Where the hell have you been?"

"What? Sorry, the traffic is kind of noisy." He repeated it, louder. "Oh. Northern New Mexico, the Red Land. That's what the Egyptians called the desert. It seemed appropriate at the time."

"I called your house every couple of hours until Christmas Eve. Then I tried Cleo, figured you were over there. But I couldn't get her until Christmas Day. Why didn't you come here like we planned?"

"I'm here now."

A stunned silence. "Where?"

"Uh, wait a minute." She leaned away from the phone so that she could see the street sign. "Corner of Voss and Eye-Ten."

"Why the hell didn't you say so?" he exploded.

"I thought I'd better call, see if you were even in town."

"I'll be there in ten minutes. Fifteen at most. Don't move, okay?"

"Yes, except, well, is it all right if I let Sam out of the car to—you know?"

"Not funny, Mac." He hung up and Kate went back to her car, snapped Sam's leash to his collar, and let him drag her toward a patch of tired grass.

"Can you believe this weather?" she commented to Sam. "Feels like we're on a different planet from that windy mesa where we almost froze to death. But he didn't sound too happy, so when Max gets here we better be on our best behavior. Otherwise it'll be back on the road for us . . . unless I decide to stick around long enough to look for a job. Might as well, since I'm here, if I can think of some way to keep anyone from contacting my last employer."

It seemed only a few minutes before she heard the squeal of tires and looked around to see a gray Mercedes brake to a stop about twenty feet away. Sam started barking as the driver's door swung open, then lunged at the leash with the strength of his namesake. Kate let go and he tore off, too excited to slow down before crashing into Max's legs.

"Okay, boy, take it easy," Max said as he ruffled the dog's fur, then let Sam kiss him on the chin while he grabbed for the leash.

Kate stayed where she was, trying to read his face as he came toward her. When he was still a couple of feet away, he stopped and just looked at her. Then, in what couldn't have been a practiced greeting, he stepped closer and wrapped his arms around her. It wasn't the breezy cheek-to-cheek embrace she'd seen at museum fund-raisers, but a real, honest-to-God hug—as if he needed to confirm physically what his eyes were telling him. She knew then that something had changed between them, even if she wasn't sure how or what that might mean.

"I haven't had a decent sleep in days," Max confessed. "Kept seeing a little red car mashed flat between a couple of eighteen-wheelers." He stepped back then, to confront her. "I know you don't owe me anything, but—"

"Yes, I do," she whispered.

"I didn't mean the scan."

"Neither did I." What she owed him was an explanation. The truth, even if it hurt. It had taken a couple of days for the anger and humiliation to dissipate under the vast expanse of blue sky and red cliffs, eroded by eons of time, and for her to realize that she had reacted like a child, without considering anyone but herself. "I wasn't thinking very straight. I was angry, mostly at myself. Felt guilty."

"Why, for God's sake?"

"For letting us both down—you and me. This isn't the first time I've failed at something I really cared about." Admitting it was a risk she now felt compelled to take, a kind of vow she had made to herself . . . and Sam. "Before, it always helped to get away and be alone for a while, to try to get things back on an even keel. Except this time I wasn't really alone. Sam and I spent three whole days up on a mesa without any other human beings in sight. It was so clean up there, under that vast expanse of unsullied blue with fresh snow all around us. And still. A quiet so profound it made you wonder if you'd gone deaf. Except I have reason to know I'm not." His eyes never left her face, even with Sam tugging on the leash. "I don't mean to make it sound like an epiphany or anything, but something happened while I was on that mesa. Maybe it was just the place, but I guess—like Camus said—'in the depth of winter I finally learned that within me lay an invincible summer.' Anyway, Sam and I decided to come on to Houston even if it was a couple of days late."

A smile started in his eyes as he lifted a hand to skim away the strand of hair blown across her eyes by the balmy Gulf breeze. "I've got a fenced yard full of squirrels for Sam, a case of red wine laid in especially for you, and a freezer loaded with steaks. I might even let you wear your old sweats if you promise not to make a habit of it. No strings attached."

Without warning, her eyelids began to burn with incipient tears, and she reached for a joking reply. "That's what I was afraid of."

The smile reached his lips. "Sam can ride with me if he wants."

Kate followed him through a residential section, then past a neighborhood shopping center and the Rice stadium. A couple of blocks farther on, Max turned into a street canopied by huge live-oak trees, obviously one of the older—and better—parts of town. When he turned into the driveway of a Tudor half-timber with a peaked roof, Kate realized she'd been expecting something less traditional or at least not so formal.

A gate to one side of the house swung open, and she followed him back to a three-car garage with living quarters above it. Max was out of his car even before she stopped, and then Sam was racing across the grass in hot pursuit of a gray squirrel. She took it all in at a glance—the tall pines and shrubs edging the backyard, the solid wood fence that acted as a noise filter, and the fenced-in tennis court. What caught and held her eyes, though, was the swimming pool with a lily pond at one end, set at a slightly higher level so that a thin stream of water would trickle into the pool.

"Lilies are sort of a hobby," Max explained as she moved toward the purple-blue buds jutting up from the spreading flat circles of dark green. "That particular color is a hybrid I've been experimenting with for a couple of years."

Kate just nodded, accepting that some things were simply meant to be. Tashat. And now Max's fascination with the plant the Egyptians called a lotus. One with blue flowers. The color of the sky. Azure, a word derived from lapis lazuli, the blue stone prized by pharaohs and commoners alike.

He waited until she had her fill of looking, then led her toward the back door. "This is the kitchen," he explained unnecessarily, "but we could cook outside tonight if you want. You might even want to take advantage of the weather to take a dip and get the kinks out. The water's heated, but January can be pretty unpredictable." That he sought refuge in the weather at least told her he wasn't used to inviting a woman to stay at his house.

As she followed him up the stairs, he even swung around to apologize for how dark the house was, because of all the trees. "That's why I thought you'd prefer the yellow bedroom." Two windows looked out over the backyard, reflecting light onto the opposite wall of built-in closets and drawers. An arched opening beyond the queen-size bed revealed a mirrored dressing alcove and bathroom, also bright yellow.

"Nice," she commented, wondering why, if he thought the house was dark, he hadn't replaced the old-fashioned windows with floor-to-ceiling glass. Certainly he could afford to, judging by the neighborhood and that new Mercedes. Imaging machines weren't cheap, but with scans costing four to six hundred dollars a pop they quickly paid themselves out, especially in a group practice. And anything to do with the brain commanded the highest fees, which probably put him in the multihundred-thousand-dollar income bracket. Like a teenager suddenly aware that she's dressed all wrong, Kate felt acutely out of place, which only brought home how little she really knew about Maxwell Cavanaugh.

"The house belonged to my parents. I moved into the apartment above the garage when I came back from Ann Arbor. My father had died several years before and my mother was undergoing chemotherapy for breast cancer, so I wanted to be close. After she died I just stayed on." He shrugged. "It's convenient to my office and the Medical Center." As if that explained everything, he turned to leave. "I can loan you a T-shirt and shorts if you didn't bring a suit."

"I did, in case I got lucky on a motel with an indoor pool."

After a few laps in the pool followed by a relaxing bath in the yellow tub, Kate joined Max on the patio, where Sam lay stretched out with his head on his paws, keeping one eye on the fire. "What can I do to help?"

"The coals are just about ready, and I'm almost through with the salad. Don't want to overdo on the lettuce." The corners of his eyes crinkled with humor. "Think it's too cool to eat outside?"

"Not for me." She followed him to the kitchen, accepted the place mats and silverware he handed her, and carried them out to the glass-topped patio table. Max followed her with glasses and a bottle of wine, then spread the coals and laid the steaks on the grill. Afterward he settled into the lounge chair next to hers and for a minute they sipped and exchanged comments about the wine, but Kate could feel him waiting.

"Did you talk to Dave?" she asked, wanting to get it over with.

He nodded. "Paranoid bastard claimed you and Cleo were trying to make him look the fool. I told him he was doing a damned good job of that on his own and didn't need any help from you or anyone else. I also called him an ass for letting his ego blind him to what he had and he ought to be down on his knees begging you to come back."

"You actually said that?" He nodded without looking at her and drank some wine, as if he were embarrassed.

Kate was trying not to dwell on what might have been, but the sense that she'd failed was still there—one more disappointment she would have to learn to live with even if it hadn't paralyzed her as it always did before. She began to talk, and in the end gave him a blow-by-blow description of everything that had happened. Max listened without comment until she finished, then got up to turn on the lights in the pool. "What a jerk!" he muttered as he went to check the steaks, then sat back down on the side of his lounge chair, facing her. "Did you get any pictures of the finished head?"

She nodded. "I haven't stopped long enough to get them developed, but I took an entire roll, from the front, back, and in profile, with different wigs. One short and curly, the other long with tiny braids like those two wooden figures in the museum, from the same period. Isis and Hennuttab, daughters of the Sun King."

"I thought Akhenaten's daughters—"

"Not Akhenaten. His father, Amenhotep the Third, Egypt's Dazzling Sun. How I wish you could have seen her." She hesitated. "I think someone *did* try to kill Tashat, Max, but not for the reason Cleo dreamed up. Only she didn't die right away, maybe because of that other *sunu*, the one who's walking beside her on the road to eternity."

"Could be. I doubt she would have lived long enough for primary callus to form without someone at least trying to treat her."

"A physician back then was supposed to examine the patient and consult his handbook before pronouncing his verdict, to treat or not to treat. If the outcome looked hopeless, he was to do nothing. He also wasn't supposed to deviate from the teachings of the medical scrolls, and could be called before the Bureau of Pharaoh's Physicians for malpractice if he did. Maybe this physician put himself in double jeopardy, first by deciding to treat her at all, and then by *how* he treated her, if it wasn't in the scrolls. The question is, did punishment ever include death?"

Max forked the T-bones onto a platter and motioned her toward the table. Once seated he cut the tails off both steaks and set them aside for Sam. Then, while she helped herself to salad, he refilled their glasses. "Have you thought about what you're going to do next?"

"Look for a job." She gave Sam an affectionate smile. "Have to keep the ravening beast supplied with crunch."

"I ran into a professor at UT a week or so ago who's looking for someone to do illustrations for a textbook. Houston is bulging at the seams with medical schools and hospitals, but not illustrators like you. He was complaining about how all anybody can do now is computer-generated stuff. I could give him a call, see if he's still looking."

"It's nice of you to offer, Max, but I didn't come here to impose—"

"Look, let's get something straight. An orthopedic surgeon I know needs a medical illustrator and you happen to be one of the best. Maybe *the* best. For me to call and ask if he's found anyone yet is no big deal. And just because I can give you some names to contact about a job doesn't mean I'm trying to push you into anything. Maybe you just need time to think. Whatever you decide is fine with me, and I'm going to do what I need to whether you're here or not. So you can forget about imposing. You can't leave Sam cooped up in some flea-bitten motel, so stay here as long as you want or need to. Got that?" He waited for her to nod.

"Okay. So what are we going to do about Tashat?"

For the past three months Kate's every thought had been driven by the need to rescue Tashat from oblivion—to somehow make it matter that she had ever lived. To do that she needed to find out not only who she was but what happened to her. And why. So she hadn't really failed, she just wasn't finished.

"Start over," she answered without hesitation. "Follow every lead, turn over every stone." The laughter in his eyes told her she hadn't let him down, either.

He nodded. "Good. Now eat."

She did, but a sense of lightness so unexpected and unfamiliar that she couldn't help wondering where it had come from made her want to laugh, too. Partly it was relief. It also had to do with the fact that Max had actually been worried. About her.

He caught her watching him. "What?"

"Do you really think I might be *the* best?"

"Easily." He teased her with his eyes. "But I'll withhold final judgment until I see those photographs."

Kate woke to a blinding yellow light and realized she'd gone to bed with the drapes open. Sam was gone, so she threw back the covers and went to the window. The surface of the pool glistened undisturbed under the early-morning sun, and just the sight of that lush green grass made her toes itch.

A few minutes later she crept out the bedroom door, face scrubbed and teeth brushed, hoping Sam wouldn't hear her and wake Max. As she reached the bottom of the stairs, the dog came bounding out of a room a little way beyond and she bent to fondle his ears. That was when she realized Max was talking on the phone, so she motioned for Sam to go outside with her.

In the backyard she peeled off her sweats and dived in, surfaced and then struck out for the far end, where she did an underwater flip and headed back the way she'd come, holding to a steady rhythm of stroking and breathing. She could feel her brain begin to take up oxygen, lap by lap, until some noise made her lift her eyes out of the water. She saw Max first, then Sam, barking like a fool.

"What's up?" she gasped, letting the water smooth her hair back from her face.

"Time to get this show on the road. We've got to take your film to be developed, go by my office, and get to the Health Sciences Center by eleven."

"I can fix my own breakfast, Max, and take the film. Just leave me a map, if you have one."

"Uh-uh." He extended a hand to pull her out of the water. "Appointment at Health Sciences is yours, not mine."

"The friend who's looking for an illustrator?"

"Nope. I did talk to him, though, and he wasn't a bit happy

when I said you were busy today and would call him tomorrow. Think he's worried you may get away."

"I didn't bring anything but a few drawings of Tashat, but a freelance assignment *would* help tide me over while I look for a full-time job." She wrapped the towel around her waist as they started toward the house. "So who is this mysterious appointment with?" Max shook his head. "You don't know or you're not going to tell me?"

"Can't. Better for you to see for yourself." Sam ran ahead and jumped against the screen door, making it bounce open, then stuck his nose in to keep it from closing. "Smartest dog I've ever known," Max mumbled as he held the door for her. "Have you considered going into business for yourself? I'll bet you'd have all the work you could handle once word got around, probably get commissions from all over, not just Houston. You'd have flexible hours and a lot more freedom to pick and choose, not to mention more money. All you'd have to invest in is a computer to access whatever databases you need, a printer, and maybe a scanner."

"How much would all that cost?" She had been toying with the idea since she first went to Denver, but hadn't been able to convince herself that she could get work on a regular enough basis to pay her monthly bills, let alone save for an emergency.

"A couple of thousand. Depends on how much memory you need." He glanced at his watch. "I can show you mine, but later. Right now you better get dressed."

As they drove down Main Street, Max began to name the buildings that made up the Medical Center, on their left. "Women's Hospital first, Hermann Hospital behind that, then Ben Taub, where all the stabbings and gunshots end up." Next were several gray, multistoried buildings, each indistinguishable from its neighbor. "Diagnostic Center Hospital," he continued, "Houston International, UT, and St. Luke's, all about as sterile on the outside as they are inside." He stopped for the light at a busy intersection, then continued for a couple blocks before turning into the driveway of a Spanish-style one-story building set back from the street. Screened by a grove of trees and shrubs, it had the appearance of a large private residence. Except for the sign out front.

Max drove around to the back of the South Main Imaging Center and pulled into an empty parking space near the door. "I'll just wait here—" Kate began.

He was shaking his head before she finished. "Marilou wants to meet you, the voice on the phone."

Kate opened the car door and was struck again by the soft, almost tropical air, too warm for most of the clothes she had brought. Her choice had been further narrowed by the mysterious UT appointment, which called for something conservative, so she'd opted for her fringed black wool skirt because it was sedate but short enough not to be too hot, and a red-and-white-striped men's shirt, plus shadowy black hose and black suede flats.

Max guided her down a long hallway to the reception desk, a counter facing both the waiting room and "inner sanctum" presided over by a tall woman with short, flaming red hair—an exotic flower in full bloom. She glanced up as they approached and stopped talking in mid-sentence.

"My God, I think she's actually gone speechless," Max whispered.

A brilliant smile transformed the woman's entire face. "Kate McKinnon, I presume." She stuck out her hand. "I'm Marilou Bobbitt. We've talked on the phone." Her West Texas twang sounded so incongruous coming from such a striking-looking woman that Kate could hardly keep a straight face.

Kate nodded. "I recognize your voice. No wonder Max is so relaxed about his practice, with you to protect his virtue."

Marilou flashed Max a raised eyebrow, then gave Kate an openly reappraising look. "I see now why he went into decline when you slipped the hook."

"Why don't you make yourself useful around here for a change," he suggested to Marilou with a grudging smile. "Introduce Kate to Aaron and Jose for me while I make a couple of phone calls." He touched Kate's shoulder as he edged past her. "I won't be long, but watch your step. That hair's not red for nothing."

Kate laughed, envious of the easy give-and-take between them, which had to be based on more than familiarity. Max's "Girl Friday" looked to be in her early forties, but there was something so engaging about her earthy friendliness that as they walked in the opposite direction Kate felt free to ask the one thing she really wanted to know.

"Your hair is naturally curly, isn't it?" Marilou nodded. "Then would you mind telling me how you keep it from going crazy in this humidity?"

Marilou glanced at Kate's wildly curling hair. "Believe me, honey, it's all in the cut. I had the same trouble when I first came here, until I found a wizard with a scissors. He's expensive, but so are all the others who don't know doodly-squat about how to cut hair. Would you like his number?"

"Sure, why not?"

Marilou rapped on the molding of a doorway that opened into a control room situated between two scanners, where a man in a white coat sat at one of the consoles. "Brought someone to meet you," she told him. "The infamous Kate McKinnon." Marilou turned to Kate. "This is Aaron Krueger, head honcho in the T and A department."

"Kate," he acknowledged as he unfolded his tall, slim frame. Fair-skinned, with gray eyes and graying hair, he had a receding hairline that made him look ten years older than Max. "Don't mind her," he advised, rolling his eyes at Marilou. "What she meant is that I do mostly interventional radiology with breast and prostate cancer patients." He hardly paused. "Did you bring any photographs of that head?"

"We just left the film to be—"

"Where is she?" a deep bass voice called from the hallway.

"The Third Musketeer," Aaron mumbled for Kate's benefit.

"You're the famous Kate McKinnon?" Max's other partner asked from the doorway. A short, compact bundle of energy with a shock of wavy black hair, Jose Carrasco had the thick chest and shoulders of an athlete—a prophetic assessment on Kate's part since she learned later that he specialized in sports injuries.

Kate smiled at Marilou. " 'Infamous' is the word, I believe." She remembered Max telling Dave that he'd shown some of the X-ray images to his partners, but apparently she had been a subject of discussion as well, especially after she "slipped the hook," as Marilou put it.

For a second Jose stood grinning, giving her the once-over, especially her legs. "Max gets so carried away when he talks about your drawings we figured there had to be something he wasn't telling us." He glanced at Aaron. "Now we know, huh?" It wasn't until he came across the room to give her a buzz on the cheek that Kate noticed the limp.

"You're going to end up swallowing that loose tongue of yours, Carrasco," Max warned from the doorway. He didn't even look at Kate, just motioned for her to come. She promised to come back with her photographs of Tashat and some drawings, accepted the phone number Marilou slipped to her, and hurried to catch up with Max.

By the time they got off the elevator on the fourth floor of the UT Health Sciences Center, anticipation was causing her heart to race. Max guided her past several doors opening off the wide hallway, most of them equipped with lab benches, centrifuges, and other equipment, plus the usual white-garbed technicians. Tonight might be New Year's Eve, but everything continued pretty much as usual in a hospital where treatment and research went on side by side.

Even so, she was completely unprepared for what she saw when he steered her through a doorway on their left—the bank of computer monitors, viewboxes striping the walls like a ribbon of windows, and an array of skulls lined up on a long lab bench, all sizes and shapes, each on its own pedestal. Disembodied. Some grossly deformed. Bizarre.

"Kate, this is Tom McCowan," Max said over her shoulder. "And this is Kate McKinnon." He moved her with him across the big room. "Tom's the one with the software I told you about. Uses it to plan his craniofacial reconstructions, each step that needs to be taken and in what order."

It came to her then that the tall man in V-necked greens was in the business of correcting God's mistakes—rearranging the underlying structure of a malformed face by moving the eye sockets closer together to give a little girl some depth perception instead of the vision and appearance of a bird, or taking a piece from the bulging forehead of a teenage boy to give him a chin—the kind of magic that reclaimed more souls from a living hell than any preacher could ever hope to save.

Then she saw a head she recognized—Nefertiti!—and all hell broke loose inside her own head.

"You didn't tell her?" the surgeon asked Max.

"I decided to let you take all the credit."

"Then let's get to it." McCowan straddled a stool and rolled it into position at the computer. "Watch that monitor over there," he instructed Kate, pointing to show her which one. A few seconds later a straight-on view of Nefertiti's face appeared, just as she looked in the famous painted bust in the Berlin Museum.

"First we peeled the tissue away from her skull using the same tissue-depth figures you use to build the tissues up." An invisible hand began to peel the flesh from the points where Kate had applied the guides to Tashat's skull.

"That's incredible," she breathed, unable to take her eyes off the monitor. Once the skull was stripped bare it began to rotate from an anterior to left oblique anterior view, then left profile, eventually making a complete circle.

"Then we plugged the dimensions Max got from Tashat's skull into our program." McCowan pointed to a monitor to the left of the first one. "And got this. Look familiar?"

Kate glanced back and forth between the two skulls, comparing the curve of a line here with the same line there, the size of one opening against the same opening in the other skull. Except for size, they were so similar she decided to look for differences instead.

Max reached around her to point. "See the shape of the nasal sill? And the cheekbones." He raised his voice. "Can we have both of them in profile, Tom?" Tashat's skull rotated first, then Nefertiti's. "I remembered you saying that her jaw reminded you of Nefertiti. Take a look at the angle of the jawbone and extension of the chin. That's why."

As the significance of what Max was saying began to sink in, Kate waited for him to draw a more explicit conclusion. Instead, he asked Tom McCowan to change the viewing angle so they could look down at the top of both skulls.

"We ran into a small problem here," McCowan admitted. "Had to approximate the depth of Nefertiti's skullcap because of that crown. With Tashat we know the cap is longer front to back than side to side. But we can compare the cheekbones. In Mongoloids they tend to slope back and project out, producing the flat face of the Oriental. With these two the slope is almost identical, which tells us they *both* could have been either Negroid or Caucasian, or some mix of the two."

"Caucasian, from the shape of the nasal sill," Kate put in.

"Show him your pictures," Max suggested. It seemed an interruption, but she got the oversize color prints out of her purse and handed them to Tom McCowan.

He took his time looking, sliding each one under the stack to keep them in order. Kate noticed his flat, splayed fingertips, and wondered, not for the first time, why so many surgeons' hands had fingers like that. When he got to the one of Tashat wearing the blue war crown, McCowan let out a soft "Wow!"

The next thing she knew he was striding across the room to turn the bust of Nefertiti enough to eliminate the distraction of the missing iris in her left eye. Then he held the same view of Tashat up beside it.

"The similarities are striking," Kate agreed, "but we don't know if your Nefertiti is an exact duplicate of the head in Berlin, or even if the original is true to life."

"The German consul in Houston called Berlin and got a name for us," Max put in. "A professor, Dr. Dietrich Wildung, who happens to be chief curator of their Egyptian collection and a very nice guy. He also speaks fluent English. The big surprise was learning that they've scanned most of their important pieces."

Amazed, Kate glanced at Tom McCowan, who nodded to confirm what Max was saying. "He sent us everything from their scan, plus a few colored slides. The bust is made of limestone covered with a gypsum plaster. What the scan revealed that no one knew before was that the sculptor came back and added more plaster to build up her shoulders and the back of the crown before it was painted. An artistic judgment, probably for proportion, or balance. No sign, though, that he added to her face for the same reason. Yet it's nearly perfect, mathematically speaking, since the chin, mouth, and nose are almost exactly symmetrical about the vertical axis of her face. Which, I admit, is suspicious. But it doesn't really matter. Here, I'll show you why."

The image of Tashat's skull disappeared, then reappeared on the first monitor, superimposed over the skull of Nefertiti.

"I can't answer your question about whether that ancient sculptor worked from life, but the likelihood of finding this much similarity in randomly selected subjects is infinitesimally small," McCowan pointed out. "If these two women lived near the same time and in the same place, the probability of a familial connection is even higher. Remember, it's the craniofacial configuration that counts, not size."

"The only sister of Nefertiti that we know of was Mutnodjme," Kate said, "who married Horemheb, the last pharaoh of the Eighteenth Dynasty. Which could be why we know about her and not any others."

"Could Tashat be Nefertiti's mother?" McCowan asked.

Kate shook her head. "Nefertiti was at least thirty-four by Year Eighteen of Akhenaten's reign, the date inscribed on Tashat's coffin." Max filled McCowan in on the three dates and why two of them didn't fit the received wisdom about how long each pharaoh had reigned.

"Then try it the other way around," the surgeon suggested. "Could Tashat have been Nefertiti's daughter?"

Mac looked to Kate. "That would make her half royal and account for the blue coffin, not to mention the arm folded across her chest." He held up a hand to forestall the objection he knew was coming. "I know, but think about that crushed left hand."

"I don't know. Nefertiti's six daughters by Akhenaten are well documented. And Tashat's father was a priest of Amen." Kate could hardly stand still, and without thinking she started for the door, intending to walk the hall to get rid of the pent-up tension. "I have to think about all this."

"Hey," McCowan protested, "you can't just walk off and leave me in suspense! Anyway, we're not done. You haven't seen the other head."

"N-no," she stammered, turning her back on the monitors. "I've already started on him, at home." She realized how that must sound and didn't want Tom McCowan to think she was a superstitious idiot. "It may sound crazy, but once a picture begins to take shape in my head it sort of evolves over time—if I don't let anything intrude."

McCowan glanced at Max. "I understand what she's saying. Sometimes when I examine some poor kid I get kind of a halo effect—just a glimmer of the face as it could be. When that happens I don't want to see him again until I get that image firmed up in my mind. Usually that doesn't happen until I can work it out on the computer, try moving things here and there until I get a match with the picture in my head."

"Yes," Kate whispered, and felt the rush of hot tears. Tom McCowan saved her from embarrassing both herself and him by turning away to call up prints of the skulls.

"Promise you'll keep me posted?" he asked as he handed them to her. "I may even have another trick or two up my sleeve. We could try different faces on her skull, for instance, or variations on the same face, using the computer so you wouldn't have to actually reconstruct anything."

"Thanks. I really appreciate all of this." She gestured toward the monitors.

He shook his head. "Once Max told me about that head between her legs and then what the CT scan showed, I was hooked. So don't hesitate to call if you need a second opinion, or just want to try something out on me."

Kate and Max were almost to the door when McCowan spoke again. "Kate?" She turned back. "That guy in Denver has to be a real asshole."

By the time they reached the elevator, Max was grinning like the Cheshire cat.

"Pretty pleased with yourself, aren't you?" Kate chided.

"You bet. Aren't you?"

"Let's forget we ever read that monograph of Dave Broverman's," Max said as they drove away from the Health Sciences Center. "Traces of Smenkhkare's name are visible on the canopic jars holding Tut's viscera. Also on the gold bands binding his shroud. Why? Because Nefertiti was still alive when Tut died, ten years after Akhenaten, that's why."

"Akhenaten *did* send Smenkhkare to Thebes to mollify the priests of Amen. If Smenkhkare was Nefertiti, then she was playing a losing hand, because the priests were out for Akhenaten's blood. What would she do—go down the tubes with him or switch sides to save herself? Or did she simply fall in love with another man? A priest."

"I'd say it's more likely that she made a deal, one the priests would really go for. They get a half-royal child while she gets off with her life."

"But Nefertiti was a hereditary princess!" Kate pointed out. "I can't imagine mentioning Tashat's father in that inscription and not a royal mother."

Max swung into the parking lot of a strip shopping center and stopped in front of a deli-cafeteria. "Hereditary! Doesn't that mean Nefertiti's father was royal? I thought nobody knew who her father was. Ay, maybe. But he was a commoner like his sister, Queen Tiye. So who does that leave?"

"Amenhotep Three. Unless she was the daughter of some foreign ruler. But we can't be sure the title wasn't honorary."

"Maybe not, but what if we could show a probable relationship between one of the pharaohs and one or both of those skulls? All we have to do is compare our two with the craniofacial configuration and dentition of the royals, right?"

"But we don't know what, if any, artistic license that ancient sculptor may have taken," Kate pointed out, trying to slow their headlong rush to a conclusion that might be flawed in its basic premise. "So we still can't say for sure that Tom McCowan's computer-generated skull represents the real Nefertiti. Also, those X-rays of the royals threw doubt on who a couple of the bodies really are. Textual evidence says two of the royal mummies were father and son, for instance, yet the X-rays don't support that."

Max wasn't daunted. "Yeah, but if we get a positive correlation, someone we both know will have to swallow what he said about Tashat being a nobody."

" 'A piece of dung'—and I quote," Kate supplied.

"Then let's see if we can make him eat it."

I smell a change coming, a shape turning leaves in the wind.
—Normandi Ellis, *Awakening Osiris*

FOURTEEN

Year Four in the Reign of Ay

(1348 B.C.)

DAY 13, FIRST MONTH OF INUNDATION

Seeing to the welfare of my expanded "family" weighs so heavily on my shoulders, especially with Khary's wife about to give birth again, that I must retreat to my sleeping room in order to escape the dust and noise of the bricklayers and carpenters who add new rooms to my house. Tonight I glanced up to find Aset sitting cross-legged on my sleeping couch with Tuli wedged against her thigh, waiting for me to finish my writing. She held a scroll, so I laid my pen aside and waited to see what she wanted.

"I was working on a poem, a gift for my father, when the river of my thoughts ran dry," she began. "I thought perhaps you could tell me where I went wrong." I nodded and she began to read. " '*Beside the well the sycamore rises. Beside the well bright corn-flowers grow. Do they rise on their tender stalks by will? Or does some force of love drive them up? I wake in the dark to the stirring of birds, a murmur in the trees, a flutter of wings. I am flesh of my father's flesh. His sorrows are mine, his joys, his spirit. And my thoughts lie with his, in peace.*' "

I have little patience for poetry, but her way with words often leaves me speechless, for they are as playthings that take on meaning only when she puts them together.

"Well, did I put you to sleep?" she demanded when I was slow to respond.

"Such loving thoughts would please any father. Perhaps you only arrived at the natural end before you realized it."

"I wrote it for *my* father, *sunu*, not any father!" she snapped, echoing the tune her mother sings so well.

"Do not lay your dissatisfaction or your temper at my door. Even the good opinion of the most gifted poet in the land is of no consequence if it does not please you." Tuli pricked an ear, hearing something amiss in my voice.

"Perhaps if you were to read me one of yours—" she began.

"Writing verses is for those with idle hands, or a man besotted with love."

"My father says a man who refuses to let his *ka* speak is either a coward or ashamed of what he carries in his heart, yet I know you are neither."

"Perhaps your *ka* is ill-informed." Tuli jumped down to sit on his haunches, begging me to change my tone.

"If I cannot blame my *ka* for what I say or do, why should I blame those who inform me?" Mischief plucked at her mouth as she tipped her head toward Tuli.

"Tuli writes verses now?" I inquired.

Like a gust of wind snatching the flame from a lamp, her blue eyes darkened, and she snapped her fingers, bringing him to her side. "He shows me in other ways that he loves me, even when I displease him. It is just that I do not understand why you have no desire to examine our feelings as you do our bodies."

"Flowery phrases do not come easily to my tongue."

"Not even when you were a green youth mooning over the ripe breasts of some girl? Tell me, then, how does the sadness I feel when I disappoint my father bring tears to my eyes? What causes the roaring in my ears when I am alone in the dark? Why do my cheeks grow red and hot when I am ashamed of something I said?" Like a stone rolling downhill, Aset has never been one to stop until she reaches the bottom.

"Perhaps all are simply signs sent by your namesake to let you know she watches over you," I suggested, since I had no other answer to give.

"You make light of my questions?" I dared not smile, so I shook my head. "If there is a difference between knowing and believing, as you say, and the road to eternity is knowing—the open eye—then to *not* ask questions is to close your eyes. Yet the priests never question anything, though they worship the sun, the source of all light and life."

I can recognize a theological argument when I hear it. "Is that what this is all about—you miss your father?"

Her hand played with Tuli's ear. "Of course I miss him, but—"

"Then think about it and see if you can find a way to discover what causes the noise in your ears. As for the verses, I will try if you have the patience to guide me." If she worries that I may stop caring for her, I will write all the verses she wants, clumsy or not. And if something else bothers her, at least she will have an excuse to come to me.

"We could address the same subject," she suggested.

"And read our verses to each other," I added. "That way you could instruct me by example."

Delight bubbled in her throat. "What shall we write about?"

"Uh, let me think what might be . . . a possibility."

"Possibility? Oh, I like that." She unfolded her legs and slid off the couch, dumping Tuli onto the floor, but the instant her bare feet touched the cool tiles she stilled, though he ran ahead into the passageway.

"Leave your scroll and I will see that it gets to your father," I told her, ignoring her bare feet. "But you best give me a few days. I am not so quick as you."

DAY 4, SECOND MONTH OF INUNDATION

With the life-giving waters of Mother River rising faster than any-one can remember, an uneasy pall of apprehension afflicts us all. Whatever the cause, the stench of carrion hangs over the city like a deadly miasma, from the growing heap of bodies outside the House of Beautification. Everywhere I go I burn sulfur to drive off the spir-its of the dead along with the rats that invade their miserable hovels. For those who will die despite any medicine I give them, I light incense and invoke the goddess—*O Isis, great in sorcery, deliver me from everything bad and evil and vicious. From affliction caused by a god or goddess, from dead man or woman, from male or female enemy, as you delivered your son Horus.*"

At times, lately, the cold fingers of fear clutch at my heart when I glance up to find Aset standing before me, white night robe still swirling around her ankles like some ghostly wraith sent by the gods to torment me. "I thought we might read our poems," she announced on this night.

I motioned her to my sleeping couch and waited for Tuli to jump up beside her. "Perhaps I should go first," I suggested, hunting through the sheets on my table, "lest my paltry effort sound the worse for coming after yours."

She gave me an encouraging nod so I took a deep breath and began. " '*Like a child in its mother's belly, I am with you but not among you. I am water bubbling from a spring. I am the laughter in two jugs of red wine. A tadpole swimming in a shallow pool left by the tears of the goddess. I have always been here, a child in the silence of things, for I am possibility.*' "

I kept my eyes on the papyrus, expecting laughter, indulgence or even pity, but not silence. Curiosity finally drove me to look up, only to find her so engrossed in her own verse that she had not even heard mine. "I told you I have no talent for poetry," I said, to explain such a pitiable effort. "I only thought to describe some things that fascinated me as a boy, which I forgot and then rediscovered with you."

She gave me an puzzled look. "I don't—what do you mean?"

"The gods have given me a rare and precious gift in allowing me to see again with the eyes of a child."

"Mine?" I nodded. "Truly?"

"Truly," I replied, provoking the glorious smile that is the greatest mystery of all to me, since I cannot even guess where such light comes from let alone explain the effect it has on me.

"That must be why our thoughts follow the same path." Too excited to sit still, she jumped down from the couch and came to my side. "I was afraid if I said how much I like yours it would sound boastful, since mine is so like yours. Read it again."

I did as she asked, and she continued where I stopped. " '*I am the word before its utterance. I am thought and desire. An idea. A portent of impossible dreams. I know no ending for I have no beginning. Because I am possibility.' "*

DAY 21, THIRD MONTH OF INUNDATION

Only the storehouses Ramose ordered built away from the river still hold edible grain. All else, even the corn and lentils stored in the royal warehouses, has been swept away by the raging current or else lies buried in mud, fueling rumors that Pharaoh has displeased the gods by refusing to name an heir. But just as the river in flood robs its banks, the land in its turn will rob the water, a never-ending cycle repeated by stars and moon and sun, each robbing the other of a place in the sky. Whose earthly star will rise now, I wonder, to take Paranefer's place? Surely that will say more than all the gossips about who sent the High Priest to the subterranean dwelling place of night.

DAY 16, FOURTH MONTH OF INUNDATION

Sheri, Nebet, and Mena came to celebrate Aset's eleventh feast day, leaving Nebet's little brother with his nurse-mother. We ate in the garden, then Mena and I stretched out on the grass while Sheri helped Ipwet and Tamin, Khary's wife, carry the empty bowls and platters to Nofret's kitchen.

"Poor Tuli is not used to having so many people intrude on his territory," I observed, glancing to where the dog lay with his paws jerking in his sleep, while Nebet, Aset, and Ruka dangled their feet in the pond, giggling and talking.

"I'll wager Aset's new palette joins the other treasures she carries in that scruffy bag," Mena remarked. "See how she keeps one hand always on your gift, as if she expects it to walk away? Does she prize it for what it is, do you suppose, or because it came from you?"

"You don't know Aset if you have to ask."

"I know her better than you think," he grumbled.

"Lately she spends hours with my medical scrolls, to become my assistant in truth not just in name. It is as if she tries to cram two days of living into every one of ours."

"She tries to catch up with you."

"Don't start," I warned him, only half in jest. "I already have been made painfully aware of my advanced years. This morning she approached me with a mathematical puzzle. How is it possible for me to be three times her age now—thirty-three to her eleven years—yet be only twice her age when she is twenty-two?" Mena smiled with his eyes closed. "She also has taken to bringing wet clay when we go to visit the sick, to form the beasts in her stories. A pig who believes he can fly because he was raised by a flock of geese and so eventually grows wings. A crocodile whose snout is as long as his tail, so he is forever forgetting which is which." Watching the three of them together, I grew curious. "What in the name of Thoth can they be talking about that Ruka chatters like a pigeon? With me he stumbles over his own tongue."

"Aset has a talent for making him believe in himself. Would that the gods gave us all such a gift, for surely she healed Nebet in ways you and I had no hand in." His next words came to me on a sigh. "How my daughter has blossomed under the nurturing sun of your little goddess!"

"As a boy I needed more than the supporting hand of my father, someone nearer to my own years. Without you, Mena, I never would have found the courage to be what I am, unimportant as that may be to anyone else." He squinted at me, wondering, I suppose, if I had drunk too much wine. "If I speak too plainly it is because Aset has been at me to let my *ka* speak. I am conducting an experiment to see if her argument has merit."

"Isn't it time you started to look for a larger parcel of land?" he asked, changing the subject. "The addition to your house takes from your garden just when you need more ground for planting, thanks to your Eye of Horus. Surely you have credit enough in Pharaoh's countinghouse."

"You remember my neighbor on that side, who did little but complain to the magistrate about the noises at my door in the night?" He nodded. "Well, he now has all the quiet he could want. I have given his widow such a generous price for the land that she has dowry sufficient to attract a much younger man, one with more teeth than the old grandfather she had." I snapped a twig off a nearby bush and hunted for a clear spot of ground. "I plan to knock down the wall and have the old house repaired, for Khary and Tamin, who is with child again. We will plant herbs and medicinal shrubs in the new ground, and have a small house built for Ipwet and Ruka—here, where the sage and thyme grow now. With all of us wearing these—" I lifted one foot to show him my palm-frond sandals, a bigger version of those Ipwet weaves for Aset and Nebet, "and Nofret bringing more orders from her friends, I may have to hire someone to help her. I also intend to plant a tamarisk, two sycamores, and another palm—both to harvest and provide shade."

I heard a noise and knew at once who it was, though no lamps illuminated the back of my garden. So did Aset. Pagosh caught her on the run and twirled her around while she hugged his neck. "I am *so* glad to see you!" She pulled back to peer into his face. "But I wish Merit could have come, too." Without a word he set her on her feet and turned to where Merit stood in the shadows, half hidden by the thin veil wrapped around her head. Aset ran to her and they began laughing and talking at the same time while the rest of us stood mute. Pagosh sent me a curt nod, causing me to wonder if his throat tightened as mine did, which reminded me of Aset's question. How is it that our thoughts and feelings, which depart our bodies upon death so are without substance, can bring tears to our eyes?

Pagosh carried a small wooden box and scroll tied with a purple ribbon, both gifts from Aset's father. The box alone would have been enough, for it was inlaid with rare woods and ivory from Kush, but it held a gold necklace that reminded me of the one Aset had "borrowed" from her lady mother—a message, surely, as well as a gift. Nofret and Sheri made much to-do over the delicacy of the worked gold, but it was the scroll that Aset clutched tightly in her hand for the rest of the evening.

Watching her, Mena arrived at a conclusion that would never have occurred to me. "She practices the art that comes naturally to women—using anticipation to enhance the ultimate pleasure."

I scoffed at his flight of fancy and told him she only waited for a private moment to read Ramose's message without interruption. "She rarely sees him, even on her visits to her husband's villa, now that her father carries the responsibilities of the High Priest."

Indeed, I have tried not to judge Ramose, though Pagosh believes it is Nefertiti's plan for them to rule the Two Lands together, like two horses harnessed to the same chariot, she from the palace and Ramose from the temple. And he may be right. But tonight, with all those I love most in this world moving about among the fragrant flowers of my garden, their voices floating on the evening breeze, the river of happiness that flows through me by day overflowed its banks and inundated my heart.

DAY 2, SECOND MONTH OF PLANTING

Senmut arrived at the hour we had agreed upon the week before but without Mena, and by way of Khary's dispensary rather than through the garden.

"Mena has been called to the palace," he explained as we proceeded to my private place of work. My examining room and the dispensary no longer open into the place where I carry out my experiments, nor into the garden where Aset spends hours every day, reading or watching over her menagerie of animals.

"What is it this time?" I asked, since we have put our heads together more than once over the old Pharaoh's failing health, hoping to give Horemheb time to consolidate his support among the Council of Wise Men.

"The old man outlives his teeth, even the few he has left. Putrid matter drains from his gums until the numbing salve no longer works, forcing him to ever bigger doses of mandrake. But even Mena cannot replace the water in a man's clock when finally it runs dry. For some time now Horemheb handles not only the royal correspondence but in truth makes all of Pharaoh's decisions." I pulled up a stool for him at the writing table in my workroom, between the chests holding my supplies and tools, a shelf for potions, salves and other concoctions, and my collection of scrolls.

"But I bring other news," he informed me. "A messenger arrived from Aniba bearing word that my father has gone to Osiris. So I will go up the river with my brother, who takes my father's place. I came to bid you farewell, Tenre, and to thank you for your generosity and wisdom."

"You have my sympathy," I replied, though his demeanor gave

no indication that he grieved, "but I am the one who should thank you."

"What for—allowing you to listen to my foolish questions?"

"For your astute observations and willingness to share them, even your stubbornness in arguing a point," I replied, and was rewarded with a smile that, like Mena's, is still quick and boyish. "Surely it will not be long until you can return."

"With my father gone and the old ways with him, the time has come for me to serve my own people. Pharaoh's Governor in Kush looks on Hiknefer with a fond eye because my brother was friend to Osiris Tutankhamen. So Huy is inclined to indulge his wishes, which means the time is ripe for me as well."

"Ripe for what?" The heirs of Kemet's vassals come to Pharaoh's court to be educated, not only to assure their fathers' allegiance but to train them for when their own time comes. But Senmut was not his father's heir, and he traveled with Pharaoh's army only to gain experience.

"To establish a new House of Life, one that I intend to make known from the highest reaches of Mother River to the Great Green Sea and beyond for the fresh breeze that blows through its open windows." His eyes danced with enthusiasm. "A place where learned men gather to exchange ideas, whether it be how to treat the tired heart of an old man, the method used by a sculptor to shape a piece of stone, or how to increase the yield from our fields. Perhaps even you would consent to grace such a place with your wisdom." I began to shake my head. "I do not ask for your answer now, Tenre, only that you remember. Whatever direction the winds blow in the years ahead, you will always have a place of honor in my house among men who question as you do, whether they be Hittite or Syrian, Canaanite or Babylonian, clean-shaven or—"

"Will you have no women?" Aset asked from the doorway as Tuli came shooting across the room and crashed into Senmut's ankles, dropping him to his knees. Nofret keeps Aset's hair short and she goes about in a kilt and sleeveless tunic, but there is no way to hide the color of her eyes except to keep them cast down when she leaves my walls. Yet Senmut has never inquired into why she is here, and always calls her Wenis, the name she goes by as my apprentice.

"In time, perhaps." He left off petting Tuli, who put his nose into my hand to let me know that his affection for me is constant if not so exuberant.

"Mena was called to the palace," I explained, "but Senmut has come to bid us farewell. His father has passed through the reeds. Just now he was telling me about the House of Life he plans in Aniba."

"We will miss you, my lord." She appeared flustered, like a boy embarrassed by the admission. "Will you return?"

"Not to stay, but to visit my friends, yes."

"Nebet?" she inquired, watching him closely. Did she still find him a novelty or was her fascination more than curiosity, isolated as she is from boys her own age?

"Of course. And Tenre, who I have invited to teach in my House of Life. Perhaps he will bring you along, to teach others how to outline the maps you make of the vessels that carry blood."

"You know my name is not Wenis, do you not?" Her lips softened into a shy smile when Senmut nodded. "Then it hurts nothing for me to thank you again for—for saving me from that old Nubian, and explaining . . . everything." Her eyes always look bigger and rounder when they fill with tears. "I am so sorry about your little sister. Nebet told me what happened to her."

"Promise me you will remember that nothing of any importance was taken from you that day. You are as whole as I am." A flash of white teeth, then, "Or Nebet."

Aset matched his smile. "You truly would have a woman in your House of Life?"

"I just said so."

"Then I would consider it an honor if you would call me sister."

For once Senmut was slow to find his tongue. "The honor is mine, Lady Aset. Indeed, I would deem myself the chosen of Amen if you would call me brother in return."

That brought more joy to her eyes. "Is Mena invited, too?"

"Only if he brings his family with him," Senmut returned. It struck me then that the words they exchanged meant more to them than to me, as if they knew something I did not. I felt like a father whose children have moved beyond his reach, not in distance but understanding, and for the first time I envied another man simply for his twenty-two years.

"In the meantime," he added, "it would please me to receive a letter from time to time with news of my friends."

"From your . . . sister?" Aset waited for him to nod before she turned and without another word left the room, wearing a satisfied little smile.

Such behavior is a mystery to me, yet there is no one I can ask for help but Sheri. And I do not always have the opportunity before I must make a response, appropriate or not. But I still cannot think of Aset as a married woman or treat her with the decorum proper for another man's wife, even if her marriage has not yet been con-summated. The fire burning in my belly comes from wondering how long that will continue now that her monthly flow has begun.

When I looked to Senmut, he was pulling a thin scroll from the bag he carried over his shoulder. "Mena instructed me to give you this."

One glance was enough, for Aset's animals are always in motion, like the pig flapping his ears as he jumps off a bee stack because he believes he can fly. Nor do any lines separate one picture from another. "Why send this to me?"

"I came upon it in the latrine of the barracks where I am assigned. Surely you recognize her hand. She tells in pictures how the old High Priest met his end watching two of his favorites, young boys from the temple school. See the clay tablets strapped to their backs?" I nodded. "In the beginning the skittish young colts head toward the pond, where the old crocodile lies waiting—all but his nostrils and eyes hidden beneath the muddy water. One colt turns away, refusing to drink from the pond, while the others not only drink but frolic in the water. Except these two, who leave the pond to play a different game"—he pointed to where one colt mounted another from behind—"in full sight of the old crocodile. That is when he begins to change from gray to black, the color of death. The excitement was too much for his old heart. Surely you see the irony in Paranefer being brought down by the corruption of his own *ka*."

He grasped both my shoulders then, in a gesture of friendship.

"For me, Tenre, you are the brightest star in the night sky, and so you will remain no matter how many months or years lie between this day and the day we next meet."

I could not hope to match the graciousness of his words, so I embraced him as a brother. Nor did I try to hide the tears in my eyes as I walked with him to the gate to delay the moment of parting, for in truth I was as reluctant for him to leave as once I was to see Mena sail with the morning light.

DAY 21, FOURTH MONTH OF HARVEST

Like the last piece in a game of senet, the Old Master of the Horse had nowhere else to go. That he passed through the reeds peacefully was, to me, more than he deserved. Khary treated the news with characteristic equanimity, pointing out that one of the heavenly joys of departing this life is that Pharaoh now can take another man's wife should he wish, a privilege denied him so long as he occupied the throne. By the time Mena entered my garden by way of the back alley, Khary had gone to his own house and Aset was inside reading, so we settled under the canopy with a pitcher of beer, where we could speak freely about what concerned us most.

"The General will climb the steps to the throne with Ramose's blessing," he predicted. "The priests know Horemheb has garnered more favor in the past two years, not less, thanks to Ay's muddled wits. Between them Horemheb and Ramses hold the loyalty of the regimental commanders, all but a few who grumble no matter who sits above them. Amen's Sacred Council knows the next Pharaoh must have the army behind him, to protect our frontiers and gold routes if nothing else, and Horemheb has more experience in governing. It was Ay who steered Tutankhamen's hand, not Nefertiti."

"His end, as well," I reminded him. "But experience has nothing to do with it."

"I know you distrust him still, Tenre, but Ramose would not have allowed Horemheb to make life miserable for the priests and followers of Aten, thereby currying favor among Amen's priests both high and low, unless it suited him. No man pulls the High Priest's string. By now every priest in the Two Lands will know of

Horemheb's order that taxes be collected on Aten's temples and other holdings. Anyway, what other choice do they have?"

Aset, I almost said, but I did not want to tempt the gods by supplying the answer to their dilemma. "If it is so obvious to you that Ramose is pulling Horemheb's string, rather than the other way around," I pointed out instead, "Nefertiti would long since have found a way to end it."

He drained his cup, then reached for the pitcher to refill both his and mine. "She is blind even to the possibility of failure. Think what she has gotten away with, Tenre. Stealing the breath from her grandson and then the Queen, the child of her body, with her own hands." He shook his head. "Did Hathor call down the wrath of the gods on her head? No! Amen-Re made her his High Priestess, the God's Chief Concubine."

What he said had the ring of truth for I have seen Nefertiti's arrogance firsthand, even with Anubis breathing over her shoulder. But I could not forget that the Sacred Council once refused to accept Amenhotep's Shasu Queen as Consort of Amen, thereby rejecting her son as the son of Amen, and in the end provoked Akhenaten to reject *them*. "I still think the priests will reject your General, lest they sow the seeds of their own destruction. No one can deny that the blood of the Magnificent Amenhotep flows in her veins."

"As it does in Aset's," he replied.

"That is why I worry. At least Ramose does not delude himself. He may have ordered all mention of the priests' part in the catastrophe with the Heretic removed from the temple scrolls, but he did not purge his own library."

"One more reason to believe he will help his cohorts see the wisdom of choosing Horemheb and leave Nefertiti where she is. Why put more power in the hands of a woman they already distrust?"

"Are you sure no others on the Sacred Council wield sufficient influence to counter the High Priest's wishes?"

He shook his head. "The seventy days of mourning end just before the Festival of Opet, a propitious time to introduce Amen's newly adopted son. Also, because of the rampaging water, the priests must make a spectacle of Amen's visit to his southern temple."

"Ramose risks much if he *does* decide to betray his wife."

"Not if he demands that Horemheb outlaw the worship of Aten," Mena countered. "That would pull the cat's claws and keep her busy protecting her back, so she cannot attack when his is turned."

I am not so sure of that, either, but I did not want Mena to think I argued for the sake of argument alone, so I contented myself with watching the sky brighten with stars, while darkness slowly engulfed my heart. For I have come to care for Ramose the man even if I do not trust his priestly motives. Pagosh says he still shares his wife's couch, at least on occasion if not so frequently as before. Surely that will come to an end should he champion her rival. Worse, it will make Ramose the target of her revenge. And that is a lot to ask of any man.

FIFTEEN

Max suggested they go out to celebrate, but Kate begged off, saying she'd had enough excitement for one day. Which was true. "Besides, nothing could top the show you and Tom McCowan put on for me." That was true, too, but New Year's Eve was a night for noise, which she had never liked.

"Then we'll have hot chocolate instead of champagne," he decided, "at least to start. And the first one who mentions Tashat or Egypt or"—he grinned and she knew he was thinking of Dave Broverman—"has to clean up the kitchen. Why don't you heat the milk while I build a fire in my study and put on some music?" He glanced to where Sam sat with his ears pricked. "Better bring some of that new crunch while you're at it so we don't have to trek back to the kitchen soon as he sees us having something."

Kate smiled to herself as she got out the makings for hot chocolate. Sam seemed to bring out the indulgent parent in Maxwell Cavanaugh, ever mindful of the dog's welfare and happiness. Was that how he felt about her, too? Why else would he stock up not only on red wine but cocoa and marshmallows? She thought back, recalling the look in his eyes when he reached up to skim a wayward strand of hair out of her eyes, and later, in the backyard, his offended "Look, let's get something straight," then "What are we going to do about Tashat?" And now, today, the way he had turned the meeting with Tom McCowan into a kind of surprise party.

She filled the mugs and put them on a tray along with Sam's

bowl of crunch, then followed the music to his study. As soon as she crossed the threshold it felt as if she'd walked through the false door in an Egyptian tomb, passing from one world to another. She took in the dark parquet floor and lush Persian rug, walls lined with shelves bulging with journals and books, then the big blond desk and matching turnaround, complete with computer and printer. On the wall behind it, two viewboxes had been mounted low enough for Max to examine an X ray by simply swiveling his chair around.

He was kneeling in front of the slate-faced fireplace, so she went to set the tray on his desk, which was covered with a thick sheet of glass. That's when she noticed the two photographs under one corner of the glass. One was of her and Sam playing in the snow in that high meadow up behind the Flatirons. The other showed a dark-haired woman with a teenage boy and girl standing on either side of her, taken in Max's backyard. All three wore shorts and held tennis rackets, as if they'd just stepped off the court, faces flushed and hair flying every which way. Kate couldn't help feeling a poignant sort of envy, but at Max's age it would have been unusual for him not to have married, even if he wasn't now.

"Are these your kids?"

He turned to see what she meant, then shook his head. "Niece and nephew. That's my sister, Marty. She's a tennis pro at a private club just outside Washington, but the last time they were here those two demons put us both to shame, not just me. Must be in the genes since my father traveled the pro circuit for a while. He started Marty and me early, to be sure we could get scholarships to college if anything happened to him. I always suspected there was more to it than that, but—"

"You've never been married?" He didn't bother to look around, just shook his head. "How come?"

This time he shrugged. "Too busy, too involved in my work— who knows?"

"You never even came close?" She knew she should stop but couldn't.

Max didn't answer right away, maybe to let her know that she had stepped over the line. Then, "I thought about it once, but no, I wouldn't call it close." He put a match to the twisted newspapers he'd stuffed under the grate as he asked, "Were you surprised when your parents divorced?"

"Not really." She joined him on the floor when he moved back from the heat, crossing her legs and dropping down to watch the flames lick at the rust-colored bark of the Texas cedar. "They split right after I left for college, sold the house where I grew up, and took off in opposite directions. I was seventeen, a premed major, but I'd been drawing as long as I can remember so I took art courses in the summer, to learn more about techniques and materials. One summer I got a job drawing animation cels, learning to break an image down into layers, which turned out to be good experience for a medical illustrator. I thought of that when you mentioned stacking those CT cross sections to build a three-dimensional head." She paused. "No, I knew my parents had problems . . . besides me, that is. It's just—I think I was the straw that broke the camel's back."

"Why do you say that?"

Kate stared at the fire, remembering. "Something changed after we moved from a small town in central Illinois to a suburb of Chicago, when I was ten. The school was different, much bigger, and the teachers let kids talk whenever they wanted. It took me a while to catch on to what I was supposed to be doing. One teacher nagged me about not paying attention and made me sit in the front row like a retarded second-grader. Mom decided something must be wrong with my hearing and took me for tests, but they said my ears were okay. My father accused me of doing it just to make trouble or to get attention. Anyway, that's when the arguing started."

"Doing it? What's 'it'?"

"I don't know, missing stuff."

"Is that what you meant about having reason to know you're not deaf?"

Kate nodded. "Over the years I've had other tests, all with the same result. There's nothing wrong with my hearing."

"You didn't miss very much if you started college at seventeen, let alone got into med school." A piece of cedar popped, shooting sparks in every direction, and Sam ran to hide behind the couch. Kate started to get up, but Max reached for her hand and sandwiched it between both of his to keep her there. "He's all right. Tell me what happens when you miss stuff."

"I guess I'm easily distracted, because, well, sometimes I just seem to—lose it. Mostly when too much is going on at once or there's a lot of noise. It's as if I can't concentrate or focus my thoughts, or—I don't know, it's hard to describe."

He nodded, then didn't say anything for a while, making Kate wish she'd kept her mouth shut. She didn't want him to think she was making excuses for what had to be her own fault. Not that she wanted it to happen. Sometimes she could predict when it was going to happen, other times not. That was the worst. But she truly did not know what went wrong, only that something did.

"I'm not sure how to say this, Kate," he began, not looking at her. She'd heard that before and could guess what was coming—another admonition to get her act together. To try harder. "But you'd make a damn good physician, with your analytical mind and eye for detail. If you ever decide you want back in—well, I have a lot of friends in the medical community here and I'd go to bat for you in a minute." Kate kept her eyes straight ahead, afraid she might be misinterpreting what he meant. "But I'd sure hate to see you waste that other thing you've got—your own special way of expressing an idea with such fluid vitality. Nobody taught you that. It comes from what you feel and the way your mind works, not just what you see."

She didn't stop smiling until he reached up to turn her face so she had to look at him. "When you took off like that I kind of lost it. First my temper. Jesus, I was angry at you! For making me feel so damn helpless. Then I started to worry about how you must be feeling, out there alone. Now—well, maybe I'm beginning to understand what I couldn't before. Having that dumb jerk give you the boot was déjà vu all over again, wasn't it? Only this time it was me, not your parents."

"Something like that," Kate admitted, as it dawned on her that Max could be angry about what she did or didn't do and still not walk away. Like Sam. "Only I wasn't booted out of med school," she added, wanting to set the record straight. "I left because I thought it was the right thing to do."

His blue eyes searched her face, making her feel almost naked.

"I just remembered something—be right back." She pulled her hand out of his, jumped up, and ran upstairs for the small box she'd secreted away in her camera bag, then hurried back to sit on the floor again and handed it to him.

"Your grandmother's necklace. Cleo asked me to bring it, before—well, you know." Max opened the box and stared at the necklace, so long she wondered what he was thinking. "Your grandmother must've been an interesting woman," she ventured, hoping he would tell her more about the woman who obviously held a special place in his affections.

He smiled, then chuckled. "A woman with strong passions and great strength of character. She also was quite a beauty, even when she was eighty. My dad used to say his mother was 'odd,' to excuse the fact that she was different." He went quiet, staring into the fire, as if remembering something. "Ever notice how some men gravitate toward women who are the exact opposite of their mothers? Well, that was my dad. I doubt my mother ever had an opinion of her own. She always deferred to him. Not that she wasn't a caring person. But I suppose that was the way she was raised."

"Maybe," Kate agreed, thinking of her own mother, "but then you'd have to say the same thing about your father—that men back then were conditioned to be the boss. Yet from what you just said about your grandmother, that's not how she would have raised him. So it's probably more about some people needing to be in control."

That's when it dawned on her—something so obvious she wondered why she hadn't seen it before. "You knew all along that glass necklace wasn't ancient, didn't you?"

"I guess," Max admitted without meeting her eyes. "Listen, that champagne should be cold by now." He made as if to get up, then stayed where he was. "I figured I needed to know if whoever looked at this one knew what they were talking about." He hefted the box with the ivory necklace. "So yes, I knew where she got it and all the rest, because I gave it to her back when I was in college. Found it in a vintage clothes shop."

The irony of that didn't escape Kate, but she still wasn't ready to let it go. "Then I was right that she treasured it because of who gave it to her. And I'd prefer a glass of the house red, unless that would spoil your party."

Relieved, grinning, he grabbed her hand to pull her up with him. "I am *not* my father, Katie, in case you haven't figured that out."

Something tickled Kate's cheek. "Stop it, Sam," she whispered. When it happened again, she rolled over and came up against a warm, immovable object. "Get down. It's too early."

"Burning incense produces phenol." A man's voice. "Carbolic acid. D'you think the Egyptians knew that?"

"Didn't like crowds," she mumbled into the pillow. "Unhealthy. Could smell the noxious odors of their bodies."

"Ah, yes, the deadly miasmas that rise from the human body." A hand massaged her back through the covers. "Sam was getting worried." When he heard his name, Sam jumped up on the bed and nudged her face with his cold nose.

"Not fair. Two against one."

"It's almost ten o'clock. Are you sure you feel okay?"

"Sleepy," Kate mumbled. "Eyes won't open." She had spent all night trying to escape one harrowing experience after another—approaching the rapids of a river in a kayak with her arms tied to her sides, knowing she was going to turn over, not knowing if she would ever come back up, drawn into the yawning maw of a giant scanner only to emerge at the other end bound in the shroud of a mummy—until finally, too tired to fight any longer, the sense of helplessness and loneliness breached the dam she'd built to hold it back and came pouring down her cheeks, drowning her in salt. Or was it natron?

"Cold out?" she asked.

"Rainy. I thought we'd try to make the Menil Museum before lunch. They've got some things you might want to see. Marilou called. Invited us for brunch Sunday. Said to bring Sam along so he can meet her two mutts. I told her I'd check with you."

She opened one eye, took in the blue chambray shirt and faded jeans, and reached up to circle his neck with her arms. "I'm so glad I came."

"Me, too." He rested his cheek on her head.

"I almost didn't, until I remembered how you always listen and take whatever I say on its merits instead of personalizing everything, or passing judgment. Not because you're trying to impress me or anything. It's just the way you are."

"That bastard really did a job on you," Max mumbled.

"What I'm trying to say is thank you. For yesterday. Tom McCowan. Everything."

He gave her a squeeze. "I'll go scramble some eggs." He got up, and Sam jumped down to follow him. As he started out he said, "I called my old chief of radiology at Michigan, by the way, to get a name at the dental school. Thought I'd call and see if whoever has those old films will take a look at ours."

Suddenly in a hurry, Kate showered in record time, brushed her teeth, and pulled on a pair of jeans, then ran for the stairs, still buttoning her shirt.

After breakfast she called Mike Tinsley, the orthopedic surgeon who was looking for a medical illustrator, at home. He suggested meeting tomorrow afternoon, even though it was Saturday, and Kate agreed. As she hung up she was already planning to do a couple of sketches, just to have something to show him.

By the time they left the house a cloud had settled over the city, cutting off the tops of the high-rise buildings they passed on the short drive to the Menil, a museum built to house the collection of Dominique and John de Menil.

"John died several years before her, but they were a force in Houston's cultural scene. You might even say they put it on the map," Max commented as he parked along the curb. "But this building is all Mrs. de Menil. No committee of public-spirited citizens would ever have come up with anything like this." The flat-roofed, single-story white frame building sat in the middle of a double block surrounded by a vast expanse of green grass and trees. "It's too intimate. Not Texas big."

When Kate saw the floating white walls and pine floors—painted black, then left for visitors' feet to reveal the grain of the wood—she understood what he meant. From the high-ceilinged open entrance hall Max guided her to a small room where the architecture gave way to what it was meant to display—in lighted glass cases built into the walls and a large freestanding pedestal. But it was what was in those cases that spoke so eloquently of Dominique de Menil's eye for the essence of ancient civilizations—small objects from Sumer and other early settlements scattered across the plain of Mesopotamia. The Fertile Crescent.

What caught Kate's attention immediately were the sandstone fertility figures, all representing the fecund human female, mounted so they appeared to float in space. Little more than three to five inches tall, they made everything else seem insignificant by comparison, because those colorless stone objects symbolized continuity. Birth and rebirth. Something that was at the same time immense and unmeasurable.

When she finished the last case and turned to look for Max, she found him only a few feet away, waiting, giving her all the space and time she needed. That struck her as symbolic, too.

"Want to leave instead of looking at the other stuff?" he asked, anticipating her. "We can always come back another time."

Kate nodded. "Nothing could compete with this. But you knew that, didn't you?"

Back outside they were hit by a cold dry wind that sent leaves cartwheeling down the sidewalk. "Feels like a blue norther," Max muttered, grabbed her hand, and ran for the car, where he revved the motor to get the heater going.

They drove several blocks in silence, until Max couldn't stand it any longer. "Okay, out with it. I can hear the wheels spinning way over here."

"Remember how the Egyptians put small models of things the deceased might need in their tombs? Little figures they called *ushabti* to work for the dead person. A house, stables with cattle and other livestock. Surely a physician would need a scribe's palette." She turned to him. "One made of ivory, since that would exhibit the same radiodensity as old bone. Those hollow tubes could be reed pens."

"You think that's what's in his mouth, a miniature palette? Maybe to give him back the ability to speak, like touching the mummy's eyes with the sacred adze to return his sight?"

Kate shrugged. "I was thinking more of giving him the ability to write, because that's what he was known for."

"A medical treatise that got him into a peck of trouble?" Max couldn't help laughing. "No wonder Dave felt uncomfortable with you around."

"That narrow cylinder also could be a scroll instead of a reed pen."

"I don't remember any layering, but I'll check it out. Tomorrow, while you talk with Tinsley. Lift whatever it is out of the oral cavity and bring up a composite. But that fits something else I've been thinking about. Remember what I said about his eyes being open, that for the Egyptians to see was to know? Without light there was no seeing. That has to be where our concept of enlightenment came from. Maybe what we've got is a physician ahead of his time and condemned for it, just as the early alchemists, or scientists, in Europe were persecuted as familiars of the devil."

"It fits. Oh god, yes, Max. It fits."

That afternoon she worked on several orthopedic illustrations, and again the next morning. Then, after lunch Saturday, she dropped Max at his office and drove his car, since it carried a "Physician" parking sticker, to the Medical Center for her meeting with Mike Tinsley. By the time she got back to the South Main Imaging Center it was past four o'clock. The few cars in the parking lot were gone, and it felt more like six, thanks to the clouds moving in from the Gulf, another turnaround in the weather.

She rang the bell and was let in by Max, who seemed inordinately pleased to see her, hardly able to keep from smiling and in a hurry. *Shades of the Cheshire cat*, she thought, and this time was prepared for what was coming. The object they had speculated about was indeed a miniature scribe's palette, with landscapes incised into the top and two longer sides.

"I have to get this down on paper," Kate decided, digging in her purse for the little notebook she always carried.

"I can transfer all these images to a disk so you can view them at home on my computer," Max told her.

Kate continued with the quick sketch. "I wouldn't want you to think I'm not impressed with this fantastic technology," she reassured him, "because I am. That's what's so sad, that we didn't have it before—"

"Before so much was destroyed? Yeah, I know. Same feeling I get when I think how long it's been, and how wrong we've been about how the brain works." Something in his voice made Kate glance up. "That's what the latest imaging technology means, especially fast MRI. For the first time in history we can look at how the normal brain functions, not just those that are damaged. By looking at the resting brain, then asking a subject to do something, we can trace nerve-cell activity and map the brain. In the beginning we found a lot of localization. Now, because we have better machines, we're seeing more complexity—that multiple areas are activated."

"Is that what you're doing in your research?"

"A small piece of the map, yes. At least that's what it started out to be. It turns out life isn't so simple." He gestured at her sketch. "I'll bet your brain looks like the Milky Way when you do that."

"Yeah, well, this image you just manufactured is why I'm not too optimistic that I can find enough work to live on. Medical students today study anatomy with computers instead of the real thing, view one male and female cadaver that have been sliced like sandwich meat and then digitized so any organ can be put together or separated out. I'm becoming obsolete faster than the black rhino is going extinct."

"I'm not touching that with a ten-foot pole, not until you tell me what went on with Mike Tinsley," Max responded.

"Nothing 'went on.' He showed me a few photographs, described what he wants, and asked me for suggestions. I agreed to do a few examples, and that was it."

"For how much?"

"We didn't talk money."

"Why the hell not? You're a consummate artist with the knowledge and skill to equal his with a knife and chisel."

"I'm going to watch this new surgical procedure he's developed first, before I decide, if you don't mind me hanging around through Monday."

Max nodded and went to his desk to begin putting things away. "Are you about finished? Sam's been cooped up in the house all afternoon." Kate watched him, but surreptitiously. It wasn't like Max to be evasive, or impatient.

"Almost. Did you know the Egyptians used a three-hundred-sixty-five day calendar, same as ours, with twelve months, each thirty days long?" she asked. "Difference was, they had only three seasons and the new year began around the middle of July, when the Nile flooded the land—the season of inundation."

"What did they do with the extra five days?"

"Holidays, to celebrate the birthdays of the gods. Osiris, Isis, Horus, that bunch."

"Well, I find it pretty damn hypocritical for Set to kill his brother, and Nepthys to sleep with Osiris when he's married to her sister, while ordinary mortals had to stand before Osiris and swear they never committed murder *or* adultery."

"Yin and yang," Kate mumbled. "Can't have good without bad, white without black and all that jazz. What do you think of Mike Tinsley?"

"He's okay, why?"

"Oh, just—you know what they say about surgeons."

"What, that they're arrogant? Ignorant beyond belief about everything else?"

He'd walked right into it. "That they're even more antisocial than radiologists."

SIXTEEN

Year Two in the Reign of Horemheb

(1346 B.C.)

DAY 27, FIRST MONTH OF HARVEST

The place reeked of sheep's urine and rotten eggs, which meant that the *sesh per ankh* had been there before me to make sacrifice to Amen and burn the yellow powder to drive off evil spirits. Aset's husband had to be in his late sixties, yet he looked much older, especially with his eyes closed. Like a man on his deathbed.

Lamps had been set at each corner of Uzahor's couch, leaving everyone and everything else in the smoky shadows, while one old priest chanted a mournful supplication to the gods of creation. The women of his family sat cross-legged on the floor, faces half-hidden by identical white shawls—Aset among them, I assumed, since she had left my house two nights before—while several men stood talking in hushed tones. The only one I recognized was Ramose.

Tuli ran to greet me, baring his teeth in a smile and nudging his nose into my hand. He wore a new collar with prancing red horses stitched to the white leather band. I made obeisance to him first, then the family, before Ramose motioned me to the old man's side.

"Only say what you need and I will see it done," he told me straight off, ordering me to treat his old friend no matter what.

"First I must listen to the voice of his heart and examine him with my hands." From the rapid rise and fall of Uzahor's bony chest it was plain that he found it difficult to breathe. "Does he complain of pain?"

"His wife says his left arm has given him no peace for several days." Which wife, I wondered. "When I arrived some hours ago, I thought he looked pale, but he said he felt tired and nothing else."

"Has he worsened since the priests burned the yellow powder?" I took the old man's hand in mine to examine his fingernails and found them as colorless as his face.

"No. Aset was right, then?" Ramose inquired. "The sulfur can cause sickness as well as prevent it?"

"Yes, should the fumes turn noxious." I put my fingers to the base of Uzahor's throat to confirm that his heart ran shallow and fast, then leaned down to smell his mouth, seeking the sour fruit odor of the sickness that can cause a man to fall into an unnatural sleep. But I could smell little but the stench of rotten eggs. Next I exposed the old man's abdomen to feel for any hardening or swelling in his vital organs, while I tried to think of a way to get fresh air into the room without embarrassing the God's Father before his underlings. "What does his own physician say?" I asked.

"That a man's body wears out the same as a sandal."

"He is here?"

Ramose shook his head. "My—" He glanced at Uzahor. "Though he loves me well, my old friend prefers to speak to the gods himself rather than through a priest. He sent his physician to the temple to deliver a message to the Hearing Ear, just before he fell into a deep sleep, as you see him. I suppose he sent the poor man away to save his pride, for he is not a bad physician, only a complacent one."

To me they are one and the same, but I held my tongue as I bared Uzahor's feet.

"Sometimes, Tenre, you remind me of my old friend. I wonder if that is why I raised the stakes higher than I ever intended the day I asked you to join my household, when you had the temerity to haggle with me."

It is not like Ramose to ramble, if indeed that was what he was doing, or openly to exhibit emotion. But he has long been an enigma to me, so perhaps I only imagined that his thoughts wandered in the past out of distress at the prospect of losing his friend. I pressed the flesh above Uzahor's toes and around the anklebone, to confirm that the swelling was not—like oil in a goatskin bag—the kind that comes and goes under the fingers. I noticed that two of his toenails were missing while the others had turned to chalk. I recovered his legs, put my ear to his chest, and heard the beat of a distant drum muffled by shifting currents of air, a sound with the soft edge that meant he was drowning in his own fluids.

"We must raise his head."

"Pagosh!" Ramose called. An eerie sense of familiarity came over me, another experience I cannot explain. "Bring cushions to put under his shoulders." Ramose glanced at me. "Anything else?"

"His wife"—I caught myself—"his Principal Wife, is she present?"

"Her name is Sati." He motioned to a woman who hurried to join us. Despite the cloud of white hair billowing around her head, the grace of her body was reflected in her face, where the waters of life ran silent but deep. Not that I mistook her for a placid cow. Just the opposite, judging by the way her black eyes appeared to breathe in the shifting light from the lamps, like live coals in a banked fire. Nor did they waver from mine until I put my palms together and lowered my chin in a bow.

"Welcome, Senakhtenre. May the great god bless and protect you," she murmured, returning my gesture. "The house of my Lord Uzahor is honored by your presence. How may I serve you?"

"Could we send the others away? Except Aset, in case I should need her assistance." I saw Ramose motion to someone else. "Perhaps you could ask them to approach the shrine to the god who protects this house, and ask him to restore your husband to health. After that, order someone to open the windows to let the outside air blow through."

When I turned back to Ramose, I encountered a different pair of blue eyes—eyes I would know anywhere in this world or the next. Otherwise, I suppose, I might not have recognized her, for she wore a long black wig styled in a multitude of narrow braids, each tied with a tiny carnelian Knot of Isis. Around her throat lay a wide collar of rod-shaped turquoise and lapis lazuli beads, drawing my eyes down to her breasts under a white gauze robe that did little to conceal her ripening body. I forced myself to put my palms together, but my hands trembled so that I had to lower my head to them lest someone suspect we were more to each other than a tutor and his onetime pupil.

When I glanced up again her eyes danced with mischief, as if she took pleasure in my confusion. "We must raise him up," I told her.

Without a word she hurried to the sitting shelf and grabbed a cushion in each hand. Ramose went to the other side of Uzahor's couch to help me lift him, while she slid the cushions under his head and shoulders. And with every move, the tiny carnelian amulets played a muted tune. I caught the aroma of almond oil laced with cassia blossoms, ginger, and peppermint, and knew she wore the perfume I had specially blended for her to mark the occasion when she left childhood behind. It suited her, I thought, not for the first time, its sweetness curbed by something sharp and tangy, hinting at the strength hidden beneath that soft, feminine facade.

"Hyena's tongue?" she whispered when I had the old man propped up. She waited for my nod, then took what she needed from my goatskin bag and hurried away. My eyes followed her and collided with Pagosh's black scowl. A few minutes later she was back with the warmed draught, hands trembling, perhaps because she has seen too much of death in her thirteen years. Now Anubis was on the prowl again, about to steal another of those she cared for.

"I added a little ginger, to ease his stomach." She tried to rouse Uzahor enough to swallow what we spooned into his mouth, but much of it ran down his chin. Then, respecting Sati's higher status, she went to stand behind her father, who sat watching his old friend with doleful eyes.

"There is little to do now but wait," I explained, mostly for Sati's benefit, who stood with her hand covering one of her husband's. Tuli jumped up on the couch, licked Uzahor's other hand, then settled himself within reach should he wake. Everyone grew quiet after that, waiting. I glanced up at the scene on the wall, where a single hunter aimed an arrow at his prey—a wild-eyed gazelle with neck and ears erect, vibrating with the excitement of the chase—and recognized it for what it was, an image of sexual arousal. Which only drove my eyes back to Aset.

She had outlined her eyes in black and dusted the lids with yellow ocher, reminding me of all the hours we have spent in my garden, discussing some treatment while she prepared her colors—grinding the yellow earth from the base of the cliffs or the burnt almond shells that produce a dark, purplish black. Afterward she would pour the fine powder into a length of hollow reed and plug it with papyrus pith before tucking it into her drawstring bag, where she carries the little papyrus-root lion, still her most prized possession—something I have never understood. It is of little value to anyone but the children she entertains with stories of his exploits in the Western Desert, where he outwits every hunter no matter how skilled or brave.

"He breathes a little easier," she whispered. I nodded and let my eyes follow the drape of Sati's gown to the floor, only to discover that she wore a pair of Ipwet's sandals. Finally, Uzahor's eyelids began to flutter, a sign that he was waking. But I have seen many an old man return from such a sleep to a place he did not know. It took a while before he gave Sati a weak smile and tried to speak. She put her ear to his lips, then left him to go to a wooden chest standing on crossed duckbill legs, and returned with an ivory scribe's palette.

"Aset," Uzahor rasped. Tuli pricked up his ears.

"Yes, my lord husband, I am here."

"For you." He pushed the narrow pen case at her. A hunting scene was inscribed on one side, in the lifelike style of another time, now banned—thanks to Ramose and his parochial cohorts.

"Oh, no, my lord," Aset protested, "this was a token of the Magnificent Amenhotep's high regard for you, and must go to one of your children."

Uzahor groped for her hand. "You . . . send me . . . message."

"I will, my lord, I promise." She smiled despite her tears. "I will remember your generosity through all eternity, too, just as I treasure the kindness you have shown me in this world. You and Sati."

Uzahor turned his pale, watery eyes on me, so she said, "This is the physician I told you about. Senakhtenre." He stared at me for a time, then heaved a tired sigh and closed his eyes. But almost at once he came awake again, a frantic look on his face as he sought someone or something he could not find.

"Mose . . . Ramose," he called in a faltering voice, a plea so filled with heartache that I felt my gut tighten in pity.

The High Priest leaped to his feet and took Uzahor's frail hand between both of his. "I am here. Nor will I leave you. The transgression was mine, not yours. Yet you kept faith with me through everything, even at the risk of going before Osiris with a stain on your heart." Ramose eased down onto the edge of Uzahor's couch and smiled at the old man. "You were right. I cannot escape the boy I once was, so I have waged constant war with my own *ka*, until I grow tired of the battle. But I cannot lie to you, either, and say I would willingly relive those years in order to do any different." He stared unseeing into the past, at what only he and his friend could know, all the while stroking the back of Uzahor's frail hand with his thumb. "Never to have pitted myself against her quick wit? Or watched her eyes light up when she laughs? Never to feel the touch of her hand in trust, or love? The rush of pleasure that comes with knowing she is mine?" Ramose shook his head. "Even to think of it brings the chill of death to my heart."

So did the High Priest confess his obsession with the woman who had stolen his free will, yet Uzahor smiled as if he forgave him whatever offense Ramose alluded to.

"Pharaoh's jackals will not come near you," Ramose assured his old friend, "now or in the years to come. So be at peace and rest. Sati has ordered a rich broth from the kitchen, to make you strong as a bull again." That same little smile was still on Uzahor's face when he drifted into what appeared to be a natural sleep.

I instructed Pagosh to inform Uzahor's family and servants to go to their beds, while Sati sank down on the foot of his couch to keep watch. But without any warning, the old man began struggling to rise, and finally lifted both frail arms to the sky.

"Aten comes!" he cried, a joyous smile creasing his weathered face. Then, as if the effort had sapped the last of his strength, his breath escaped from his open mouth, taking his *ka* with it, and the husk of the man he had been fell back against the cushions.

Tuli let out a long, mournful howl, then began licking the old man's hand. I moved to listen to his heart, to confirm what I already knew. From the look on Sati's face she did, too, so I closed Uzahor's sightless eyes, straightened his blanket, and folded it neatly across his chest, to give her time to recover herself. She dropped to her knees beside her husband's couch, took his lifeless hand, and pressed it to her forehead as the elderly priest began an incantation to Osiris. *"Blessed be Osiris. Blessed be the son of earth sprung from the egg of the world. Blessed be the son of heaven, dropped from the belly of the sky. Blessed be the god in his names, salvation of priests and goatherds, king of kings, lord of lords. Priest and man, his body shimmers turquoise green."* When he finished she put her lips to Uzahor's hand for the last time, rose and wrapped her dignity about her like a shawl, and went to inform the others who kept vigil in the antechamber to his room.

I wondered if Ramose had known that his friend worshiped the Heretic's god even after Horemheb's proclamation made it a crime. Why else would the old man cry out to Aten instead of Amen-Re or Osiris? Unless he had only been reliving his youth, as so many old men do, in the time of the Magnificent Amenhotep, who championed Aten above other gods. By the time his son, who styled himself Aten's one and only, was gone from the Two Lands, Uzahor must have been at least fifty and set in his ways.

Aset took Tuli in her arms to quiet his whining and went to her father's side, but Ramose continued to stare at the wasted shell of his beloved friend. It was not until the mourners outside began to wail that he roused himself to give her instructions.

"Go and change into whatever you wear as the physician's boy. Pagosh will be waiting at the rear gate to take you from here. Speak to no one along the way and keep your eyes cast down." She reached up and gave him a hug, then darted a wide-eyed glance at me. Ramose watched her until she was out of sight before turning to me. "It was Uzahor's wish to return to Abydos, the place where he entered this world. Those who have outlived him here consider him eccentric in any case, in part because he preferred one woman to several." He came near to smiling then. "He always claimed his sexual pleasure was the more intense because of it, but—"

"How, then, did he explain taking a second wife?"

"By sacrificing the truth of his wisdom and experience to the jibes of his friends, out of love for me." Ramose gazed at the lifeless face. "He always found his own path. Even more so since Aset. He once told me that she was my greatest achievement, no matter how high I rose in position or wealth." A bittersweet smile took his lips. "Just knowing he was here—" His throat worked to swallow his grief, so I stilled my curious tongue instead of asking what he planned now and stood like an accused man before Pharaoh's judges, waiting to hear my sentence pronounced. Expecting exile.

"Now I must ride the storm alone," he mumbled when he found his voice again, then fixed his blue eyes on mine.

I spoke first, clothing my promise in a warning. "I will do whatever it takes to keep her safe."

"If ever I doubted it, Tenre, that time is long past. But we must move quickly. His daughter goes to Memphis to a marriage already arranged. Sati will accompany him to Abydos and live nearby in the house that has been in his family since the time of the great Thutmose. For the next few weeks, while we mourn him here, no one from this house will mention Aset, but you must put a guard on her lest she leave your walls."

"Her word will be sufficient," I replied, then dared to ask, "Uzahor left no sons?"

For a moment he stared at me. Then he shook his head and continued as before. "For now Merit and Pagosh must remain here."

"And afterward?"

"You would add two more to your menagerie?" I nodded. "Then I will leave it for them to decide. Pagosh will bring her clothes when he can, probably after dark, but if at any time you get wind of something that does not smell right, send word to me by your man Khary, so I will know the message is not a ruse."

It was not the first time Ramose has aroused my suspicions even as he granted me reprieve, for it is one thing to know that Khary manages my dispensary and another to recognize him by sight, even for a priest who is on speaking terms with the king of the gods.

DAY 4, SECOND MONTH OF HARVEST

I was finishing my midday meal when I looked up to find Khary hurrying along the path between his private garden and mine, followed by a man carrying a large basket on one shoulder, whom I took for a vendor. As they neared I saw that Tuli led the way, wagging his tail, and felt a twinge of uneasiness at his acceptance of the stranger who wore a striped nemes and dirty rag looped over one eye and cheek.

"Where do you want it?" Khary asked, as if I had ordered what the man carried.

"How in god's name should I know?"

When the one-eyed man lifted the basket from his shoulder and set it on the ground, the stink of his unwashed body descended on me like a cloud of flies on a pile of fresh dung. I did not recognize the crisscrossed sticks he carried, so I picked one up and held it to my nose. He bent to push the sticks aside, revealing a folded length of unbleached linen. I shrugged, wondering why Khary bothered me with replenishing our supply of bandaging, but before I could speak he lifted the cloth to reveal something blue. Lapis, from the look of it. And turquoise!

I grabbed his arm, turning him until I could see the satisfied smile break across his bronze face. "By Thoth but you stink, Pagosh." I had been expecting him in the dark of night, not with Re-Aten high in the sky. "Your sense of humor grows bold with age." Khary began to laugh, setting Tuli to running circles around our feet.

"It was not meant to be funny, *sunu*." Pagosh pulled the dirty rag from his head and waited for the commotion to subside. "If I can fool you, I need not worry."

"I'll wager you did not get past Aset." He shrugged and refused to meet my eyes. "Surely you must have seen her. She watches Khary's son on the mornings Tamin goes to market to sell Ipwet's sandals."

"We spoke."

I motioned him to the other chair. "You brought her belongings?"

"And a bundle of scrolls from Uzahor's library," he replied, dropping onto the empty stool. "There are more, but my donkey is all skin and bones. The others were already taken to haul grain from the fields. It will require one more trip at least." I filled a clay mug with beer and handed it across to him. He feigned indifference, but even the date palms and willows were wilting under the brutal onslaught of the sun.

"I will unload the other basket from your poor beast," Khary offered, probably to let us talk in private, "and put him to graze in what remains of the kitchen garden. A mouthful or two will sweeten his temper."

Pagosh chewed a bite of bread and cheese, then washed it down with beer. "Mena came this week as usual?" he asked. I nodded. "He encounters nothing unusual across the river?"

"Horemheb worries about what the Hittites do now that Mursili sits in his father's place. An envoy from Hattusas arrived and demands reparation for the untimely end of the prince they sent to Ankhesenamen. It seems he was full brother to Mursili."

"So the crow comes home to roost," Pagosh muttered.

"Does Ramose expect trouble from that quarter?"

"Is Pharaoh bent on ridding the Two Lands of the Heretic's followers?" he replied, since it is forbidden now even to speak the rebel's name, let alone worship his god.

"To worship Aten is not necessarily to follow the Heretic," I pointed out.

"Tell that to Horemheb."

"His Edict of Reform has been inscribed on the temple wall, to assure that ignorance will be no defense when wrongdoers are called before Pharaoh's judges. Horemheb must have had the Sacred Council's approval, so they all have a taste for blood. Even a petty thief fears the words he cannot read once he has seen a man's hand chopped off." I tipped up the pitcher to refill his mug. "Pharaoh has made no move toward Nefertiti, so Aset will be safe for the same reason, even if word gets around about Uzahor. Anyway, the man who signed the marriage contract now is High Priest of Amen." Pagosh kept his gaze trained on the plot where the fennel and purple thyme bloomed, as if to delay telling me the bad news.

"Does Ramose say what he plans for Aset?" I asked.

"I know that his love for her is that of a father. If he cares more than most fathers for their daughters—well, Aset is not like most daughters."

I recalled Ramose saying the same, but a lot of silt has come down the river to muddy the water since then. "The question is, does he love someone or something else more?"

"After so many years of your tutoring, *sunu*, it is a wonder Aset trusts anyone."

"I could say the same about you," I countered.

"Ramose told me of your offer," he said, still not looking at me. "I thank you from my heart, Tenre, but it is better that we return to him."

"We are not without resources here now that so many physicians from the House of Life send their assistants to the Eye of Horus for pills and potions, if that is what worries you. Khary hears more about what goes on than an entire army of spies, especially if it is to do with which officer is Pharaoh's latest favorite, or whose wife lies with another man. Or woman."

He bit into a fig from the bowl on my table. "Netted like a bird in your garden, I might do something foolish and betray you both."

"You? Foolish?" Bemused, I could only shake my head. "What about Merit? Or did you give her a choice?" He bent to retrieve something from the basket, then handed me a scrap of papyrus.

"She sent this to show that she practices what Aset taught her." I looked at what had been written on it. *My thoughts go with you.* "From the beginning whenever Aset came to Uzahor's villa, she would read to Merit. A love poem written in another time or a story with a lesson hidden in it, turning it into a game. Once she read to her from the journal kept by a great Queen whose heart was torn asunder by the loss of her babe. Afterward Merit told me she could feel the Queen's pain in her own heart. It made her believe in the magic of words. And to know that a Queen could suffer as she did made her feel less alone. Not so—so flawed." He scowled. "That is her word, not mine, and I have forbidden her ever to use it again."

He fell silent for a moment, leaving me to wonder how he can say so much with so few words. "That Merit never had more babes I believe to be the will of the goddess, who intended us for another purpose. So Merit returns willingly to the High Priest, to mingle with the women who serve his *tahut*." He drained the last of his beer and heaved himself up, disturbing Tuli's dreams of chasing a rabbit. "My wife would never admit it, but having Aset taken from her has allowed her time to become friends with other servants in the neighborhood." He twirled the dirty rag around one forefinger. "A young widow named Amenet, for one."

"If you wonder why I do not go there anymore," I said to save him the trouble of asking, "it is nothing to do with her. Amenet is pleasing enough to look at, and talented in the ways to satisfy a man. But it is not *maat* that I continue with her when I have no intention of making her my wife. Already I have too many women in my life. Nofret and Tamin. Ipwet. Surely that is enough for any man to put up with."

"Wait much longer, *sunu*, and you will leave no children to say your name after you pass between the mountains to the west."

"If what I do in this world is not reason enough to be remembered, then my name does not deserve to live. Like you, Pagosh, I believe it is the will of the gods that I care for the children of others rather than my own." He nodded, and I breathed a sigh of relief, too soon as it turned out, for he had one more arrow in his quiver.

"I notice you did not mention Aset among the women you must put up with. Why is that, I wonder?" He did not wait for an answer, but started off across my garden, leaving me to ponder what he left unsaid.

DAY 29, THIRD MONTH OF HARVEST

A man Khary knew as a boy came to him in the night seeking help for his wife. Lulled by the darkness, and because Aset has not been outside my walls for two months, I allowed her to come along, a thoughtless act that put her within a breath of disaster.

On the way Khary told us that Pepi had been sentenced to ten years' hard labor in the mines of the Sinai for stealing bread, and on returning to the city of his birth found work cutting stones for the pylon Horemheb erects before the temple of Amen. The mud hovel Khary led us to looked clean enough, except for the smoke issuing from a single oil lamp. But that a workman has no salt for his lamp, to keep it from fouling the air he breathes, is a sign of unjust wages and more a measure of the one who pays him.

"I believed my god would heal all sickness if we but followed his example to be clean and treat all living things with love," Pepi confessed, "but I could not stand and do nothing but pray." Some of his teeth were missing, and his breath was noisy, a sign of the lung sickness that afflicts so many men who work cutting stones, but his only concern was his wife.

"That she bleeds is not a good sign," I agreed. I could feel no movement in his wife's belly, so I gave her a potion to help expel the babe—whether breathing or not—while Aset tried to soothe the woman with words of encouragement. Khary had stepped back outside, I thought to preserve the woman's dignity though I know now that it was to stand guard.

When the contractions came harder she began to cry out, curling her body over the agony in her belly. When Pepi tried to comfort her, Aset came to where I knelt on the floor between her legs. "Is it time yet?"

I shook my head. "But not much longer."

"Did you notice the face of Aten on the wall above the lamp?" she whispered. "The orange disk glows as if the sun still lives. And her name is Thuya, like the mother of old Queen Tiye." I nodded but made no reply, for we already knew that Pepi had lived for a time among the nomads of the Sinai, as does the Heretic even now, and had married the daughter of a Shasu shepherd. But in worshiping his god here they went against the law of the Two Lands.

"Take me, my god, I beg you," Thuya cried at the height of one long tightening, in a voice that brought tears to my heart. "Let Mose be my shepherd to show me the way, for I can bear no more." So did she call Akhenaten what his followers name him among themselves now.

"Aten's face shines upon you, Thuya," Aset assured her, moving to take her hand, "even now, though you walk in the shadow of the valley of death. Be not afraid, for he is with you." Her words seemed to comfort Pepi's wife, or perhaps that was when the babe's head finally pushed through the barrier that had held him back.

"Pharaoh's wolves are coming!" Khary hissed as he burst into the room. "Pepi, snuff that flame." The stonecutter leaped to his feet while Khary grabbed Aset and shoved her into a dark corner, unwrapped his kilt and threw it over her, head and all. That was when I first noticed two small children asleep on the floor.

"Not a sound," Khary warned, and to Pepi, "do what you can to keep her quiet."

In the silence that followed we marked the approach of Pharaoh's Aten police by the dogs they roused, and I thanked the gods we had not brought Tuli. Only a tattered rag draped the doorway to shield us from prying eyes, nor was there another way out. We were trapped like rats in a cage, in the dark. But I could feel with my fingers, and knew the babe's head was about to emerge from his mother's body. A minute later I cupped the babe's head in one hand, and felt for a tiny shoulder with the other. Coated with the slippery paste that greased his way, I almost dropped him when he kicked his feet and let out a pitiful mewling, a sound more catlike than human.

I breathed a sigh of relief though my hands shook at the thought that his cries might bring Pharaoh's police down on our heads. But a babe hungering in the night for his mother's breast, or a cat on the prowl, are common enough to pass without notice by men with an eye only for the telltale light of Aten. I cradled the babe in one arm to ward off the night air, stroking his cheek with my finger while we waited for them to pass, hardly daring to breathe.

Finally, after what seemed an eternity, the sound of barking dogs faded away. "Stay where you are while I make sure they left no one behind," Khary whispered, and slipped through the ragged doorway. I did not hear him return until he spoke again. "It is safe to light the lamp again." No one stirred. "Pepi?" he whispered.

A heart-wrenching cry rent the dark room. "My god has forsaken me—" the stonecutter sobbed. I felt the air stir as Khary moved past me, fumbled with the lamp, whispered a curse, and finally got a flame going.

Aset saw the babe in my arms, and hurried to take him from me. "Oh, Thuya, what a beautiful babe you have! Look, Pepi, a boy." She glanced at Pepi and fell silent, sensing that something was wrong.

He still held his wife, but tears were running down his cheeks.

"Beloved of my body, mate of my *ka*, without you I am an empty husk," he wept into her hair. "Oh, Aten, mightiest of the mighty, from whom all life flows. Let your light shine upon her face that she may breathe again. Come back to me, Thuya, come back." He went on pleading with his god to restore her to life or take him instead, calling her name, begging Thuya to forgive him—for what, no one could bear to ask. Whether Pepi smothered his wife while trying to keep her from crying out, or Thuya chose that way herself rather than bring us all to grief, I cannot say.

The followers of Aten believe it is only in the wickedness they embrace in this life that one man differs from another. But is it wickedness simply to believe in the wrong god, whether it be Amen-Re or Aten, two faces of the same sun? That is the crux of my disaffection with all the priests.

DAY 30 FOURTH MONTH OF HARVEST

Flocks of white ibis have begun to appear in the shorn brown fields, for like Thoth they know the secret of the flood that renews our soil and so do not have to depend on the dog star to tell them when to fly north. Surely the rising waters of Mother River cannot be far behind, but waiting to learn if there will be enough or too much, sweeping away our homes and animals along with the canals that feed the higher fields, is an uneasy time for all. In the meantime, Aset makes corn-husk dolls for the shrine of Hapi, to celebrate the New Year and placate the capricious river god.

Most days she assists Khary in the dispensary, but the routine of our lives changes in other ways as well. In the evenings now she puts on one of the gauze gowns she wore as Uzahor's wife before joining me for our meal, and tonight I noticed she is letting her hair grow. But when I mentioned it she just shrugged and smiled, a little guiltily, I thought. Afterward I sought her advice about a sick child, only to have her recall the man whose leg drew up until he could not put his foot flat on the ground.

"Yet everyone beset by fever does not end with a useless leg." I waited, for she has the habit of fitting one thought to another the way a master bricklayer constructs a wall. "A woman's womb tightens when she labors to expel her babe, and that causes pain, as well, but the tightening comes and goes like waves washing ashore after a passing boat. What of the pain in Uzahor's arm? Could that have been a tightening, too?"

"His pain was a sign that the heart begins to falter."

"So the tightening is in the cardia, not the muscles of the arm." I stopped eating, curious as to where she would go next. "In both kinds of vessels, or only the ones I painted red on your map?" It seemed to me an echo of my own voice, telling Senmut that somehow we must learn to ask the right questions.

Always before I asked what path the blood takes through the body, not how it gets there. But that, I believe, may finally be the right question.

SEVENTEEN

The sun made Kate squint when she came out of the hospital, and a summerlike blast of heat hit her when she opened the door of Max's Mercedes. That's when she decided to go shopping. By three o'clock, when she breezed into the Imaging Center, she was feeling happy in a way she hadn't for a long time. And comfortable, thanks to the cotton outfit she'd just bought.

Marilou spotted her right away and beckoned her to the reception desk. "Boy, am I glad to see *you*. He's been driving us—" She broke off as the devil himself appeared.

"Hi," Max said, eyes moving all over her, then back to her face. "I was beginning to worry, thought you might've gotten lost or something."

"I went shopping." She turned to make her skirt flare out, showing off the embroidered camisole top and overshirt to match. All three pieces were the same color, a dusty cinnamon that made her eyes look almost green.

"I noticed. Does that mean Tins¹ through with a fat check?"

"Mostly it means the clothes I brought with me are too warm for this weather," she said as she followed him down the hall.

"So tell me about it," Max invited, once they were in his office.

Kate spread the sketches she'd done at the hospital across his desk, showing the steps in Mike Tinsley's new procedure for repairing a fractured kneecap. Max gave them a cursory glance, then picked up the one of Tinsley with his binocular magnifying goggles pushed up on his forehead.

"I thought he'd use a photograph to show the setup with all the equipment in place," Kate explained, "so I was just trying to get down the way it felt to me there—the aura of excitement at the beginning and how the tension builds, then the letdown after the procedure climaxes and everyone begins to settle back into familiar territory, closing up. But that one seemed to turn the tide." She paused. "Did you know he plays Mahler while he operates?" Max shook his head and waited.

"I'm going to illustrate the entire book, use my own judgment about what needs illustrating, and how. Tinsley wants to frame each procedure with scene-setting sketches like that one, to bring in the psychology that colors everything a student or resident does or doesn't do, no matter what level of skill they acquire—what we all share in common: the human factor. It's one thing to draw an anatomically accurate picture and something else to present it in a way that keeps everyone reminded that they're dealing with other human beings. I guess that's what made me realize I was being handed the chance to do something really important, not just work for hire."

The instant she said it Kate realized that the need to portray the humanizing aspect of medicine had been the driving force behind her illustrations from the moment she dropped out of medical school, coloring not only her drafting style but how she chose to present her subjects. That was what Max had been trying to say about her drawings, from the very beginning.

She tried to smile at him, but her lips began to wobble, so she just hugged him instead. He held her and rubbed his cheek against her hair.

"I'm not a gambler," she told him when she recovered her voice and could pull away without revealing how close she'd come to tears, "maybe because I've never been able to afford it, but, well, I agreed to do an unlimited number of illustrations—to be determined by me after I see Mike's text, plus suggestions from him. He gets final approval, but my name appears on the title page." She paused, watching Max's face, but he seemed to know she wasn't finished.

"I'm also planning to learn all I can about the latest computer-graphics stuff so that I can use whatever works best in a given situation. That way I'll also be in a position to enlarge on what I can offer other potential customers. Not that I told *him* that. What I'm gambling is that I'll make enough to cover all the time this one project is going to take. I hope it isn't just ego, but he thinks we've got the makings of a classic, so I asked for a percentage of the royalties plus a piece of whatever advance he gets from his publisher. He thinks that will go way up when they see my illustrations and know I'm going to do the whole book."

"Tinsley actually told you all that?" Max asked, incredulous. "Not much of a businessman, is he?" Kate hoped that wasn't just a variation on his habit of going silent when faced with something unexpected or unknowable.

Without thinking, she reached out and tugged on his hand. "Come on, Max, say what you really think. Did I give away the store, make the deal of a lifetime, or what?"

"It doesn't matter how much money you make if it's really important to you, but I call it an act of faith, not gambling."

Tuesday morning, after Max left for his office, Kate put Sam on his leash and jogged down to the office supply in Rice Village, the neighborhood shopping center just a few blocks from Max's house. When they returned she spread everything out on the kitchen table, which sat in an alcove framed by floor-to-ceiling windows, and went to work. First she made several anatomical drawings of the human knee, in pencil. Then she selected the best one and refined the lines with India ink, slipped it into a folder, told Sam to behave, and hurried out to her car.

Two hours later, when she emerged from the hair salon Marilou had recommended, a languid Gulf breeze had turned Houston into a humid hothouse. "Great!" she muttered, sure her hair would be up around her ears by the time she reached the car. Back at Max's house she showered, taking care not to look at herself until she was out and dressed, then stood in front of the full-length mirror—and almost didn't recognize the woman she saw! Anxious now, and in a hurry, she returned to the kitchen and pulled the cork on a bottle of wine to let it breathe, then went back to work.

She was trying to decide which tendon to do next when she heard a car door slam. Suddenly nervous as a cat, she dipped her paintbrush into the jar of water and hurried to where she'd left the wine, filled the two stemmed glasses, and turned just as Max come through the door.

"Hi. Sorry I'm so late," he apologized, dropped his briefcase on the floor, and bent to fondle Sam's ears. It wasn't until he slipped off his suit coat and threw it over the back of a chair that he noticed the wine. "Are we celebrating something?"

"Maybe." She handed him a glass, not wanting to make a big thing of her hair. Cut just to the edge of her jaw, it was at least three inches shorter and for the first time in her life held a shape rather than curling up in a frizzy mess—not to mention the highlighting she thought made it look healthier and more alive.

She knew the instant he noticed, mostly by the way his eyes changed. "Turn around," he ordered. She did a quick spin and felt a smile begin inside her head. "Again, slower." He slid his arms around her from behind and laid his lips to her ear. "I'm beginning to understand why a man might risk his head for a woman."

Kate turned and threw her arms around his neck, only to have him reach up and slowly pull them away. It took her a second to realize that the wineglass she held was empty. "Oh God, Max, I'm sorry."

"I need to shower, anyway, and change for supper. Then you can pour me another glass and tell me what you did today." He ruffled her hair. "Besides this."

She made herself go back to the illustration and tried to concentrate on what she was doing instead of thinking about what Max had just said. Or rather, what he could possibly have meant. Surely it was nothing more than a halfway joking sort of compliment about her hair. Or was it?

She jumped when she felt a hand on her shoulder. "Sorry. Don't stop."

"I'll be done in a second. Plastic doesn't absorb paint, so if I stop now, I'll have to overpaint a dry edge and leave a raised line."

He refilled her glass as well as his, set it on the table out of her way, then pulled out a chair and sat down. "What kind of paint is that?"

"Opaque watercolor."

He didn't speak again until she tipped her brush into the murky water. "Tell me what you're doing."

"What you see as you go into the knee, enhanced by color shadings to distinguish one tendon or piece of cartilage from another— instead of those." She gestured at the stack of axial scans Mike Tinsley had given her. "It was my idea to—here, I'll show you." She reached for one of the inked outlines. "I had this copied onto transparent sheets so they'd all be identical. Now I'm putting in where and how the tendons attach to the bone, but on different sheets so you can peel them away one at a time to reveal the shape, color, and texture of everything you have to deal with surgically, one at a time." She stacked the three painted transparencies she'd finished and handed them to Max. "Think it's going to work?"

"You wouldn't have taken it this far if it didn't." He lifted the first sheet, then the next. "Ever think of doing a book on forensic art, maybe combine your drawings and the kind of illustrations you're doing for Tinsley with MRI or CT scans?"

"I doubt the market would be big enough to interest any publishers."

"Even if you build it around Tashat? You could describe the coffin inscription and how the X rays disprove her age but confirm those paintings—that she was left-handed. Show her injuries and the gold glove. Include photographs of the computer-generated composites and compare it with the cartonnage mask. Pose all the unanswered questions and suggest poss answers, about Ptah and Khnum, the plants in that garden- He stopped. "Did Dave ever venture an opinion about that, by the way?" Kate shook her head. "Does he even know they're medicinal?"

"Not from me."

"Then you're home free."

"He'd never give me permission to use my illustrations, let alone a photograph."

"Maybe he doesn't have to. All they own is what they paid you to do, which you left with them. What about the photographs I saw at your house?"

"I bought the film and used my own camera. Dave was going to have a professional photographer come in after everything was done. But that doesn't mean I can publish them without permission."

"He said it, Kate. You were a hired hand. Phil and I donated our expertise and the scan with no strings attached. Dave never asked us to sign a thing, so I doubt he could stop us from giving someone else permission to use those films, but I'll check with my lawyer."

"I don't know, Max. Maybe I should talk to Cleo."

"Okay. I guess you owe her that much. While you're at it, ask if she knows what Dave is planning to do with the head and your drawings." He paused. "What's the hieroglyph for artist?"

"There isn't one. They had sculptors and craftsmen and different kinds of scribes. An outline scribe was top dog because he laid out the register on the tomb walls and drew the figures, then others came behind him and filled in the colors, or chiseled away the lines to create reliefs. Why?"

"We talk about the art of medicine. I thought they might have the same figure of speech. Okay, so that's a dead end. How about the glyph for Osiris?"

Kate reached into the wastebasket for something to write on, drew the glyph for Isis—the staired-stepped throne—added an open eye with a brow to the left of it and a seated man to the right.

"So her name was derived from his?" Max asked.

"Or his was built by adding to hers, the same way the human fetus develops as female before undergoing modification to become male—as you very well know, *Dr.* Cavanaugh!"

"You and Marilou go for the jugular every time," he muttered, shaking his head. "Must have the same short in your neural networks."

She caught the little twitch at the corner of his mouth, so she let him have the other barrel. "The Egyptians didn't use a horned viper as the sign for the male pronoun for nothing."

. . .

Kate volunteered to fix her specialty, a tuna-noodle casserole they could share with Sam, while Max prepared a salad, just to keep it simple. Now that she'd committed to the Tinsley textbook, it was time to bring up the subject she'd been avoiding.

"If you're finished with the paper, Max, I thought I'd look at the want ads, see what may be available for rent."

"There's no rush," he mumbled without looking at her. "Better wait until you've have a chance to case out the different parts of town, unless—"

"I've already stayed longer than—"

He turned to confront her. "I like having you here—you and Sam."

"I like—we like being here."

It was as if they were using code and the words had another meaning, but Kate was worried that she was reading more into them than he intended. In the past few days she had become painfully aware that she was far more interested in Maxwell Cavanaugh the man than she was in Dr. Cavanaugh the radiologist. But she still couldn't be sure that his feelings for her weren't strictly platonic, and she didn't want to embarrass him, let alone herself.

Later, while they were cleaning the dishes away, he told her he was going to go search the Net for a while, which she interpreted as a subtle hint that he wanted to be alone, until he asked, "Want to see what the Egyptology groupies are talking about? You might learn something."

"That the sphinx was built by aliens from another planet?" she replied. "No thanks. I better finish those transparencies for Mike Tinsley."

It seemed only a few minutes until he was back. "Did you know the Ebers Papyrus was found between the legs of a mummy?" He could hardly contain himself. "A mummy from the necropolis at Thebes!"

"Seems like I read that one of the medical papyri was. Why?"

"She has to ask why?" he asked Sam, who looked to Kate, then back at Max. "Has to be some reason. Why wrap a medical handbook with a physician's body instead of just leaving it in his tomb like all the food and other stuff he was going to need in the afterlife?"

"I don't know, but Cleo might."

He started to leave, then turned back to ask, "Is there anything else I should know that you neglected to tell me, besides where the Ebers was found?"

Kate thought for a minute, then beckoned him to her. While he watched, she dipped her straight pen into the bottle of ink and drew an arched brow, a circle for a pupil, then a wedge-shaped cheek mark of a falcon near the inside of the eye. Another line started just below the pupil but angled toward the crest of the cheekbone, ending in an open coil. "That's the tear line of a cheetah. Look familiar?"

"The magic Eye of Horus."

She nodded. "Each part of the eye is also the sign for a fraction. This line stands for a half, this for a quarter, an eighth, this a sixteenth, a thirty-second, and a sixty-fourth. Physicians used those symbols to designate the amount of each ingredient in a medicine. That's why the Eye of Horus is the symbol of health, of being whole."

"You must've left one out. The fractions you mentioned don't add up to one."

"The rest is for the magic that makes the eye shine with life." She drew an R, extended the leg as she had the tear line, and then crossed it. ℞ "You're still printing the Eye of Horus on your prescription pad."

"Remind me never to play Trivial Pursuit with you," Max muttered. "Anything else?"

Kate fluttered her eyelashes in an exaggerated show of thinking. "Uh, let me see." Something in her voice caused Sam to wag his tail. "Oh, but surely he already knows that," she said to the dog.

"Try me," Max insisted, daring her.

"One medical papyrus, an old one, suggests that the Egyptians believed a woman could get pregnant through the mouth."

As the slow grin she liked to watch started in his eyes, then spread to his lips and took a decidedly devilish turn, Kate felt her cheeks go hot and knew she was blushing.

He said it anyway. "I guess that tells us something about their sexual practices, doesn't it?"

She was saved by the phone. It was Cleo, and Max handed her the receiver, then absented himself so they could talk in private. The first thing Cleo asked was when she was coming back, which she avoided answering by describing her arrangement with Mike Tinsley. When Kate asked about Tashat, Cleo told her the mummy was back in storage.

"I've got the head and your drawings in my office." Cleo paused. "I knew you were good, Katie, but—damn, this is going to sound maudlin, and maybe it's just the time of day or the amount of light coming in through the window, but I could swear the expression on her face changes. Sometimes it feels as if she's watching me with that little smile, like she knows something I don't."

Kate recognized it for the compliment Cleo meant it to be. "Well, you might want to hold off using any of that stuff for a while. Max and I are working on something that could change everything. Nothing definite yet, but it could send Dave to the showers with his tail between his legs. Are you sure everything's okay, Cleo, that he isn't going to take what happened with me out on you?"

"Listen, when I heard what he did I got to thinking about some other stuff that never sounded quite right. Decided to conduct what you might call an urban dig, inside the museum. I've also got Phil playing the rich collector with a couple of New York dealers. So not to worry. If what I suspect is true, Dave's the one who'll be out on the street, not me."

After breakfast Max made no move to go change, and then surprised Kate by suggesting that they play a few games of tennis.

"I haven't played since college, and I never was very good. Certainly no match for you. I wish you wouldn't feel you have to entertain me."

"I don't. Wednesdays are my day at the Health Sciences Center, but I already called Ben, told her I wouldn't be in until after lunch. Thought you might want to come along, see what we're doing and get a look at one of the imaging machines I told you about, that you're not going to run into outside a major medical school. Fast MRI."

"What does that mean?"

"That we can watch the brain while it's functioning—that it can produce pictures quick enough to catch a fleeting thought."

"Are you sure I won't be in the way?"

He shook his head. "Go put on your Reeboks, or whatever, while I get a couple of rackets. Maybe we can teach Sam to retrieve the balls."

Curiosity got the better of her. "Who's Ben?"

"Beth Casey, one of the bright new stars in the Department of Neuroscience. Everybody calls her Ben—you know, the doctor in that old TV program?"

Kate didn't have a clue, maybe because TV had been off-limits a lot of the time when she was growing up—punishment for "not paying attention." When she didn't respond, Max quickly dismissed it with, "I guess that was before your time," making Kate wish she hadn't asked.

Cute as a bug's ear—that was Ben Casey. But it didn't take Kate long to discover that appearances could be deceiving. Despite the pixie smile and demeanor, the young neurophysiologist was dead serious about "what makes us tick"—the same driving force that had cooled Max's youthful ardor for Egyptology.

"From what Max told me, you're probably familiar with a lot of this," she began, "but if you have any questions, about anything, don't hesitate to ask." She glanced at Max. "Klaus is in the hole, waiting. Harry's in there with him."

Max nodded and led Kate into the adjacent room, where a man stood talking to a mop-headed, bespectacled teenager, who sat in what looked like an oversize club chair. Unlike the scanner chambers Kate was familiar with, this one had been designed to allow a patient to sit up, which she realized was necessary for someone to perform a task like writing, or fitting pieces into a jigsaw puzzle.

Max addressed the man standing beside the scanner. "Harry Blanton masquerades as the psychologist on the team, though he's too sane to be very convincing," he began by way of introduction. "And Klaus Rodenberg is our resident software genius, a man of multiple talents. He's not only bilingual but ambidextrous. That's why he spends a lot of time in here letting us try to figure out how he does it."

Close-up Klaus looked closer to fifty than fifteen. It was only the unkempt hair and rubbery posture that gave the impression of a perennial teenager, that made him look immature or at least unfinished. Kate wanted to ask the psychologist why, if they were really creative or innovative, so many computer nerds looked like clones of Bill Gates.

"Klaus, Harry—this is Kate McKinnon." Both men smiled and nodded. That Max didn't bother to identify who she was made her suspect that they already knew.

"How long is it safe to be in there?" she asked Klaus. She had only a superficial familiarity with research on brain function, mostly from newspaper reports that were frustratingly devoid of details about how the experiments were carried out, which left the findings impossible to evaluate.

"We limit ourselves to an hour at a time since we're not sure about the effects of long-term exposure to electromagnetic fields. But we don't have any evidence that it scrambles your brain, if that's what you mean. No injection of radioactive glucose, either, which you have to do with PET. That's why these fast little babies have changed the entire landscape of brain research."

"We better get out of here, give you time to slow down," Max said, motioning for Harry to proceed with the blindfold and earphones.

Kate followed him back to the larger room, where Beth Casey waited. While Max set up the machine he explained to Kate how the process worked.

"With these beefed-up magnets we can watch the brain's circuitry as it thinks, talks, imagines, or just listens—by exploiting the fact that activated brain cells use more oxygen than cells at rest. As the red cells give up oxygen the blood moves toward tiny veins that carry it back to the lungs." He glanced up to make sure she was following what he said, so Kate nodded. "What the scanner detects is this blood flow, because deoxygenated blood gives off a different magnetic signal than oxygenated blood. The machine captures the magnetic waves from the shifting blood supply in the brain, the software converts the electronic data into detailed images and gives us moving pictures of the activated networks."

She nodded again, and Beth picked up where Max had stopped. "We start by eliminating as much sensory stimuli from the outside as possible, to get a baseline image of the brain at rest. We have a pretty good idea of what that should look like from previous sessions with Klaus, but we still have to wait for the brain to settle into a passive mode. The protocol we're following today deals with the silent generation of words and images. First Harry will give him a letter of the alphabet and ask him to silently sound out every word he can think of that begins with that letter. Generally we see a lot of variation between subjects on this task, with different areas of the known language regions lighting up but synchronized with one or more of the hearing areas." She stopped talking when images began to appear on the monitor of the command console.

For a while neither Max nor Beth spoke except to clue Kate about what Klaus was being asked to do. Fascinated by the constant ebb and flow of colors—mostly yellows, greens, and orange— she couldn't take her eyes from the monitor, even to search for a stool.

"Here's where Harry asks him to picture a black cat," Beth explained. One area glowed bright yellow, and not far from it, a section of dark green turned yellow-green. "And now he's thinking about drawing the cat with his left hand. The right motor cortex lights up because he's preparing for movement even if he doesn't actually do it. But watch what happens when he's asked to imagine drawing the cat with his right hand." Kate saw both the right and left motor cortex light up. "The same thing happens when a right-handed person is asked to draw with his left hand," Max added.

"Now we're heading into the final run," Beth told her. "This is where Harry gives him a list of technical requirements related to processing information with a computer, and asks him to try to solve the problem in his head, without any feedback from outside to stimulate the visual cortex." The monitor began flashing like a neon sign, colors going on and off as signals raced along unseen neural pathways from one part of the brain to another. "That's complexity of the highest order—abstract analysis and then synthesis," Beth observed.

"Look at the energy it takes, and the extent of involvement. See where the yellows burn orange and even red in some places." Max shook his head in wonder.

"What?" Kate demanded, wanting to know the reason for the look on his face.

He gave her a self-conscious smile. "Watching the human brain perform still gives me the shivers. I can hardly believe my luck in being alive here and now instead of back when Tashat lived." He got up, as if suddenly realizing that he'd been sitting while Kate was standing. "Would you like to give it a try?"

Kate hesitated for a second, then shrugged. "Sure, why not?"

Twenty minutes later she was the one in the hot seat, trying to follow the directions being fed into her ears—to not think about anything—without success. How could anybody be conscious and not think? Didn't that define consciousness?

"You're still racing your motor," Max told her through the earphones. "We're going to pipe in a mixture of frequencies called white noise for a few minutes, see if that helps you slow down."

The utter silence that followed was so profound it brought a new thought. Was this what it was like to be entombed?

With no competing outside stimuli, the sense of déjà vu that had been waiting in the wings of her mind moved center stage, coloring and shaping every picture that flashed before her inner eye. How it had looked and felt as she passed through the big cylindrical CT scanner, aware that the people outside could see through her skin. See all the places that hurt.

"Kate? Are you okay?" Silence, then, "We don't have to do this. You can come out if you want." Max sounded concerned, worried. Anxious.

"No, but I'm probably too new at this to clear my mind. Do you think it might help if we started some task?"

"Okay, but anytime you want to quit just say so. Harry's going to hand you a pad of paper and a pencil. First we want you to picture two animals. Any two animals." She did what he asked. "Now draw them." She did that, too, sketching quickly, and was barely finished when he spoke again. "Tell me what the animals are doing." She tried to, but a song by the Beatles came over the earphones, drowning out the sound of her own voice. Then, without warning, the music stopped and she heard several sharp clicks, followed by more instructions, this time from Beth Casey.

Kate wished they would decide what they wanted her to do. Or not do. It was frustrating, not being allowed to complete the tasks they asked her to do, but she tried to put a lid on her feelings, to be ready for the next one.

"Bear with us a minute, Katie," Max murmured into her earphones. She waited, wishing they would get their act together, which finally made her smile. How many times had *she* been on the receiving end of that one?

"Next we're going to read you a list of animals. We want you to say yes when you hear the name of any animal you think is dangerous. Ready?" She said yes, then waited.

"Monkey." Pause. "Dog. Sheep." Pause. "Cat."

"Yes!"

"Horse." Pause. "Owl. Lion." Long pause, then "Mouse."

"Yes!" As soon as she said it she tried to take it back. "I must've been thinking rat."

"That's okay. Let's just go on." Pause. "Armadillo."

"Yes . . . no. I'm not sure."

"Scorpion."

"Yes!"

"Sam."

She started laughing, and felt the tension drain from her body, freeing her of the confusion and frustration born of never being sure she would be able to decipher or understand what was going on around her.

"That's our pie in the sky, Kate—discovering the functional basis for humor," Max said through the earphones with a smile in his voice. "You just lit up the entire universe. Time to quit."

I am an idea wrapped in flesh that sprang from the belly of the sky. Like a hawk I sail beyond the known into the realm of the unknown.

—Normandi Ellis, *Awakening Osiris*

EIGHTEEN

Year Four in the Reign of Horemheb

(1344 B.C.)

DAY 3, THIRD MONTH OF PLANTING

Mena brought us news today that Senmut is on his way to Waset, to recruit physicians for his House of Life.

"Now that Pharaoh commands the outline scribes to draw in the old way," Aset pointed out, "he will have to look elsewhere for one such as he wants. Horemheb even ordered the walls of my grandfather's House of Jubilation painted over."

Mena's worried eyes sought mine, for she has never referred to the Magnificent Amenhotep as her grandfather before, at least not in our presence.

"Not in his wife's apartments," Nebet told her. "Mutnodjme forbids it." Now that she is in training to become one of the favorites who one day will serve the Queen, Mena's daughter comes less often than before. At eleven she favors her mother, but in every other way is herself, especially the smile that mixes an air of mystery with sensuality. Aset says Nebet lives in a place of her own making, which is as good an explanation as any.

"Pharaoh only tries to restore the proper respect for our laws," Mena tried to explain, "to rid the Two Lands of the corruption that comes close to beggaring us."

"Enforcing just laws and fair wages for a day's work is one thing," Aset argued. "Clipping the wings of a bird is something else."

"At least no one lacks for work." If Mena was stubborn in his defense, it was out of loyalty to his General, who has named him Chief of Pharaoh's Physicians. But I do not criticize how my friend plays the game of politics. That he remains true at the core despite the duplicity that runs rampant among those near the throne, I credit in part to his wife and the kind of love I see between them still.

"Only because he tries to bury the truth," Aset insisted, equally unbending. "He has ordered the names of the Pharaohs carved into the temple wall. Yet not only the Heretic's name is missing from the list. He also leaves off Osiris Tutankhamen and Smenkhkare. And if *she* never existed, then what am I—a vision conjured up by some priest drunk on henbane?"

DAY 16, FIRST MONTH OF HARVEST

I tucked the scroll I brought away with me last evening into the belt of my kilt, but I had to wait until Nofret left us to confront Aset. Then I simply unrolled it and asked, "How do these get across the river? For one to somehow fall into the hands of a palace guard I could explain away as a trick of the gods. But one of Senmut's friends who gathered at the Clay Jar to celebrate his return said he recognized the hand!"

"How should I know?" she replied without looking at me.

"You would be disingenuous with me now, after all this time?" I stopped short of asking her why everything has become so stiff and awkward between us, but at least her eyes met mine.

"I do not mean to be. It is just that I don't want you to blame Tamin or Nofret for taking them to the market. They only want something to laugh about with their friends." Ipwet has enlisted other women to help her meet the growing demand for her sandals, and now Tamin needs another hand to help her sell them.

"I see nothing humorous in this. The story is not only violent but seditious." I was not being entirely truthful, for Aset can make even the most vicious animal appear comical just by the way he bends a leg or raises one eyebrow. But lately her wit has sharpened and her picture-stories begin to exhibit a bite they did not have before. This one showed a big baboon with his mantle puffed out and ears extended like the brown quartzite figure that once stood before the tomb of the Magnificent Amenhotep—until Horemheb had it removed to his own tomb. Next to him a big rat stood on his hind legs cracking a whip over a herd of goats, whose feet were shackled by the wooden blocks used to restrain prisoners. The baboon cleared a path with his axe, lopping off a goat's foot here, an ear there, then a nose, while behind him a river of blood rose until it spilled into the green fields on either side.

"People see what they want in them."

"They see exactly what you mean for them to!" That I raised my voice in anger to her shocked me more than her, but still she refused to leave off defending what she did.

"It is the act of a barbarian to chop off the hand of a man who steals bread because his children are hungry. If I do not say it, who will? Clean-shaven men like my father?" She shook her head. "To commit such an act in the name of a god does not make it *maat*."

I would not disagree and she knew it, but that did not lessen the danger to her. "Any more of these and you could lose your own hand," I warned, intending to leave it at that. Instead, my injured pride took control of my tongue. "Do you consider me so—so tiresome, then? Lately it seems that you—

Her left hand moved as if to reach out to me, then stilled. "What ties my tongue is fear of disappointing you, of failing to be what you want me to be, for I am not and never will be all you believe me to be. Who do you see when you look at me—an innocent young girl, free of guile or evil intent?" She shook her head. "How could I be? I am my mother's daughter. In that at least I have no choice."

"In no way are you like the woman who gave you life, either by nature or intent," I assured her. "Sometimes I think you care more for others than yourself. A little girl with a malformed hip, clumsy Ruka, Resh the potter—all open like a flower to your sun because you shower them with kindness and love. Even a street dog."

At that a smile began to tug at the corner of her mouth, giving me the courage to let my last arrow fly. "Do not forget that you are your father's daughter as well. Should you need proof of that you have only to look in your mirror." The smile spread from her mouth to her eyes. "What is the secret of those blue eyes, I wonder?" I mused, to keep her smiling. Instead she took me seriously.

"Surely you do not believe that nonsense about the hard parts of the body coming from the father and the soft from the mother!" she chided. "Uzahor once told me that his father's mother had blue eyes. Yet none of her children did, nor their children. If my eyes are a gift from my father, why did Uzahor's grandmother have no children with eyes like hers?"

I shrugged and spread my hands, for I have no answer. But the news she imparted so carelessly confirmed what I already suspected—that Uzahor was Ramose's father. Indeed, that would help explain why Aset inherited not only Uzahor's vast collection of scrolls but his villa in Western Waset, making her a wealthy woman in her own right. For now it sits empty, maintained by one of the old man's faithful retainers, a constant reminder that Ramose will have no trouble arranging an advantageous match for her. Nor can that be long off now. Already Aset is five months beyond her fifteenth feast day, and it has been two years since Uzahor passed through the reeds.

As we parted, she touched my hand and gave me a bittersweet smile. "What I fear most, Tenre, is that you will tire of my questions—my childishness."

Surprise took my tongue and scrambled my thoughts. Surely she understands me well enough to know that I have never considered her questions childish. Could she have heard something in one of the letters Pagosh brings from the High Priest? Why else imagine that I might leave her, unless someone—Pagosh, perhaps?—put the idea to her that I contemplate marriage?

"It is far more likely that *you* will be the one to leave me, precisely because you are no longer a child." I thought surely my sad smile must have given me away, for she curled one arm around my neck and put her cheek to mine, an embrace as unexpected as it was different from the hug of a child.

I suppose she loves me in her way, just as she loves Pagosh and

Mena, or Khary. But mine for her is not that of teacher or guardian. Asleep she invades my dreams. Awake my eyes seek her even when she is absent, until I have no peace whether with her or away from her. Let her walk into a room and the blood races to my loins as well as my face, while the roaring in my ears deafens me to all but what I cannot have and should not even contemplate. Lately, in the dark of night, I even feel the touch of her lips and hands on me, torturing me until I must guard her from myself now, as well as the strangers who come to my door.

Year Five in the Reign of Horemheb

(1343 B.C.)

DAY 12, FOURTH MONTH OF PLANTING

Never has the feeling come over me so strongly that life repeats itself as when I followed Pagosh across the courtyard of Amen's great temple. Yet much has changed there. The black granite statue of Tutankhamen standing between Amen's knees lies shattered on the ground, a sight that overwhelmed me with sadness and longing for a time of innocence long gone. The Heretic's temple to Aten, where Nefertiti once lifted the sword of battle above her crowned head, has been torn asunder as well, leaving only a heap of rubble to mark where it stood.

"Would it not be wiser for us to meet somewhere else?" I had protested when he came for me as Re's fiery orb slipped behind the western cliffs. "Better to meet where he holds audience with any who have reason to approach him," Pagosh had muttered, with the same tight-lipped urgency, "whether it be Pharaoh's emissary or the High Priest of Ptah. Anyway, it is not for others to question who the High Priest sees."

Yet now, as we skirted the base of Horemheb's new pylon, which dwarfs even the great gateway built by the Magnificent Amenhotep, he tried to reassure me. "The way we go no one will see us, and the walls of Ramose's private chamber are thick as a tomb."

We approached the chambers that surround the sanctuary, each more sacred and secret by virtue of its nearness to the dwelling place of the god, and passed under a columned arcade where perfumed oil filled the wall sconces. In the distance I could hear the drone of chanting priests performing their ablutions on the shores of the Sacred Lake, and a moment later we stepped out into the open again, into the glorious glow of a copper sky. I slowed my steps to savor Re's parting gift, a spectacle that always awakes in me an intense awareness of being alive, even as the great god goes to his death. When my eyes returned to earth I confronted a massive stone block stained with the blood of countless cattle, geese, and goats, a grisly reminder of where I was. And why.

I hurried to catch up with Pagosh and found him waiting for me at a small pond, which we crossed on stepping-stones. By the time we came to a narrow wooden door I was completely lost, and told him so. "Only the apprentices charged with keeping Amen's house come this way," he explained, "so do not get your feet tangled in the brooms."

The vestibule was lit by two small oil lamps sitting atop a half wall, one of which Pagosh took to light our way along a narrow corridor. On the walls were the bearded enemies of the Two Lands, hands bound behind their backs, with the great Thutmose leading the parade atop his favorite elephant. Pagosh put his hand to the great beast's belly, and a section of the wall slid back without a sound.

"Quick, before it closes again," he said, then went to touch his flame to one wick after another, until a golden glow suffused the entire room, a place so wondrously alive that I recognized it at once as the zoo Aset had been searching for when she wandered by mistake into the god's sacred place. "I see you recognize it," he commented as I turned round and round to take it all in.

"Does Ramose know—"

"Why else choose this place for his sanctuary? At least here she is with him in spirit, if not in the flesh."

Ramose came through the door at that moment, and I went

down on my knees in deference to the High Priest, if not the man. "On your feet, *sunu*," he ordered as he swept by me. "There is no use presenting a false face to me now. I know you too well."

I rose and watched him strip off his priestly trappings, tossing them onto a stone bench heaped with colorful cushions—first his white nemes, then the finely pleated robe, followed by two gold armlets and a heavy ring, and lastly, his jeweled pectoral. When he turned to face me he wore only a pleated hip wrap tied with a purple belt.

"Well, can you no longer control her?" An angry scowl creased his brow. "What must I do, bury her in some cold temple with a gaggle of shriveled old crones to watch her day and night? Deny her even a chip of stone to write on lest she commit treason against her god? Not to mention her King!"

I held my tongue to let him vent his frustration rather than have him act in the heat of anger, then be bound by an unreasoned decision. When he reached for the scroll on his writing table and slapped it into my hands, I felt the cold fingers of fear squeeze the air from my lungs.

I took my time, unrolling it bit by bit to see a ram kneeling on the bricks to give birth to a lamb. Next, the lamb—a yellow globe with rays ending in human hands over its head—is led to a big stained stone block, where a giant ram waits, ready to make sacrifice to the god. I unrolled it more and saw several ram-headed mice dripping gold and jewels huddled over a brazier, imbibing the fumes from a bowl of burning yellow seeds. One held an orange coal between his fingers. A bone needle penetrated the protruding tongue of another and blood dripped from the dagger embedded in the cheek of still another. Hands, ears, and noses dripped blood from a cloud of smoke above their heads, even a dismembered female breast. At the end, a huge ram-headed rat stood on his hind legs, trying to keep three balls in the air. I puzzled over how he fit what had gone before, until I noticed that he wore a pleated hip wrap with a purple belt. Since the ram is the holy animal of Amen, the ram-headed mice had to signify his priests—in this case, priests of the highest order, all under the influence of some hypnotic substance. Sabean frankincense from the look of it, a shrub with resinous yellow seeds.

"Well?" Ramose demanded, his patience at an end. "Will you dissemble and say her intent is simply to amuse, that she means no disrespect and commits no disloyalty?"

"Surely the meaning lies in the eye of the beholder," I replied. It is known that certain priests and oracles use hallucinatory plants to induce visions in order to forecast or interpret certain events, but to suggest that the Sacred Council is guided not by Amen but the smoke of self-indulgence and greed is a sin of the highest order. Some would even call it treason.

Ramose laughed, but not because he was amused. "This is only the latest, not the first. Another time it was the baboon who so fears the lambs that he must slit their defenseless throats, leaving the ground beneath *him* barren and brown while the earth under the lambs is made fertile by their blood and so sprouts green. She is not satisfied with skewering the rich and royal. Now she ridicules Amen's Sacred Council as well."

"Your daughter has always been one to stand up for the runt of the litter," I pointed out. "Surely it comes as no surprise that she feels as she does about the shedding of blood under Pharaoh's Edict of Reform."

He sighed as if the wind had died from his sail, leaving him suddenly becalmed. "It appears that she believes Amen himself gives life to the Rebel's flock by trying to eradicate them. Did I mistake her meaning?" I shook my head and he stared at me for a moment. "Even I will not be able to keep her safe if she continues," he admitted finally.

I could not say that in the very act of begetting her he had put her in danger. "Aset will never be safe so long as any man believes she is his path to the throne," I pointed out instead, "but she follows the teachings of Thoth and Isis, as you intended. Surely you take pride in her strong sense of *maat*."

"Never speak to me again with an oily tongue!" he thundered. "Whatever she has become, you and I must share the blame as well as the credit!"

"But you are the one who chose me," I replied, "just as you are the solid rock on which she built her house, the light that holds the darkness at bay for her. No wonder she holds you so high . . . too high, perhaps, for even the High Priest of Amen to rise to her expectations. If you drop one of the balls now and then—" I shrugged, for I had no doubt that Ramose was the juggler at the end of her picture-story.

The bargain he had struck with Horemheb to erase the Aten heresy from the memory of the People of the Sun and at the same time constrain his lady's boundless ambition has always been a double-edged sword. That is because, instead of falling into disarray after Akhenaten went into exile, the Heretic's followers kept faith with their god by erecting shrines and approaching Aten themselves. In this way did they discover they had no need for a priest to intercede on their behalf. And should such a practice spread, the power of the Amen priests would be threatened as never before, even under the Heretic. Now Aset threw the risk Ramose took for her back in his face by portraying his god for what Horemheb made him—as cruel and evil as any mortal who ever lived.

But he said nothing of this to me. Instead he asked, "And her mother? What does Aset expect of her?"

"Since the night her sister went to Osiris, it is as if her lady mother does not exist." I held up the scroll. "But she is here, too." I pointed to the tabby with yellow eyes and bared teeth, who lurked behind the lotus column.

"Bastet. Of course." He sighed. "Can you not find another way to fill her time?"

"She does not sit idle now, but looks after Tamin's children when she is not helping Khary with our medicines."

"My daughter is a servingwoman to children?"

"In this as in all else she follows the dictates of her *ka*."

"To my utter despair and heart's delight," Ramose admitted, glancing to where Pagosh stood in the shadows at the edge of the room. "Word has come that Horemheb makes his way to Waset as we speak, so guard her well, even against herself. Both of you." With that he turned and strode to his writing table, picked up the ring he had taken from his finger, and slipped it over the end of a tightly rolled papyrus. "Tell her I—no, just take care this does not fall into any hand but hers."

As we came away from the temple I glanced up at the twin pylons, soaring high into the starry heavens, banners waving in the evening breeze, and could hardly believe my good fortune—unless I had misread Ramose's intentions. As usual, Pagosh brought me back to earth.

"High Priest or not, he dances to her tune."

Apprehension quickened my breath. "Nefertiti?" I asked.

"Do not act the fool," he muttered.

I decided to hold my tongue, not wanting to spoil what I have with anticipation of what may yet come to pass.

But I understand now why some men cling to this world with such tenacity rather than embrace the heavenly one that lies just over the western horizon, where the pure in heart go to join Osiris. Which I am not and never will be. For I not only love but lust after the half-royal daughter of the High Priest of Amen, a god I neither believe in nor respect, and feel no regret whatever for one transgression or the other.

NINETEEN

It was Thursday. The week was running out and so was her time for deciding what she was going to do next. But tonight Max was taking her to dinner at some Greek place, and Kate was determined to make the most of it. So she'd brushed her hair into place while it was damp, sweeping it back from her face on one side to reveal a single earring with a hundred tiny slivers of silver. It was the earring, in fact, a souvenir from Cleo's last trip to Istanbul, that had demanded the little black dress.

Almost painfully plain, the soft wool jersey hugged her throat in front, draping her breasts and throat in fluid shadows before plunging to a deep *V* in back. "Ready?" She offered her coat to Max and waited for him to take it before turning around.

"Jesus!" he whispered to himself. Kate turned to look at him and inadvertently brushed her lips across his cheek. Max backed away while she slipped into the sleeves, then gave her shoulders a quick squeeze. Not exactly what she had in mind.

When they arrived at the restaurant, several male diners were lined up on the small dance floor, arms on each other's shoulders, while three musicians plucked out the theme from *Zorba*. Max requested a table away from the music, where they sat scanning the menu in silence while the waiter went to get the bottle of wine Max ordered. When he returned, Max waved him away and filled their glasses himself, then waited for her to taste it.

"It's different," she acknowledged. "I like it."

Satisfied, he lifted his own glass. "I'm going to tell you something, McKinnon. And if you laugh, I'm taking a hike. Remember me telling you I'd been thinking about switching to academic medicine so I could spend more time on research?" She nodded. "Felt like I needed some fresh air, but I couldn't seem to get myself off the fence, about that or anything else. I finally decided I had to do *something*, even if it was less drastic, so I grew a beard. Then I walked into that museum, ran into you and Tashat, and suddenly there wasn't a fence anywhere in sight."

Kate smiled, but she could tell by the look on his face that he wasn't finished. "A few days after I got back from Denver that first time, I got a call from a guy I knew back in high school who's now a patrolman with the Houston Police Department. It was pretty late and EMS had taken his father to Ben Taub." Max paused, apparently in a storytelling mood. "Hank and I still have a beer together every now and then, and he knows I'm fond of his father, partly because his old man didn't act like most parents. I never will forget the night the three of us sat on their back steps eating watermelon, having a seed-spitting contest—his idea, not ours." He smiled at the memory and drank some more wine. "Anyway, some idiot wanted to give him heparin without knowing what was going on inside his head. Hank's no dummy. He knew an anticoagulant could be a disaster if his father was hemorrhaging. I went down there, did an MRI, and located the clot. Afterward I hung around for a while, just to keep Hank company. It was coming up on five the next morning by the time I got home. I went into the bathroom to shower and made the mistake of looking in the mirror. Want to know what I saw?" Bemused, Kate shook her head. "Twenty-five years between you and me! That's when I shaved the damned beard off, right then and there."

The punch line was so unexpected she couldn't help laughing. "Are you hung up about my age?"

He gave her a look she hadn't seen before. "Let me put it this way. I think that *sunu* walking the path to eternity with Tashat had to have a damn powerful reason to risk his life for her. Ask yourself what that could have been. Gold? Land?" He shook his head. "Uh-uh. The odds were stacked too high against his being able to save her, and I'll bet he knew it. That means he had a far more com-

pelling reason for trying to keep her alive. More irrational. Yet
Tashat was somewhere between twenty-two and twenty-five, to his
forty to forty-eight. At a minimum that's eighteen years between
them, twenty-six at most." By that time his eyes were bright with
suppressed laughter. "I'm not looking to lose my head, but I figure I
ought to be able to handle twelve."

Kate stared at him, her heart clogging her throat, hardly able to
trust what she thought he was saying, not wanting to make a fool of
herself. Without thinking, she lifted her glass to sip some wine, half
hiding her face behind the rim of the glass. The moment passed
when the waiter arrived carrying a tray filled with small bowls of
hummus, cucumbers in yogurt, dolmathes, and a couple of other
dishes she couldn't identify.

Max had ordered the tasting dinner, so that's what they did for
a while, forcing whatever was going on between them to wait.
Somehow they made it through the entree, talking about the food
and the ancient Greeks.

"So what else did the Greeks get from the Egyptians, besides
fluted columns?" Max asked as the waiter took their plates.

"Those four golden goddesses guarding Tut's viscera look so
sad and vulnerable—the way their heads are turned, their outstretched arms and softly draped bodies, like the Elgin Marbles.
That kind of genius didn't come from following a set of rigid con-
ventions no matter what historians say about Egyptian art being so
stylized that it all looks alike, the product of a totalitarian system
rather than a democracy like Greece." The smile in his eyes
reminded her of something. "Maybe it was the newspaper I picked
up in New Mexico that made me think of it, or going over my photographs of those scenes on Tashat's cartonnage, but—do you read
the comics on Sunday?"

"Sometimes."

"Each cel has a frame around it, yet we read them as one con-
tinuous story, right?" He nodded. "Well, I decided to ignore the
gold bands and read the hieroglyphs as text, not just isolated pic-
tographs. This is what I came up with." She dug for the piece of
paper in her purse, unfolded it, and handed it to him.

Kate watched his eyes and knew when he finished reading what
she had written. Then he went back to the beginning and read it

aloud. " '*Enter me and I shall make you a god! Enchantress and wife, she dances and draws down heaven. Under her spell I come to myself. Under her body I come to life. I take her in my arms. I taste her lips. I lose myself in beauty and chaos. To love is to believe in goddesses.*' "

He glanced up. "It's a love poem."

"Yes, but the operative word is '*wife.*' That means it was written by her husband, or by someone's husband, which someone had copied onto her cartonnage."

"Then why—?"

"I don't know."

Max looked around, searching for their waiter. "Do you want dessert?" Kate shook her head. "How about some coffee?" She shook her head again. "Then let's get the hell out of here." He pushed back from the table. "I'll settle with the waiter on the way out."

She slipped her coat on without any help from Max, who seemed suddenly impatient. Watching him pay the bill, she wondered if he could be feeling what she did—an attraction so strong it was difficult even to think about anything else. It wasn't just physical, either. What she felt was more complicated—the physical attraction intertwined with intellectual stimulation in a way that made them inseparable. The way his mind worked turned her on as much as the touch of his hand, and for the first time in her life she realized that, at least for her, one could not exist without the other.

As they walked across the parking lot he took her elbow, then let his hand slide down into the pocket of her coat to clasp hers. But once in the car they drove several blocks in silence, Kate wondering if he had any idea how she felt about him. And then what he was thinking. Max certainly wasn't the careless type. He would need to know more about her, personally, before—maybe he just didn't know how to ask.

"I don't sleep around, Max, in case you were wondering. I've been with one man and that was a long time ago. Six years"—she tried to put a humorous twist on it—"back when I was young and foolish."

He glanced at her, then back to the car ahead of them. "I never thought you did. Sleep around, I mean."

Kate waited, hoping he would say more, but instead of encouraging him to be equally forthcoming, her confession seemed to have the opposite effect.

Back at his house, Max held the door for her, then muttered something about having some work to do before he could hit the sack. When he beat a hasty retreat to his study, Sam looked as crestfallen as Kate felt, obviously torn between following him or going upstairs with her.

In the yellow bedroom Sam jumped on the bed, slumped against the pillows, and gave her a doleful look. "I know how you feel," Kate told him as she kicked off her shoes, peeled off her dress, and tossed it over a chair. "Maybe *he* can handle the twelve years between us," she muttered under her breath, "but I'm not so sure I can."

What was it with him, anyway? Maybe it was a case of smothering the fire with too much fuel—too much togetherness. She stomped into the bathroom, echoes of Cleo's warning reverberating in her head. Had Max been pulling her string all along, only she'd been too thick to see it? She scrubbed her face, brushed her teeth, and put on her pajamas. When she came out of the bathroom, Sam watched her with sleepy, bloodshot eyes, until she jerked the pillow out from under him and pointed to the foot of the bed. "There or down on the floor."

He chose the bed, so she stacked the two pillows and picked up *The Cerebral Symphony*, a book she'd lifted from the shelves in Max's study. The jacket blurb called it "a lyrical documentation of the inner voice that gives form to our thoughts, passes judgment, and makes choices—the narrator of our mental life who convinces us that we exist as individuals." Just the ticket to cool the blood and induce sleep.

Except it didn't work worth a damn. She kept seeing the smile in his eyes, feeling his hand on hers, then on the back of her neck. Had she imagined the special sense of intimacy she felt when they were bouncing ideas off each other, in recognizing that their minds were different yet matched in some fundamental way? Something she had never felt with anyone else. *How did we end up at such an impasse?*

She threw back the covers, unable to lie there any longer. When she went to the little table by the window to draw, Sam jumped off the bed and ran to the door, waited a minute, then scratched to let her know he wanted out.

"Dammit to hell and back, Sam!" she exploded, strode to the door and jerked it wide open. The dog trotted down the hall to Max's bedroom. "Traitor!" she hissed after him in a half whisper.

The stairwell was dark but she could see that Max's bedroom light was still on because he'd left the door open a crack for Sam, who liked to check on him in the night. Before she could get cold feet, Kate marched down the hall, tapped on the door with her knuckles, then barged right in.

Max glanced up over his half glasses, snapped his book shut, and slid it under the covers, guilty as a teenager caught with a porno magazine.

"What's wrong?" He started to get up.

"Nothing. I just wanted to tell you, uh, that I'll be leaving tomorrow, after my meeting with Tinsley. It's time I got back . . . to Denver."

He froze with one leg dangling over the side of the bed. "Why? What's your hurry?"

"I've already stayed much longer than I intended." Too long, she thought, taking in the white T-shirt and boxer shorts. Somehow it didn't surprise her that Max wasn't a pajama man.

"That was when you still had a job to go to."

"I know." She glanced around the room to avoid meeting his eyes. "But I have bills to pay, need to pick up my mail, stuff like that."

"Your rent must be paid through the end of the month, and you can always call Cleo, have her forward your mail."

Kate took a step back and came down on a soft paw. Sam let out a wounded yip, then circled her with his tail tucked but wagging, to let her know he forgave her.

"What are you running from this time?"

That hurt, more than she wanted him to know. "I wish you wouldn't treat me like a truant child."

"Then stop acting like one. At least tell me what rubbed your fur the wrong way."

"You're driving Sam crazy, that's what!" Her voice sent the dog scurrying for the folded quilt Max kept on the floor for him. "How can you be so great at figuring out what's wrong with people's brains and not see that having to run back and forth between my room and yours all night is making him schizo."

Hot tears stung her eyes, putting a brake on her runaway tongue. "I appreciate all you've done, really. Letting me stay here. Tom McCowan. Putting me in touch with Tinsley, showing me around Houston. I even kind of liked it at first . . . that you weren't coming on to me. I know you said—" A tic at the corner of his mouth hinted at a smile, making her see hot, raging red.

"I guess maybe I *am* too young for you," she exploded, "because I resent the hell out of you playing games with me. Eager to talk one minute, stony silent the next. And you think Dave is a control freak! Not that it isn't my own fault for getting into a position where I'm beholden to you, so you can call all the shots."

He started to say something, but she raised her hand. "Don't bother. I'm not letting you pull my chain any longer." She wheeled around, needing out of there.

"Come back here, dammit!" he yelled, freezing Kate in her tracks. She'd never heard him raise his voice before, even when he cursed Dave that day after they left the museum.

When she turned around, he was pulling out the top drawer of the night table next to his bed with one hand and motioning her to him with the other. Curious, she moved toward the table and saw that the shallow drawer was full of what looked like different-colored candies, all individually wrapped.

"I fantasize about making love to you a dozen times a day," Max confessed. That's when she realized they were condoms, some packaged in shiny foil, others in colored plastic. "I even wake up in the night reaching for you, only to discover—well, just say I've developed an irrational fear of being caught without. Lately, every time I get near a drugstore I have this overpowering urge to go in and buy a few more, just to be sure I'm prepared. If ever."

Kate tried not to laugh at the thought of him loading up at the Village drugstore and word getting around, scandalizing his neighbors in this upscale Republican neighborhood. "You must have quite a reputation as a ladies' man by now," she mused. "Then why—"

"I promised no strings attached, remember? Almost fell off the wagon more than once. Then tonight, well, I was beginning to think this might be it. Talk about schizo! *You're* the one who warned me off, with that little tidbit about how you don't sleep around. I figured that meant you weren't interested, or didn't know me well enough yet, or something." He wrapped his arms around her and put his lips to her hair. "I really made a mess of it, didn't I?"

Kate shook her head. "We both did."

"Think it's too late?" He lifted her chin to meet the kisses he began scattering with agonizing slowness across her cheeks and eyelids, then around the corners of her mouth, before finally taking pity on her. And himself. Kate opened to let his tongue slide between her lips, ending the waiting and wanting.

At some point in the last few days, watching his hands sketch invisible objects, Kate's awareness of them had turned to longing. Now those hands were evoking sensations that intensified her awareness of herself even as she learned him by touch, too, creating an entire sketchbook of new pictures in her head.

"Sometimes, late at night," she murmured against his neck, "I used to wonder if I had conjured you up out of my imagination." She smiled as he backed toward the bed, taking her with him. Then he was sliding his hands down to the curve of her hips, to hold her against him while he slipped the buttons on her pajama top. A moment later he leaned forward to caress the heartbeat in her throat with his lips and tongue, before moving down to her breast.

"Where's Sam?" Kate whispered into Max's neck, never able to drop off to sleep unless she knew.

"Curled up on the floor next to me, snoozing away peaceful as you please."

She smiled with her eyes closed and moved her lips across the warm skin beneath his jaw, then rolled over onto her other side. As the emotional roller coaster she'd been riding all day finally began to level out, she became aware of the steady rise and fall of his chest against her back.

"You remember that first day in the museum?" he asked, giving the lie to the old saw that men don't like to talk afterward. "What was your first impression of me?"

"Beard. Pushy."

"I thought I kept it pretty neat."

She moved her head against the pillow. "Not bushy. Pushy."

"Oh!" He sounded surprised or maybe insulted. "How old did you think I was?"

"Too old," she teased. "Fifty . . . until you smiled." She snuggled down into her pillow. "I'm too sleepy to play true confessions. Can we do this in the morning?"

"Just one more thing." He paused long enough for the fogginess of encroaching sleep to settle over her again. "There's nothing keeping you in Denver anymore, is there?" She could feel him holding his breath.

"Only Cleo and all my stuff."

"Then stay here. Take however much of the house you need for your work. We could rearrange or redo—"

"You're asking me to stay here, with you?" She turned to look at him. Moving to Houston was one thing. Living with him was something else. "Shouldn't we think about this for a while, not jump into—"

"If that's what you want, but I already have—thought about it. Too long."

"How long?"

"Since the last time I was in Denver, but I figured you weren't about to desert Tashat, that she was the real reason you were putting up with Dave Broverman. God, Kate, you *have* to want to finish what you started—both heads and the life-size figure—for publication if nothing else." Kate didn't want to talk about that, not now, anyway. And she couldn't be sure he hadn't thrown it in as a diversion, to keep her from saying no.

"I just think we both need some time, to see if we can learn to talk to each other. Be straight with each about our feelings. Not let things get all muddled like they did tonight."

At the ends of the universe is a blood red cord that ties life to death, man to woman, will to destiny. Let the knot of that red sash, which cradles the hips of the goddess, bind in me the ends of life and dream. I walk in harmony, heaven in one hand, earth in the other. I am the knot where two worlds meet.

—Normandi Ellis, *Awakening Osiris*

TWENTY

Year Six in the Reign of Horemheb

(1342 B.C.)

DAY 15, THIRD MONTH OF PLANTING

Waking to find Pagosh standing beside my couch no longer overwhelms me with panic, but this time he was not alone. A man swathed in the shabby garments of a supplicant priest stood behind him. I leaped to my feet, grabbed a kilt from the nearby chest, and wrapped it around my hips all in one, ready for whatever would come. In that same instant—call it a premonition or something in his stance—I knew who it was.

"Wake Aset and instruct her to prepare to travel down the river," Ramose said, pushing the coarse brown linen from his clean-shaven head. "Quickly, for we must be away before Re-Horakhte lights the morning sky."

Out of habit I put my palms together, then stood paralyzed as it struck me that he meant to take her! "Why?" I blurted out.

"Rouse her, then we will talk."

"I will see to it," Pagosh volunteered, pausing only to light a lamp from the one in the shrine to Thoth before disappearing down the hall. I lit another lamp and led Ramose to my examining room, for I am accustomed to being in charge there and I felt in need of every advantage I could get.

Tuli came running ahead of her, and Ramose went down on one knee, even allowing the excited little dog to lick his bronze face. Aset stopped at sight of her father, confusion flooding her face when he stood to greet her. Then a delighted laugh bubbled from her throat, making me smile in spite of myself.

"Father!" She threw her arms around his neck, knocking him off-balance. Ramose showed no sign of objecting and instead buried his face in her hair, savoring what he had been denied so long. "Oh, how I have missed you." Aset sighed.

"As I have missed you, little goddess," he whispered.

Pagosh went down on one knee to stroke Tuli's ear, despite having cursed the little dog's affectionate ways only moments before, while I watched and waited.

"The High Priest of Ptah leaves for Mennefer at dawn," Ramose told her, "and has agreed to take you with him. You will be under his protection there, not because I order it but as a favor to an old friend. It remains but for me to prepare a document transferring a block of credit in gold from my name to his, for your use."

"Why?" By keeping her eyes on his face she tried to learn more than he might be willing to say.

"It has become too dangerous for you here."

She rephrased the question. "Why now, after all this time?"

Ramose looked in the wrong direction if he expected succor from me. "Why?" he repeated. "Your picture-scrolls."

She stepped away from him as if from a blow and dropped her eyes for the first time. Yet she did not make excuses or apologize. "Horemheb has more friends in Mennefer than in all the rest of the Two Lands together," she pointed out. "It is where he came into this world."

"Someone has learned that Aset did not go to Abydos?" I inquired.

"I had a message only an hour ago. A royal emissary came to Abydos with orders to return Aset here. Sati delayed him long enough to give her messenger the advantage before informing him that Aset had gone on pilgrimage to Dendera, to the temple of Hathor. It will not take him long to discover she is not there. A day or two at most and Pharaoh's emissary will be at the temple, asking what I know of your sacrilegious picture-stories."

Aset's face flushed, but she stood her ground. "Suspicion will fall on you no matter what you say, unless you point the finger at me."

"I can fend for myself, daughter. It is you I can no longer protect . . . from your mother. It was she who stirred Pharaoh to inquire after you in Abydos."

"Oh!" Aset looked at her feet, yet she refused to apologize or beg forgiveness. When her head came up she gave me a haughty stare. "I am a woman now, Tenre, despite what you think. A woman of some property."

"As if I needed reminding," I muttered.

She turned to her father. "It would not be *maat* for me to leave you or Tenre to face the consequences of what I did with knowing intent. I shall go to my own house, the one Uzahor left to me."

"Refusing to do as I say would not be *maat*, either," Ramose countered, closing the trap she set for him. "I am still your father."

Seeing her defenses crumble, Aset scooped Tuli up in her arms, a sight that tore my heart. For it means what it always has—-that she believes the only one she can depend on never to abandon her is a scruffy street dog. "I will not go," she insisted, setting into motion her carnelian *tyet*, which she wears day and night in the belief that the knot in the girdle of Isis has the power to protect her, even from her own mother.

"It will not have to be for long," Ramose tried, hoping to persuade her rather than order her to obey him. "When your scrolls no longer heat his blood, Pharaoh's attention will be drawn to something or someone else, and you can return."

"I will not go without Tenre." She moved to my side, clutching Tuli to her breast.

Pagosh emerged like a wraith from the shadows. "We waste precious time," he advised Ramose. "Send both of them, but up the river to Aniba. Pharaoh will never think to look there, and Prince Senmut can see that no harm comes to her better than any servant of Ptah, High Priest or no."

Ramose opened his mouth—to object, I think—but closed it when she spoke first. "Oh, Paga, yes. What a wonderful idea!" She set Tuli on the floor, hardly able to contain herself. "You could hint to Pharaoh's man, Father, that I tricked Sati with that story of a pilgrimage. And confide to him that you suspect I have run off with a lover. That would solve everything, wouldn't it?"

Ramose's blue eyes sought mine. "Speak up, *sunu*. Are you willing to take my daughter to Aniba?"

Old suspicions about her feelings for Senmut burrowed into my flesh like a fiery serpent, causing an itch that demanded scratching. "On one condition," I replied, risking everything on one throw of the sticks. "That you sign a contract making her my wife."

I thought Aset's eyes would pop from her head, though the High Priest did not move a muscle. I held his gaze, determined that he should believe I would not waiver in my demand, for he is a man of consummate skill at hiding his true feelings.

"And why should I do that?" he inquired, as if I had suggested he pay me two cows or a horse for my services.

"To give me legal right to have her with me at all times, to keep her safe."

"You want me to believe a marriage that is merely a legal convenience would satisfy you?"

"No." It seemed as if he and I were destined by the gods to bargain over his daughter, again and again. But this time I wanted something *from* her, not for her. "Nor am I willing to enter into any arrangement with you unless your daughter agrees to it."

"Agrees to what?" he snapped.

"Stop talking as if I am not here, both of you!" Aset burst out. "You behave like a cat with a mouse," she admonished her father, then turned to me, "and you like a snake with no backbone. My father would no more force me to take a man I do not want than you would." That was news to me. "It is for me to decide if your offer has merit."

I glanced at Pagosh and got a curt nod, along with a look that said it was up to me now—that my time finally had come.

"Then I will spell out exactly what I would expect. I will not be another Uzahor, a grandfather to you in all but name. I want a wife who will share my thoughts and cares and fears in the light of day, as well as my couch at night."

"*All* night, like Sheri and Mena?" Surely she asked only to be sure she did not mistake my meaning, making me worry that *she* would be the one to deny me, not her father.

I nodded and told her what only she might understand. "That and much more, I think, if we are willing to find our own way."

She studied me for one long, excruciating moment. "Truly?" Her face remained too solemn to bode well for my prospects of winning this game, but I gave her the only answer I could. "Truly."

Her entire countenance lit up, eyes sparkling like stars, even before her lips parted in that glorious smile. "I believe we could have that, too, and more. Much more."

Was she agreeing to become my wife or to something my stumbling wits could not take in? I could not say, for there are times when I feel like a dumb ox in the presence of her nimble wit, led by a ring in the nose across a fresh field.

An instant later she stood at my side, slipped her hand into mine, and turned to face Ramose. "I will take the physician Senakhtenre for my husband, Father."

A smile started somewhere inside me while my heart threatened to leap from my chest, yet somehow I managed to keep my feet on the ground while I waited for Ramose's reply.

"To make such an important decision in haste—" he began.

Had I Pagosh's faith in him I might have believed the High Priest picked his way carefully out of concern for his daughter's happiness, but I found it more likely that he weighed the loss to his bargaining power should she come to me.

"I have waited for Tenre a long time, haven't I, Paga?" She barely paused. "Surely the goddess meant us for each other from the moment we each set foot in this world. Otherwise, Osiris would have taken me that night I was so sick. And it was Isis who sent him to bring me forth from my mother's body. You yourself once told me *that!*"

His eyes grew suspiciously shiny as he gazed at her, until I wondered if he saw her as she had been then, but he shook off his memories and gave me a hard look. "Have you no more to say? Time grows short and Pagosh chafes at the rope."

"All that needs saying has been said," I replied, "except what is to be written into the marriage contract."

"You should be kissing my feet, *sunu*, not haggling over terms!" Ramose muttered, half-angry and half-amused—or so I thought from the way his lips toyed with a smile. But then, as I have said before, he is a man of infinite guile.

"Aset's property and possessions are to remain in her name," I told him. "Nothing is to be conveyed to me. She also is to have the right to manage and receive property without my approval."

"Why does that not surprise me?" he said, shaking his head. Aset squeezed my hand, telling me to hold my tongue. "What else? Spit it out so we can be done."

"She must approve all rights and obligations required of either party, but should she divorce me, for any or no reason, the entire marriage settlement, no matter how small or large, is to be restored to her, not the usual one-third portion." In truth I wanted nothing from him, but to refuse it would be to negate her worth.

I saw him glance at Pagosh. "Anything else?"

"There also is no need to make provision in case of adultery, on her part or mine. The rest is for Aset to say. And you." This time I squeezed *her* hand.

"Such charity! The man leaves me crumbs and expects my gratitude!" Ramose exclaimed to the ceiling.

"As Thoth is my witness, my lord," I dared to add, "I vow to protect and care for your daughter in sickness and health, through the dark of night the same as when Re sails his boat across the sky, from this hour until my final breath. And beyond, if that is possible." I started to say I would willingly risk any hope I might have of eternity for his daughter, but did not want him to accuse me again of speaking with an oily tongue.

Instead I glanced at Pagosh and found a smile hovering about his lips. I knew then that the contest was mine. Mine and his, since he is the one who sowed the seeds of Ramose's trust in me.

A soft glow lit the eastern horizon as we readied to sail. Merit came to the river to see us off, issuing a flurry of last-minute admonitions to Aset. Then they hugged one last time, both weeping and talking at the same time. Afterward they stood waving to each other as that place on the shore grew smaller and smaller, then disappeared from our sight. And so, with the wind at our backs, we embarked on a new life in a place neither of us can even imagine.

For a time Aset's face alternated between glowing happiness and a terrible sadness, reflecting a sense of exhilaration at the prospect of the unknown adventure that lies before us, and sorrow at leaving everyone she holds dear. Except Tuli. Pagosh is to return to Waset after he sees us safely into Senmut's hands, though he promises to return within the year, bringing us word of Ramose and Nebet. And Khary, who continues the Eye of Horus but with Mena to oversee it.

We stood together on the deck watching the passing scene, first a few mud-brick hovels edging the green fields—shelter for the fellahin who work them—then a man guiding a plow hook drawn by a single oxen, the blade set at a sharp angle in the wooden shaft in order to dig deep into the soil. Beyond the green strip to the west lay rocky hills and cliffs, while to the east a vast expanse of desert stretched to the spine of the mountains, forming an impenetrable barrier to the marauding peoples beyond the Red Sea.

It was not until we passed a long line of women and children carrying pitchforks and rakes that Aset broke her silence. "You are giving up so much, Tenre. The city you call home. Your friends. The Eye of Horus. The garden it has taken you years to grow. Even the place where you carry out your experiments."

"My friends are your friends as well, and the Eye of Horus continues without me. In time, as your father said, the risk to you will pass. Until then we will continue healing the sick as before, perhaps in Senmut's House of Life." I tried not to allow the suspicion lurking in my thoughts to come forward—that in the end she had found a way to join her life to his.

"What did I risk, really?" she mused. "A month, another year perhaps, imprisoned within the walls of your garden, living half a life, hiding my true feelings?" She watched the sail fill rather than meet my eyes, then, "Did I force you to what you now regret?"

"Is that what you think?"

"No," she admitted with a funny little smile.

"Oohhh?" I dragged it out. "Why not?"

"Did you think I could not see the hungry look in your eyes when you forgot to hide it? How you watched me when you thought I was not looking? What happens to your body when you look at my breasts?" She turned to me finally. "I tried to be patient, to wait for you to speak first, but—"

"I have thirty-nine years to your seventeen! Have you considered that?"

"Between some people, age counts as nothing. You and Senmut, for instance." She was right. That I follow a different path than most physicians has more to do with my natural inclination than age or experience. And Senmut's approach to the causes of sickness, not only his impatience with unsatisfactory answers to old questions, mirrors my own. That is why he was drawn to Mena.

"I spoke of our mortal bodies, not how or what we think," I replied, trying to say what my *ka* told me to even if my heart refused to believe it. "What if in five years I am no longer able to satisfy the yearnings of your flesh?"

"Not if you teach me how to please you."

Pagosh was at the stern talking with the man who navigated our course, so no one was close enough to hear us. I curled an arm around her shoulders and pulled her close. "We will teach each other," I murmured, against her soft curls. I wore a long-sleeved tunic and kilt, while she had wrapped a woolen shawl around her shoulders, for the wind never ceases on the river, and it is cool at this time of year even with Aten high in the sky. That I touched no bare skin made me even more aware of the way her smaller body aligned with mine—how her head fit under my chin and her breasts in the hollow below mine, while her pelvis cradled my genitals.

My bliss was short-lived, however, for she leaned away to look into my face. "Is that why you insisted there be no mention of adultery in the marriage contract?" I shrugged, but her eyes held mine. "We are different in more than age, Tenre. Some ways I cannot change, so it is more likely that you will tire of me."

I turned, enclosing her in my arms. "Never. I vow to keep you by me until Re sails across the sky for the last time, or Isis ceases to weep for Osiris, whichever comes first."

"Truly?" Her lips moved against my neck, sending a shiver down my spine. And more. I moved my hips against hers to let her know I cherish her in that way, too, and that reading about a man's rising organ in my medical scrolls or even seeing it under his kilt, is not the same as taking it into her body. In part I did it to arouse her curiosity, but also to change possibility to probability in her thoughts, which in turn can provoke sexual desire. By full dark I wanted her as eager for that experience as I already was.

Our felucca carried cargo beneath a second deck across the belly of the boat, offering protection from the sun and any spray that might come over the side, yet it was not so large as to call attention to our passing. Our cargo consisted of baskets and chests packed with clothing and other personal things, a supply of herbs and medicinal extracts from the Eye of Horus, and enough bread to feed us all for several days. When midday drew near, Aset and I sat cross-legged on this higher deck to share the meal Nofret had pressed into our hands when we left.

"It is too salty," I commented after a taste of the roasted goose.

"Probably from Nofret's tears," Aset returned. "Want some of these?" she asked, offering me the basket of dates just as a spray of water hit her in the face. Startled, her arm jerked, sending the dates flying over the side into the river. "Oops! We just made an offering to Hapi." She grinned, glanced at me, and burst out laughing.

"What is so funny?"

"You! Your face," she sputtered.

"Were you on your way north as your father wished, you would be moving with the current rather than fighting it," I pointed out, for we had to dodge the spray every time the captain tacked across the current, to keep the sail filled with wind.

"Better to get wet than go to the High Priest of Ptah."

"You find my face funny?"

"You have a wonderful, beautiful face." Reaching out her hand, hesitant at first, she smoothed the lines between my eyes, then let her finger slide down my nose, over the end to my upper lip. "And lips," she murmured. "Did you know that I can read what you think in the way you hold your lips?"

"Can you?" I whispered, hardly daring to breathe. She nodded, cupped my face in her palm, and stroked her thumb across my cheekbone.

"One morning I opened my eyes and there you were, sitting

beside my couch, waiting for me to wake. From that day to this, whenever the terrible sadness comes to me in the dark, I close my eyes and see you smiling at me, just as you did then." I turned my mouth into her hand and touched my lips to her warm palm.

For a time, then, we talked about what might await us in Aniba. I asked if she would teach Senmut's outline scribes how to paint maps like the ones she draws for me, but she only shrugged and continued to gaze at the passing scene. Still, I hope the idea will take root and grow, to displace any urge to continue with her story-scrolls.

All around us on shore we could see men working the shaduf, dipping the leather buckets attached to the end of a wooden beam—which can be swung in a circle from the point where it rests on three legs—into the river. Afterward the stone counterweight lifts the filled bucket, which then is tipped into canals that carry water to the upper fields.

"Since the shaduf we get two harvests a year from the freshened fields," I said, changing the subject, "and can count on at least one from the higher areas where the flood rarely reaches, the reason more land is under cultivation. Did you know that?"

She nodded. "It is such a simple thing. We have lived with Mother River from the beginning of time, yet the idea came to us from the people who live between the Tigris and Euphrates rivers. Why do you suppose we did not think of it?"

It is never *how* with her, always why. "Do you remember the first time we played Jackals and Hounds?" I asked, for surely there can be no answer to such a question. She nodded. "And afterward, sitting atop your father's villa?" When she looked at me I saw the curious little girl she had been then, blue eyes bright with hope and expectation. "You captured my heart even then, with just one word. Why."

She laughed with delight, that soft gurgling sound that bubbles from her throat, and squeezed my hand in understanding.

A little later, while she talked with Pagosh, my thoughts returned to that day again, and the way she had tested me with the field of blue lotus. There is evidence aplenty that she possesses her mother's skill at bewitching men, but the Beautiful One's eyes lie hooded and still, like a serpent's, while Aset's leap with joy and curiosity. More than that, Aset possesses an innate love for others—Tuli, Pagosh and Khary, Ruka and Resh, and many more. Surely those are the true reasons other men worship my wife. The little goddess with dirty feet. I looked to the west, suddenly impatient to be alone with her, and found Re's bright orb beginning to turn orange. Another hour or two, at least, before we would stop for the night.

Pagosh came forward soon after, leaving Aset talking with the man who steered our course. "We are little more than an hour from Edfu," he informed me, "and will put in there for the night."

"A propitious place, surely," I replied, "since it is home to the sacred temple of Isis built on the site of Horus's victory over Set—by Imhotep, the greatest physician and architect of all time."

"The boatmen and I will go ashore to replenish our supply of water in the town, and afterward spread our pallets on the bank of the river. That way we can be on our way at first light." He gave me a second look. "Unless you fear riding at anchor alone?"

"I will not be alone." He nodded. "Thanks to you," I added. The white scar on his cheek stood out against his ruddy skin, the effect of the chilly wind, I suppose, and his eyes were hard as ever. I had much to thank him for and nothing to give him but words. And words have never counted for much with Pagosh. I put a hand on his shoulder. "I am fortunate indeed to have such a friend."

Startled, he blinked at me, then muttered, "As you have been to me. But it is your wife you should thank for refusing every other man her father proposed."

Without another word he began moving away, leaving me shaking my head. "Pagosh?" I called. He turned around. "Could you persuade Tuli to go ashore, too?"

A glint of humor came into his eyes. "That depends on your wife"—he let me dangle a moment—"whether she trusts you enough to let him go."

When finally we had the boat to ourselves I could find no words to breach the unfamiliar silence between Aset and me. She proceeded to spread our pallets, assuming the work of a servant as if born to it. For a time I stood watching her place them side by side and edge to edge—the only way they fit the space just forward of the raised cargo deck—before moving to help her. Too late. But I got a smile for my trouble, and then an invitation.

"Come sit by me out of the wind and we will drink a cup of wine in celebration of this new beginning."

"W-wine?" I stammered.

She motioned to the clay flask wedged into the narrow space where the sides of the boat form the pointed prow. "A gift from Pagosh, along with a rare piece of advice."

I crossed my feet, bent my knees, and dropped down beside her. "He believes to mark the truly important events in our lives helps us to remember and cherish them in the years ahead."

"Pagosh is a man of so few words I am inclined to listen when he speaks," I said, watching her work the stopper from the flask. "What do you think?"

"I have always found him wise beyond measure." She handed me two glazed cups, then tipped the flask to fill them. Afterward I handed one back to her. "May your *ka* live on, Tenre, and your two eyes behold happiness forever."

"And yours," I whispered. We tilted our cups at the same time, watching each other's lips. I have always been slow to produce words fitting to the occasion, needing time for deliberation and reflection, but I searched for a way to make my own contribution to mark this day.

"I came away unprepared and so have no gold or jewels to give you, but I am not entirely empty-handed." I left her to search the chest I had filled with medical scrolls, including those I have written myself rather than leave such dangerous testimonials behind for others to come upon. But the scroll I wanted was soft to the touch from frequent handling.

"It is of no value, I fear," I explained as I placed it in her hands, "except to assure you that I did not fall victim to your overbearing willfulness." A spark of curiosity lit her eyes and I expected her to unroll it at once. Instead she asked, "What is it?"

"Verses. Mine." Still she waited, watching my face. "In which I tried to describe the many ways I have loved you, from the day I became physician to your father's household until now." I smiled, remembering the night she chided me for not allowing my *ka* to speak, and how long I had worked over my first attempt, about possibility.

"Oh, Tenre, why did you never tell me?"

"How could I?" I asked, hoping she would understand that I, too, had been living only half a life.

She reached out to touch my face again and I put my hand over hers, to keep it there. "May I read a few of them now, just to myself?"

"As you wish." I released her hand and lifted the flask to refill our cups while she held the scroll up to catch the last light from the gold-streaked sky. Watching her I knew which one she was reading, just from the way her eyebrows drew together, then from how her lips flirted with the beginnings of a smile, finally twitching with suppressed laughter. When she straightened suddenly I wondered if something I had written shocked or offended her.

"What?" I asked. Instead of answering she put the scroll down and looked at me, not with the fleeting enthusiasm of a child but the abiding joy of a woman, a woman secure in the knowledge that she is deeply loved. It mattered not to me if I only imagined that her wonderful eyes were shining with love for me.

The sun died and night came with startling suddenness, stars springing to life in the vast darkness of the sky while we sat in silence, sipping our wine, watching the moonlight spread a silver path across the black river.

" 'To love is to believe in goddesses,' " she whispered, repeating a line from the verse I had written only two nights before. "Perhaps you have worried too long about my *ka*, husband, and so forget my *akh*, the spirit within me that quickens every time you enter the room. Sometimes when I looked up to find you walking toward me across the garden, my heart would thump so loud I could hardly hear what you said to me. I have a constant need to draw your brown eyes to mine, so I can watch them soften with the love you feel for me. Or to find some way to provoke that slow smile you give only to me and so experience the warm glow that invades my entire body, stealing both my wits and my will."

How could I have been so blind?

I did not wonder for long, for I felt so alive at that moment, so full of love—and terror—that I thought my heart must burst.

Instead, I took her in my arms and told her the truth as it came to me, letting the gods guide my hands and lips and body.

Only once did my thoughts cause my desire to falter, when I recalled the child whose feverish body I had tried to cool with water. In that moment it struck me as perverse that now I tried to arouse her until she burned with want—a want only I could satisfy. When I hesitated she stilled as well, and whispered, "Is it because of what that old crone did to me?"

I gathered her closer so she could feel the voice of my pounding heart. "I am overcome with desire for you is all, and fear hurting you. Not only that, but I may reach my end before you if we continue without pause."

"I am not a fragile thing to be protected from my own pleasure, Tenre. We promised to teach each other, remember?"

"Every word you uttered last night is engraved on my heart," I replied. And so we continued as before, pausing from time to time only to make the end more intense when it did come.

Afterward I kept her in the curve of my arm, loath to let her leave me even then. As our bodies cooled I reached to pull a blanket over us, and saw that already she slept. But I lay awake for a long time, looking up at the stars that made night seem almost as bright as day, trying to separate dream from reality. My thoughts went back in time to what my days had been like before she came into my life. I realized then that she had given my very existence not only direction but purpose, and that without her this world would be as colorless as the desert around us.

When next I opened my eyes, the stars were bright in the dark sky as before, making me wonder if I had dreamed that someone painted my chest with a brush made of downy feathers. But I was awake now and still felt it sweep back and forth across one nipple and then the other until they formed hard knots. A moment later the feathery brush took a new path, over my rib cage and down across my abdomen. I felt at the same time a tightening in my gut and swelling surge in my loins—as if my body responded to someone else's command. What dark fantasy was this, I wondered, that tortures me even as I sleep? I put a hand down and encountered a mass of soft curls.

"Aset?" I whispered, for I could not be sure she was awake enough to know what she was doing.

"Sshhh, be still," she whispered without interrupting her exploration of my body, leaving nothing untouched by her hair, nimble fingers, and soft moist lips. Each time I lifted a hand to touch or caress her, she stilled it with one of her own, refusing me even the tiniest distraction from the sensual feast she prepared, until I could do nothing but give myself into her tender keeping.

Her head moved down, blazing a trail of anticipation with her lips and darting tongue, a weapon that turned languidly gentle as it reached my turgid penis. In a haze of anticipation, an unimaginable ecstasy shook my entire body as her mouth closed around me. Then, just as the pleasure flooding my loins threatened to erupt, she pulled away, leaving me suspended between this world and the next, unable to go either forward or back. In the next instant she swung a leg over mine, to kneel astride my thighs and raise herself slowly, teasing and torturing me with her pouting nether lips until, finally, her wet sheath took in my entire length. For one interminable moment she held perfectly still. Then, watching my face in the moonlight, she began sliding up and down. Near the end I thrust up as she came down, my hands grasping her hips to pull her hard against me, so she would know the instant I spilled into her. When I was done she fell forward to lay her cheek over my heart and listen to its frantic pace.

"That was so you will never again think of me as a child, Tenre . . . or as my father's daughter. From this night forward you and I embark on a different voyage."

Now she lies just behind me, lulled to sleep by the gentle rocking of the felucca riding at anchor. The moon is bright enough in the cold dry air to cast a patina over the landscape all around me, from the murmuring ribbon of water to the grassy bank where Pagosh and our oarsmen spread their pallets for the night. In the distance I can make out the roofs of the slumbering town, mudbrick hovels all hugging the earth while only the temple of Isis reaches high into the sky. A moment ago a big white ram came down to the water to drink, yet I cannot help wondering if unbridled pleasure causes me to confuse dream with reality. I even won der if I have passed through the reeds without knowing it, for everything is changed, not only the world around me but within me. I am a man fully grown, yet I see with the eyes of a babe and imagine all the adventures yet to be dared. Only one thing remains constant and real—love, the gift of the goddess.

TWENTY-ONE

Max was pouring syrup on a cut-up pancake when she came down the next morning, while Sam sat clicking his nails on the floor in anticipation. As soon as Max set the plate on the floor she made a beeline straight for him, not caring how she looked without any makeup, hair curling wildly after a hurried towel-drying. He caught her in his arms, then held her close.

"No regrets?" he asked.

"Only that the night was so short." The touch of his hand had quieted all the little doubts that set in the instant she opened her eyes. "Aren't you supposed to be at your office pretty soon?" It was already after nine.

"Not today." He seemed reluctant to let her go. "Ready for some pancakes? Weather forecast says a wet front's on the way. I thought we might get in a few games of tennis while we can. Unless you'd rather do something else."

Whatever he wanted to do was fine with her so long as they could be together. After last night it felt as if another Max had taken the place of the one she had eaten breakfast with yesterday. They were going to have to learn to talk to each other all over, in a new way.

By the time they finished the first set Kate was really worried. Max's mind definitely wasn't on tennis or on her. She didn't think he'd thrown the set to her on purpose, either. Which made her wonder if he was having second thoughts about asking her to stay. As they headed into the house to get a drink he never looked at her, or held the door or anything. Maybe he was worried about one of his patients. If so, she wished he would say so, not leave her wondering.

"I need to tell you something," he said, so abruptly she felt a jolt of premonition. He motioned her toward the kitchen table and waited for her to sit down, then took the chair beside her facing the windowed alcove that looked out to the backyard. "Do you know what dyslexia is—what happens in the brain to cause dyslexia, I mean?"

Confused, Kate nodded, then shook her head. "Not really. Just that it has to do with how some children process visual stimuli, which makes it difficult for them to learn to read."

He nodded. "That's what we used to think. Turns out the problem is in how those kids hear, how the brain processes language, not how they see." She wondered why he was telling her this. And why now.

"The medial geniculate nucleus—the area of the brain that receives incoming signals from the ear and sends them to the auditory cortex—has fewer neurons that process fast sounds, mostly stop consonants, in dyslexics than the brains of normal readers. Since they never hear these sounds, dyslexic children can't construct the mental dictionaries that enable us to recognize a sound the next time we hear it—to make sense of it. Are you with me?"

"Yes, but I don't have any trouble reading, Max, really."

"I know that. And I'm probably doing this badly, but—what you *do* have is sort of a twin to dyslexia. It's called central auditory processing disorder, a hearing problem that has nothing to do with the ears. It's in how the brain processes complex auditory signals."

He waited for Kate to say something, but a kind of mental white noise had wiped out everything but the sensation that she'd been hit from behind—by something she never expected and hadn't seen coming.

Then it began to sink in. Something was wrong with her brain. She kept her eyes on her hands. Didn't know what to say. Couldn't think.

"I suspect you fell between the slats, timewise," Max continued. "Until ten years ago there was a lot of debate about whether CAPD even existed. Then a team of audiologists at Baylor, here in Houston, confirmed that it did, using topographical brain mapping."

She still couldn't look at him. Face him. "How long have you known?" she asked.

"I suspected from what you said New Year's Eve about the trouble you ran into after you started going to a bigger, noisier school. Then the other day, while we had you in the scanner—" He reached out to touch her arm and Kate pulled back, dropping her hands into her lap.

"Why didn't you say anything then?" she asked, keeping her eyes cast down.

"I thought about it. But I didn't want you to think that's all I do—that everything's just another diagnosis with me. That I'm detached, impersonal. Didn't want to ruin what I felt happening between us, the sense of closeness. I've never felt that with anyone else." He dropped his voice. "The way we can be with each other is important to me, what I think we can have together. That's why I'm telling you now, even if my timing is off. I didn't know if last night was ever going to happen, let alone when. So there's never going to be any better time."

Kate finally looked at him, searching for any sign that he wasn't being straight with her—for the slightest hint of a smile or disingenuousness—and was surprised to find his face naked, without the beard. Another trick of her psyche.

"Then tell me everything you know about this—this brain disorder," she replied. "I'll yell uncle when I've had enough."

He nodded. "Each sensory system has specialized neurons that are activated by sounds, sights, and other stimuli, and these receptors create a sort of map or spatial diagram of how this information is processed. Except in the auditory cortex, which contains cells that appear to be unlike any others in the nervous system." His eyes never left her face. "These cells are able to detect sounds anywhere in space around us by emitting signals in a temporal code, not spatial. There's a lot we don't know yet, like whether the signals are passed on to other brain circuits to help us understand or whether they're secondary sites, artifacts of another process. But it looks pretty certain that these temporal codes are used by other sensory systems to tie several spatial maps together. Anyway, that's where I think CAPD originates, some flaw in the temporal coding process that makes you unable to handle a lot of signals at the same time."

He paused again but Kate waited for him to go on. "I can dig out the latest stuff in the literature so you can read about the research for yourself. That's really what you've been doing for a long time, Katie—converting everything you can to visual stimuli, taking in more of the world around you through your eyes than your ears. The happy result is your unusual ability to construct mental images. Vision is a linking together of subsystems—*what* is in the temporal lobe, *where* is in the parietal lobe—combined with associated memories. When we see an apple we not only know it's red and round but that it has seeds inside and how it tastes. Every visual area that sends information upstream also receives information back along those same neural pathways. In most people, input from the eye is much stronger than signals coming the other way, from the imagination. Not with you. I wish you could've seen Ben's face when I asked you to think of two animals and then draw them."

"I was thinking more about what *you* were seeing on that monitor than what I was doing," Kate told him. "I don't even remember what I drew."

"Wait here," he said, jumped up, and left the kitchen. She sat staring out the window, wondering where Sam was. Then Max was back, handing her a pencil drawing of a lion and gazelle playing some kind of board game.

As she stared at the hastily sketched "cartoon," other animals began to appear on either side of the lion and gazelle, the lines fainter and slightly out of focus—reminding Kate of the halo effect Tom McCowan talked about.

"It looks vaguely familiar," she admitted, "but I don't remember doing it." She looked up. "Does that mean I've got more than one disconnect in my brain?"

He shook his head. "We try to put subjects into a resting state before a test by eliminating outside stimuli, but the brain isn't just reactive. It's constantly generating stuff. At night, with almost no sensory input, it's free to do whatever it wants. During the day the senses limit the types of images you can generate, but it's still going on. Daydreaming. A mixture of fact and fantasy. Problem is, sometimes our mental maps get so elaborate that we get lost in them. Happens to everybody."

This time when he reached out to smooth her hair back from her face, Kate accepted the gesture for what it was, a sign of caring not only about what happened to her but how she felt about herself.

"Is there any way to fix this . . . disorder?" she asked.

"Stay out of crowds, all the things you already figured out to do."

"Medical school?"

"If that's what you want. You probably ought to stay away from emergency medicine, but anything else?" He shrugged. "*Is* that what you want?"

"I don't think so. No. I was just asking. Where's Sam?"

"Asleep on the couch in my study. Watching us play tennis wears him out."

"I've had enough, haven't you? I think I'll go shower."

Max nodded and watched her go. She knew he wanted more from her, but she didn't have more to give. She needed to be alone. To think. To get a second opinion from her inner voice.

She stood letting the spray pummel her back, but the hot water only seemed to intensify the conflicting emotions pelting her brain. Anger mixed with relief. Resentment with gratitude. Relief at finally knowing why some perfectly intelligible voices would suddenly turn into gibberish. Grateful that she no longer needed to fear the day when the gibberish wouldn't go away. Angry with herself for letting her guard down.

She turned to let the water mix with the tears running down her cheeks until she couldn't tell which was which. Max was stimulating yet easy to be around, even when they didn't see something the same way. *Because he's not judgmental. Just because he takes a different approach than you do doesn't mean you're wrong—not to Max. What drives him is curiosity, not control. The need to question. To ask why. Not only with his patients but Tashat. So why not you?*

With Max she felt connected instead of "different"—a thought that triggered a recollection of Max telling her about his grandmother. But she wasn't the same person she used to be, either, maybe because of Sam. She thought of the day they hiked across the top of the mesa, her carrying a backpack with water and their lunch, Sam breaking trail for her through the virgin snow. She had talked it over with him, telling him everything, and decided that, no matter what, she wasn't going to abandon Tashat. Now, thinking about it, she knew someone else had been with them that day—that it was Max's unwavering faith in her that was helping her to believe in herself, despite all the Dave Brovermans, past and present. That her inner voice, the one the ancient Egyptians called the *ka*, was beginning to speak with assurance instead of the self-doubt she had lived with so long.

Now Max had given her another priceless gift—self-knowledge—releasing her from the clutches of the vulture that had been sitting on her shoulder for years, watching her stumble, waiting for the fall that would bring her so low he could peck out her golden eyes. And she had turned her back on him. Again.

She turned off the water, towel-dried her hair and then her body. With water still trickling down her back, she pulled on a pair of panties and was hunting for her bra when she heard a door close downstairs. She grabbed her robe, slipped her arms into the sleeves, and grabbed the folder from the table by the window as she went. She flew down the stairs—had to catch him before he left—pivoted around the bottom post and ran for the kitchen.

He was sitting right where she'd left him, staring out the window, until he heard her and turned.

"I thought I heard the door," she stammered.

"Sam wanted out." He turned back to the window. "He catches on so fast to everything else, why can't he learn to return the tennis balls to that bucket?" It sounded to her like a halfhearted attempt to say something to cover an awkward moment.

Kate began to worry that what she held in her hand wouldn't be enough, that she had waited too late. But that was a chance she had to take because she didn't have anything else—only the drawings she had been doing of him from that very first day, in the museum. A story she would never be able to put into words.

"Sam is too intelligent to find chasing balls inside a fence any challenge," she said as she went to him. "He just indulged you a few times because he didn't want to hurt your feelings." She laid the bulging folder on the table in front of him.

Max glanced up, then at the folder. As he opened it and saw himself as she had—a middle-aged hippie with a beard and one eyebrow raised—he smiled but shook his head. Then he discovered the hastily sketched cartoon beneath it—a man in a mouse-colored suit with a long tail trailing behind him, timidly knocking on one side of a door, emerging from the other side as a roaring lion. That one brought a laugh, and he began turning the sheets like the pages of a book, anxious now to see the next one, and the next, as it dawned on him that they were all depictions of him—seen through Kate's eyes. The look of consternation when he realized she had pulled his leg about Sam. Standing on her front porch in the dark, eyes and mouth cold as the blanket of snow behind him. Stepping out of his car at the gas station in Houston, angry yet overjoyed to see her.

When he came to the last one, a pen-and-ink drawing of his hands, he looked up with a question in his eyes. Kate wasn't sure what he was asking—why just his hands, or why any of them. " 'Let me count the ways,' " she whispered, hoping he would understand what she meant.

When his eyes came alive with a smile that told her everything she needed to know, Kate bent and wrapped her arms around his neck. Then, after a minute, Max pulled her down on his lap and wrapped *his* arms around *her*.

He began spending more time at his office, but nothing like the twelve to fourteen hours he'd been putting in before Kate came to Houston. He didn't *have* to, he told her, and now he didn't *want* to.

One afternoon he came home early to give her a tennis lesson before it got dark, followed by his special mesquite-grilled chicken. That was what Kate really looked forward to, eating at home and discussing the day over a glass of wine while they worked on the meal together.

She spent another morning at the hospital to observe the post-operative knees of Mike Tinsley's patients and picked up a copy of the chapters he'd completed so far. After that she worked on illustrations in the morning, then spent a couple of hours in the afternoon reading, making notes about what needed illustrating, and sketched any ideas that came to her.

She also fell into the habit of waking just as it was beginning to get light and would lie in bed letting her imagination float ideas and images to the surface of her mind. One was pure serendipity, like the watercolor wash born of an accident during surgery, when Mike nicked a blood vessel with his bone drill, flooding the entire field with a quick rush of blood. More often than not, though, she found herself trying to construct a series of events to account for Tashat's premature end. And then, inspired by the transparencies she'd done for Tinsley, she began painting Tashat as she saw her in those early-morning half dreams.

The following Saturday Max insisted that she come to his study for a different kind of lesson. He'd clipped the printout of the superimposed skulls of Tashat and Nefertiti to the viewbox mounted on the wall behind his desk, and she assumed he was working on something to do with that. Instead, he turned the monitor of his PC so they both could see it and brought up a picture with text, an axial "slice" across the human chest cavity. Kate skimmed the first few lines of text.

"Because of the obliquity, only a portion of each rib is seen in each axial cut. One can see the articulation of the rib with—"

"This software package is called Radiologic Anatomy," Max explained. "Mostly it's used as a teaching tool, but it's fairly encyclopedic so I like to keep it around as a reference. I thought you might want to get familiar with how to use it. What you do is click on any part of the body to get a CT image like this one. Or a regular radiogram. Or a dissection slide. The arrows and other icons at the bottom of the screen let you move it left or right, or zero in on a particular part and blow it up."

He moved the mouse, clicked on the head of da Vinci's famous drawing of a man with his arms outstretched inside a circle, and the image disappeared, then was replaced by an axial view of the skull and brain. Next he demonstrated how to move in and out, then called up a dissection slide of a matching area of the brain.

"Here, you try it," he said, turning the mouse over to her. She did, and was hooked. It wasn't until he called her to lunch that she realized she'd been sitting there for two whole hours.

"You should've booted me out sooner," she mumbled by way of apology for taking over his study.

Max just grinned. "I've got some other stuff you might want to look at now that you've got the feel of things. I think Jose has an orthopedic tutorial, but I'll ask around at the office and see what else is available. If you want."

"I want. But only if someone else won't be needing it for a couple of days."

By the end of the following week she was almost finished with Tashat. Hurrying in case Max should come home early, she fitted the last two transparencies into the small glass panes. Afterward she paced the kitchen, watching the alcove as the light changed with the moving sun, trying to decide if she needed to change anything.

When she heard Max's car in the driveway she was overcome by a sense of déjà vu, and realized she was playing the same scene she'd set up the day she had her hair cut. This time she stood out of his line of view as he came in the back door.

"Jesus!" he whispered under his breath. "For a minute I thought she was alive."

Kate had fitted the plastic sheets over the small glass squares, turning the multipaned alcove window into a life-size viewbox lit by natural light. Now, with the sun almost directly behind her, Tashat appeared to be walking toward them.

"It's in her physical attitude, too, not just her eyes," he mused.

"Something she has to keep the lid on. So much energy, so much . . . life."

"I saw a dress like that in the Petrie Museum in London," Kate explained, "from a much earlier period. Cleo would be all over me for taking historical liberties, but I thought it suited her." Tiny stitched pleats ran across the yoke of the white-linen sheath and down the long, tight sleeves. Otherwise, it was perfectly plain and fell straight to her ankles.

Kate had painted Tashat's hair gathered into a knotted filet with sky-blue beads at each intersection of the twisted linen string. Other than that her only adornment was a garland of red berries mixed with waxy green leaves—that and the drawstring bag swinging from one shoulder.

"The berries are a nice touch," Max commented as he pulled Kate in front of him, wrapped his arms around her from behind and put his cheek against her temple. "D'you suppose she carried medicines in that bag?"

"It's big enough to hold lots of things, even a scribe's palette."

"Think about it, Kate. She had to be a member of the aristocracy or she wouldn't have been mummified and painted with anything like the skill we saw on that cartonnage. So what could have been going on back then to get an Egyptian of her class in trouble?"

Kate could feel the tension in his arms and knew he was either excited or upset about something. She also knew he would tell her in his own good time.

"If she didn't die during the reign of Tut, Ay, or Horemheb— the three pharaohs who are missing from the list on her coffin— then she must have lived either just before or just after them. Before would be under Akhenaten, a period of social and economic upheaval. If she lived afterward, well, none of the three pharaohs who followed Akhenaten left any heirs. That could mean a power struggle, probably between the priests and the army."

"If Tashat's father was a priest, she would have been aligned with them. Maybe she came out on the losing side."

"Or her father did," Kate suggested. "Say he got crosswise of Horemheb and didn't survive her. Given their habit of wiping a person from history by banning his name or destroying his body, sometimes both, that inscription may not give his real name. Nebamen means favorite of Amen, which must have been as common as Smith back then."

"Then maybe her name isn't Tashat, either. If the inscription is a red herring, the truth of who she is lies in that portrait and the scenes on her cartonnage, plus the ones inside the coffin lid." Max straightened and turned her to face him. "Take a flying leap, the first thing that comes to mind. What's her real name?"

"Isis. Aset in ancient Egyptian."

He nodded. "It's also more fitting for a royal princess."

"Even if it is, where does that get us?"

"Say she *was* someone important, either because of something she did or who she was. Having to hide her identity after death doesn't fit an act of adultery. That's what I came home to tell you. I got a call from Ann Arbor. Bill Ragsdale finally got around to looking at those films I sent, and wants to know who we're looking at." His lips twisted into a devilish grin. "I told him I wasn't at liberty to say yet."

"No fair, Max. Give. What did he say."

"One of our skulls exhibits the cluster of craniofacial features they've identified with the Eighteenth Dynasty royal family. But it gets complicated after that, so hold your fire, okay?" Kate nodded. "Do you remember telling me that there was some doubt about who a couple of the royal mummies really are? Well, it's more than a couple. Ragsdale thinks some of them probably were misidentified back in the Twenty-first Dynasty, when the priests rewrapped and reinterred a whole bunch of the royals together—the cache of mummies found in the late 1800s. You still with me?"

Kate nodded, hardly able to breathe. "Jim Harris and Ed Wente, who put together that *X-Ray Atlas* you showed me in Denver"—she waited while he pulled a piece of paper from his pocket and unfolded it—"think the mummy identified originally as Thutmose Four probably is Amenhotep Three. Because of the similarity in the craniofacial morphology of both Tut and the skull found in Tomb Fifty-five—who they assume is either Smenkhkare or Akhenaten. What you'd expect if Amenhotep III is their father." He shrugged. "Not that that's conclusive, or they wouldn't still be looking for any confirmation they can get. Anyway, one of our skulls exhibits features similar enough to the mummy they now believe is Amenhotep Three to be his daughter."

Kate blurted, "Nefertiti!" Max nodded. "What about Tashat?"

"Definitely related. Close enough to be the granddaughter of the Magnificent Amenhotep—the third Amenhotep. If that's who that mummy really is. That means she could have posed a threat to someone who coveted the throne simply by existing."

"That's why she was killed—so she couldn't legitimize the opposition's claim to the throne by marriage to a half-royal princess?" Kate felt something crumple inside her. "Oh, God, Max, I hope not. What a terrible waste."

"I know, but suppose she did die at the hands of some power broker intent on claiming she never even existed. And that her friends arranged for her to be named the wife and daughter of two fictitious men, a diversionary tactic to protect her body so she can come forth another day. Her child isn't mentioned in that inscription because that might put him or her at risk, too, assuming the kid was still alive."

A new thought fought its way to the surface of Kate's consciousness. "Do you think we could twist this Ragsdale person's arm one more time and ask him to look at the male skull, give us a second opinion about whether he could be her father? Not that I doubt your—"

"I already sent the films this afternoon, FedEx overnight." Max held out his hand to take her with him. "But I need to E-mail him so he'll know they're coming."

He was keyboarding the message to Bill Ragsdale when Kate had another brainstorm. "Remember the juggler—the mouse who's performing for an audience of animals? He's wearing a ram's head mask, like a priest. Rams were the sacred animal of Amen, so maybe he's her father."

"So maybe we're looking at another Aesop's Fables, or Brer Rabbit, where all the animals wear clothes and talk like humans?"

"Not just any human. What if each of those animals represents a real person, someone Tashat actually knew? Do you remember the big yellow tabby cat sort of half-hidden behind a bush, so only one eye shows?" She picked up a pen and drew the magic eye of

Horus, with the tear mark of a cheetah but without the cheek mark of a falcon. "Whoever that cat is, something is wrong with her. She isn't whole."

The following Friday Max came home early again, using the excuse that he just wanted to beat the traffic. But he seemed preoccupied, and after changing his clothes, he went to his study to work.

Kate decided to give Sam a bath and was in the yard brushing him dry when Max came flying out the back door. "Ragsdale, the guy at Michigan, just confirmed my reading on the head between her legs. He's no relation. Can't be her father."

"I never thought he was, but at least we can rule that out."

"I asked Ragsdale whether any of the mummies in that attic room at the museum in Cairo were missing any parts—a leg or an arm, something like that." Max eased down on the edge of a lounge chair, then jumped back up, too excited to sit still. "You're not going to believe this, Katie. One, he says. A physician." He waited for her to look up. "No head."

She dropped Sam's brush. "Did he know where this mummy was found?"

"Necropolis at Thebes. He gave me the name of a professor at Cairo University, someone who has an in with the curator of mummies at the Egyptian Museum. Otherwise, he says, you can wait months for them to answer a letter." He paused before spilling the rest. "I already called him. Name is Seti Abdalla, but he speaks English like a native. Of England."

"And?" Kate urged, impatient that he wasn't telling her faster.

Somehow Max managed to hold off grinning long enough to deliver the coup de grâce. "Don't just stand there burnin' daylight, girl. Better go start packing your duds."

TWENTY-TWO

Year Seven in the Reign of Horemheb

(1341 B.C.)

DAY 16, SECOND MONTH OF HARVEST

My daughter has curly black hair and tiny toes, like her mother. She
gasped for breath but soon quieted, as if sensing she was safe in my
hands.

"What about her eyes?" Aset whispered, weak from her labor.

"I think yours were not so dark, but it is too early to say."

"I offered to Amen every day, begging him to make them
brown."

I did not have to ask why. Instead, I handed our babe to Kiki,
the girl Senmut sent from his own household because Aset refuses
to have servants, probably to guard our privacy for the times when
the impulse to couple comes upon us without warning. Even my
examining table has been the site of experiments I could never have
imagined, but surely that will change now, just as she must care for
our daughter instead of waging war on the women of Aniba who
cut the genitals of their daughters. Which she has done with Senmut's encouragement.

Tuli clicked his nails on the tile floor as he pranced in place. "Soon, Tuli," she assured him as I pressed down to expel the membrane, which I collected in a clay crock and set aside. When I pressed again, though, a rush of blood spilled from her body.

"Bring the babe and a roll of that clean bandaging you set in the sun," I called to Kiki as I lifted Aset from where she knelt and carried her to our sleeping couch. She cradled our daughter and directed a nipple to the babe's mouth. Soon I felt her uterus tighten and knew a great sense of relief.

By the time I finished cleaning up, both of them had dozed off, so I watched them a while, storing the sight in my memory to be able to bring it before my eyes at will in the years to come. Then I carried the bloody membrane to the back corner of our garden and buried it under a struggling young tamarisk tree—and finally gave vent to my great need to tell *someone* about my new daughter. Tuli.

Afterward he watched me bathe and slip a tunic over my head, tie my best kilt around my hips—the one I wore only for special occasions. At that he ran to his basket of toys and collars, took the strip of crocodile hide decorated with white cowrie shells in his teeth, and brought it to me.

Mother and daughter were wide-awake, looking at each other. "Does she please you?" I asked, easing down on the couch.

"I find her truly beautiful, don't you?"

"Almost as beautiful as her mother," I agreed, for Aset's beauty remains unsullied by sun or wind or the rigors of daily life. I would have said more except for the cold nose nudging my leg. "Our friend's patience wears thin."

When she called him by name he stilled, ears perked, waiting for one word. "Come." He leaped up, stumbling over Aset's blanketed legs in his haste. "The little girl I told you was coming is here at last." Twisting with excitement, he licked the tiny fist, causing my daughter to kick out her legs.

"You told me it was a son you carried," I reminded Aset.

"To learn whether you would be disappointed in a daughter. Also"—a smile pulled at her mouth—"because I enjoyed hearing you argue in favor of a girl."

I put my lips to hers. "I would love any child of yours, though you fill my thoughts and my heart until I fear there is little room for another."

She cupped my face with her hand. "As you do mine, but already I feel a new kind of love, different from any I have known. Surely our hearts are amazing in that way, something else the ancient ones left out of your scrolls. Did you send word to Senmut?"

I nodded and handed her the scroll I had tied with a blue ribbon. "But she must have a name before you can introduce her to our friends." I had taken Pagosh's advice and prepared ahead of time for this momentous event, so the papyrus was larger than need be for the few words it contained, in order to surprise her.

"What a gorgeous thing!" she exclaimed as her eyes fell on the inlaid box. Made of wood from the yew tree, it feels smooth as water to the touch, even where the triangles of ebony and ivory are set into the wood. "I asked Senmut to name the finest craftsman in Aniba, who turned out to be the Assyrian's woman."

"The physician who can make the old ones see again? He mentioned no wife to me." Aset makes it her business to meet all those who come to Senmut's House of Life, to learn the customs of people from other lands.

"I did not say she was his wife. Nor have I seen her. I passed a message through the Assyrian, asking only that it suit the occasion and be large enough to hold what is inside." Until then Aset thought the box itself was my gift, but inside on a piece of light blue linen lay a string of ivory beads, each perfectly formed and polished. What made it unusual was the clasp—a delicate ring that hooked over the head of a ram.

She stared at it so long I began to think she found it crude, but when she looked up I saw tears in her eyes, along with the beginnings of that glorious smile. I tried my best to match it though a rush of emotion blurred my sight.

"The ram honors Khnum," I said, "who guided us through all the cataracts in your short life to this place of happiness." I alluded to the rocky place in the Nile where all is turmoil and danger, and to the god who watches over it, because I do not want her to associate the ram with Amen or her father, and so be reminded every time she wears it of what she left behind.

"Go on, read what I have written," I said as I took my daughter in my arms. "It is time she learns her name." Though it is customary among the People of the Sun for the mother to name an infant, Aset had asked me to do as her own father had. "Tuli, too." He stood when he heard his name, to be ready for whatever Aset commanded. First, though, she fastened the ivory necklace around her throat, positioning the ram's head over her heart.

"The night was bright, and Sopdet, evening's brightest star, had spiraled into being. A white ram came down to the river's edge to drink. In the distance I could hear men singing, water rushing.

I held my wife's hand—we were new lovers then—and learned the art of inundation. 'Enter me and I shall make you a god.' I take her into my arms, taste her lips, lose myself in beauty and chaos. In her body I come to life.

I am he who stood in the rising water and washed himself in love. I am he who heard beneath the music of hurrying water the laughter of she who in nine months became my daughter.

I am he who names her beloved of the River God. Hapimere."

DAY 10, THIRD MONTH OF PLANTING

At Senmut's insistence we occupy a remote wing of his brother's palace, with its own private garden, which he claimed for the use of honored visitors to his Per Ankh. The royal residence in no way compares with Pharaoh's House of Jubilation, but is a compound of one-and two-story apartments that have been added on as needed.

Meri's eyes begin to turn brown, but in all else she is the image of her mother, even the way she studies my face when I cradle her in my arms—until I look down and catch her. Then she kicks her feet, wanting me to play with her toes or make a growling sound in my throat while I hold her fingers to my lips. At three months she is unusually responsive, but then not every mother talks to her child as Aset does.

The two outline scribes Aset instructs come to our rooms now, and Senmut drops by every day or two to see how my daughter does, he claims, though I suspect it is really his "sister" he comes to see. I realize now it was jealousy that caused me to misread her feelings for him, to my everlasting shame, and that she sought only to determine if he was good enough for her beloved friend. For it seems that Nebet even at that tender age had sworn she would have no other. Nor does it appear that Senmut will be satisfied with any other woman. He sent a letter to her along with Aset's announcing the arrival of our daughter. But he is first in line to inherit the throne and so cannot speak for her until his brother gets his Principal Wife with child, since Mena would never let his daughter go as second wife to any man, even a prince.

Today we were relaxing in the garden when Kiki came running with the news that an emissary from Pharaoh had arrived in Aniba. "His entourage is on the way to the Hall of Ambassadors even now. They say he carries a message for King Hiknefer."

Tuli lifted his head and sniffed the air, his ears pricked to catch some distant noise, then leaped to his feet and began racing around the garden. I looked toward the gate and saw Pagosh, but he motioned for me to stay where I was. In the next instant I saw Nebet just behind him, and my heart leaped with joy, for I knew with absolute certainty the identity of Pharaoh's emissary.

Aset and Nebet hugged and laughed and hugged some more. Then Aset went to Pagosh and threw her arms around his neck. Before he could protest she had kissed his cheek, whispered something in his ear, and hugged him, too. What surprised me was seeing him lift Meri from her basket. She stared at his scarred face without making a sound, until a smile welled up from within him and broke like the sun across his face.

"I would know you anywhere," he told her, perfectly serious, then glanced at me. I nodded, letting him know that I, too, see the disconcerting likeness.

They came bearing many gifts, from Nofret and Tamin, Sheri and Ramose. Aset's father sent a length of pink cloth from the land of the purple dyers, and a delicate openwork bracelet dotted with tiny granules of gold, sized to fit the wrist of a babe. But nothing gave Aset more pleasure than the little wooden monkey with movable arms and legs from Merit, along with a letter written in her own hand.

By the time Mena got free of his duties at the palace I was no longer fit company for anyone. We had moved inside, for the nights are colder here than in Waset, just as the days are hotter. Even so, seeing Mena in the flesh made me newly aware of how much I miss the city of my birth, in spite of Senmut's efforts to see that I meet every scholar and dignitary who visits his brother's court. And there are plenty of those, since Aniba lies on a busy corridor of trade, halfway between the First and Second Cataracts. It is a fortress town built long ago to guard the mouth of a desert wadi that leads to the gold mines to the south and east.

Senmut brought him to us, for we have rooms aplenty and can accommodate all three of our guests. "He carries the flail to Khai," Senmut burst out at once, unable to hold the news any longer. For good reason. Huy, Pharaoh's longtime Viceroy in Kush went to his eternal home some months ago, but Khai had been his deputy. Since Khai's Principal Wife comes of a Nubian mother, his own children feel at home in Wawat—and Senmut is assured that Pharaoh's overseer will continue to indulge him in his Per Ankh. "Merenptah of Waset, Chief Physician to Pharaoh, is to place the gold ring on his finger."

I looked to Mena and found a grudging grin on his face. "I have little experience of such occasions," he joked, "but Prince Senmut is to guide my hand, if not my tongue."

"Will you wear wild cattails on your arms," Nebet asked, "and ostrich plumes in your hair?" Senmut makes the rest of us look colorless by comparison, for he wears the colorful tunics of his people along with the white headband of a prince. But he does not ape the antics of an uneducated tribesman.

"I will do what I must to see Khai named Pharaoh's Son in Kush," he told her.

"And tasseled earrings?" Nebet persisted. At fourteen, she combines the earthy coloring of her father with an aura that becomes ever more ephemeral with time.

"Not if I can help it," he muttered, chagrined that she teased him.

"Oh, I wouldn't want to miss that for anything"—Nebet looked to Aset—"would you?" Aset smiled and patted the bench beside her, inviting Senmut to her side with a gesture that took the sting from Nebet's teasing.

Later, when Nebet made much ado about Meri's cradle, Senmut informed her that it had served both him and his little sister. He not only named the many woods used in its construction but pointed to the teeth marks on the edge, which he made as a boy watching over his baby sister. Afterward their eyes kept meeting and looking away, only to seek each other again and again. For the remainder of the evening Senmut was to Nebet as a flower is to the sun—eyes following her wherever she went.

Watching them made me wonder if Mena came to Aniba for reasons of his own, perhaps to see if the place is so uncivilized that even a prince could not assure his daughter's safety. Or did he come to make sure that Senmut's wife is chosen for him? If so, I would not fault him, for I cannot say what I would not do to see *my* daughter safe.

After Senmut left, Pagosh, Mena, and I sat talking while Aset and Nebet went to another part of the house. I was eager for news from Waset, but Mena jumped in ahead of me. "What of your latest experiment, or does instructing Senmut's recruits eat all your time?"

"Senmut builds on his experience with you, so instructing and investigation are one and the same. Each student spends three months assisting me. But you will see for yourself tomorrow, at the House of Life." I wanted to save the rest until I could show him Aset's new map, so I inquired about Khary and the Eye of Horus.

"He let supplies fall too low for a time, which brought a lot of grumbling when he could not fill all the orders, but he begins to catch up."

"An infestation of insects devastated our herbs?"

Mena shook his head and glanced at Pagosh. "Pharaoh's police finally caught up with his father. Also his friend Pepi. You remember him?" I am not likely to forget the woman who died to keep from betraying her family to Pharaoh's Aten police. "Tamin and Khary have taken Pepi's children, since the followers of Aten are sent north when they are apprehended, for Ramses to use in building a new store city within the fortress at Zarw. That way the labor costs nothing but the gruel to keep them alive."

"How does Khary take it?"

"He and some others sailed down the river under cover of night and smuggled two hundred sacks of oats and wheat into the camp where the prisoners are held."

"Is Ramses a man who finds satisfaction in rubbing their noses in the dirt from whence Akhenaten came?" I asked. Mena shrugged. "What need has your General to be so miserly that he dispatches workmen to scavenge the Heretic's city for stone?"

"I will speak plainly, Tenre, though Pharaoh instructed me to keep it to myself. My real purpose here is to learn why the flow of gold from Pharaoh's mines is less this year than last, and less last year than the year before and the year before that."

"Your General grows feeble indeed if he sends a physician to oversee the extraction of gold," I chided. The Nubians rule at Pharaoh's pleasure only so long as they hold their people to a steady flow of gold from their lands to his, so it made more sense to me that Horemheb communicate his concern to Hiknefer.

"He trusts few men to tell him the truth."

"Who can afford to speak the truth if he risks being accused of treason should Pharaoh not like what he hears?"

"I do not tell him only what he wants to hear, Tenre, and never have," Mena protested, indignant that I should suggest it.

"Nor do you go against him without good reason," I pointed out. "But Horemheb does not *expect* dishonesty from you. Your history with him was built on trust from the time when you saved his arm, if not his life."

Mena softened his words with a smile. "We have had this discussion before, and I still think you mistake Horemheb's intent. He sends a message to Khai along with the flail of office, instructing him to give Senmut what he needs to continue his Per Ankh, and his full cooperation. Do you assign Pharaoh an ulterior motive for that, too?"

"He pleases you as well," I pointed out, "since he is aware that you look on Senmut with fondness."

I did not want to confirm Mena's opinion that I find a self-serving motive in all Horemheb does or does not do, but I find my old friend too gullible by far where his General is concerned. Horemheb knows it is not with Hiknefer but in Senmut that the seeds of unrest lie, which is the real reason he moves to assure that the prince is otherwise occupied.

Year Eight in the Reign of Horemheb

(1340 B.C.)

DAY 21, FOURTH MONTH OF PLANTING

I stopped on the threshold to our garden to watch my daughter step from shrub to shrub, holding on to a branch here and there. At ten months she is wobbly on uneven terrain, but I find watching her infinitely fascinating, especially the way her face lights up with each new discovery. I was trying to imagine what it is to smell a flower for the first time when the leaves she grasped stripped off in her hand. Before I could move, she plopped down on her bottom and let out an indignant howl.

"Just get back up, Meri," Aset told her from somewhere nearby, hidden from me by a row of shrubs. "Tuli will help you." Poor old Tuli nudged Meri's thigh with his nose until she bent forward and pushed to get her bottom in the air, then grabbed his ear so she could straighten up and find her balance. He still follows wherever she goes—first crawling and now walking—though his joints ache with age.

"Are you so helpless that you must stand by and wait for what may never happen?" Aset asked. I thought she spoke to me, so I started toward the shady arbor where she often sits, then stopped when Senmut answered.

"What more can I do? She has tried everything Tenre suggested and still does not conceive, until Hiknefer complains that she is too demanding. Most nights now he lies with one of his other women."

Since Nebet returned to Waset, nothing pleases Senmut, and everyone displeases him, until his colleagues at the Per Ankh grow weary of his unpredictable moods. But I know what it is to want one particular woman and only one, so I cannot help pitying him.

"I cannot put off writing to Nebet much longer," Aset told him, "and she asked especially for news of you."

"She did?" He drew the words out, relishing them on his tongue.

"Has your brother gotten any of his other women with child?" I suppose Senmut shook his head, since she murmured, "Then *he* is the reason, not her. Could you not go to your brother's aid?"

"Me? How?"

"Lie with her yourself. The child would still carry the blood of your father, and it cannot make much difference which woman you lie with, given how you have been spending your nights. Or does it take more than one now?"

"What can you know of how I spend my nights?" he muttered, more embarrassed than angry.

"Everyone in Aniba knows," she replied. "Surely you do not expect a woman who lies with the next king of Aniba not to brag of it to her friends! Or do you not care?"

"You will not tell Nebet?"

"My *ka* does not like having to choose between you, brother." It came to me then that I was spying on my own wife, but before I could creep away in shame, my daughter pitched forward and hit her nose on the hard ground. She let out a howl that brought all of us running.

It wasn't until later, when Aset told me of Senmut's visit, that she mentioned he was having the walls of his great room white-washed in preparation for Nebet's next visit. It seems he has become so obsessed with the scene she painted on the wall of Meri's room—a windstorm on the desert with all manner of sprites and fairies tumbling head over heels across the endless sand—that he wants to fill his private quarters with her visions of the river, hills and swirling sand dunes that surround us. Senmut believes it is *how* we learn to see that determines *what* we see, but I took it as an opportunity to ask Aset if she knows the source of Nebet's unique visions.

"There was a time," she replied, "when Nebet would not allow herself to sleep for fear that the evil spirits who lived behind her eyes might steal her *ka* in the night."

"Mena never told me."

"I doubt he knew. But Sheri did. That is why Mena began to bring her along on the days when he came to see you. Remember?" I nodded. "By then Nebet refused even to speak of it, afraid the demons would strike her dumb. I pretended not to notice how scared she was, and drew pictures as fast as I could while I talked on and on about how my *ka* guides my eyes to see what they do and then speaks through my hands." Aset lifted a hand to my cheek. "You are the one who taught me that." For her simply to touch me has always been enough to bring my body alive, driving all else from my thoughts, and tonight was no different.

Thinking back on it now, though, it is not what she said that concerns me but what she did not say. For I remember another conversation we never had, about why she persisted with her story-scrolls. Had she done otherwise, though, she would not now be my wife. So who am I to question how the gods direct our fate?

DAY 3, SECOND MONTH OF HARVEST

I rose early and was at my writing table when I heard Aset cry out. I ran first to the nursery, then to our sleeping room, and found her sitting on the floor with tears streaming down her cheeks. She held Tuli to her breast, rocking his lifeless body back and forth, begging the gods to let him stay.

When I put a hand on her shoulder and she looked up at me, I saw the haunted look I had glimpsed only once before—the night her beloved Ankhes died at the hands of her own mother. A mother they shared.

"He did not open his eyes wh-when I rose from our couch, s-so I thought to let him know I—" She stopped for breath. "H-he was already cold."

"His aching joints gave him little peace these past few months," I whispered, trying to console her. "Sixteen years is an advanced age for a dog."

"But it is not like Tuli to go without waking me, to—to at least bid me farewell." The anguish in her voice sent cold terror rippling through my flesh, born of the fear that I was losing her to a desolation so deep she might never return. Surely Tuli had loved her beyond life itself, nor did she hide from him the secrets in her heart as she does from me. She would deny that, but then he knew her better than she knows herself.

"His *ka* slipped away in the night so as not to cause you sorrow," I murmured, and was relieved when she gave in to great racking sobs that shook her whole body.

Afterward she bathed him with her own hands, wrapped him in fine linen, and carried him to the House of Beautification, but not before she sent word to Senmut, asking him to counter the priests' objections so I could be the one to gut her beloved friend. Together we packed his body with crushed spices and herbs, laid him out with his legs positioned as if he were chasing a cat, and covered him with natron. But nothing I say or do lightens her sense of abandonment, and she has withdrawn to a place where no one can reach her. Not even Meri.

DAY 11, FOURTH MONTH OF HARVEST

Aset helped the *sem* priest place him in the special box she had made of fragrant wood, the top bearing a painting of Tuli's heart being weighed against the feather of truth, with the scale tilted in his favor. Afterward she carried her faithful companion to our garden, where Senmut and I placed him in the ground under his favorite tree, a drooping old willow. Kiki held Meri's hand while I spoke the verses Aset had chosen from the Book of Coming Forth by Day, then we settled ourselves near his eternal home to break our fast. As we lifted our cups of wine to speed him on his journey, I could not help wondering—if I still miss him baring his teeth in a smile whenever I return to the our rooms—what it can it be like for her?

Year Ten in the Reign of Horemheb

(1338 B.C.)

DAY 10, THIRD MONTH OF PLANTING

Hiknefer's wife brought forth a son, and Senmut has sailed for Waset with the rising sun. While Aset waits to learn the outcome of his campaign, she begins the drawings for a medical text I am writing about problems that beset women, something she has urged me to do for some time. She already has illustrated my other medical scrolls, one set for Senmut's archives and another for Mena's personal library, which Senmut carries with him.

DAY 14, FOURTH MONTH OF PLANTING

Sleep did not come easily to either of us tonight. "You hold my body so tenderly," she whispered against my chest. "Do you fear I will tear?"

"I thought only to enhance what you feel. Next time, if you like—"

"Do you know why I have not conceived again?" In that instant I saw the blood gush from her vagina, but I shook my head. "Do you not long for a son to carry on what you have begun?" she persisted. "And to praise your name after you are gone?"

"Surely you know I am happy with my daughter, except when she gets into one of her stubborn moods. Do you encourage her to shed her sandals the minute I leave the house?" I teased, though I am pleased beyond measure that my daughter wants to find her own way. "Why does conception happen one time and not another," I went on, "though a man and woman lie together on the same days, month after month—or does not happen at all, even when there is no apparent sickness or injury to the genitalia or womb? You are twenty-one, a flower in full bloom, while I—" I felt her stir. "No, let me finish. More likely it is my forty-three years than anything to do with you."

She stayed silent for a while, but I knew she did not asleep. "How did you come to call Nebet 'little lotus bud'?"

"No reason that I remember. Why?"

"I used to wonder why you never called *me* a pet name—'dusty toes' or 'funny monkey' or something. Nor do you now."

"I served at the pleasure of your father while hers was my dearest friend. It is only natural that our history influences how we deal with each other."

"Because it would not be proper—is that what you mean? Must I always do without just because the blood of the Magnificent Amenhotep flows in my veins?"

Perhaps she only revealed to me what she said to no one before, except Tuli—how deeply she still hurts—reminding me of how little her childhood resembled mine. Though she occupied an entire wing of a grand white villa, with servants and all manner of fancy foods, toys, and clothes, she did not know the steadying love of a generous mother, or the freedom to roam at will without every man, woman, and child deferring to who she was.

I pulled her closer and put my lips to the corner of her eye. "I have always found words inadequate to express my feelings for you, though I tried in my verses. As for a pet name, I love you too much to find satisfaction in naming you anything but what you are to me, and always have been—my reason for living, what I care most for in this world. You and Meri."

She sighed as if she had been holding her breath, and turned her head away. "If you and I cannot overcome our history, Tenre, what hope do I have of escaping the destiny demanded by my blood?"

Year Eleven in the Reign of Horemheb

(1337 B.C.)

DAY 16, FOURTH MONTH OF INUNDATION

Aset's feast day always brings back the night she came into this world—the sudden pounding on my door, Pagosh ordering me to come at once "or the lady who kneels on the bricks this night surely will die." But this one—when I am twice Aset's age instead of thrice—has been the happiest day I can remember since Tuli passed through the reeds. Nebet chattered on and on about their new home, while Senmut and I took our satisfaction in watching and listening to our wives.

"Do you still feel you made a wise choice then?" I asked, though it is obvious.

"I am no fool, Tenre. I know the choice was hers, as it was with her mother before her." He sent me a crooked smile. "As it will be with your daughter as well."

DAY 9, THIRD MONTH OF PLANTING

Pagosh arrived earlier than usual with news that Ramose sickens with a malady his physicians can neither name nor heal, and we are to leave for Waset within the week. This time we sail on Hiknefer's royal felucca, not under the tattered banner of a lowly fisherman to hide our true identity.

So our sojourn in Aniba comes to an end, five years of tranquillity and happiness born of the freedom to be true to myself, thanks to Senmut's generosity of spirit. It is here, too, that Aset and I learned to know each other anew, as lovers and then husband and wife—and, finally, as mother and father—without the encumbrance of who Aset is and I am not. For that and more I shall be eternally grateful to the man who is both brother and son to me, a man I not only honor but love.

TWENTY-THREE

From the elevated pedestrian walkway above Tahrir Square, they could look down on the meleé of converging cars, buses, and donkeys hauling refuse carts to garbage dumps on the edge of town. The stench of exhaust fumes coupled with the constant blast of horns pushed Kate to a running walk, until Max pulled on her hand and yelled, "Slow down, Katie, we've got plenty of time."

Kate felt disoriented, partly because her internal clock was still on Houston time. Everything had happened so fast. Arriving in Cairo on Sunday, meeting with Seti Abdalla on Monday, trekking out to the pyramids Tuesday morning and that evening to the medical school, where Max and Dr. Mahmoud Hamid performed another scan, this time on the headless physician from the Egyptian Museum. Since they were meeting Seti at the museum, it had to be Wednesday.

Winter was high season for tourists, when daytime temperatures in Cairo rarely rose above seventy-five or eighty degrees compared with the torrid heat of summer, and they found hordes of tour groups milling around the entrance to the big yellow building. Just inside the door they came face-to-face with a recumbent Anubis, the first thing Howard Carter had seen when he broke open Tutankhamen's tomb—still on guard. Beside him stood their Cairo University contact, looking nothing like his ancient ancestors in a tweed Norfolk jacket. So British, Kate thought, yet his English smacked more of the Sorbonne than Oxford. And his mother, as he put it, was a *force majeure* in the Egyptian antiquities organization.

"You rested well?" Seti inquired solicitously. Kate and Max both nodded and smiled. "And the pyramids—you found your guide adequate?"

Kate gave him another noncommittal nod, not wanting to sound ungrateful since he had arranged their tour. The problem was people. Fifteen million of them. That and the urban sprawl encroaching on the sandstone escarpment like some alien invasion from outer space. But the truth was that the remains of a group of people who had existed twenty-five hundred years before Tashat was even born struck her as irrelevant, and with each passing day she found it increasingly difficult to contain the simmering impatience that made her feel so uneasy.

They followed Seti up the stairs to a foyer where the smaller masterpieces were on exhibit—including the wooden figure of a young Nubian girl carrying a clay jug on one hip that was Kate's favorite—through a door marked private into a dim passageway that smelled like the nineteenth century. From there they paraded single file through a narrow hallway to a door with peeling letters. Except for the bank of fluorescent tubes overhead, the Mummy Conservation Laboratory reeked of the past, too, from the dark woodwork to the wall of glass-fronted cabinets. In the center of the room lay the mummy—the ancient physician they had come to see. Beside him stood two men wearing white coats and face masks.

"Come in, come in," Nasry Iskander invited, pulling the mask down below his chin and extending his hand. His close-cropped white hair and bronze face made everyone else look pale by comparison, including the man beside him, who turned out to be Hosni Nabil, the museum's chief conservator. Nabil's hair was only graying, but his back looked as if he had spent his entire life bent over a yellowed papyrus, and it was his age that worried Kate. Was he even aware of the recent advances made in preserving textiles and paper? As Seti was performing the introductions a third man arrived, who turned out to be a photographer.

"We are ready to begin," Iskander informed them, catching Kate by surprise, "but perhaps you would like first to look at how he came to us." He motioned to a table across the room, drawing their attention to a mummiform coffin that was nothing like Tashat's. The head was shaped like a *nemes*—the cloth headdress worn by Egyptian men—and the eyes were outlined in black, with round black irises that gave him a wide-eyed look. Other than that there was only a band of red down the center, crossed by four more bands of the same color, but the rounded curves and satin-smooth wood made Kate itch to run her hand over it, the mark of a master craftsman. Another paradox, since the quality of the wood spoke of money and position while the lack of decoration or gilt marked the deceased as a person of little consequence. Even the inscription give him no position or lineage of importance, except to Kate and Max. *Sunu.*

All they knew was that this body fell within the age range of the head between Tashat's legs. Now a part of him was about to come forth to a new day, and with it, Kate hoped, the secret of what had happened to him. And Tashat.

She glanced at Max and found him staring at the banded coffin, so still he seemed to have stopped breathing. For one panicky instant she imagined he was someone else, until he glanced up and gave her a wistful smile.

The mummy itself was plainly wrapped, like those the team at Manchester had performed autopsies on, except for the Egyptian blue faience amulet sewn over the place where his heart would be.

Iskander pointed to the amulet. "That is Thoth, the god of wisdom. The inscription on the back says, 'I hold in my hand a figure of Thoth made of *tjehnet* so that I will not die a second death.' *Tjehnet* means brilliant, or divine light. That is what my ancient ancestors called the ware we know as faience. Of course it is not true faience at all but a nonclay material containing ground quartz, soda ash, and lime, along with copper or cobalt salts for color. It is not so difficult, I think, to believe in magic when to simply apply heat to such drab materials turns it a brilliant blue or green, colors that are reminiscent of the sky and vegetation that sustained them."

As Iskander stepped to the head of the table to make the first cuts with a pair of scissors, Kate almost cried out for him to stop. The purr of a tiny motor sounded in the still room—the photographer, she realized, and felt reassured. At least they knew to document everything. She watched Iskander peel the bandaging back with a gloved hand, one layer at a time, keeping the cutting to a minimum until he reached the linen that had been soaked in resin to make it impervious to moisture, insects, and sand. Then he stepped back for a moment to give the photographer a clear field, before switching to a small chisel and wooden mallet. When he picked up a miniature keyhole saw, Kate mentally winced each time he pushed it forward, worried that he might cut more than the resin-hardened cloth. Then, after a few last snips with his scissors, he lifted the small flap away and laid it on the prepared sterile bandaging, and took the flashlight Nabil handed him and bent to peer into the opening.

"Uh-huh," he murmured. "It may come without enlarging the opening any farther. At least it is worth a try." He paused long enough to allow the photographer in for a better angle, then, using a long tweezers to grasp the cloth-wrapped object Max and Dr. Hamid had discovered during the scan, Iskander tugged until he met resistance. He pulled gently, testing to see if the bundle was stuck to something or had met an obstruction, then asked for another tool, this one long and thin but with a blunt tip. While he probed around the bundle, trying to free it by using the forceps to vary the tension on the cloth, Kate put her hand under Max's elbow, then slid it down to clasp his, and found it as clammy as her own. So much for the cool, detached physician, she thought, as she hugged his hand to her side. He squeezed her fingers, but didn't say anything. Neither did Seti.

"Aahhh, now it will come, I think," Iskander murmured. Finally. A minute more and the bundle was out. Iskander handed it to Nabil, who held it out with both hands—his attitude that of an ancient worshiper offering his most prized possession to his god.

The photographer raised his camera to record Nabil's prayerful stance, then the older man carried his precious bundle to another table and began picking at the cloth with his gloved fingers, searching for where it might come loose. The torn, discolored edges fell away easily, revealing a thick roll of papyrus. He touched it with one finger, testing for flexibility, then slipped a thin piece of plastic under one curling corner.

"It appears to be in very good condition," he concluded. "There is little sign of brittleness, but I must apply a backing for support before going any further. Only then will it be safe to lift the edge a bit more, perhaps enough to tell what we have." Kate sighed with relief as Nabil looked to Iskander for instruction.

"Our friends have come a long way for this," Iskander pointed out. "Perhaps you could put aside your other work for a time?"

"Of course." Nabil seemed eager to please. He turned to the photographer. "Ashraf will record everything just as it appeared upon recovery. Also to work with." He gave Kate an apologetic smile. "The ancient papyri are too fragile to handle more than is absolutely necessary. I cannot say what difficulties we may encounter, but I will work as quickly as possible."

Kate thanked Nabil and then Nasry Iskander, though she doubted any of this would have happened except for Seti Abdalla. And his mother. They were the real reason she and Max had not been left to cool their heels for a week or two, waiting for an appointment to talk with some minor functionary. But it wasn't until they were leaving the museum that Kate had a chance to mention her—obtusely, by way of thanking him.

"I showed her everything," Seti was quick to confess, "not only the photographs of the cartonnage and your head, but also your drawings. I knew my mother would become involved the instant she saw them, but perhaps you know of her work. Her name is Danielle duPré."

Kate went still, unable to put one foot in front of the other, then stammered something about being familiar with his mother's books. In fact she owned every one of them, because Danielle duPré was an authority on ancient Egyptian art with a reputation as a maverick who didn't run with the herd. Yet she had survived with her scholarly virtue intact.

"Of course, but I—I didn't know she *lived* here."

"She came to Cairo fresh from the Sorbonne to work with the French Archaeological Mission, never intending to stay so long. But within one month of arriving she met my father." He smiled and lifted his shoulders in a typically Gallic shrug.

"How long do you think it will take Iskander's man to unroll that scroll?" Max asked, impatient with their small talk.

"It is difficult to know. I will call him tomorrow to learn how it goes, but surely you will stay a few more days?"

Max nodded. "I think we'll go to Luxor for a couple of days, though Kate's afraid that seeing it might displace the picture she carries in her head—of what it was like three thousand years ago."

"The temple at Karnak?" Max nodded. "Then you have only to stay away from the sound and light shows," Seti advised. "In ancient times Amen's great temple slept while Re sailed his boat below the horizon of this world, so there would have been no more than a torch here and there to light the way of a watchman."

He dug a card out of his European-style wallet, wrote a number on the back, and handed it to Max. "Call me at home, tomorrow night. Anytime after seven. Perhaps I will have something to tell you by then."

Seti turned to Kate for a parting word. "Florence Nightingale recommended to see Egypt in solitude and by night, with the stars as lamps. A hundred and fifty years ago, Africa's angel of mercy found 'the savages of the present in the temples of the past.' But who is to say there were no savages in the temples back when your ancient physician lived? That, I think, is what we are about to find out."

In my hand I took the sword I was given and I learned to use it.
—Normandi Ellis, *Awakening Osiris*

TWENTY-FOUR

Year Twelve in the Reign of Horemheb
(1336 B.C.)

DAY 23, SECOND MONTH OF INUNDATION

Perhaps to cast his eyes on my daughter was enough to renew the High Priest's faith in eternal life—the promise of his God—for the withered muscles in his legs grow stronger each day. Pagosh says he turns more and more of the running of the temple over to his underlings, to spend his remaining time with her and Aset.

While we were away Nefertiti took up residence across the river with her sister, after Pharaoh ordered Amen's Sacred Council enlarged and reorganized—to lessen the power and influence of the High Priest—then packed it with men of his own choosing.

"The war between chaos and order is never-ending, but this time the battle for the throne of Horus will be like nothing we have seen before," Ramose predicted today. "Already any word of Pharaoh falling ill, true or not, sends people to the temple in panic, because Horemheb refuses to name an heir. 'Let the one who is strongest take the throne, as I did,' he says. But what if to do so that man must sell his soul?"

"Or woman," I added as a reminder.

His eyes sought mine. "That much, at least, I share with

Horemheb. They are *tahuts*, both of them." Queen Mutnodjme has long been known for her lascivious behavior, but I never thought to hear Ramose call his wife a whore, as Pagosh does.

"My mother's eyes were blue, too, did you know that?" Ramose asked as we sat watching Aset and Meri splash each other with water from the garden pool. "One of the few times he spoke of her, Uzahor told me they were like the sky Re leaves behind as he descends toward the western horizon." That we are willing to risk surprising the other is a measure of how far Ramose and I have come to trust each other, now that I no longer fear he will take from me what I care for more than life itself.

"You have no memory of her yourself?" I asked.

"She went to Osiris two days after giving me life. All I have is a gold necklace and a wisp of her hair." He grasped the carnelian scarab hanging from the gold chain around his neck and pried it open with his thumb, to show me a curl of reddish brown hair. "According to my father, she was a woman of infinite beauty, of unusual stature and coloring."

"I find that easy to believe," I replied, for Ramose is still a hand-some man. At fifty-nine he looks no older than most men of forty-five, though his eyelids are a bit heavier than before. If his hair and brows have gone white like Mena's, no one can tell it, for he still keeps his body clean-shaven as well as his head. It is only when he tries to rise from a chair that his age shows.

"Flattery from you, *sunu*?" he asked with a wry smile.

"The truth," I denied.

"Then tell me why a son repeats the sin of his father, even when he is duly warned and can see for himself the grief it caused every-one around him?"

"Some things can be learned only by doing, from making our own mistakes."

"You have always been too generous, Tenre." Whether he com-plimented or insulted me I cannot say. "She was the daughter of a merchant from a land north of the Great Green Sea, whose mother had recently died. Her father could not bear to leave her behind, so he brought her with him to Waset, where he was taken by some pestilence, leaving her alone among strangers. I tell you this now only because my father's blood is joined with your father's, in your daughter. And my father was a fool! Whether I have been one as well I leave to you, but that was how Uzahor judged himself for abandoning my mother while she carried his son in her belly."

So I had guessed right about Uzahor being Aset's grandfather.

"I have little memory of my early years, by choice I suspect," he continued, "since the life of a street dog is better forgotten. But I do not blame him. There was little to be gained by marrying a woman with no standing or property but her father's ship. Aren't we advised that 'A woman of strange parts, like an eddy in deep water, is of unknown depth"? I recognized the warning from the old Book of Wisdom. "So he married another. To Uzahor's credit, he could not forget her. But he waited too late. When he learned she had departed this world he began another search, this time for a boy of five who bore her mark." He paused so long I thought he was finished.

"Uzahor warned me that I deluded myself if I thought retribution for the sins we commit in this world is delayed until we stand before Osiris. He said the gods punished him every time he looked at me and saw her eyes, reminding him of all he had lost. And for what? A fine house, more gold than any man needs?" Ramose's voice trailed off while he wandered through his childhood, when the lessons he learned must have been bitter indeed. "He placed me in the home of a childless friend to see that I was educated, but Uzahor from then on was a presence, a friend of the family I thought, until my sixteenth feast day, when he told me about my mother." He heaved a tired sigh. "But nothing in my entire life prepared me for what I would feel when my daughter slipped her small hand into mine."

Like a streak of light from the sun, I heard his confession to Uzahor just before the old man died—that given the chance to live his life again he would do the same. "Never to have pitted myself against her quick wit, or watched her eyes light up when she laughs? Never to feel the touch of her hand in trust, or love? The rush of pleasure that comes with knowing she is mine?" It was Aset he had spoken of, not her mother.

"We are more alike than you think," I admitted. "I cannot imagine what my life would have been without her." I described to him the time she had waited for me with her Jackals and Hounds, and afterward, when I took her to the roof, how I thought to entertain her by pointing out the sights around us. "Instead of a field of blue lotus, Aset saw a herd of elephants waving their ears to create a breeze."

He smiled. "You thought the fever had taken her wits?"

"Not after she twice whipped my Jackals with her Hounds. No, I shaded my eyes and looked again. She was right. They could as well have been elephants . . . with blue eyes. So Aset has been my tutor as much as I have been hers, from the start. By the time we came down from your roof I was caught in the web of a girl whose eyes sparkled like sunlight on running water. All it took was one word. Why?" Ramose gave me a startled look, so I hastened to explain why I told him the story. "I just thought you might like to know the real reason I accepted your offer."

He actually laughed at that, giving me another glimpse of the man behind the priestly facade.

DAY 18, FOURTH MONTH OF INUNDATION

"If you wish to return to Aniba you have only to say so," I said, watching Aset work a wooden comb through her tangled curls. "Why go about it like a thief in the night?"

"Say what you mean, Tenre. I am too tired for riddles."

"Do you consider it an adventure, having to leave everything we own behind, fortunate to escape with our lives?"

"Sarcasm does not suit you."

I felt an urge to shake her, physically to tear away the veil of complacency she wore—that would, in the end, offer her no protection. "Nor deceitfulness you," I replied. "Do not pretend ignorance with me. Or innocence, as if you believe me to be an addled old fool!"

She turned, her yellow robe flaring open over her thighs. "If I hurt you in some way, my love, I am sorry. Truly. It was not by intent."

"Then perhaps you can explain what you *do* intend." I grabbed her hand and pulled her with me out the doorway. In the room where I keep my medical scrolls, I touched the flame of the lamp from a wall niche to the standing lamp beside my writing table, one of those we brought from Aniba. Aset has placed them in every room, because the fish-shaped bronze bowl is supported by a tall wooden column, putting the twisted linen wick above eye level so the flame illuminates the ceiling and fills the entire space with light. I pointed to the two scrolls spread open across my writing table. "Look at those and tell me they do not say what I think they do."

Before Aniba she crowded everything onto one piece of papyrus, coiling a snake around a chair leg or half a cat behind a tree. Now the pictures follow one after another for the length of a cubit rod or more, and tell a more intricate story. In one a fat gray tabby held audience for a parade of mice carrying bread and fruit, as if they made offerings to some goddess—obviously the Queen from the two identical vervet monkeys. As the mice passed before her, each stood on his hind legs to expose himself, and so offered to lie with her even though he held a lotus to his nose to ward off the foul odor emanating from the object of his desire. In case anyone should miss her point, the tabby's chair carried the symbol for coitus in the sacred language of the gods—the female pudenda crossed with the male penis and testicles.

In the next scene a parade of gray cats hobbled about on crutches with blood dripping from the soles of their feet, the punishment meted out to adulterous women under Horemheb's Edict. Among them strolled the same fat tabby, draped now in a purple-fringed shawl, but without crutches. And *her* feet dripped no blood. In the other scroll several mice ran about attending the fluffy-furred, preening cats. One mouse brings a goblet of wine, another a platter of roast duck, a wig, or a mirror. One even washes her mistress's feet. Then, in the scene that follows, all is reversed, with the lady cats on their knees serving the little gray mice.

"What you suggest here—that the natural order be changed—would breed nothing but chaos."

"Such thoughtlessness from you, Tenre, though you seek to change the way things have always been by learning what the gods try to hide from our eyes? Why fault me then for trying to plant such ideas in the thoughts of my people, lest in time, like a pool of stagnant water, we rot and begin to stink."

"I seek to learn how to cure a sickness or repair an injury," I argued, "not alone to change something."

"Must we kill the joy in the eyes of a child by sending him into the fields as soon as he can walk, just because that is the way of his father and his father before him?" She held out her left hand. "Surely the gods gave me this for a purpose."

So it begins again, a campaign like the one she mounted in Aniba to stop the practice of cutting away a woman's ability to feel pleasure. Only this time she aims much higher. "My people." That means she seeks nothing less than to direct the destiny of the Two Lands—like her mother and the glorious Amenhotep before her—just as some demon drives me to try to discover what it is that keeps the blood flowing through the vessels after the heart gives it a push. So how can I command her to stop, knowing she believes as I do that to oppress any man, whether in the name of a king or a god, is to enslave peasant and noble, slave and master alike?

DAY 25, FOURTH MONTH OF HARVEST

I am ordered to appear before the Bureau of Physicians to answer charges brought by a physician named Herihor. He accuses me of not following the instructions handed down by Imhotep in his Secrets of the Physician, and claims that I subvert the sacred profession of healing by revealing magic incantations never meant for the uninitiated. Mena says he targets the Eye of Horus and advised me not to worry, since he himself appointed the committee of inquiry. But I suspect there is more to it than that, unless I listen to Pagosh too much—who lately has been muttering that Nefertiti sits like a vulture, waiting for Horemheb to sicken and die.

DAY 29, FOURTH MONTH OF HARVEST

"A man comes to you with a painful swelling. It is warm to the touch yet you find no tear in the skin, only an angry redness. How would you treat him? Or would you?" Herihor reeked of ladunu, the fragrant oil used by the Babylonians to tame their beards, perhaps to cover the stench of his breath, for his teeth have begun to rot. He wore a pectoral bearing the image of Sekhmet, the lion-headed goddess of pestilence and slaughter who is fond of blood, which marked him a surgeon.

"There is no evidence of pus under the skin?" I inquired, expecting a trick. He shook his head. "Then my verdict would be to treat him with warm vinegar soaks."

"Nothing more?" he asked, hoping to shake my confidence.

"If the redness is on an arm or leg, I might instruct him to keep it raised, and have him drink an infusion made from ground willow bark to ease the pain."

"You would not call in a man of the heating iron, or consult your calendar to discover whether the swelling arose on a malevolent day? Why not?"

"You said there was no putrefaction."

"Would you not even prescribe an amulet or spell, to cast out the evil spirit that inhabits his body?"

"Perhaps. It would depend on whether he believes in such things."

At that he sent a sly smile to his fellows who sat in judgment, Khay-Min among them. Mena's father by marriage holds his age well enough to pass as my friend's older brother, perhaps because he has always found the questions of younger men more stimulating than threatening.

"Then you subscribe to the notion that a man causes his own illness?" It had the sound of a reed trap snapping shut on a greedy goose.

"He only states what every man here knows," Mena put in, coming to my defense. "A spell is of more use with some men than others."

"There are many sources of sickness in the body," I explained. "Some come from overuse, as walking wears the soles of my sandals. Other maladies come from without. A worm, or the stinger of a bee, which can cause havoc to equal an enemy's arrow."

"Aahhh, you claim expertise not only in birthing babes, but in treating the wounds of battle as well?" Herihor scoffed.

"By now every physician in Waset has learned to treat such wounds," Mena replied before I could, "thanks to Pharaoh's Edict of Reform." It was not the first time for him to say what no one else dared, yet he remains Pharaoh's favorite. And that, I suspect, is the biggest mystery of all to a man like Herihor.

"Tell us then, *sunu*, why any man should seek a physician in the House of Life when he can obtain all manner of pills and potions from your Eye of Horus at no cost?"

"Most poor devils who stumble into the Eye of Horus cannot afford the services of any physician," I replied, "let alone one in the Per Ankh. And they pay according to what they have, when they can. Otherwise"—I shrugged—"nothing. But perhaps it will put your worries to rest to know that my man dispenses certain medicines only to other physicians. Ground mandrake root, for example, and fetid nightshade."

"I send my assistant there at times," a physician named Irenakhty put in, "and find his herbs fresher because they do not sit on the shelf so long."

"You worry without cause, Heri," Khay-Min added. "Tenre's man requires me to send a list stamped with my signet ring, to be sure it comes from me."

"His untrained man can read?" Herihor scoffed, then fell silent at Khay-Min's nod.

"How often does he ask you to settle with him?" one of the others asked.

"Every month," another answered, revealing that he does the same. "If I forget, he sends a reminder. Once it was a few pills shaped like tiny birds, another time a sample of black alder bark, from Kush." He glanced at me. "A man with ideas like that is worth his weight in gold."

What I feared most—that they would condemn me because it is the rule of my profession that if no one knows why, then no one may seek to know—never came up. So I escaped with my skin intact, thanks to Mena's talent for shaping a group of men to his will, though he let them believe the decision was theirs. Surely it is a paradox that in Aniba, where Senmut has gathered the outcasts from many lands—most of them considered poor or uncouth by comparison with the land of the Pharaohs—we exchanged all manner of ideas and findings from our investigations, and gained because of it. Like plants in the field, our learning thrived and grew through exposure to the light of day.

Afterward I treated Mena to a pitcher at the Clay Jar, where his levity lasted no longer than our first mug of beer. "Horemheb's end is closer than the others suspect," he confided in a low voice. "But before I say so I would have you examine him. It is my decision to make, but perhaps you could cover yourself in the robes of a priest to ease your way." For a moment his eyes sparkled with humor. "I don't suppose you would consider shaving your head?"

DAY 30, FOURTH MONTH OF HARVEST

Horemheb's body is like a battlefield under attack from many directions at once. His bowels run day and night until his anus turns inside out, making it painful for him to sit or walk. But he vomits up most of what he eats as well, and that, along with the yellowing of his eyes, suggests something amiss with his liver.

Mena talked openly before his General, describing to me how he had administered enemas containing honey, moringa oil, and sweet beer for the pain in Horemheb's anus, adding a little frankincense to ease his stomach. I recommended suppositories made from the seeds and pods of itasin, white lotus leaves, and juniper berries steeped in sweet beer for him to drink, "And no more wine made from grapes."

"For one day only," Pharaoh muttered, "to see if you are as wise as he makes you out to be." He motioned to Mena but kept his eyes on me. "Hand me the scroll." When he had it in his hand, Horemheb raised himself up and slapped it against mine.

I knew without looking what it would be, but what I found shocked even me. The yellow tabby finally was revealed as a savage wildcat, gray stripes and all. With one swipe of her paw she destroyed one after another in her path, then turned on her own young to devour them as well, until—blood dripping from her mouth and claws—nothing remained but the double crown of the Two Lands.

"Take care, *sunu*," Pharaoh warned me as he collapsed against his cushions, "lest the she-cat eat your kitten as well."

Year Thirteen in the Reign of Horemheb
(1335 B.C.)

DAY 16, FOURTH MONTH OF INUNDATION

Aset is accustomed to my being called away, especially with the pestilence following the flood worse than usual, so my leaving raised no alarms. Meri was busy helping Merit decorate the garden for Aset's twenty-fourth feast day, and Khary, Tamin, and their children were due within the hour. That Nebet and Senmut are expected any day only adds to the excitement, for they bring their firstborn to meet his grandfather. A son named Senakhtenre!

By the time I arrived at the palace, Pharaoh lay senseless and motionless, except to cry out and try to rise from time to time as if his *ka* still fought the enemies of Kemet. Once he protested, "But for me the Syrians and Hittites would have overrun us!" He did not exhibit the tendency toward sexual arousal that accompanies an injury to the spine, so whatever afflicted him resided in his intestines, kidneys, and lungs—a conclusion confirmed by the odor of feces and urine that pervaded his room.

Imhotep, the only man to become a god without climbing the steps to the throne, had placed the heart at the center of a network of forty-six vessels, any of which could become overfilled or obstructed. He also believed that they carried blood, air, food, sperm, mucus, tears, urine, and feces, just as our canals carry water and life-giving mud from Mother River to our fields. But Mena and I have learned that some vessels carry only blood, in both the living and dead—the ones Aset has entered on our map.

"Look well, Tenre," Mena murmured. "Is this what you and I look toward in ten years' time?" Mena's hair is as thick as ever, though the white begins to conquer his eyebrows as well, turning his bronze face even darker. The skin under his chin is not so tight, either, but his back remains straight, maybe because he wills himself to stand eye to eye with his wife. That, surely, is why we both flourish when other men begin to wilt on the vine.

"Sheri and Nebet," I murmured for his ears only, "Aset and Meri, beloved in truth as well as in name. *They* are the ones who cause the blood to rush through our bodies, washing away the hatred and disappointment and envy that shrivel other men's souls."

As darkness fell over the city of Amen, Pharaoh's ministers and advisers began to gather, along with the High Priest and his entourage, to send Horemheb on his journey with appropriate ceremony and prayers. Nefertiti made a brief appearance as his life force leaked from his penis along with his urine, but not his Queen. Only one man shed any tears, recalling a time and place when he marched into battle with his General. Nor do I fault my boyhood friend for that, though I found Horemheb's passing far too gentle, given the pain and violence he has visited upon his people.

DAY 18, FOURTH MONTH OF INUNDATION

Senmut and Nebet arrived in Waset as the workshops and taverns were closing their doors, but they came across the river anyway, to show their son to his namesake. At eight months the babe is as happy as he is handsome, neither as dark-skinned as his father nor so light as his mother but a blend of the two. Senmut insists he takes after me in always wanting to explore where he is not wanted.

Aset bubbles with laughter now that her friend has come, more than at any time since Tuli went to Osiris, despite the cloud that hangs over all of us because no one knows who the General's successor will be. Ramose spends his days at the temple offering prayers for Osiris Horemheb's soul and overseeing everything else, for priests both high and low are overburdened at such times. Even the priests who teach classes for the young spend their days copying out prayers and spells for others, who are reminded of what the future holds for them.

DAY 24, FOURTH MONTH OF INUNDATION

A rheumy-eyed old wickmaker selling his wares in the street yelled to me as I passed this morning, warning one and all that the Heretic returns to Waset with an army at his back. When I asked what army, he babbled on about the Shasu, or Abiru—he was missing so many teeth I cannot say for sure. "The Shasu follow their grazing sheep," I told him, hoping to put an end to one rumor at least, "not the Heretic. They are a clannish bunch, so someone plays you for a fool if he says men who mistrust all but their own blood follow an outsider. Anyway, they have no weapons, only their shepherd's crooks." He reminded me that Aten already has sent a plague of insects to devour our crops, and withheld the life-giving waters of Mother River because the priests drove the rightful king from the Two Lands. Now, he claimed, Mose came to wreak his final vengeance, on one and all.

DAY 5, FIRST MONTH OF PLANTING

It has been twenty days and still no word. That can only mean the sides are evenly drawn between those who back the High Priest's choice and Horemheb's appointees to the Council. Khary believes that the priests cannot deny the army commanders, and so will choose Ramses.

"That may be," I agreed, "but why choose a man in his sixtieth year?"

"He was Horemheb's right hand, and has sons who have sons of their own, evidence that his family's roots have not become shriveled with age."

"Like the roots of the great Amenhotep's family?" I replied. He shrugged. "Do you think to spare me an insult to my wife? If so your concern is misplaced. There is no love between her and her mother." Still he pretended ignorance, leaving me to worry more about what he did not say than what he did. We were finishing the inventory we do before ordering more medicinal roots and such from the trader who brings them by caravan from ships that ply the Red Sea, when a woman came in asking for the magic potion Khary had given a friend. She said her husband upbraided her for not bearing more children, leaving him short-handed in the fields. While Khary prepared what she wanted she regaled him with the story of another friend, who can see into the future and predicts the High Priest will become coregent to his daughter, who is of royal blood!

"Surely that bucket will never hold water," Khary told her.

"The High Priest's daughter is not only married but a woman of twenty-four years, who has no need of a regent to guide her hand."

I thought nothing could shock me anymore, but she did. "The husband is of no consequence and easily done away with, a commoner. And you are not of this world if you believe the Sacred Council would trust a woman of any age alone on the throne."

DAY 12, FIRST MONTH OF PLANTING

"You believe it is true, then, that the two Queens lie together?" one of the men peering over his shoulder asked the amulet carver. I slowed my steps and Senmut did the same, pretending an interest in his wares to get a look at the scroll in his hands. Aset and Nebet had gone to Ipwet's shop to choose sandals for her to take back to Aniba, with Pagosh watching over them despite my wife's objections.

"Whoever draws them always has spoken the truth before," the amulet carver replied. "Why doubt him now? Better worry instead whether the Heretic's Queen will name another woman her Principal Wife if she takes the throne. The only one who can satisfy both the priests and generals is the High Priest's daughter, granddaughter of the great Amenhotep. What they should do is get rid of her aging husband and marry her to Ramses' son."

Senmut nudged my arm, and we moved on. "Do not listen to such rubbish!" he advised, keeping his voice low. "Aset tries to damage Nefertiti's cause out of fear that her father might fall under her mother's spell again."

I shrugged as if it were of no consequence to me, but her picture-stories are on every tongue, wherever I go. Last week I saw them passed from a dockworker to sailors who carry goods from one town to another, even into Nubia. One shared with me a scroll in which she repeated the story of the sacrificial lamb, but this time after they cut his throat, the priests set his body afire. Out of the smoke a new shape began to take form—the lamb's ears stretching to become arms while his haunches straighten into the fleshy thighs of a man. In the end, his head is one with the sun, and his hands reach toward the priests of Amen, who cringe in horror at what they have loosed on themselves. She had exaggerated the man's thick lips and pendulous earlobes until he looked sad. Then, in the very next scene, angry flames leap from his eyes as he raises his bronze staff of kingship—the one with the serpents twining themselves upon it—and calls on his god to bring insects and pestilence down upon their heads.

It is because I know what feeds her stories about the Heretic returning to claim his throne that I cannot help shuddering at the thought of what she risks.

DAY 17, FIRST MONTH OF PLANTING

It was after dark when Ramose called us both to his high-ceilinged reception room. When we learned that he had sent Pagosh for Mena as well, we knew something threatened us all. "The Heretic's Queen intends to seize the throne," he said without preamble, watching Aset in case the news should knock her from her moorings, "without waiting for the seventy days of mourning to end."

Aset's breath came like the wind filling a sail. "How can she if you withhold the blessing of Amen?"

"She claims already to have Amen's blessing. Otherwise, she could never have ruled as coregent. She also has the support of the mangy dogs who complain that they get nothing but crumbs from Amen's table."

"Priests of Amen?" I asked, to be sure I understood him.

Ramose nodded. "Renegades, along with the nomarch of Waset and others of the same ilk, who chafed under Pharaoh's Edict because it cut into their take."

"When will she make her move?" Mena asked.

"My men question one of the traitors even as we speak, but I doubt it will be long now. Thirty-two of the seventy days have passed already, so we must act."

"It is all my doing," Aset murmured, and sank onto the edge of the sitting shelf like a rag doll with all the stiffness washed out of her. "I have brought nothing but trouble down on you, Father, from the moment I came into this world."

Ramose is not a demonstrative man, but he went to her and took both of Aset's hands in his. "I would have you no other way, daughter. You have always pleased me beyond any other. I am the one who lost my way, until you came."

She stared at their hands. "But I asked too many questions and went where I wasn't supposed to. You said so yourself."

His lips twitched. "I was wrong." At that she looked up, then threw her arms around his neck and held on as she did when a child. "Come, we must see what is to be done." She nodded against his neck, then gave him one last squeeze.

Ramose looked to Mena. "If you cannot find your way to doing what I ask of you, only say so and I will understand." Mena nodded. "Someone must send a message to Zarw." Mena nodded again, without hesitation. "Say whatever you must to convince Ramses he is needed, with troops enough to secure both the palace and city."

"But the royal guards hold the palace already," Mena told him.

"Their commander is her man," Ramose answered.

If Mena doubted the truth of that it was not for long. "Then I will go myself. We cannot afford to trust anyone else. The river flows swiftly at this time of year—"

Ramose held up his hand. "Hear me out before you decide." He turned to me next. "Can you get a message to the Sinai?"

I knew then what he intended—and that he, too, had seen Aset's cartoons. Yet the sheer audacity of it took my breath. "I know just the man," I told him, and saw a wry smile light his face.

"I thought you might." So he has known all along and simply let sleeping dogs lie, in case the day should come when he needed one of Akhenaten's followers.

"Khary says Zarw is much changed from the days when you were there with Horemheb's troops," I told Mena, "so you better travel together." Horemheb had long since appointed Ramses the Two Eyes of Pharaoh in the North, making him overseer of the king's fields, serfs, and granaries in Lower Kemet, in addition to commanding his troops. More than that, Ramses has collected taxes enough to build a grand new town near the fortress at Zarw. "From there Khary will find a man to carry the message, someone the Heretic trusts not to set a trap."

"Are you sure his father is not too old for such a journey?" Ramose inquired, at the same time suggesting who to send.

"What message?" Aset asked, done with evasion and secrets.

"That we will accept him back as Pharaoh with certain conditions, which I will put in writing for Tenre's man."

"Khary is his own man!" she blurted, fighting the helplessness that threatened her sense of *maat*. "A man of learning and wisdom. And you would do well to remember that. Nor will he carry a message he finds offensive just because it comes from the High Priest of Amen." With those words Aset let him know that neither she nor Khary would countenance whatever he intended simply because of who he was.

Ramose must have recognized that, for he quickly laid out the conditions he would impose on Akhenaten—that he must allow the People of the Sun to worship any god they chose, and leave all military decisions to Ramses. Also, he would be allowed no more than one quarter of his treasury in any one year for the glory of Aten. "I am informed that the Heretic wearies of having no one to command but his wife and her father's sheep," Ramose added, "and so is likely to be amenable to such demands. It is a risk, I agree, but—" He shrugged.

"The Sacred Council agrees to this?" Aset asked.

Ramose shook his head. "That is my part—to convince enough of them *and* the Council of Wise Men that we are best served by setting a precedent for imposing conditions on the next pharaoh, which has always been our goal. Already they believe the Heretic's Queen has her own agenda and could bring the Two Lands to its knees, ripe for the taking by the Hittites—or worse."

Where once Ramose gave up his chance to sit on the throne for his daughter, this time he risked his life for her. And Aset knew it. "Is there nothing *I* can do?"

"No!" Mena and I shouted, but it was her father who gave voice to our thoughts, harsh words born of his fear for her. "You have done enough, daughter. Now I speak to you as plainly as you did to me. In following the path you believed to be *maat*, did you even once stop to think of the man who loves you more than life itself? Or Meri? Would you have *her* grow into womanhood without a mother, too, as you did?" Aset's face flushed, and I felt the urge to go to her, but I kept my place.

"Perhaps I expect too much of you," Ramose continued. "If so, that is because you gave me reason, not just your quick tongue and ready wit but your compassion for others. Once you were drawn to those who limp through life like poor Ruka. Now you talk of 'my people'—an arrogance that does not become you."

"Enough," I said, unable to stand by and see him tear her heart asunder. "More than enough." I kept my voice low, a warning to both of them. "Some things once said, even by those who love each other, can never be undone."

Mena heaved a sigh and got up to leave. "I must be away. Have Khary meet me at first light in the place where we put in our skiff. Tell him to come equipped to hunt waterfowl, in case anyone should see us."

"I leave for town as soon as the message for Akhenaten is ready," I agreed, and turned to Ramose. "I will make sure Khary knows what it says so he can pass the message by mouth if it comes to that."

Aset went to bid Mena farewell. "Shall I send Pagosh to watch over Sheri while you are gone?" she whispered, still feeling the lash of her father's tongue.

"Senmut and Nebet are there, but I thank you for remembering her." He did something then I have never seen him do before—put both arms around my wife and pull her close. "Your father only loves you too much," he whispered. "I recognize the sickness because I suffer from it myself." He looked at me then, with that boyish grin. "Not that Tenre would know anything about that."

I walked with him to the gate, to have a few words in private. "The Heretic is not worth even one of the white hairs on your head, so part company from Khary when you draw near to Zarw, in case he has been seen consorting with the outcasts."

"Will he go willingly into the lion's mouth?"

"If not, it will be me you see on the bank of the river at first light. At the very least he will give me a name and the way into their camp."

He nodded. "Guard your goddess well, my friend. The tabby will try to rid herself of whatever dirties her golden coat, lest even the street dogs she runs with find her too flea-bitten."

I took his advice and warned Pagosh not to let Aset out of his sight, then made my way into town in the dark, alone, wishing all the way that Tuli was with me to warn off any marauding street dogs. Also because I needed someone to talk to. As I expected, Khary accepted the mission to Zarw without hesitation, his eyes sparkling with eagerness for adventure. But I warned him to take care lest he leave his children without a father, then rubbed salt in the wound by reminding him that Tamin is still an attractive woman, and would be even more so should she inherit his considerable worldly goods.

Aset was still awake when I returned and so eager to couple with me that once was not enough. When I was slow to become aroused the second time, she took me into her mouth to coax my penis erect with her tongue and lips, then lifted her hips to meet my thrusts with a ferocity that set my blood afire, calling forth a burst of bright stars behind my eyelids. For a while I floated among them in the night sky, until Aset clasped me to her with a desperateness that brought me plummeting back to earth.

I rolled away to let her know that I could do no more. Still she continued to cling. "Do you think I deceive you and will go with Mena after all?" I asked. She shook her head. "You are afraid?"

"Not really. It is just—"

"You are safe within these walls, but I will see to putting more men on the gates."

"It's not that," she whispered, her voice thick with tears. "The only thing I truly fear is—is that you will leave me behind. Like Tuli."

TWENTY-FIVE

Max and Kate spent the afternoon wandering through the great temple of Amen-Re, with its Sacred Lake and magnificent columned hall, which hadn't yet been built when Tashat lived. Then, as the sky came awash with crimson and gold, they retraced their steps to sit on the remnant of an ancient stone wall to watch the sun slip behind the weathered cliffs beyond the Valley of the Kings.

"Do you read hieroglyphs from right to left or left to right?" Max asked.

"Both," Kate answered. "Also up and down. But the scroll will be in hieratic."

"Yeah, you're right. I forgot." He paused. "Why the hell didn't they write any vowels? Does that make sense to you?"

"Certain sounds could have a magical effect, so they were considered sacred. Remember when you called me an artist of consummate knowledge and skill? You can call it whatever you want, but that changed everything for me, beyond reason or explanation." Max smiled and brought the back of her hand to his lips.

A half hour later they headed back to the hotel, where he ordered a bottle of wine and grilled sandwiches from room service, claiming he was too tired to go out. But Kate knew he was chomping at the bit, anxious to be near a phone when seven o'clock rolled around. He surprised her by holding off until ten after before putting in the call.

"Nabil has discovered there are two scrolls, one inside the

other," Seti told him straight off. Beyond that he was pretty close-mouthed, except to say that it probably would take Hosni another full day and perhaps more, to complete unrolling and photographing both scrolls. "You might as well stay a few days more. Nabil will work through the weekend, but I cannot say if he can be finished by Monday."

"Any idea yet what the illustration is?" Max asked.

"It appears to be some sort of anatomical drawing, but that is more for you to tell us—you and Kate."

In the end Max accepted that they wouldn't know any more before Monday, if then, but he wasn't willing to wait any longer than that to return to Cairo. As soon as he hung up with Seti, he put in his usual call to Marilou, who was keeping Sam.

The next morning they got up early, took a ferry across the river, and hiked into the desert to the Colossi of Memnon, two huge misnamed figures that once stood before the funerary temple of Amenhotep III. From there they could see the sandy foothills where the noble families of Thebes had built their tombs, most of them opened by archaeologists and simply left to weather, without their inscriptions and wall paintings ever being documented.

Traveling on foot took longer and was exhausting, but Max seemed to understand that Kate was trying to experience what it was like to walk the dusty town, or ferry across the river to join a funeral procession into the desert. At times she gave him a running commentary that would have put most tour guides to shame, other times she would fall silent as the tomb. Too tired for anything else by the time they returned to Luxor, they decided to leave the antiquities museum to Saturday, and found it far more intimate than the one in Cairo, especially the rooms where the smaller artifacts glowed like jewels.

That night after dinner they were dawdling over coffee, loath to call it quits, when Kate brought up something that had nothing to do with Egypt. "What does it mean to forget, Max—to not be able to remember something that you once could but can't anymore. Are the things we forget still there in our brains only we've lost the directions for finding them?"

"It depends on how strong the memory was in the first place.

Things that didn't make much of a mark, that weren't very 'memorable,' tend to fade with time. But a visceral reaction to something—what some people call a gut feeling—is actually a product of our memories. Even minor emotional stress, if it pumps adrenaline and noradrenaline into the bloodstream, can prime the brain to take special note of the circumstances that instigated a particular reaction. Why? Did you forget something?"

"I don't know." She picked up the pen the waiter had left for Max to sign their credit voucher and began doodling on the back of the bill. "Sometimes it feels like it. Other times I—I remember things I have no reason to. Like yesterday, at Karnak, inside the temple. I knew what was coming around the next corner, in the next . . . whatever. The whole time we were there I felt on the verge of remembering more, kind of like a word on the tip of your tongue." She glanced up. "I need to go back, Max. Do you mind?"

He didn't answer, nor was he looking at her. He was staring at the little monkey she'd just drawn—with her left hand.

Kate dropped the pen so fast it rolled halfway across the table.

"You know," Max began, covering her hand with his, "everyone used to think that female chimpanzees hung out only with the males in their own neighborhood. If one did happen to get it on with a nonresident, their offspring would be killed by the resident males. Then DNA testing came along and guess what? It turns out that female chimps have been sneaking out to meet other guys all along, because they found a whole bunch of extracurricular babies, all alive." A smile lit his eyes. "Anybody who thinks we've got everything all wrapped up in a tidy package needs his head examined."

They were passing through the great pylon gateway built by Horemheb, the last pharaoh of the Eighteenth Dynasty, when Kate heard what sounded like a long, eerie scream. She cringed as the shadow of a huge bird passed overhead and then stopped, hesitant to go on, afraid of what she would find ahead.

"Something the matter?" Max asked.

"Didn't you hear it?"

"Hear what?"

"I don't know. A screeching bird, maybe."

Max took one look at her face and said, "Let's go sit in the shade for a while." He pointed to the nearby bench.

"Not here. Please. I need to—I can't breathe." She left him standing there, dumbfounded, and started back the way they had come. When she broke into a run Max took off after her. By the time he caught up she had slowed to a walk and was looking around, searching for him.

"Where did you go?" She was on the verge of tears and knew he could hear it in her voice. "I couldn't find you—"

Max guided her over to a fragment of wall facing away from the temple and pulled her down beside him. "I didn't go anywhere, Katie. You took off so fast it took me a few minutes to catch up, that's all. Let's just sit here and catch our breath, then you can tell me—"

"Something awful happened back there," Kate whispered without looking at him. "Not . . . just now. A long time ago. It felt—I don't know." She wrapped her arms around her ribs and held on, trying to stop the shivers that were shaking her whole body. "I've never been to Egypt before, yet this place feels familiar." Afraid he would see how terrified she was, she stared at her feet. "Is something else wrong with my brain, Max—something you haven't told me?"

"No! Nothing. Truly, Kate. Sure, you probably feel a greater empathy for the ancient Egyptians, because of Tashat. But the minor disconnect you *do* have—your word, not mine—is unimportant in the global sense of brain function."

Several older women in shorts and floppy-brimmed hats, obviously a tourist group traveling together, turned curious eyes in their direction. Max ignored them. All he cared about was her.

"This place is enough to make any of us question our own reality—everything we learned in school and accepted as true until now. So our brains have to search for ways to make sense of what we're seeing and feeling, to somehow make things fit our existing memories. For most of us this place is a miracle. It dwarfs us. Inspires awe. That puts it right at the edge of comprehension, something else we share with the people of Tashat's time. We may have developed a lot of technology they didn't have, and we certainly know more about the laws of physics, but I doubt they loved their dogs any less than we do. Or that they weren't driven by greed and meanness and love, just like we are. Seti told me a story the other day. Seems the museum had some ancient flutes restored and asked a couple of professional musicians to come in and play them. Guess what?" He paused. "The ancient Egyptians used the same scale we do."

That got Kate's attention. She looked at Max and dropped her arms.

"That means the spatial maps in our brains have stayed pretty much the same." He paused, letting that sink in. "Do you remember what I said about Egyptology and medicine having a lot in common, that's there's still too much we don't know?" Kate nodded. "Well, what we *do* know is that genes can mutate as a result of environmental carcinogens. And that severe trauma—extreme fright or pain—can affect the brain, not just the psyche. Some recent studies even showed shrinkage of both the right and left hippocampus among veterans who suffered combat trauma. So it's possible that extreme experiences, whether intense emotions or physical trauma, are in some way impressed on the genes, probably by chemicals generated within our own bodies which cause changes that are passed forward in time from one generation to another."

She soaked up every word, grateful for the balm of reason he was applying to her runaway fear, and in that moment realized that he knew her better than she knew herself. Max was her touchstone, her path to the reality of who she was. And who she would become.

"Thanks to a few molecular biologists who, like you, weren't content with the conventional wisdom, we know now that genes determine a lot of our behavior. The fact that we learn from experience, for instance, because we can remember. Genes are our ancestral memories, of life as the human species has lived it on this earth." When he took her face between his hands and looked into her eyes, the great temple of Amen faded into oblivion. "Something unexplainable happened to you back there. Let's just leave it at that for now . . . and keep our eyes wide open."

She smiled into his eyes, then leaned forward to brush his lips with hers before grabbing his hand to pull him up with her. "Don't just sit there burnin' daylight, Max. Time to go pack our duds. That plane to Cairo leaves at seven-fifteen, remember?"

Back at their hotel, Kate repacked her bag, then wandered out to the balcony for one last look across the river. She raised her camera to zoom in on Hatshepsut's funerary temple, trying to pretend the cars and tourists didn't exist, only the brooding, waiting desert and wind-eroded cliffs.

Swinging around to her left she picked up remnants of the time-worn pylons that once soared a hundred feet or more into the cloudless blue sky, and beyond that the massive columns shaped like bundles of papyrus reeds. Amen's great northern temple was, as Max said, immense, in both concept and actuality. But like a work in progress, its ruined walls, stelae and gateways looked unfinished, as if waiting for completion by the next mortal god to sit on the throne of Horus.

"We'll come back, Katie," Max said from behind her. "Next time we'll hire a felucca and sail up the river to Edfu, camp out under the stars, and visit the place where Horus triumphed over evil." He came to lean on the railing beside her, and waved an arm at the scene spread out before them. "It just grabs hold of you and won't let go, doesn't it?"

Kate lowered her camera. "The sky is bluer than I've ever seen it, even in Colorado, and the greens greener, maybe just by contrast with the desert. But the sun feels hotter and the nights colder. Darker. Like death. It's no wonder the Egyptians were obsessed with the sun and haunted by what they couldn't see. By what lay in shadow." Reluctantly, she turned to go back inside, but Max caught her arm, then stroked the side of her cheek with two fingers.

"Remember when you asked me why I never got married, and I said I was too involved in my work, that it took all my time?" Kate nodded. "Well, I lied. Or maybe I didn't really know. I do now. I was waiting for you."

He fished in his pocket and pulled out the ivory necklace, let it slide through his fingers for a second, then unhooked the catch and slipped it around her neck, keeping the oval ring toward the front so he could see to fasten it again. When he dropped his hands, the timeworn ram's head lay where it belonged, Kate thought—over her heart. A wave of happiness tinged with regret made her want to laugh and cry at the same time, but she put the sadness away. The past was just that—behind them.

Instead she touched her lips to his and whispered, "I'm glad you didn't get tired of waiting and take up with an older woman. She would never have been right for you."

TWENTY-SIX

Osiris Horemheb

(1335 B.C.)

DAY 3, SECOND MONTH OF PLANTING

I found Pagosh first, lying faceup in a pool of blood with one arm stretched out straight. His other hand still clutched his gaping throat, as if he had tried to hold it together to keep the blood from escaping his body—and with it his *ka*.

In the instant I realized he was gone, I glanced to either side of the path ahead, searching for some sign of Aset. Expecting—I don't know—to find her the same, I suppose. But I could not find even a footprint in the sun-baked dirt to indicate what direction they had taken. Surely there had to be more than one to have taken Pagosh. I looked back at him and saw that the blood had not yet soaked into the hard-packed earth. That meant the murderous act had taken place only a few minutes before I arrived. Not that it would have mattered had I come sooner, for no man can survive such carnage, not even Pagosh.

I knew he would already have been urging me on my way, yet I puzzled over his stretched-out arm—as if he reached out to Amen for help. But that did not fit the man, so I squatted down to sight along his arm, and looking up saw the colored banners flying from the twin towers of Horemheb's massive pylon. Then, with the bile of fear rising in my throat I got up and ran, imploring Thoth as I went to let me find her before it was too late—that I would not come upon her as I had him.

Nor did I slow my steps when finally I came in sight of the temple. The area in front of the great gateway stood empty, and the place struck me as eerily still. Then, in the distance, like an echo from across the valley, came a long, keening cry. Mourners in the Place of Truth, I thought, or an injured animal.

I looked up as a shadow passed over me, and saw what appeared to be a giant bird silhouetted against the brilliant sky, wings outstretched in flight. But instead of soaring higher it came toward me, just as Tutankhamen's Horus of the Sky had plummeted toward earth on that day so long ago.

I could do nothing to stop what was happening this time, either.

She struck the stone parapet of the balcony where the god makes his appearances on special feast days, across the center of her body. She seemed to bounce, for her legs flipped back into the air, then she disappeared over the edge, toward the inside, onto the god's platform.

How I got into the pylon I do not recall, but the soldiers who stand guard there must have had been paid to absent themselves, which I realize now was why the forecourt struck me as too quiet. Inside, I started up the spiral stairs and was perhaps halfway to the door to the balcony when two priests came down from above, so fast that they knocked me out of their way, making me lose my footing.

When I straightened I looked into the brown eyes of a woman who wore a veil across the rest of her face. "You are too late, *sunu*. The game he played is over."

My blood went cold, but I forced my way past her, intent on reaching Aset before it was too late. When I burst through the door that opened onto the god's balcony I saw her lying on her side with her right shoulder slumped forward, both knees drawn up toward the center of her body. Blood spilled from the soles of her feet, but I put my hand to her neck first, to see if she still lived, and felt my heart leap with joy.

I tore off my kilt, ripped it into strips, and wrapped them around her feet to slow the bleeding. When I turned her over, cupping her head in my hand to keep her neck straight, I found blood on her tunic, just below her breasts, and lifted her carefully into my arms. A few broken ribs for sure, I thought, then stood up and started down the stairs, careful to guard her feet in the enclosed space.

It was not until I was in the light again that I noticed her left hand—all bloody and mangled, with the fingers bent at odd angles. Two fingernails had been ripped off and the others were so engorged with blood they had turned purple, as if an elephant had stepped on them, mashing the flesh and splintering every bone.

I tried to run, but pink foam oozed from the corner of her mouth with each agonizing breath she tried to take, so I knew that at least one lung had been punctured. But she was alive!

At Ramose's gate I sent the gateman scurrying for Ruka, the one person I could count on to fetch Senmut and Mena without delay, then instructed the gateman to take enough men with him to carry Pagosh home.

Merit met me at the door of our quarters, took one look at what I carried, and asked, "My husband is with Osiris?" I nodded, for in truth I could not utter a word.

"Hurry," she urged, and led the way to our sleeping room. I put Aset on our couch, trying to cushion where I knew her bones were broken, and prayed to Thoth that she would not come awake until I had them set. That is not possible with ribs, of course, yet I must find some way to ease her breathing.

Merit brought blankets to help hold her body's heat, which is necessary to maintain life, then water and clean cloths to wash away the dried blood. I was anxious about her labored breathing and worried that Ruka might not be able to find Senmut, who is more experienced at reading the signs of internal injuries that result from a blow to the body. Nor do my surgical skills equal his.

Merit bathed her lacerated feet while I worked over her hand, supporting it with a piece of dried oxhide. First I straightened the fingers as best I could, though they already had swelled to twice their usual size, and still bled where the nails had been. Then I taped her entire hand to the hide with strips of linen moistened with hoof glue.

Senmut brought Nebet as well, and I told them everything, how and where her body struck the parapet, and all the rest—leaving out only my encounter with the woman who gave her life, for that score no one else can settle. Not even Aset's father.

Senmut pulled the blanket away and put his ear to her chest, just above her left breast, then moved his head to the other side. Except for her wheezing it was so quiet we might have been holding our breaths. Nor was there any moaning or crying from Nebet and Merit, as some women are prone to do.

"Has she awakened at all?" he asked.

I shook my head. "Not even when I aligned the bones in her fingers."

"Probably because she cannot get enough air. The fluid in her chest keeps her lungs from filling. The only way to relieve it is to insert a hollow reed, but I will be honest, Tenre. Even that does not always succeed. The reed can become clogged with blood or mucus, or the lung may be so torn it cannot hold air."

"Then we waste time talking." Merit brought more cloths and water for Senmut to cleanse his hands while I purified the thin, narrow blade of his own design in the flame of a lamp.

He went in through her right side, five or six finger widths below her armpit, holding the reed tight against the flat blade but back from the tip. In that way he inserted the reed as he cut. She cried out once, a sound more catlike than human, making tears start behind my eyelids. The instant he punched through to the chest cavity, a stream of bloody fluid began to run from the end of the reed into the bowl I held ready.

Senmut pulled his blade free, leaving the reed protruding from her side, and motioned for me to hold it there. Then he circled her extended arm to stand at her head and squeezed her jaws to force her lips open, put his mouth to hers and blew into her, to breathe for her. Again and again, until I lost count.

"Something pushes back," I said. He instructed me to withdraw the reed a little at a time while he continued blowing into her mouth. By the time the reed came free, her breathing was no longer so noisy.

While he pressed a pad to the cut to slow the bleeding, I had to sit down until I could get my legs back. Afterward he helped me wrap her ribs to prevent more damage, and for a time then the hours crawled so slowly I wondered if Re had thrown the anchor from his boat.

When finally she did stir it was only to move her left hand, which brought another mewling cry. "A good sign," Senmut commented, but I knew it for a mixed blessing. Her eyelids began to flutter, and finally opened.

She stared at the ceiling, trying to place where she was, then tried to draw a breath. Her face crumpled with pain, and I hastened to take her right hand in mine. I spoke softly, so as not to startle her. "Stay quiet. All is well." She turned her head toward me. "Senmut has bandaged your chest, if you wonder why it feels so tight. Better not try to breathe too deeply." She tried to squeeze my fingers. "Nebet is here, too. And Merit."

"Meri?" she mouthed.

"She spends the day with Khary and Tamin, remember?" A shiver of apprehension made the hair rise on the back of my neck, for until that moment I had forgotten my daughter.

"I will go fetch her," Senmut volunteered, "so you can know she is safe."

"And I will look after her until you mend," Nebet added, tears clogging her throat.

Aset's eyes sought mine. "You must . . . find a way . . . her safe," she whispered. "From—" The pain struck without warning when she tried to lift her hand, and a wild look came into her eyes. She moved as if to raise up and see what was wrong, bringing a scream from her throat. Then she fell back, eyes closed, and Senmut rushed to put his ear to her chest.

"We must give her something for the pain, but not so much that it slows her breathing. A child's dose of mandrake, until we see how she does with that much."

I was glad for his advice and left her only to get what he needed. When Aset came awake again I explained that her fingers were broken as well as a rib, but she refused to take any mandrake until she knew Meri was safe.

A few minutes later, Nebet and Merit wandered out into the garden, to leave us alone, but I could not bring myself to question her for fear of reviving memories that are better left buried—especially if she saw what they did to Pagosh. So I held her good hand and stroked the back of it with my thumb, the only caress I could offer her without causing more pain.

"Mother?" Meri called a while later, as she came toward our couch all big-eyed and solemn. I could tell Senmut had prepared her for what she would find, and thanked him with my eyes. He nodded, then took himself elsewhere for a time.

"Come here . . . sweetie." Aset pulled her hand free of mine and reached for Meri's. "I only . . . need . . . to rest . . . few days. You go . . . Nebet . . . until—"

"Until I come for you," I finished for her. "You are not to leave Mena's walls with anyone else, understand?"

"Not even Paga?" Meri asked, looking at me.

"Paga is with Osiris," Aset whispered. So she did know.

"Truly?" When her mother nodded, Meri's little face dissolved in tears. Without warning, tears flooded my own eyes, forcing me to turn away, for it hit me suddenly that I would see his intransigent face no more, nor have to guess at the meaning behind his cryptic words. The rock I had leaned on for so long was gone from this world.

"There is . . . no shame . . . in crying . . . for those we love. As I have. Many times." She meant it for me as much as Meri, so I turned back to let her see that I mourned him, too.

After Nebet and Senmut took Meri away, Aset accepted a few swallows of the mandrake and finally dozed off. Yet I continued to hold her hand, to let her know I was there even while she slept. Or perhaps I actually believed I could keep Osiris from taking her, should he come again in the night.

My memory grows blurred after that, but sometime during the night I turned to find Ramose staring at her pale face—the rage that burned in his eyes making the veins in his forehead bulge and throb. I knew then that he had seen Pagosh's body.

"They left proof of their cowardice behind, atop the god's

gate," he informed me, keeping his gaze on her ruined hand. "A rock the size of a man's head. Did they use the razor on her as well?"

I told him what they had done to her feet, then wished I hadn't when he caught sight of the blood already soaking through the bandaging. An instant later he turned and strode from the room.

As Re went to his death in the west, Merit brought me a carafe of wine, bread, and dates, for she knows I will not sleep. Nor, I suspect, will she, so I asked her to sit with me for a while. "Your husband tried to save her even as his *ka* departed his body," I told her, and explained how I knew to look in the direction of the temple.

She nodded. "Aset changed him, gentled him."

"Not only Aset," I added. "Even his voice changed when he spoke of you."

"He told me once that he never truly trusted any man before you."

"Would you like me to accompany him to the Per Nefer?"

"Ramose had him carried there an hour ago, but I would appreciate your advice, Tenre. My lord has offered us a place in his own eternal home. And to be with the High Priest of Amen is a high honor indeed, but . . . well, we planned our own place, to be together forever when my time comes."

"In this you must do as you wish, Merit, or what you know Pagosh wanted, not someone else." She let her tears flow, then, for the first time, but not for long. Nor did she voice her fear for Aset, out of kindness to me.

"I will be nearby," she said as she rose from her chair, but paused to tell me more. "The High Priest has caused four men to be hoisted to the top of the god's gate, where they hang by their feet as a warning to others who may think of deserting their posts. Already the vultures have pecked the eyes from their heads."

So it begins. Ramose must know whose hand arranged it all, for it carries her mark. Revenge in kind—ordering Aset's feet slashed to brand her an adulterer in retribution for the cartoons where she accused Horemheb of turning a blind eye to his own unfaithful wife, crushing the hand that exposed Nefertiti as the murderer of her own child and grandchild, so Aset will never draw another, in this life or the next. And finally, throwing her from the pylon

Horemheb built—the Pharaoh whose edict Aset branded as cruel and unjust.

DAY 4, SECOND MONTH OF PLANTING

"The first twenty hours are always the worst," Senmut reminded me.

"It is not only the pain. She relives falling, again and again."

"Two more men hang from Horemheb's sacred gate."

"Ramose is driven by revenge, but the trail will end as it always does, at the river." Senmut sent me a sharp look. "The deed is done. What harm can come now from speaking the truth?"

DAY 6, SECOND MONTH OF PLANTING

Still there is blood in her urine, nor does she eat, despite Merit's efforts to tempt her with sweet cakes and bits of fruit. That could be the mandrake, yet during the night she is tormented by visions that make her cry out, despite her laboring lungs. Only when I bathe her hot cheeks and neck with a cool cloth does she appear to gain respite from the pain.

DAY 8, SECOND MONTH OF PLANTING

Nefertiti has convinced enough of the royal guard that their fortunes lie with her to form a force big enough to incarcerate the others in the palace barracks. So she holds not only the palace but the royal treasury, and has declared herself Horus on Earth, son of Amen and Lord of the Two Lands. Smenkhkare.

I apply dried honey to the cuts on Aset's feet, then wash it away with water, but she complains now of pain in her left shoulder. I cannot dismiss the possibility that she senses what is wrong inside her, especially since I give her the drug that seers use to gain insight into the mysteries. I once listened to my father question an old priest who claimed that to smoke the fetid nightshade plant allowed him to see what before he could only hear. I would learn from Ramose what he knows of such things, except that I doubt he will return from the temple anytime soon—or that any priest will close his eyes this night.

DAY 9, SECOND MONTH OF PLANTING

She takes nothing but fruit juice or a little goat's milk, but it has been a full week now. Surely that in itself is reason to hope. Senmut brought a letter from Mena, who wrote that "good physicians are too rare for any commander to risk throwing one to the crocodiles," which means he succeeded in his mission. But I worry that he may bring Nefertiti's wrath down on his own family, for Ramses is an ambitious man and it would not surprise me should he find his advantage in an arrangement with the one who styles herself Pharaoh.

DAY 11, SECOND MONTH OF PLANTING

Ramose is deposed and a cat's-paw sits in his place, so as Re dropped behind the western cliffs, I went to find a captain about to sail down the river, who agreed to deliver my message to Mena. Now Ramose hides himself like a wounded lion, even from his daughter, who somehow senses something amiss. She grows more restless with each hour, forcing me to try to put an end to his self-indulgence. But his heart is so filled with self-loathing—for failing her—that he punishes himself by staying away. Even so I will try again tomorrow, for he needs her as much as she needs him.

DAY 13, SECOND MONTH OF PLANTING

It was just past midday when Aset motioned me closer, for she still cannot draw breath enough to speak with any strength. She refuses to take any more of the mandrake potion, saying she would rather know that she is still in this world.

"Shall I send a message for Senmut to bring Meri home?" I asked, anticipating what she wanted.

"Soon. Not yet." She looked toward the doorway. "Garden . . . feel sun."

I called to Merit to fix a pallet by the pool and also bring dates and persea fruit, hoping this meant she would begin to eat, as well. But when I lifted her from our couch, the flesh around her lips turned white, a sign that I caused her excruciating pain despite my attempt to be gentle.

"Where . . . my father?" she asked, watching my face to see if I spoke the truth.

I took her whole hand in mine and told her everything, ending with the message from Mena. She closed her eyes, I thought to sleep for a while, until I saw a tear seep from the corner of her eye. I leaped to my feet, determined to pull Ramose from his lair.

She stopped me with one shake of her head. "Get my . . . goatskin bag. I will . . . be all right. Not alone. Tuli . . . with me." A chill came over me, but I did as she asked and hurried back, determined to cheer her spirits.

"Perhaps I should give your little papyrus-root lion a wash," I teased as I opened the drawstring bag and pulled him out.

She reached her good hand in to feel for what it contained. "Bring . . . ram's-head necklace," she whispered. Overjoyed that she wanted it, since vanity in a woman is a sure sign of returning health, I fetched the necklace I had given her on the occasion of our daughter's birth. But instead of letting me fasten it around her neck, she added it to her bag, then looked at me.

"Listen well, husband. This . . . my legacy . . . to Meri. Lion and . . . ivory necklace. Not gold one . . . from father. Scribe's palette . . . given my grandfather. Amenhotep. Poems you gave me . . . first time we . . . came together . . . husband and wife. Nothing else. So no one . . . can learn . . . who she is. Now. Or in future. Give rest . . . to Merit."

"The time to talk of such things is when you are well again," I protested.

"Promise me. Please . . . my love."

"Of course, only—"

She put the tips of her fingers to my mouth. "Not . . . finished." I nodded but held her fingers to my lips, so starved am I for her touch. "You. Meri. Return . . . Aniba. So when . . . your time comes to join me—" She gasped for breath. "Pact with Nebet. I would care . . . for hers and . . . she mine." She smiled at some memory. "Nebet had written . . . into marriage contract."

"Surely your father—"

She rolled her head back and forth. "Throne of Horus . . . casts a long shadow. Make sure . . . does not fall across her . . . as it did me."

"Senmut says Meri grows anxious. I will fetch her home in the morning. Then you can talk with her yourself."

She shook her head again. "Better that she . . . remember me . . . as I was. Not like this." Her eyes closed, then opened again. She looked straight at me. "This cannot be all there is for us, Tenre. It would not be . . . *maat*."

Is it maat to leave me to walk toward the western horizon alone? I wanted to shout, to stop her from the path she followed.

"Let the blood . . . on my lips . . . taste sweet . . . as berries," she whispered between shallow breaths. "Give me magic. The spell of . . . living well."

Whether she spoke to me or the gods I will never know.

*Knowing his end, a man feels tomorrow's sorrow, but today's
joy. He looks toward heaven and lives without regret. He
grieves, therefore he is a man. He becomes the heart and tongue
of god. He creates of mortality something immortal.*
—Normandi Ellis, *Awakening Osiris*

TWENTY-SEVEN

Seti Abdalla was waiting when they arrived at the museum Friday
morning. He sat at the long table in the center of the room where
Iskander had retrieved the scroll, bare now except for the stack of
papers under his hand. Courtly as always, he rose to greet them and
inquired about their trip to Luxor, though Kate could tell his heart
wasn't in it. Something was weighing on his mind.

"I am afraid I was not entirely truthful on the telephone," he
admitted to Max as soon as they sat down. "The papyrus was in
such good condition that Hosni was able to unroll most of it in only
a few hours. By the time you reached me I had the first photographs
in hand and had already begun the translation. You must forgive
my little deception, but I hoped by the time you returned at least to
be able to say for sure if this is your man." He smiled. "I told you
there were two scrolls?"

Both Kate and Max were quick to nod.

"Perhaps it is easiest to simply show you the illustration." Seti
began laying out several eight-by-ten photographs, edge to edge,
two across and four down.

As a form began to take shape, Kate rose to avoid reflections off
the glossy prints, and felt a shock of recognition that shook her to
the bottom of her soul. It was an outline of the human body, with

scriggly red and blue lines growing inside it like the bare branches of a tree. A tree Kate had seen before.

"Perhaps, Dr. Cavanaugh, you would be willing to render a professional opinion?" Seti suggested.

Max could hardly tear his eyes away, but he finally glanced at Kate, then Seti. "I'd say it's a diagram of the circulatory system. A damn good one, considering."

"Yes, considering that the whole world believes no one made any distinction between veins and arteries until A.D. three or four hundred, at least," Kate agreed.

"That's not all," Max added. "This also shows the blood passing from one side of the heart to the other through the lungs, and no one came even close on that for—what?" He glanced at Kate. "Another thousand years?"

"Fifteen hundred. Vesalius," she supplied, then glanced at Seti.

"So," he breathed in his French way, "the history of medicine is being rewritten." He smiled and began rubbing his hands together. "Then we have much work ahead of us to discover the path this knowledge may have taken from my ancestors to the Persians, perhaps, and the Greeks. If it was in the library at Alexandria, of course—"

"Was the other scroll a medical text like we thought?" Max inquired, impatient to learn the rest.

Seti shook his head. "I found no recipes or spells for treating an illness or injury, if that is what you mean. I would say it is more a kind of personal journal kept by the physician named Senakhtenre, this *sunu* who accompanies your Tashat on her journey through eternity." He paused. "Except her name is Aset. Isis we would call her today."

Kate and Max exchanged a look. "How can you be so sure he's our man?"

"Many times in this journal he speaks of a dog—a small white dog named Tuli."

Kate felt a rush of tears, of relief intermixed with a terrible sadness. So long as they didn't know for sure she had been able to fend off the awful certainty of Aset's death, despite the evidence before her eyes—the mummy itself. Which didn't make much sense.

"I believe she is the reason he began to write such a journal."

Seti paused to give his next words the import they deserved. "There is no doubt now that your Tashat—his Aset—was the daughter of the Heretic's Queen by a priest of Amen."

"Nefertiti," Kate murmured.

Seti nodded. "But there is more, much more." He patted the stack of onionskin sheets under his hand.

"If it's a journal it must be dated." Max was looking for an explanation for the three dates on the coffin, but Seti put him off.

"It is best that you read it for yourself. I must be at the university soon, so I will leave these with you. But before I go I would like to ask you to be my guests for dinner this evening, at my home." He looked at Kate. "My mother wishes to meet you. Already she knows all about this—" He waved a hand, meaning everything that had happened and what they had learned. "From the time I showed her your photographs and drawings she can talk of little but the book you must write."

Max kept glancing at Kate with an "I told you so" smile, even while he was getting directions to Seti's house. Then their linguist friend pointed to the rumpled sheets of paper. "Remember, it is all backwards. In the beginning is what appeared first as Hosni unrolled the papyrus—a section written in another hand he found attached to the end of the physician's journal. Following that is the end of the journal itself, as much as I had time to translate till now."

After the door closed behind him, Kate went back to the table and sat down. "Why don't you read it to me?" she suggested, wanting to hear it in a man's voice, as if the ancient physician himself were speaking.

Max nodded, took the chair across from her, and picked up the top sheet. "It's dated the eighth day, fourth month of planting in Year One of Ramses." They looked at each other, both thinking the same thing—that *was* the most significant date on Tashat's coffin.

I speak to the gods who judge Senakhtenre, Physician of Waset, friend and brother to me for forty years, that both Thoth and Osiris may know the compassion and honesty of the man who comes before you, and to make sure he is not held accountable for what others have done.

In Zarw I found Ramses skinnier and more impatient than I

remembered him, but he greeted me as an old friend and conducted me on a tour of the city he builds. So it was not until evening that we could talk. Even then his son Seti was present, as he had been throughout the day, for his father has appointed him mayor as well as his deputy in the North. When I told them why I had come, Ramses informed me straightaway that his elite guard prepared to sail for Waset even as we spoke, to confront the High Priest and his Sacred Council, and that all his commanders already had pledged their support to him. So it did not take much to convince Horemheb's old friend to move quickly, lest Nefertiti consolidate her position by gaining the support of the nomarchs, police, and judges who enforce the laws of the land.

I did not know then, of course, that she already had declared herself Horus on Earth. Or that Ramose was no longer High Priest of Amen. But by the time Tenre's letter reached me, it no longer mattered. Akhenaten and his straggling band of followers were camped outside the main gate of the fortress, demanding not only entry but homage as rightful Lord of the Two Lands. Day after day he came to stand before the gate, ranting and waving his rod with the entwined serpents, the staff of kingship given to him by the priests who initiated him into the rituals made known only to the son of Amen.

I suppose he would be there still had a block of stone not fallen from one of Ramses' construction sites, crushing the overseer who stood below. That the stonemasons were forced to labor as punishment for worshiping Aten soon gave rise to rumors that the Heretic had caused the wrath of his god to topple the stone, a story that spread like fire in dry hay, growing ever more wondrous as it passed from one tongue to the next. Finally, as heavy black clouds began rolling across the sky, a crowd gathered in the market square, where other stories joined the first. It was said that the Heretic's god visited a plague on the People of the Sun, causing their children to vomit everything they ate until they starved even in the presence of plenty. Surely that could only be the work of a vengeful god! In the end, the people of Zarw called on Ramses to send Akhenaten and his brethren back to the Sinai before all their children were taken. Yet he hesitated, torn between how to deal with this new rival for the throne and at the same time arrive in Waset to wrest power from the Heretic's onetime Queen before it was too late.

It was Seti who finally ordered the Heretic and all his follow-ers—rope stretchers, stonemasons, and lowly water bearers alike, along with their women and children—to be gone from sight when Re-Horakhte next showed his face on the eastern horizon. Otherwise, he promised, not even the thunder of their god would stay the hand of his father's troops.

The following morning we climbed to the ramparts and found their striped tents gone, leaving only the dust stirred up by a hundred feet to show the direction they had taken. Seti declared it no great loss since those who left Zarw with Akhena-ten numbered only fifty men, who long since had taught their skills to those who labored beside them. So it was done, and at first light the following day, we sailed for Waset.

When I arrived home I found the message Tenre left on the writing table in my library, a single sheet of papyrus weighted with the iron-bladed dagger given him by Osiris Tutankh-amen—a sight that brought dread to my heart.

Osiris has won the game we played for twenty years. I only hastened their meeting when her eyes pleaded for me to release her from the unbearable pain. I have prepared her for eternity, as well, leaving the key to her whereabouts with the one who was conceived in the arms of the river god.

Know that I tried to stay, for Meri, though for me the sun is gone from the sky. But then perhaps it is better for her to live in peace without me than in fear with me. Know, too, friend and brother in my heart, that I would not be the man I am but for you. Whatever comes to pass, you have my love and trust, now and forever—if there is such a thing. If not, I am still the most fortunate of men.

As I read his words the chill of the tomb crept into my bones, and I felt a terrible sense of loss caused by the gaping hole in my heart. When Senmut came I saw at once by his face that a piece of him is missing as well. Even worse, he saw it happen.

Tenre would know that his only opportunity to get close enough would come at the mouth of Horemheb's eternal home, when she stepped forward in the leopard skin of the new Pharaoh. How he found the will to look on the face of the woman who had given life to his beloved and then taken it away, I cannot say, but while all eyes were watching her touch the sacred adze to the once mighty General's mouth, Tenre slipped unnoticed through the crowd—and with one quick thrust of his thin-bladed dissecting knife severed the big vessel in Nefertiti's once-beautiful neck.

He would know exactly where to strike, too, and that such a wound always brings death. Only how long it takes the body to empty itself of blood differs from one man—or woman—to another. So that had to be what he intended. What he could not have expected was to die quicker than she did, while a hundred mourners stood by watching in disbelief. No one could anticipate that the hot-blooded young commander of Nefertiti's guards would swing around and with one stroke of his sword cleave Tenre's head from his body.

That sight I thank Thoth every morning and night for sparing me, leaving my memories of him unsullied by blood and gore. Even now I catch myself glancing up from time to time, expecting to see his sober countenance break into a smile at something I said, or to find a jest brighten his warm brown eyes, usually at my expense.

No one could have saved him, though saying it does little to ease the guilt Senmut feels for standing by like all the others, stunned by what took place before their very eyes. At least he managed to save what was left of the man he loved as father and friend, kicked aside in the dust and left to rot in the sun. But it was not until after dark that he dared take Tenre's body to the House of the Dead, where Nebet's husband is as well-known as the man he carried. Nor is Senmut without the means to salt the palms of those who hold out their hands. Otherwise he would have been turned away from the place that is forbidden to any who kill. All, that is, but the mortal gods who sit on the throne of Horus.

So it came to pass that three Pharaohs claimed the throne of Horus in quick succession, almost, you might say, at the same time. To confuse any who would seek to destroy her a second time, Aset starts her journey through eternity in Year 4 of Smenkhkare, Year 18 of Akhenaten and Year 1 of Ramses. Since she also travels under a false name, as Tenre wished, Nebet has put her own hand to painting her beloved friend's mask and bindings, to assure that Aset's soul will recognize her body.

As for my part, just as my boyhood friend rid this world of evil to save his daughter, I have cleansed the hereafter of a mother who murdered at least two of her own daughters—by stealing Nefertiti's body away in the night and carrying it to the bank of the river where the crocodiles lay their eggs. I confess, as well, that I did not act alone, though it is not for me to reveal the identity of my accomplice. That I leave to him when his own time comes, though I willingly admit that we both found joy in what we did. And in knowing that she-cat has made her last kill, in this world or the next.

Tenre once said that without Aset he could never be whole. Nor, I believe, was she without him. So I arranged for the part of him he considered the true seat of our thoughts and feelings to make the journey in her company. He goes with his eyes wide-open, too, though he truly believed that the road to eternal life lies in what we are able to learn and leave for others to build on, not in our worn-out bodies which in time turn to dust. But who can know for sure? And what good is an open eye without the tools to record what we see? So I have seen to that, as well.

This message goes with his body, that Osiris and his judges will know the truth of how my friend lived. If Tenre was right, then his journal and her map will stand in place of his head, along with his heart. The map shows the location of the vessels that carry only blood. The ones Aset painted red carry blood away from the heart, in spurts, while it runs darker and not so fast in the vessels she painted blue. Which may be why it is not so dangerous to cut into one of those.

Tenre's medical scroll remains with me, a gift copied out by the most talented scribe ever to inhabit the Two Lands, for it was Aset who embellished the papyrus with all manner of color-ful animals who tell their own story—vignettes that add insight to what Tenre learned from his experiments.

Since Nebet and Aset arranged many things between them, Hapimere will sail for Aniba with Senmut and my daughter, as her parents wished. As will Merit, who I pray will come to love my grandson as she did his namesake.

Senakhtenre. Father, brother, and son to me all in one. Com-panion of my youth, the anchor on which my skiff dared to ride the rough currents of this life. Mirror image of my ka. How alien and empty the city of my birth feels without him. But not so empty as my heart.

Max sat staring at the last sheet for a while before he remem-bered to add, "It's signed Merenptah, onetime Master of Physicians to the Army of the North and Chief Physician to Pharaoh, now *sunu* to the people of Waset, as was my boyhood friend before me." He glanced up and saw the silent tears running down Kate's cheeks. "Would you rather wait and read the rest another time?"

She shook her head. "I have to know what happened to her, don't you?"

He nodded and picked up the next sheet. "I found Pagosh first . . ."

Kate's heart thundered in her ears when Tenre looked up to see Aset's spread-eagled body against the blue sky. She recognized the thin, high-pitched scream she'd heard once before, ending with a sharp crack. Bones snapping. When Aset appeared to bounce up into the air, it was because the momentum of her legs flipped her over onto the god's balcony. In her mind's eye, Kate watched the pink foam ooze from Aset's lips, and in the next instant saw the monochrome X ray of Tashat's chest.

Later, when Tenre mentioned the pain in Aset's left shoulder, Max mumbled, "Ruptured spleen." Finally, as if dreading what he knew was coming, he reached across the table to grasp Kate's hand.

Day twenty, second month of planting. It is as if she occupies two worlds at the same time, and travels back and forth between them. Still, she recognized her father, though he has taken on the appearance of an old man. For a time Ramose sat watching her labor to breathe, speaking to her from time to time, then waiting for her to respond. I was too far away to hear what passed between them, except when she cried out in the voice of a child. 'I will never . . . borrow my . . . lady mother's . . . eye paste . . . again, Father. I promise. Will you love me then, please?' Despite the pain it brought her, she sniffed again and again, trying to stifle her tears, while images from the past flashed before my eyes, leaving me without pity for the man who had hurt her in ways no physician can heal.

An instant later, a wild look in his eyes, Ramose leaped to his feet and fled the room. So does Sekhmet punish him for staying away so long, I thought, for only one person has ever touched him at the core. Now she lies suffering the agony of the damned, and he is helpless as a babe.

Since our return from Aniba, Ramose and I finally have

learned to talk to each other. I understand now that it is not a golden idol he puts his faith in so much as the need for structure and order. And that, he believes, requires higher beings who act as larger-than-life parents to set the course for their children, to bring them to the proper behavior. Otherwise, all would be chaos.

So, after Re abandoned us, letting darkness fall over the land, I called Merit to come sit with Aset while I searched him out, and found him at the table in his library. There he often stays through the night writing theological treatises that he keeps hidden from his priestly colleagues, just as I do with my medical scrolls. He sat with his chin resting on his chest and one arm flung out across the papyrus on which he had been writing.

For a minute I hesitated, believing he had fallen asleep at his task. Then I noticed his other arm hanging by his side, and in the silence of the night heard the slow drip . . . drip . . . drip of his life's blood into the bowl he had placed on the floor beneath his now lifeless hand. I knew then that Ramose had taken revenge on the one he judged more harshly than any other, even before he went to face Osiris and his forty-two judges.

Max laid the onionskin upside down on the stack of sheets he'd already read, pausing to straighten the edges before taking up the last page. Someone else might think he was simply being careful with the delicate paper, but Kate knew better. She turned her hand to clasp his, to remind him that they were walking this road together.

Day 21, Second Month of Planting. I cannot chance offending the gods, so I recite every spell exactly as prescribed in the scrolls of the priest-physicians. 'Oh Isis, great in sorcery, deliver her from everything bad and evil and vicious. From affliction caused by a god or goddess. From dead man or woman. From male or female adversary. As you delivered your son Horus. Dispel the disease in her body, the ailing in her limbs. Osiris call away your serpent. Protect the one who suffers, who is pure of heart.' I even burned the yellow resinous seeds from the land of Punt, which give off the hypnotic fragrance I hoped would allow me to feel or see what she does—so I can see into her body and in that way find a way to heal her. All to no avail.

Day 22, Second Month of Planting. Because she taught me

even as I taught her, we grew in understanding together. And love. Did I ever use that word before she came? From her I learned, too, what it is to be brave. Pagosh was right about that as he was about so many things.

So it is done. As her breath began to slow, I took her in my arms to wait for Osiris. When next I glanced up his rigid green form was beginning to take shape in the shadows of the room. "This time you may take her," I told him, "for only you can make her whole again."

A moment later I felt her ka brush the back of my hand. A final caress as she left me.

So did the god claim what once I had denied him, yet for a time I stayed as I was, letting the knowledge that she is gone sink into my bones—to know that never again will my thoughts be enlightened by her quick wit. To never again feel the fire in my body flare up at the touch of her lips. Nor will my ears ever hear her take me to task simply by calling me husband.

Then as Re-Horakhte crept above the eastern horizon, I wrapped her in a soft linen sheet and carried her to the Per Nefer, to accomplish what once she asked me to do for her beloved Tuli. When I saw how broken and torn she was inside, not only her ribs and lungs but her liver and stomach, I wondered that she could have stayed so long, strong-willed or not. Afterward I registered her under the name she once talked of taking to hide who she was, to protect her even in death should I not succeed in what I intend.

But first, while Senmut and the others make the long trek to Horemheb's eternal home, I will go to Mena's to leave Aset's goatskin bag for our daughter. I have added my own legacy to hers—Aset's map of the vessels that carry blood, along with this journal—that one day Meri may know her mother as I did. Also that she may come to understand what happened to Aset, and why. I want our daughter to know, as well, should I fail to return, that I do what I must to make sure the same is never visited upon her. Hapimere. Beloved of my heart.

So for now I bid you farewell—daughter conceived in joy, favorite of the River God. May you rise like the sun, rejuvenate yourself like the moon, and repeat life like the flood of Mother Nile, forever and ever.

AFTERWORD

The mummy of a Lady Tashat does, in fact, exist, and is on display in the Minneapolis Institute of Art. The inscription on one of her two elaborately painted coffins reveals little beyond her age at death (15), and that she was the daughter of the treasurer of the Temple of Amen at Karnak and the wife of a Theban noble.

X rays taken in 1975 show a broken and contorted skeleton—and a second skull between her legs. Curators at first thought the extra skull might have been an embalmer's mistake, but a CT scan by Dr. Derek Notman, a radiologist at the University of Minnesota, revealed that it was the head of an adult male, "carefully embalmed and wrapped in layers of linen before being bound with the mummy. Notman saw further that the back of the second skull had been beaten in—whether before or after death is not clear—and that fragments of the skull had been set back in place with a mudlike packing material. Since Tashat's outer bandaging appeared to be undisturbed—each layer of thin linen bandaging is visible in the axial scans—this means the head was placed there intentionally at the time of mummification, and that its placement was not the work of vandals or grave robbers" (*The New York Times*, Nov. 22, 1983).

Whether Tashat's injuries occurred before or after death remains a mystery, as does the identity of her companion and how or why his head came to be where it is.

AUTHOR'S NOTE

The names of the ancient Egyptians are as foreign to our eyes as they are to our tongues, providing few clues even as to gender. Many incorporate the names of gods, especially aspects of the sun god such as Aten and Amen. There was Amenhotep, meaning Amen is content, and Ramose, son of Ra, and Ankhesenpa*aten*, so named by her father, Akhenaten, later changed to Ankhesen*amen* but still a tongue twister. Yet "to speak of the dead is to make them live again," so we cannot simply change Senmut to Sam, or Tenre to Tom.

Far more difficult to comprehend, I believe, is the length of time these people lived as a coherent culture, a span equal to the "distance" from Stonehenge to modern-day England—so long that by 450 B.C., when Herodotus wrote his famous history, the Egyptians themselves could no longer read the hieroglyphs of their ancestors. So it was not until 1822, when Jean-François Champollion found the key to deciphering the stone uncovered by Napoléon's troops at Rosetta, unlocking the door to that long-lost language, that modern Egyptology truly was born. Now another door has been opened by nondestructive techniques such as computerized tomography, endoscopy, and DNA analysis, all capable of revealing a mummy's "secrets" while preserving these artifacts of human history for the even more sophisticated technologies to come.

Some missing pieces of the puzzle are gone forever, of course, thanks to the avaricious thieves of both antiquity and modern times, the tomb-robber mentality of so many early excavators, and the widespread belief that powdered "mummy" could cure everything from gout to impotence (coincidentally contributing to the spread of the plague in sixteenth century Europe). And then there were the ubiquitous tourists on the Grand Tour! Not all the "souvenirs" they carried home ended in the dustbin of time, however. The mummy of Lady Tahathor, for instance, purchased in 1856 for the sum of seven pounds by one George H. Errington of Colchester, England, eventually was presented to his hometown museum. Several such mementos have found their way into museums in the United States as well, where they are being examined with techniques that allow them to continue their voyage through eternity.

So the history of the ancient Egyptians is still being written. And rewritten.

Through much of this century, Amenhotep III was dismissed as the strong-willed Queen Tiye's amiable but indolent husband. His fame, such as it was, derived from his son, Akhenaten, who probably established the first monotheistic religion. Yet today the thirty-eight-year reign of the Magnificent Amenhotep—"Egypt's Dazzling Sun"—is recognized as Egypt's Golden Age, when painting began to depict life instead of death, literature described human experience rather than divine, and Egypt's physicians were in demand throughout the Middle East. Indeed, it appears now that the legacy of Amenhotep III was individualism and naturalism in artistic expression, the foundation on which classical Greece was built.

There also is evidence that Amenhotep III favored the god Aten over Amen even before his "heretic" son came to the throne. Certainly he physically and symbolically distanced the throne from Amen's great northern temple (Karnak) by building his royal palace across the river, a move he would not have made without reason. Not when the only residents of the land west of the Nile at the time were the souls of the dead. So it is likely, at least in the beginning, that Akhenaten was driven by the same political imperative: the need to constrain the growing power of the Amen priests. But the father never fell victim to the religious fanaticism of the son, who eventually outlawed and then confiscated the property and wealth of the other gods—just as Henry VIII did to the Catholic Church of England twenty-eight centuries later. In the process, though, this ancient Heretic swept away both the organizing structure of his people's lives and the source of their livelihood—employment in the fields and workshops of Amen-Re and a host of lesser gods—plunging the Two Lands into social and economic chaos.

With Akhenaten's passing, the resurgent power of Amen brought a return to tradition, repression, and conformity that led eventually to the degradation of artistic expression and science, even of their highly developed embalming techniques and funerary art, while magical incantations began to dominate the practice of medicine—the kind of regression we see today in the rise of Muslim fundamentalism and, closer to home, in demands that "creation science" be taught in our schools.

No one knows what happened to Nefertiti, Akhenaten's Queen, not even when or where she died. Nor do historians agree on her parentage. Or on Tutankhamen's for that matter. Only that both Nefertiti and Tutankhamen as well as Akhenaten *could* have been sired by Amenhotep III. Egyptologists J. R. Harris, Julia Sampson, and others have asserted, based largely on an accumulation of physical evidence, that she assumed the public representation of a man and ruled as Akhenaten's coregent during the final three years of his reign—that "the elusive" Smenkhkare was none other than Nefertiti.

As for the plausibility of a political cartoonist in the time of the pharaohs, the satirical papyri in the British Museum along with the many cartoonlike sketches found on limestone chips (ostraca) all up and down the valley of the Nile suggest that was not only possible but highly probable.

The sun god Re (or Ra), the father of creation, was the universal god of the Egyptians, but several aspects of the sun also were worshiped: Re-Horakhte, the early-morning sun (Horus Rising); Aten, the full face of the sun; Re-Atum, the afternoon sun; and Amen, the hidden or midnight sun. Yet it was the goddess Maat and the concept she represented—an amalgam of truth, order, and justice—that constituted the moral ideal of the People of the Sun. Thoth, on the other hand, was unique among all gods, then and now, in trying to dispel the darkness with learning.

The Egyptians followed a twelve-month calendar but with three seasons of four months each. The New Year began with the reappearance on the eastern horizon of the dog star Sopdet (Sirius) after seventy days of absence because of the halo of the sun, signaling the flooding of the Nile in mid-July. The Season of Inundation extended through October, when the average high temperature in present-day Luxor ranges from 98 to 107° F. The Season of Planting was November through February, while the Season of Harvest ran from March through June.

I chose to use the Egyptian Amenhotep rather than the Greek Amenophis, and the spelling convention followed by most American Egyptologists today. The city of Amen—Luxor today—was called Waset by the Egyptians, Thebes by the Greeks. Ipet-isut, Amen's great northern temple, in Arabic became Al-Karnak (the fort); Ipet-resyt, the southern temple of Amen built by Amenhotep III, became Al-Uqsur (the palaces), since corrupted to Luxor. The Shasu were foreigners of nomadic habits including several Semitic tribes. Some sources suggest that the name Hebrew did not come into use until after the Exodus, but when that event took place, if indeed it ever did, is still the subject of debate.

I also chose one chronology of the pharaohs from several, none of which rests on uncontested ground. But it is during the twenty-five years following the reign of Akhenaten, when the glorious Eighteenth Dynasty came to an end, that *The Eye of Horus* plays out.

ACKNOWLEDGMENTS

The lyrical verses used in the text and as epigraphs for the Egyptian chapters are from *Awakening Osiris: A New Translation of the Egyptian Book of the Dead* by Normandi Ellis (Phanes Press, 1988). In leaving behind the archaic language of earlier translations, Ellis allows us to see the changing color of the desert sky through the eyes of a people who lived thousands of years ago—to share their aspirations and disappointments and come to realize they were capable of both soaring flights of imagination and the most mundane ordinariness—until, in the end, we hear ourselves in their voices.

Dr. Robert Pickering, physical anthropologist and former chairman of the Department of Anthropology at the Denver Museum of Natural History, opened the door for me to forensic reconstructions based on CT scans of a mummy, sharing not only his expertise but his enthusiasm for learning more about how the ancient Egyptians lived, not just their way of death. It was an exhibition, *Egypt's Dazzling Sun: Amenhotep III and His World*, organized by the Cleveland Museum of Art in collaboration with the Réunion des Museés Nationaux, Paris (catalog by Arielle Kozloff and Betsy Bryan, 1992) that truly opened my eyes to this artistically magnificent period of Egyptian history. And while there were many other collections and exhibitions along the way, none were so thought-provoking (indeed, mesmerizing) as this one, set against the backdrop of architect Louis Kahn's equally magnificent Kimbell Art Museum in Ft. Worth, Texas.

Many people had a hand in shaping this book. Eunice McWharter was every ready to read one more draft, allowing me to test one idea after another. Dr. George Beddingfield provided insightful observations on the story and how to tell it, Christina Harcar gave generously of her time and editorial expertise, and Leslie Kronz lent her ear for voice and tone when I needed it most. In between, the Sunday Afternoon Connoisseurs read and offered thoughtful counsel, then came back for more. Perhaps it was for the wine. Jennifer Sawyer Fisher, my editor, provided not only editorial guidance but unfailing equanimity and good cheer in the face of one more read. Elizabeth Ziemska and then Nick Ellison, my agents, opened still another door for me, all the while giving generously of their wisdom, confidence, and enthusiasm. My thanks to all.